A CELESTIAL AFFAIR

Daphne Neville

Copyright © 2016 Daphne Neville

All rights reserved, including the right to reproduce this book, or portions thereof in any form. No part of this text may be reproduced, transmitted, downloaded, decompiled, reverse engineered, or stored, in any form or introduced into any information storage and retrieval system, in any form or by any means, whether electronic or mechanical without the express written permission of the author.

This is a work of fiction. Names and characters are the product of the author's imagination and any resemblance to actual persons, living or dead, is entirely coincidental.

The views expressed in this work are solely those of the author and do not necessarily reflect the views of the publisher, and the publisher hereby disclaims any responsibility for them.

ISBN: 978-1-326-59262-2

PublishNation, London
www.publishnation.co.uk

Other Titles by this Author

The Ringing Bells Inn
Polquillick
Sea, Sun, Cads and Scallywags
Grave Allegations
The Old Vicarage

1999

Chapter One

Across the clear azure sky, one sunny afternoon in late June, a solitary white cloud gently drifted above the picturesque Cornish fishing village of Trengillion. Comically shaped like a giant muffin, it floated over the roof tops of cottages and houses, the post office, the school and a large sycamore tree which flourished in the corner of the village hall's uneven concreted frontage.

The sycamore, a tree much loved by the village youngsters because it was easy to climb, had developed and grown outside the village hall for more than half a century and during its lifetime had played host to many different species of birds, as in early April of the current year when it became home to a pair of magpies.

Under the watchful eyes of near neighbours and children, the magpies meticulously built a nest high up in the sycamore's leafy branches and then over the ensuing weeks dutifully reared their young.

The children talked much of the two birds to their teachers which inspired a competition in the school to name the pair; hence before long, the two magpies came to be known to everyone in the village as Kernow and Kate.

The village hall stood in the heart of Trengillion on its main street and was one of the oldest buildings in the village. Built of granite in the early sixteenth century, rumour decreed it had at one time been a large thatched cottage which had fallen into disrepair following a fire at the beginning of the eighteenth century. For many years afterwards it had stood empty and then eventually was converted into a single storey hall for village use.

As the muffin shaped cloud passed over the hall, Kernow and Kate strutted along the ridge tiles of its slate roof, oblivious of the cloud and everything else that went on around them; for their attention was solely focused on rearing their young who were almost ready to fly.

Once satisfied their four offspring were well-fed and safe within the nest, the couple took flight, casting small shadows onto the gardens below as they moved swiftly southwards towards the sea.

Above the church tower they circled the flag pole and then settled on the turrets to devour insects crawling through the brilliant green summer coat of the Virginia Creeper. They then took off once more and within the sound of the sea lapping against the cliffs, swooped down onto the rim of a granite bird bath where they splashed and flapped sending water cascading onto the freshly cut grass below. Once bathed they flew up to the rooftop of an attractive house overlooking the cove and flapped their wings to remove excess water before preening one another in the warm sunshine.

To anyone watching the antics of the birds from a distance, it might seem their coats were of simple black and white, but to the jackdaw resting on the west gable chimney pot, it was obvious their plumage was subtly coloured. For in the bright sunlight, their wing feathers gleamed shades of blue and purple, and their long, straight tail feathers, shone green tipped with blue.

On the cliff tops beside the house where the magpies preened, with her knees closely tucked beneath her chin, Elizabeth Castor-Hunt, rocked on a patch of grass surrounded by dense clumps of golden gorse and feathery bracken. A south easterly breeze tousled her brown curls as she watched a fishing boat on the beach below clumsily sliding over evenly spaced logs on its journey to join other boats already home. Above it a flock of seagulls swarmed and squawked, their cry almost inaudible against the chugging of the elderly winch.

The boat belonged to Matthew Williams and on board was Elizabeth's son, Wills, who had been out fishing: his first day as a temporary crew member to while away the long summer university vacation and earn some cash.

Wills acknowledged his mother with an inconspicuous wave, conscious that fishermen already on the beach might think him a molly-coddled mummy's boy, should his gesture be observed. But he need not have worried, for the men of the cove knew and liked Elizabeth well. Since the death of her grandmother, Molly Smith, she appeared to have taken on the persona of the deceased lady; her clothing was flamboyant in style and vivid in colour, but she was especially held in esteem because like her grandmother, it was rumoured she had the ability to see beyond the grave.

When the activity on the beach drew to a close, Elizabeth rose, stretched her long arms and walked the few yards home to Chy-an-Gwyns. As she opened the gate her movement disturbed the magpies who expressed their protests with a mechanical caw and then flew away back over the village towards the sycamore to check their young family had come to no harm.

Elizabeth closed the wooden gate and took the path which led to the back door of Chy-an-Gwyns, home for the past year to herself, husband, Greg and their two children, Tally and Wills. The move had occurred following the death of Greg's mother, Tabitha, after which he and his sister, Lily, had inherited the house. Their late father, Willoughby, who passed away in 1995, had many years before, expressed his desire to see one of his children live in the house when he and Tabitha were both gone. Greg therefore, was only too happy to grant his father's wish and buy-out his sister, Lily, in order to take up residence in the family home.

Elizabeth loved Chy-an-Gwyns. She loved the name - Cornish for house in the wind - and she loved the location, perched high on the cliff tops. The views out to sea were breathtaking and she never tired of looking down onto the village she had known all her life; the village she would always call home. Additionally, the house itself was a joy to behold, solidly built of cut granite with two equidistant attic windows on the front elevation tucked snuggly beneath the eaves. Its rooms were spacious and airy, the ceilings high, and every nook and cranny oozed character, yet at the same time, it felt cosy, friendly and always inviting.

As she neared the house she picked a sprig of mint from a wooden tub alongside the herb garden to cook with new potatoes she had dug that morning. With mint in hand she closed the back door; simultaneously the telephone rang. Elizabeth hurriedly kicked off her sandals, dropped the mint onto the kitchen table and rushed to lift the receiver. It was her father, Ned Stanley, retired headmaster of the village school.

"Ah, good, got you at last, Liz. I've rung several times during the last hour or so but you've obviously been out gallivanting somewhere."

Elizabeth smiled. "Yes, but I've not been far away, just out on cliffs watching Wills and Matthew get the boat pulled up the beach, first day and all that. Is there a problem, Dad? You sound rather agitated."

Ned groaned. "Do I? Sorry, but yes, I probably am agitated. It's this damn new mobile phone, Liz. How the dickens do I get it to store numbers? I've been trying for ages and I can't fathom it out. I'm not at all keen on these new-fangled gadgets, you know, and I'm sure I'll never use the damn thing in spite of what you youngsters say."

Elizabeth laughed as she pulled out a chair and sat at the kitchen table. At forty five she thought it amusing to be called a youngster.

"It's impossible to tell you over the phone, Dad, so the best thing is for me to demonstrate, and to be honest, I only know how to do it myself because our Wills showed me when I got mine."

"Damn! Shall I pop up and see you then?"

"No need, I shall be down later today because it's Keep Fit night, so I'll call in and show you what's what on my way to the village hall."

"Oh, bless you, thanks Liz. I'd appreciate that and it'll save me the walk up to you. It's hot work climbing that hill especially this time of day. Not that I'm complaining about the weather, it's lovely to see the sun, but today's been marred by this phone. I've been messing about with the wretched thing all morning, you know. And your mother's no wiser than me, not when it comes to technology, anyway."

Elizabeth sighed. "And I'm not much better; like you and Mum, we didn't do technology and stuff when we were at school. Mind you, it's probably just as well because I'm sure I'd have been a right dunce if we had."

"What! Not you, Liz, you were always top of the class back in your school days."

"Not in science," she laughed, "and I'd put technology in a similar category. You know, mumbo jumbo and gobbledygook. Anyway, I must go, Dad, I'm gasping for a cuppa. I'll see you later about half six."

"Thanks, Liz, I look forward to seeing you. Bye."

Ned sighed as he put down the receiver, Elizabeth sounded more like his mother with every passing day. She even looked like her sometimes too. He laughed. At forty five, Elizabeth was roughly the same age as his mother had been when first she set foot in Trengillion, and sometimes he had a strange feeling that history was repeating itself.

Once the fishing boat was back in its rightful place on the beach, Wills Castor-Hunt left the cove with empty lunch box in hand and headed home to Chy-an-Gwyns; and Matthew Williams, tired after the early start, crossed the beach to do likewise, but before he began to climb the long path home he called in at the Pickled Egg café to see his sister, Jane, who insisted he join her for a cup of tea.

"How did young Wills do?" Jane asked, as she placed a mug in front of her brother. "It seems like only yesterday that he was born."

"Oh, don't, you sound like Mum when you say things like that and I like to pretend we're still youngsters ourselves and not on the verge of being middle aged."

Jane laughed. "I don't think we're on the verge, Matt, surely now we're in our forties we're already there."

Matthew groaned. "I suppose so. Anyway, Wills did well, very well in fact. I'm sure he'll be a great asset to me this summer. He's good company too and a credit to Greg and Liz."

"Good, I hated you going out single handed, it was silly and dangerous. It's a pity Jim ever gave up because he was a good worker, wasn't he?"

"Yeah, but the poor bloke was prone to sea sickness so he's much better off working on the land. I'm surprised he managed to go out with me for as many years as he did."

Jane sat down at the table opposite her brother. "He must have enjoyed your dynamic sense of humour and wit," she teased.

Matthew grinned as he stirred a heaped teaspoon of sugar into his tea. "I think it was more he got a liking for the taste of crab. Anyway, it really hasn't bothered me going out alone these past two years. I'm happy with my own company, having said that it's good to have an extra pair of hands because it means we can work more pots and I have to keep up a good supply of crabmeat for you as well as the Newlyn market. How is business?"

"Not bad. There are a few visitors around but nothing like there will be later in the summer. Lunchtimes are good and I'm making a living, but I'm happy, and if the truth be known, I like this time of the year when trade is steady. I feel everything is prepared with a little more care and attention than it is during the hustle and bustle of the high summer madness."

Matthew nodded as he sipped his tea. "Is Janet helping you again this year?"

"Yes, bless her, and her two daughters. Jess is joining us as well which is fantastic as she was a great help last year." Jane reached for a tin of biscuits and offered one to her brother. "I had told Janet that I'd manage without her if she was too busy with her interior decorating business. But she insists on helping and I must admit I'm glad. She's good company as well as a good worker."

"Well, you'll probably find things are a bit quiet on the decorating front in the summer and she's glad to have something else to do."

"Yes, I daresay you're right."

Matthew quickly drained his mug and then stood up. "Thanks for the tea and biscuits, Jane. I'd better be getting back now because Rebecca said she'd be home at half past four and it's my turn to cook dinner."

"What are you having? Anything nice?"

Matthew picked up his empty lunch box. "Prawn curry, it's my speciality."

"Curry! Isn't the weather a bit too warm for that?"

"No, we'll eat it outside in the front garden, al fresco like. We often do if the weather's good. So if I make it a bit too hot today we'll be cooled down by a gentle sea breeze. Pure bliss. Must go, bye Jane."

Matthew left the Pickled Egg and headed for the track at the top of the incline which led onto the coastal path and home; for like the Castor-Hunts he also lived on the cliff tops but on the opposite side of the cove in one of the old Coastguard Cottages situated near the ruins of the old Penwynton Mine.

The coastguard houses, after their restoration by a property developer in the 1960s, were initially furnished and let out as holiday homes, but over the years, one by one, they came up for sale. Matthew, having a substantial deposit, managed to get a mortgage and buy the smallest one on the end of the row, with just two bedrooms. It had by far the largest garden so they knew that should they ever be able to afford it, it would be possible to build a substantial extension on the side of their modest home.

As promised, Elizabeth called in at Rose Cottage before her Keep Fit class and found both her parents sitting at a wooden table in the front garden enjoying their dinner in the early evening sun.
"The garden's looking beautiful," she said, bending to smell a particularly stunning yellow rose as she walked up the path, "Grandma would be so chuffed to see you're taking good care of it for her."
Ned smiled; Elizabeth still regarded the cottage as belonging to her grandmother even though it was twelve years since she had passed away and left it to Ned in her will.
"The mobile phone is in the kitchen by the bread bin, Liz, if you want to go and get it. I've nearly finished my dinner."
The inheritance of Rose Cottage back in 1987 initially caused a dilemma for Ned and Stella, as they already owned their own home and Stella was naturally reluctant to leave it, for it was the place where their daughters, Elizabeth and Anne, had been born and grown up. Ned likewise, was unwilling to sell Rose Cottage, the house his mother had loved and tended for thirty five years. Eventually a compromise was met and they sold the Old School House to Steve Penhaligon and his wife, Susan, who was their daughter, Anne's, sister-in-law; therefore it felt as though they were keeping the house in the family.
As Ned finished off the last mouthful of his steak pie and laid his cutlery neatly across his plate, Elizabeth returned outside with the troublesome phone.
"I don't really know why I ever let you talk me into having that damn thing," said Ned, wagging his finger at the mobile as his daughter sat down on the grass beside the table. "I'm sure I'll never use it. It's fiddly as well as complicated and I can't see any of the silly little digits unless I've got my specs on."

Stella laughed. "Oh be fair, Ned, you need your specs on for most things these days, especially reading."

"That's what I said when Wills bought me mine for Christmas," said Elizabeth. "About not needing it I mean, not the specs bit. But actually it's come in quite useful on several occasions when I've been out shopping and I'm getting quite a dab hand at texting."

"Texting! I'll never be able to fathom that out, it'll be as much as I can do to use it as a phone."

Stella smiled and gently shook her head in amusement. "Your dad's such a Luddite, Liz, though he'd never admit it. He didn't think we needed a microwave and showed off rotten when I insisted we had one last year, but now he uses it more than me."

"Well, that's because it's really easy to heat up soup in it and you don't have to dirty a saucepan…"

"Exactly," laughed Stella, "and I bet one day you'll sing the praises of your mobile too."

"I won't. Anyway, perhaps you'll both stop picking on me and you'll show me how to store numbers, Liz."

Elizabeth dutifully copied family numbers from her own phone onto Ned's and showed him how to select them. "You ought to have a mobile too, Mum, and then you and Dad would never lose each other while out shopping."

Stella threw back her head and laughed. "We've been married for forty six years and never lost each other yet, so I think it's unlikely we shall now. Besides, one mobile in the family is more than enough. I really don't need one as well."

"Yes you do," said Ned, didactically wagging his finger, "you often go into town without me and you also go for great long rambling walks. If you had a phone and something went wrong then you could call for help. We'll get you one next time we're in Helston."

"See," smiled Elizabeth, slipping the phone back into its leather case, "you're seeing the useful side of them already. Well done, Dad."

Chapter Two

Trengillion's inn was built during the 1740s around the same time as Penwynton Hotel, formerly Penwynton House. Originally it was called The Ringing Bells Inn and belonged to the estate of the wealthy Penwynton family, but in 1919, a few months after the end of World War One, it was sold to a farmer from the Helston area who sadly neglected to maintain it and eventually he was forced to close it down. For the next ten years the inn remained empty, until finally, in a derelict state, it was put up for sale by auction. This occurrence was in the nineteen thirties, and the purchaser was a stranger to the area, a young man from Derbyshire called Frank Newton.

Following extensive restoration and much hard work, the ivy covered, abandoned building finally re-opened under its original name, The Ringing Bells Inn.

On Frank's retirement in 1967, the Inn, a free-house, was bought by Raymond and Gloria Withers, after which, Raymond, a gun crazy devotee of the Wild West, renamed it The Sherriff's Badge. However, because of an unfortunate incident in Trengillion which took the life of a young man and the cause of his death was a gunshot wound, Raymond renamed the inn, the Badger, since many of his clientele called it the Badge anyway.

In 1983 the Withers sold up and moved to Falmouth and Trengillion's new licensees were Gerald and Cassie Godson, who, not overwhelmed with the inappropriate name Badger, renamed it the Fox and Hounds, a reflection of their passion for fox hunting. The Godsons remained at the inn until January of 1999, when they retired to Bath.

The new and current landlord was Justin Thornton, a young man in his mid-thirties, recently pensioned off from the Royal Navy. And he, in the tradition of his predecessors, changed the name yet again. Very much against blood sports, Justin opted for a name close to his heart and the pub was renamed The Jolly Sailor.

In the short time Justin Thornton had owned the inn he had proved to be very popular with the locals, especially the females. He ran the establishment with strict military precision and made everyone, young and old, feel very welcome. Furthermore, as a bachelor, slim, handsome and humorous, he was eligible to boot, and having no immediate family in the area to aid his running of the inn, he also provided employment for several people, all local, with the exception of the talented newly appointed chef, Maurice Lamont.

Following his advertisement in a national newspaper for a chef, Justin was faced with a considerable number of applicants, many with qualifications far exceeding those required for a modest village pub. But after sifting through the applications and interviewing dozens, he finally chose Maurice Lamont for no other reason than he liked him and felt they would get along well together.

Very little was known about Maurice and his life prior to recruitment at the inn, other than he was a former resident of Plymouth where he had worked in a popular, fashionable hotel.

When he first started work at The Jolly Sailor, Maurice, also a bachelor, asked Justin if he could put a caravan on the inn's disused vegetable plot where a previous landlady had once grown produce to feed the guests. This was because he was reluctant to take up accommodation offered inside the inn which would deprive Justin of a letting room. He was also unenthusiastic about living over the shop, so to speak. But his dilemma was solved when he heard that Valley View, a fully furnished, detached house was coming up for rent on a long-let, and after viewing the house he decided it was the best option for all concerned.

Valley View was not far from the inn and situated opposite the village hall, hence it was far enough away to ensure he got a little exercise each day before and after work. Having failed a driving test on six occasions, Maurice had no car and thought it unlikely he ever would. But he didn't mind, for the money he saved on petrol, insurance, road tax and maintenance he was able to spend on his passion: computers and the latest technology.

Ever since they had begun in 1997, Trengillion's Keep Fit classes had been a popular event with ladies of all ages but especially those on the wrong side of forty. Each week they exercised vigorously for one and a half hours under the watchful eye of their physical training instructor from Polquillick but then put back all the calories they had burnt off with a visit to the pub for a drink or two and quite often crisps, peanuts and chocolate as well.

The Keep Fit session prior to which Elizabeth had visited her parents regarding her father's mobile phone, was no exception. She and her friends, eager for a chat, went to the inn as usual and made themselves comfortable around a rectangular table at the far end of the public bar.

"I wish Justin had a nice wife to help with this place," mused Anne Collins, Elizabeth's sister, as she and Susan Penhaligon returned from the bar with a round of drinks. "He works so hard. In fact he never seems to do anything but work, poor lamb."

"That's because he's trying to get well established before the holiday season gets underway," said Susan, one of Justin's part-time employees, as she took a seat. "He told me so. But I think he'll let his hair down more in the autumn when he feels settled, and he's already talking about and looking forward to Christmas."

"Christmas!" screeched Elizabeth, rolling up the sleeves of her purple fleece, "we've not even got into the summer properly yet."

Susan nodded. "I know, but I think he's looking forward to it because he's not quite sure what the summer will bring, it being his first."

"He'll cope alright because he's got a great sense of humour," said Candy Bingham, watching the young landlord hand change to Ian Ainsworth. "In fact if I were twenty years younger and not married, I'd be hanging up my hat for him."

Elizabeth laughed. "Just as well Larry's not around to hear you say that, I think it'd make him pretty jealous."

"No, not Larry, he's not the envious sort. Anyway, he knows full well he's the only bloke for me. In this life anyhow."

"I hear young Stephen at the post office and his girlfriend, Nessie, have split up," said Susan, slipping her feet onto the rung of Anne's stool. "I can't really say that I'm sorry because she was never my cup of tea. I can't understand what she's saying half the time and it drives me mad when I hear her call Stephen, Laddie."

"Och aye the noo," giggled Anne, "I find her difficult to understand as well."

Candy frowned pensively. "I've an aunt who's a Scot and I'm sure I've never heard her say och aye the noo."

"Well, to be fair I've never heard Nessie say it either," said Anne, "and I've not the foggiest idea what it means."

"It most likely doesn't mean anything at all," said Elizabeth. "It was probably made up by us English as ridicule: a joke or something like that."

Candy nodded. "Maybe, but then I do know aye means yes, and I believe och means oh and noo means now, so if you put it all together it would sort of mean, oh yes, the now."

"What! That makes even less sense than och aye the noo," laughed Susan. "Anyway, if she's gone for good, and I hope she has, that means Stephen's an eligible bachelor once again."

Candy whistled. "We're starting to get overrun with them now. What paradise Trengillion must be for a single girl in her thirties."

"Hmm, but it's a shame," said Anne, "for Stephen, I mean. It'll be hard work for him running the post office on his own, especially with summer coming up. They've got a brisk little business going there."

"He spends much of the time on his own anyway," said Susan, disparagingly. "Nessie was never much help because she was too busy looking down her nose at everyone and scoffing toffees."

"And playing the bagpipes," giggled Candy.

"No, she didn't surely. Did she?" said Elizabeth, surprised.

"Of course not," said Candy. "Not to my knowledge anyway."

"So, putting bagpipes aside, and best place for them, who left who?" Elizabeth asked, pouring the remainder of her tonic water into her gin.

Susan shrugged her shoulders. "Not sure, but apparently they had a blazing row and either he chucked her out or she went off in a huff. There are two stories doing the rounds, but whichever it was it's claimed that after she'd thrown some of her things in the boot of her car, she drove out of Trengillion like a maniac."

"I should think he chucked her out then," said Anne, thoughtfully, "because I went in the post office this morning on my way to work and thought how happy Stephen looked."

"Wonder where she's gone then, because she gave up her rented flat last year when she moved in with him, didn't she?"

"Probably back home to her parents in Scotland," said Anne, "I rather liked them when they came down at Easter, her parents, I mean. Especially her dad, he seemed very jovial."

"A jovial Scot, surely not," said Rebecca Williams. "Aren't they supposed to be dour?"

"Oh, come on, that's a bit unfair," said Anne, "I can think of several Scots I've come across over the years who have been perfectly friendly, but right now I can't think of any, apart from Nessie's parents. Having said that, I can't really say that I dislike Nessie. She's always seemed perfectly sociable to me,"

Candy giggled. "Yeah, and on reflection her parents must have a sense of humour otherwise they'd never have called the poor girl Nessie." A puzzled look suddenly crossed Candy's face. "Hey, I've just remembered something. The other week I went into Helston and as I was driving up Godolphin Road I saw Nessie standing by a garden gate with some bloke who was giving her a hug. I didn't think anything of it at the time, but I wonder if she's got another bloke."

"Really!" Susan chuckled. "What was he like?"

"Dashingly handsome, if I remember correctly, and it was definitely Ness he was with because she was wearing her green jeans and leather jacket."

As they spoke, Maurice the chef sauntered into the bar having finished cooking for the evening. He nodded politely to the ladies in the corner, conscious they were watching him, and then after Justin had poured him a pint of lager he disappeared into the games room to join Charlie and Sam Bingham for a game of pool.

"He's another one who ought to have a wife," said Rebecca, removing her jacket. "I feel so sorry for him living all by himself in that big house."

"Well, he's got his computer thingy," said Elizabeth. "Tally says it's his pride and joy and all he ever talks about."

"He should have bought an iron instead," giggled Candy, "his clothes always look so crumpled and neglected."

"Ah, but at least he's able to cook," said Susan, who because she worked with him often had a lot of time for the new chef, "so he'll not starve or have to live on junk food either, like most bachelors do."

"Why do women always feel sorry for any poor chap that isn't wed?" laughed Jim Haynes, who unbeknown to them was leaning on the games machine listening to their comments. "Some of us enjoy being footloose and fancy free and I can cook too. But I don't have or need a computer for company and I couldn't afford one anyway. However, you'll be pleased to know that I do have an iron, and if I might be permitted to say so I'm pretty good at using it, although the only thing I ever iron is the white shirt I wear when working on the Hotel bar."

Susan blushed. "I didn't see you there, you flappy eared bugger and if I had it would have jogged my memory and you'd have got a mention too. Anyway, you might think you enjoy your freedom now, but you wait until you're knocking on a bit and you have to slow down. It won't be much fun then being on your own with no family to care for, or to care for you."

"Hmm, you've got a point," agreed Jim, helping himself to one of Susan's crisps. "In fact it's a very good point. So if you see any potential wives lurking around please let me know. I mean to say, there could be an abundance this summer with Trengillion being paradise for unattached females in their thirties. I'm not too fussy, but they must be attractive, be able to cook, love gardening, have a terrific sense of humour, like old buildings and graveyards, like walking, fresh air and cycling, but most important of all, they must not nag."

"Blimey, if that's not fussy I'd hate to hear what is," laughed Candy, "but we'll keep a look out, won't we girls? In fact we'll try and get you all paired off before the year is out. You, Maurice, Justin and poor old Stephen."

Prior to Elizabeth and Gregory Castor-Hunt's move to Chy-an-Gwyns, they had for many years lived in Cove Cottage, a modest house situated at the top of the beach alongside a similar house called Sea View. Cove Cottage was their first home, bought for the sum of twelve thousand pounds in 1977, the year of their marriage, and it was where their two children, Talwyn, known as Tally and Willoughby, known as Wills had spent their childhood. The Castor-Hunts reluctantly sold Cove Cottage in order to raise money to buy-out Greg's sister, Lily's share of Chy-an-Gwyns, and their house was bought, much to their delight and the surprise of many Trengillion residents, by a British actress of some note, Iris Delaney.

Iris Delaney loved Cove Cottage from the moment she first set eyes on it and over the months had come to regard it as her haven, her sanctuary, her rural retreat: somewhere she could let down her hair and be herself away from prying eyes and intrusive camera lenses. Usually she stayed at the cottage alone, often for just a couple of days, and her short breaks were as frequent as her busy lifestyle permitted. The locals enjoyed her visits and the abundant glamorous quality she brought; for her fine features, designer clothes and eloquent discourse added a touch of class otherwise missing in the everyday life of the village. Nevertheless, she forbade anyone to raise the subject of her work, for when she was in Trengillion she wanted to live as normal a life as possible and be treated by the locals as a friend and not a celebrity.

In her long periods of absence, bachelor, Jim Haynes tended Cove Cottage's small garden and kept the place looking spick and span on the outside. Jim, a fanatical gardener in his mid-thirties, was renowned for his horticultural skills and was the founder member of a movement to acquire allotments for villagers which flourished in a field accessed by a track running off the lane leading to the Old Vicarage. His own property prevented him from growing more than a few flowers in tubs and window boxes, for he lived in a converted Ebenezer Chapel situated by the cross roads. Hence most of the land surrounding his property was sown with grass, and much to the astonishment of many holiday makers, graves and tombstones.

Nevertheless, Jim's relaxed lifestyle was frequently the envy of city dwellers and holiday makers. He had no full time job to tie him down, but worked part time on Long Acre Farm and at the Penwynton Hotel, when required. He also sold some of the produce he grew on his allotment to the post office, the Pickled Egg and the inn, and had an unmanned stall with an honesty box on the roadside outside the gates of his home.

Jim had done much of the chapel's conversion himself, piecemeal over a number of years, but for the plumbing he had called in Larry Bingham. Charlie, Larry's son, a newly qualified electrician, had recently rewired the entire building. Upon completion, Jim aptly named his new home Ebenezer House in honour of the chapel it once had been.

Chapter Three

On Tuesday afternoons throughout the year with the exception of Christmas week, Trengillion's senior citizens met in the village hall for the Over Sixties' Club, where they played cards, partook of light refreshments and once a month watched entertainment in the form of a magician, a singer, a practical demonstration or someone giving a talk or a slide show on a subject they felt might be of interest to others.

Ned and Stella usually went to the Club along with their neighbours and close friends, Rose and George Clarke, although Stella dearly wished the Club's name was a little more subtle, such as in Helston, where their senior citizens met weekly in similar circumstances but under the banner of Darby and Joan.

Twice a year the old folks went on an outing in a mini bus owned by the village for the use of its various clubs and organisations. In December the outing was always a trip around West Cornwall to view the Christmas lights and in the summer it was a trip to a seaside resort in the county, the location of which differed from year to year.

The choice for 1999, after much deliberation, was Mevagissey and the date nominated was August the seventeenth. Normally they would have gone a week earlier but that date was vetoed because it would fall during eclipse week and would not be practical in view of the anticipated crowds threatening to bring the county to a standstill.

"Do you know I've never been to Mevagissey," said Gertie Collins, sipping tea, served by volunteers Candy Bingham and Gertie's daughter, Susan Penhaligon. "I think that's amazing since I've lived here all my life."

"Ned and I went there a few years back one August Bank Holiday Monday," said Stella. "It was very crowded because the streets are so narrow. Having said that it was really nice and a good day out and we had a wonderful cream tea with fantastic strawberry jam."

Ned nodded. "We did, didn't we? I'd forgotten that. Anyway, at least I won't be driving this time, all that reversing was a real nuisance. In fact it will be really nice to relax properly and I won't have to worry about parking either."

"Have you heard about poor Stephen at the post office?" Rose asked, carefully pulling the marzipan off her slice of Battenberg cake and dropping it onto George's plate. "Apparently Nessie's gone and left him in the lurch."

"I heard he asked her to leave because she's been seeing another man recently," said Stella.

Gertie leaned forward across the table her eyes shining at the prospect of finding out and spreading gossip. "That's what I've heard. Someone told me they had a blazing row when Stephen found out but I don't know whether or not that's true. I do know her new chap lives in Helston though; Godolphin Road, I believe."

Rose sighed. "Dear, dear, what a shame, although I'm sure Milly won't shed too many tears over Nessie going. I believe she didn't really approve of her and dreaded the prospects of having her as a daughter-in-law and her being the mother of any grandchildren. I hope Stephen's not too upset."

George frowned. "Who told you that?"

Rose shook her head. "Hmm, I'm not sure."

"Well, I think it's all poppycock," said George, clearly annoyed. "Nessie's a great laugh and I've seen her and Milly together on lots of occasions and they always seemed to be getting on fine and minding their own business, unlike numerous other busy-bodies I could name who frequently put two and two together and seldom make four."

"Are Milly and Johnny going on the outing this year?" Stella hastily asked, in an attempt to move the subject on and thus avoid more conflict.

"Err...Milly is," said Gertie, sheepishly, "but I'm not sure about Johnny. Milly's going to keep an eye on Madge because the poor thing's not too good on her legs now."

"Hmm, I noticed that when we had the old time dance band playing at the last meeting," said Stella. "Shame, she's always been such a lively soul."

"Not always," whispered Ned, "she was overweight and lazy when she first arrived in Trengillion and it wasn't 'til after she'd married Albert and done some work on the farm that she lost some weight."

"I remember that," tittered Gertie, hand over her mouth, "she was a peroxide blonde back then who wore loads of make-up. That must be donkey's years ago."

Ned grinned. "Yes, it was 1953. We were on honeymoon at the time, weren't we, Stell? And if I remember correctly Madge was making eyes at George for much of the summer."

George choked on his tea. "Christ, I'd forgotten that. I never think of her as the same person as she was back then. God, she was a nightmare and twice the size she is now."

Stella sighed. "What a lot of water has gone under the bridge since those halcyon days. We really must make the most of our time together now, because like it or not, one by one we'll each pass on to that unknown place yonder."

"Oh, don't say that, Stella," gasped Gertie, feeling tears prickle the backs of her eyes, "you've made me go all goose-pimply. We're all of us far too young to think of leaving this wonderful world just yet."

"I agree," said Stella, "and it'll be really sad for whoever is the last one of us left. I mean, there will be no-one to reminisce with, and no-one…"

"…to compare aches and pains with or challenge to a Zimmer frame race," laughed George. "The last won't be me though, nor will I be the first, because I've no intention of falling off my perch yet awhile or living to be a crabby old fart in an old folk's home, treated like an idiot by the world and his wife."

"Don't tempt fate, George" said Rose, horrified, "you really mustn't jest. Death sadly is something over which we have very little control. Anyway, you're a crabby old fart already."

For many years three farms had thrived on the outskirts of Trengillion; Home Farm, Higher Green Farm and Long Acre Farm, but now only two were run as operational businesses.

Long Acre Farm, in the vicinity of the old Penwynton mine, was successfully managed by Tony Collins and his wife, Jean. Through choice the couple had no children and had profitably run the farm since it became too much for Tony's grandfather, Cyril Penrose.

Much of the farm's produce was traditional; they grew wheat, potatoes and cauliflowers, had a herd of bullocks and a flock of sheep. Their more unusual diversity, however, was the growing of Christmas trees, a project which began in the early days of their marriage and had since expanded to take over several acres of farm land.

Home Farm was situated down a leafy lane and for many years was owned and run by the Treloar family, the most recent member being the late Albert Treloar, who with his wife, Madge, had run the farm until their retirement in the nineteen eighties; the administration had then passed to Madge's grandson, David and David's wife, Judith. In order to keep a watchful eye over his beloved farm, Albert had ordered the construction of a modest two bedroomed bungalow near to the farm house, into which he had then moved with his wife, Madge.

Following the death of Albert Treloar, Madge's only daughter, Milly and her husband, Johnny, offered Madge a home with them, but she refused, claiming she treasured her independence and thought it wrong for elderly parents to disrupt the lives of their offspring. For those reasons, Johnny and his mother-in-law were the best of friends and he was frequently at her bungalow doing odd jobs and making sure she was warm and comfortable.

Until their retirement, Milly and Johnny had run Trengillion Post Office, but they now lived at Sea Thrift Cottage, nestled on the cliff tops near to the Witches Broomstick.

The third farm was Higher Green Farm, also located on the cliffs near to the Witches Broomstick. In spite of its one-time success it had not been a viable farm since being involved in a scandal, after which it had been sold to the highest bidder. Sadly, following the sale it was never worked as a farm again, for the new owner auctioned off most of the farmland and then also sold the farmhouse along with three acres, including an orchard, which he had retained as gardens for the farmhouse.

The current owner of the Higher Green Farmhouse was a property tycoon who lived up-country and let the place through an agency for most of the year to holiday makers, with the exception of a week in April when he visited the farmhouse himself to inspect its décor and general state of repair.

Johnny and Milly Pascoe, although retired, still worked part time as housekeepers and caretakers at Higher Green Farmhouse. They were offered the job on application, due to their many years of experience in dealing with the public at the post office and the close proximity to the farmhouse of their home, Sea Thrift Cottage. The work did not take up a great deal of their time as it only needed their attention on change-over days, but it was enough to keep them occupied and give them an interest.

Chapter Four

"I think I'll cut a nice bunch of lilac from the old tree and take it down to the graveyard for Mum and the major," said Ned, flinging the daily newspaper onto the floor and rising from the settee. "Would you like me to get some for your mum and dad too?"

Stella looked up from the book she was reading and smiled. "That would be nice but I think you've left it a bit too late, the lilac's gone over now."

"Has it? I'm sure it was fine when I last looked." Ned walked to the window to view the lilac tree at the top of the garden amongst the shrubbery by the roadside. "Humph, you're right, the flowers are all dead and brown. Well I never, it didn't last long, did it?"

"It never does really, but then it usually comes into flower in early May around Flora Day and we're nearing the end of June now."

"Bother! I'll have to find something else then. When will the dahlias be in flower?"

"Not today," laughed Stella, "they're only just coming into bud so I'm afraid you'll have to wait until next month. Take some roses from the rambler out the back instead, it's smothered in flowers this year and you can put a few sprays of gypsophila with it. The white will break up the colour nicely."

With bunches of sweetly scented roses and delicate white gypsophila resting across the sleeve of his faithful old Navy blue fleece, Ned left Rose Cottage for the short stroll to the churchyard. Once through the lichgate, he walked along the gravel path and in the shadow of the turreted tower, he split the flowers into two bunches and placed them on the graves of Stella's parents, Tom and Connie Hargreaves, and his mother, Molly, buried beside his stepfather, Major Benjamin Smith.

With the exception of blackbirds sitting on the branches of a rowan tree, Ned was alone in the graveyard, and so he sat on George Fillingham's memorial bench to enjoy the peace and warmth of the

June sun, high in the sky, peeping through the tall trees which separated the churchyard from the back yard of the inn.

Looking across the tops of the nearest tombstones, he sighed, his thoughts, nostalgic. All but one of the older generation had passed away in recent years. Dairy farmers, until their retirement, Pat and May Dickens. Local builder Harry Richardson and his wife, Joyce. Farmer, Cyril Penrose's widow, Nettie. Arthur Bray, campanologist of the church in his younger days. The Inn's one-time, much treasured, first landlord, Frank Newton and his sweet wife, Dorothy. Retired, stoic, village police constable, Fred Stevens and his wife, Annie. And farmer, Albert Treloar; all gone. The only real old-timer left of her generation was Madge Treloar, Albert's strong-minded widow.

Ned grinned, his expression tinged with both amusement and sorrow, realising, that to the younger generations, he and his contemporaries were unquestionably the new batch of old timers. After all, Sid Reynolds was eighty one and his closest friend, George, was nearly eighty, so in reality they were not far behind Madge in years. Where had the time all gone?

Before returning home, Ned called at the post office for a copy of the *Radio Times* and some second class stamps. He was served by Stephen Pascoe, who with every passing day looked more like his father, Johnny. Ned curiously glanced through the open door leading into the living accommodation just on the off chance he might see evidence that Nessie had returned, thus quashing the rumours regarding her hasty departure, but the rooms beyond stood silent and devoid of everyday female possessions.

"How's your grandmother?" Ned asked, taking his wallet from his fleece pocket. "I've not seen her at the Over Sixties' Club for a week or two now."

"Fine I believe, though her knees have been bothering her lately and she's a bit forgetful, but then who isn't at that age?"

"Hmm, I know the feeling. Exactly how old is she now?"

"Goodness knows. Eighty something or other, I'm not very good at remembering ages and birthdays. I do know she's determined to reach ninety though and I've a feeling she doesn't have to wait too long 'til she gets there."

Ned laughed. "And I expect she'll make it." He put the stamps inside his wallet and tucked the *Radio Times* beneath his arm. "Please convey my regards to your parents, Stephen, when next you see them."

"Thanks, yes I will. In fact I'm popping up tonight after I've closed. They have a change-over in the farmhouse tomorrow and need some light bulbs."

"Are they happy in their retirement?"

"Very, thanks, and they love Sea Thrift Cottage. Mum says she wakes up every morning and is just happy to be alive. I can see her point, it's a beautiful spot: so quiet and peaceful."

"That's really good to hear and it certainly is a nice position. You know, your parents are the third couple I've known to retire there. George and Bertha Fillingham were the first way back in 1952, then Stella's parents of course, and now your mum and dad. It makes me feel quite old. And you needn't reply to that, young man, platitudes aren't necessary."

Stephen grinned and nodded as Ned reached for the door handle and made his exit.

Inside the Old Vicarage, armed with vacuum cleaner, duster and furniture polish, Anne Collins walked down the wide passage way, her mind set on spring cleaning the living room, known by the family as the big room since the children, Ollie and Jess, were small. There had not been a fire lit in the hearth for over a month and on waking that morning Anne had reluctantly conceded that the yearly chore was long overdue. However, to make the task more enjoyable she decided to move around the furniture. She knew it would annoy John who liked things left boringly the same, but housework was her duty and she decreed that a change was the only way she could possibly take satisfaction from the otherwise tedious job.

After three hours' hard labour the room was thoroughly clean, but changing around the furniture left a space beside the door which looked in need of filling. However, to find something to fill the gap was not a problem, for the Old Vicarage garage housed a vast array of furniture, surplus due to various family house moves over the years.

Anne took the padlock key and went out to the garage to look for a suitable piece, and after deliberation settled on a Windsor chair which had once adorned the living room of her late grandparents' retirement home, Sea Thrift Cottage. As she lifted the chair down from the table on which it stood alongside two matching bedside lamps, Jess peeped around the garage door clutching a rolled up towel. "Just going down to the beach for a while, Mum. Gosh, look at all that junk. Can't you give it to a charity shop or something?"

"Oh, Jess, how can you call it junk?" said Anne, blowing dust from the seat. "Lots of this stuff has been in the family for years. You must remember some of it in the various family homes."

"Yeah, I suppose so. I certainly remember that little bookcase; it used to belong to Auntie Liz and Uncle Greg when they lived at Cove Cottage. It's where Tally kept her Famous Five books."

"Well, it still does belong to them, I suppose, but now they have neither room for nor need of it. That's the trouble with all this chopping and changing, your dad and I are the only ones that have stayed put."

"And you're the ones that have been lumbered with it all."

Anne smiled. "We don't mind, Jess, besides we volunteered to store it. One day it'll come in useful, you wait and see."

Jess, only half listening to her mother's words, pointed to the back of the garage where several items were neatly stacked on the surface of a large table.

"I recognise that wash stand too. It belonged to Great Grandma Molly. I remember it being in her bedroom with a pretty jug and bowl on top. I used to think it looked really creepy when I was little. Grandma and Granddad should have left it there."

"Well, to be fair they did keep a lot of Great Grandma Molly's things but they naturally wanted to have their own things round them too, and the Old School House was considerably larger than Rose Cottage."

"Hmm, and I think you'll find it still is. Anyway, I'm off to meet Tally on the beach, she has this lunchtime off work, so we're going to have a lazy day and get a delicious tan."

Anne laughed. "Every day's a lazy day for you, Jess. You've done nothing since you got back from university but eat and sleep."

"And drink," said Jess, impishly, "I've been a pretty good customer at the Jolly Sailor, but then that's because there's nowhere else to meet my mates and Justin's an absolutely divine, delicious hunk."

Anne tut-tutted.

"Anyway," Jess continued, "I shall be starting work at the Pickled Egg soon for the rest of the holiday so it's only right I take my ease now and charge my batteries for the busy times ahead. Bye Mum, don't work too hard."

Tally was already on the beach, not sunbathing, but talking to her brother, Wills, who had just finished a day's fishing with Matthew Williams. Jess waved and then went over to Matthew's boat to greet her two cousins.

"Caught much?" she asked, removing her sunglasses to peer into the boat.

"Hmm, we've had a good day but there's nothing to show for it because the crabs have all gone into store pots."

"Yes, of course. I sometimes wish I'd been a bloke," said Jess, wistfully, "you have much more fun jobs than us. I mean, the only seasonal jobs for hard up students are cleaning holiday places, waitressing and bar work."

"Hey, there's nothing wrong with bar work," grinned Tally, who had a summer job at the Jolly Sailor, "and I'd rather work in the pub any day than handle beastly, creepy crawly crabs looking for fingers and toes to bite."

"Pinch," laughed Matthew. "Crabs pinch with their claws, they don't bite."

Tally blushed. "Well you know what I mean."

"Anyway," said Jess, "when I talk of fishing being fun I'm meaning the delights there must be of being at sea, not the fishing side of things. You know, like setting out into a beautiful sunrise, the freedom and all that. What's more if you're feeling tired or hungover, you could just lounge around and do nothing while the boat bobs about on the ocean and nobody would ever know."

"Humph," grunted Wills, "just as well the sea is traditionally no place for women. Lounge around indeed."

"I didn't mean I'd never do any work," Jess added, hastily, "just that, well…"

Matthew laughed. "We know what you meant, Jess. Anyway, if ever you want a jolly jaunt on the old briny just say the word. I often take Rebecca out for a trip to give her a break, so you could all go out together sometime."

"Cool," said Jess, patting the boat's stern, "I'll take you up on that and you must come too, Tally."

"Hmm, I think I'd like that, but it'll have to be soon before the eclipse because they reckon it'll be really busy down here then."

"That's five weeks or so away yet," said Matthew, "anyway the offer stands, just let me know, but Sunday's a good day for Rebecca because the hairdressing salon's closed then. And I promise to make sure there aren't any creepy crawly crabs lurking in the bottom of the boat."

As with many relationships it was quite by chance that Rebecca Bray had met Matthew Williams during a trip in 1987 when she had accompanied her father, Walter, a keen genealogist, to Trengillion in search of their ancestors.

Rebecca had trained as a hairdresser on leaving secondary school in her Devonshire home town and quickly discovered she had a natural flair for the profession. This enabled her to get work in one of Devon's most prestigious salons where she rapidly became a popular choice for its middle class clientèle.

However, destiny decreed her future lay not in the county of her birth but across the Tamar, way down west on the Lizard Peninsula. Her father's research revealed that Matthew and Rebecca were distant cousins several times removed and on their first meeting both knew their fate was sealed. Rebecca always vowed it was love at first sight and even Matthew, although a pragmatist, admitted he found it hard to disagree.

Chapter Five

In 1993, when twins, Ollie and Jess, were fourteen years old, Anne Collins happily returned to work part-time on the reception desk of the Penwynton Hotel. It was not for financial reasons she chose to return; her husband, John, was doing very nicely with his brother-in-law, Steve, in their building business and their mortgage repayments were modest in comparison to the early years of their marriage when much of their income was spent on renovating the Old Vicarage. The reason for her return was partly to meet people in a job and environment she had always enjoyed, but mainly because Linda Stevens had asked if she would like to return to the fold.

Anne liked Linda, the two women got on well and had known each other since 1967 when Linda's parents, Mary and Dick Cottingham and her aunt and uncle, Heather and Bob Jarrams, had jointly bought the then Penwynton House and converted it into a hotel.

In 1993, the joint owners had decided to take their ease and gradually retire from running the Hotel. They unanimously agreed to pass its administration on to Linda and her husband, Jamie, who gave up his bank job in order to give the Hotel his undivided attention.

In the early days following her return, Anne worked just three mornings a week, but after a couple of years she found herself offered more and more hours until eventually she became full time throughout the busy summer months.

During the last week of June, as Anne put down the telephone receiver following an enquiry, Mary Cottingham, one of the Hotel's proprietors, returned from a shopping trip in Falmouth and entered the Hotel by the main front door. Due to the heat she looked flustered, but in spite of her obvious tiredness, as usual, not a hair was out of place.

"That's the third enquiry this morning already for eclipse week," said Anne, sighing and smiling at the same time to welcome her boss. "We could have booked out every room ten times over I reckon."

"I know," laughed Mary, putting three carrier bags onto the black and white tiled floor and as she flopped wearily into a Regency chair by the reception desk, "and it's the same everywhere apparently. Phew, it's warm out there, I need to get my breath back."

Anne smiled. "You do look a little flushed. Would you like me to make you a cup of tea?"

"No, don't worry, Anne, I'll have one when I get back upstairs."

Mary removed her shoe and rubbed the sole of her foot. "I note what you said about booking out the rooms several times over in the eclipse week. Linda told me they had a phone call at three o'clock this morning from America." She slipped her foot back into her shoe and sighed. "It's a pity really that we can't have an eclipse every year."

Anne looked aghast. "Oh no, I don't think I can agree with you there; it's all starting to look a bit nightmarish to me. You know, I read the other day that there are likely to be half a million more visitors here than we usually get for that week in August, and August is already the busiest month of the year. We won't have room to move."

Mary smiled. "Well we mustn't forget the media are inclined to exaggerate, but even so I daresay everywhere will be a lot busier than usual. We'll have to make sure we get orders for supplies in early though, just in case things run short."

Anne laughed. "Absolutely, it'd be dreadful if we had nothing to feed the guests."

Mary patted her round stomach. "It wouldn't hurt me to miss a meal or two. In fact I often look back wistfully on the days after the War when food was still rationed. I know I was a teenager then but I had a twenty three inch waist and I'm sure we were all a damn sight healthier."

"So Grandma Molly used to tell us. I don't know how you all did it. I mean, the thought of little or no chocolate seems pretty harsh to me."

"Yes, and so it was, but then when things got back to normal we all appreciated everything the more. People are so wasteful today and they expect too much from life. Very few would be happy, or able to rough it like we did, but then we had no choice."

"Very true," said Anne, "and you mentioning roughing it has reminded me that Jess told me the Recreation Ground Committee have decided to open up the field for campers during eclipse week in order to raise a bit of money, and good old Justin has agreed to let them have access to the inn's toilets through the side door. Mind you, it should do him a bit of good as well and like us they've had all their rooms booked for ages."

"Really! Now that is a good idea, so you'll have campers as near neighbours for a while."

"Hmm, I suppose we will, but only when we're in the garden, we won't be able to see them from the house, or hear them for that matter and hopefully they'll be well behaved anyway."

"I'm sure they will, I can't see that the eclipse is likely to attract riff raff. Having said that you never know, I suppose they might be as interested as anyone else. Which reminds me, Jim Haynes was telling me some people are actually renting out their homes for large amounts and moving in with relatives for the week too. I don't think I'd like to do that, not just for a week anyway, it wouldn't be worth the hassle of moving one's personal possessions. Jim said he thought about it but soon gave up the idea. After all, an Englishman's home is his castle."

Anne grinned. "I agree and when all's said and done, I expect it'll be a miserable day anyway so there won't be anything much to see."

"Tut, tut," smiled Mary, rising from the chair having cooled down and recouped her energy, "you mustn't be such a pessimist, Anne."

"I'm not being a pessimist, I'm being a realist. After all I've lived in Cornwall all my life and know the weather often spoils the best laid plans and all that. Remember Linda's wedding day? It chucked it down from dawn 'til dusk and that was during a drought in flaming June."

Mary laughed, recalling the atrocious weather on the day of her daughter's marriage. "Enough said, but I do hope you're wrong on this occasion, Anne. I really do."

When she finished work, happy to be out in the fresh air, Anne walked home through Bluebell Woods, where the vibrant colours of the pink and mauve rhododendrons were beginning to fade and her favourites, the white flowers, were each tinged with brown.

She followed the contour of the stream, sporadically edged with clumps of golden marsh marigolds and pastel coloured lady's smocks, both shimmering together in the dappled shade. Pensively, she considered options for dinner; should it be salad or pasta bake? While deep in thought she encountered Jim Haynes wheeling his bicycle along the woodland path, homeward bound following a day's work at Long Acre Farm.

"Lovely weather," said Anne, cheered by his tuneful whistle.

"Smashing," he agreed, standing aside for her to pass, "but it's a lot cooler here in the shade, thank goodness. It was damn hot out planting cauli in the fields today, but at least we got them all done."

"I bet. I must say you do look a little hot under the collar."

Jim shook the neckline of his grubby tee shirt and laughed. "I bet I don't smell too sweet either. Still, never mind, I'll be in the shower in a few minutes. Meanwhile, I'm half tempted to take off my trainers and paddle in the stream, but I'm put off by the possibility of standing on something sharp and knackering my poor old tired feet."

Anne nodded. "I see your dilemma, because it does look rather inviting when it's as clear as crystal. Mind you, as well as the likelihood of treading on something sharp the chances are the water will be damn chilly too."

"Ah, chilli, that reminds me, I'm glad I've seen you. Would you like some chilli plants? Far more germinated than I'd anticipated and now they're getting bigger they're taking up too much room."

"Chillies! Wow, yes please. I've never grown them before and we use quite a few because John does like his curries. Are they difficult to look after?"

"No, not at all. I treat them a bit like peppers but I don't water them as often. I've got three different varieties so you can have one of each. They make attractive houseplants too if they're kept on a sunny window sill."

"Brilliant. When shall I call round and collect them?"

"They're in my greenhouse up at the allotment, but if you like I can drop them in to you on my way to the inn tomorrow morning as I've a load of stuff to drop off there for Maurice."

"Yes, okay, do that then; if I've already gone to work Jess will be there, that's if she's up."

Jim laughed. "It won't be too early, around twelve; I said I'd drop the veg in to Maurice at lunchtime."

"That's fine, thanks, Jim and I'll leave a couple of fuchsias with Jess for you. I took loads of cuttings last year and they all rooted bar one. They'll look lovely in your numerous tubs."

"That'd be fantastic, I do have a few gaps because sodding slugs and snails ate most of my petunias before the poor things even had a chance to flower."

Anne sighed sympathetically. "That's one of the reasons I like fuchsias, because the slugs and snails don't seem to bother with them and of course they have such a long flowering period too."

"Good point," said Jim, glancing at his watch. "Blimey, it's later than I thought. Gotta dash, Anne, because I want to see the tennis. Henman's third match on Centre Court today and it should be a good one."

"Is he?" I'd like to see that too. He always puts up such a good fight and he's doing well again this year, isn't he? In spite of the dreadful weather on Tuesday."

Jim nodded. "Yeah, and I'd dearly love to see him win, he certainly deserves a break. Trouble is there's always Pete Sampras to beat. Still, you never know."

Anne smiled wistfully. "I really thought he was going to beat Sampras at Queen's, but Pete's such a formidable opponent that I don't think anyone stands much of a chance against him."

Although Justin Thornton had little or no time for gardening, he was still very fond of certain flowers and sunflowers in particular, partly because he had been encouraged by his granddad to grow them as a child and partly because they seemed such happy, cheerful flowers and reminded him of the lazy hot summer days of his youth. For the latter reason he decided to run a competition in the village, open to all to see who could grow the tallest sunflower. The date he chose for the close of the competition was August the eleventh, the day of the solar eclipse.

The competition caught the imagination of all generations when first it had been publicised back in the spring and Justin was surprised by the competitive spirit demonstrated by his clientèle, especially the quiet, shy ones. He decided, however, after hearing talk of super-size species, that to make entry fair everyone must grow the same variety from seed, which he would provide. The sunflower seeds therefore had been available from the inn since Easter. No starting date or deadline for the sowing of the seeds was specified but allocations were restricted to just three per entrant.

The first house of a row of four known as Coronation Terrace, had once been the home of Susan and Steve Penhaligon, but since March it had been occupied by a family new to the village of whom very little was known. However, following dedicated detective work by curious members of the community, it was eventually established that the names of the new inhabitants were Trevor and Valerie Moore. Observation also revealed they had two young children, both girls under school age.

The Moores, the investigations exposed, were brought into the village by the local authorities from further up the line and many people initially resented the fact that the house had not gone to a local couple. However, attitudes softened a little when it emerged that Trevor Moore was, according to his next door neighbour, Gertie, on the sick although she, like everyone else, was a little mystified as to what might be the justification.

Gertie discovered quite by chance shortly after the family moved into Number One that Trevor was in receipt of benefits. It had been a chilly, windy evening in mid-April and she was hurrying home after a WI meeting in the village hall. The following day the rubbish was due for collection, hence along the road, dustbins and black bin liners had stood in serried ranks by nearly every garden gate, including Number One Coronation Terrace.

Ugly black threatening clouds had rolled rapidly through the sky that night, frequently blotting out the moon, and as Gertie lifted the latch of her own gate, eager to get inside and out of the wind, she felt cold raindrops brush against her rosy cheeks. Hunching her shoulders she turned to walk up the garden path; simultaneously a strong gust of wind had whipped down the road, rustling the bulging black rubbish bags in its path, and rattling dustbins so violently their plastic lids were knocked to the ground.

Gertie paused thoughtfully as the lids span and tumbled in the road, and after deciding she had no desire to have the neighbourhood's rubbish strewn over her front garden, and likewise neither would her neighbours, she dutifully stepped back out into the road and securely replaced the lids of the bins nearby. It was as she lowered the lid on the bin from Number One, that a crumpled piece of paper from the Benefits office, caught her eye in the light from the street lamp opposite. Gertie furtively glanced over her shoulder, and seeing the coast was clear in all directions, snatched the paper from the grasp of a greasy margarine tub and quickly pushed it into the pocket of her coat.

Once inside her home, Gertie hurriedly called Percy's name. He did not reply and so she assumed he had gone to the pub. Glad that she was alone in the house she pulled the letter from her pocket and read it through; its content was in regard to a change to disability benefits following his recent move. Gertie was delighted to have unearthed this useful piece of information and as she screwed up the letter and tossed it onto the low burning fire in the living room, she hoped it might help find out more of the family's situation as the future weeks unfolded. But as neither, Trevor nor Valerie worked and the children were too young to attend school, it soon became apparent they had very little reason to socialise and therefore kept themselves pretty much aloof from the village and its activities. Hence, to Gertie's annoyance, the nature of Trevor Moore's disability remained a mystery to her and everyone else to whom she had conveyed her findings.

Tally was sitting in the public bar drinking a glass of Coke after finishing her lunchtime waitressing shift when Maurice the Chef came out from the kitchen. With a pint of cold lager in his hand he sat down by her side.

"It's probably a silly question, Tally, but are you any good at sewing?"

Tally screwed up her face. "What, like with a needle and cotton?"

"I think they're usually two of the main tools needed for the job."

Tally laughed. "Well, it all depends what type of sewing. I mean, I've stitched on a button or two before now but nothing more complicated than that. Why do you ask?"

He sighed. "I bought a new pair of curtains for my living room off eBay because the flowery ones already there weren't really me, but they are far too long and drag on the floor. I thought about stapling them up but I can't find my stapler."

Tally whistled. "Oh, that's too complicated for me but don't worry I'll get Mum to do it. She's quite good at sewing because she learned it from her granny."

"Her granny was good then?"

"Brilliant! Mum says she used to make all her own clothes. I don't remember her too well because she died when I was quite young, but I do remember her clothes were really vivid. And that's not criticism because I like bright colours but not as bright as Great Grandma, or Mum either for that matter."

Maurice nodded. "Would you ask her for me? I'll pay her of course, but please stress there's absolutely no rush, especially now it's summer and the nights are light."

"Yes, I'm off home now so I'll ask her when I get in. You won't need to pay her though because I'm sure she'd be only too glad to do it as it would give her something to do."

Chapter Six

Late one afternoon in early July, after a busy morning on his allotment weeding and sowing fresh salad crops, Jim Haynes settled down in front of the television with several cans of cold lager and a pizza to watch Tim Henman's semifinal match against Pete Sampras at Wimbledon.

Jim held out very little hope of the young Brit defeating the American colossus, in spite of Tim's huge support both from spectators lucky enough to have Centre Court tickets and those watching on Henman Hill. Nevertheless, he knew he could rely on Britain's Number One to put up a good fight and get the adrenaline of all British tennis fans pumping.

The match started well: Tim won the first set, 6-3 and raised the hopes of tennis fanatics throughout the nation.

Jim waved his fist as the second half began. "Come on Tiger Tim." But to his disappointment Pete Sampras fought back and won the second set 6-4. The third set also went to Pete, 6-3. Jim's heart sank. In spite of Tim's obvious determination, Jim knew the match could well be over and done with at the end of the fourth set. And it was. Pete Sampras took the fourth set 6-4 and with it the match, dashing the hopes and dreams of a nation once again.

Jim rose, disheartened and switched off the television set. He then went outside and lay on the grass in the warm sun, hugely disappointed. To him the All England Lawn Tennis Championships were as good as finished once Tim Henman was out and there seemed little point in continuing to watch.

"Still, there's always next year," said Jim, sardonically, to long deceased Thomas Symonds, on whose grave he rested his head of dark brown curls, "and the year after that and the year after that."

However, in spite of his decreased interest following Tim's defeat, Jim still watched the Wimbledon final on Sunday afternoon and was greatly heartened when Pete Sampras beat André Agassi in three straight sets.

"At least," Jim smiled, switching off the television set, "Tim was beaten by the best. *And* he took a set off Pistol Pete, so he's one up on André."

On Sunday July the eleventh, Matthew and his wife Rebecca met Tally, Wills and Jess on the beach for a trip out to sea. As it was a Sunday and he had the day off work, Jess's twin brother, Ollie, joined them too. The weather was fine and the sunshine hazy as they pushed the boat down the beach over the evenly spaced logs and into the gently rippling waves.

"Which way would you like to go?" Matthew asked, taking control of the rudder once they were all aboard. "West or east?"

"I'd like to go to the west," said Tally, excitedly, waving her hand in that direction, "then we'll pass beneath Chy-an-Gwyns. But I expect you'd like to go east wouldn't you, Rebecca, so you see the Coastguard Cottages?"

"No, no, not at all. I've seen them from the sea several times before. In fact I've been both ways so the choice really must rest with you lot."

"I'm happy to go either way," said Jess, shrugging her shoulders. Ollie agreed and so it was decided they would go to the west beneath the cliffs on which stood Chy-an-Gwyns.

The wind was light and the sea calm as the small fishing vessel chugged away from the shore with gentle waves splashing idly against the fibreglass hull. No-one spoke until they were some way out and Matthew turned the boat towards the west.

"Trengillion looks so different from the sea," Jess whispered, "I don't think I'd have been able to have recognised it even if shown it on a picture."

"Wouldn't you?" Tally laughed, surprised, "I'd know it anywhere from any angle but then I suppose I've had the advantage of living within sight of the sea all my life, so it's only right I should."

"And you have an aerial view photograph of the coastline hanging in your bedroom," teased Wills, "which, I might add, you gaze at frequently."

Rebecca laughed. "Do you miss it when you're away? The sea I mean, not the picture."

"Yes, often, especially on lovely sunny days and when I'm stuck indoors studying or when the wind is blowing a gale and I know the seas will be rough and enormous."

Wills nodded in agreement. "That's when I like the sea best, when it's stormy, wild and choppy. I love the tremendous roar of the enormous waves and the thrill of trying to remain in a vertical position as the crazy winds attempt to take one's breath away."

Rebecca nodded. "Absolutely, my favourite time too, though days such as this are also wonderful. How about you, Jess, do you miss it?"

"Well, actually I'm at Swansea University and it's near to the sea. Having said that it's not quite the same as being here. Trengillion is home and there's nowhere in the world to touch it."

"Hear, hear," laughed Tally, tilting her head to view the cliffs. "Just look at Chy-an-Gwyns. Isn't it superb? I love it to bits and I feel as if we've lived there always. I don't think I'll ever be able to move away from here, not permanently anyway."

"It is lovely," agreed Rebecca, admiringly, "and I can see your point of view because I love living on the cliff tops too, albeit our home is very modest compared to Chy-an-Gwyns. But won't you all have to move away when you get your degrees? I mean, West Cornwall doesn't hold a great deal of potential for graduates, does it?"

"I might be alright," said Wills, flicking a fly from his arm, "I'm studying law and lawyers are needed all over the country, though I might go on to be a barrister, it all depends how well I do."

"Wills is the cleverest of us all as you can see," laughed Jess.

"No, I'm not. Ollie and I got pretty much the same results in school tests, didn't we, Ollie?"

"Well, yes, but I could never have gone on to study like you do. I'm more of the hands-on type and I like to be outdoors like Dad."

"Fair enough. I must admit I am studying pretty hard at present and I'm enjoying the challenge as well, but I don't know if the enthusiasm will last. Going back to the original topic though, I wouldn't mind living up-country for a spell, but I think I'd like to come back here in my dotage so I can be buried in the churchyard with folks I'm familiar with."

"Christ, Wills," Matthew chuckled, "that's a bit premature isn't it? Planning your funeral, I mean. You sound like one of the old timers talking of being buried in the churchyard with your cronies."

"Wills is a bit of a romantic, aren't you, Wills?" Jess giggled. "Like Great Granny Molly was."

"And he's lucky too," sighed Tally, "I wish I knew what I wanted to do when I finish university. I shall probably end up teaching like Mum."

"I didn't know your mum was ever a teacher," said Rebecca, surprised, "when was that?"

"Oh, ages ago, before Wills and I were born. She taught up-country for a while after she first qualified and then came down here and taught over at Polquillick. She always vowed she'd go back to it when we grew up but she never has."

"Yeah, but that's because she doesn't need to," said Wills, "Dad earns well and Mum says it's morally wrong to work unnecessarily if it's taking work away from others."

"Which is her way of saying she can't be arsed," laughed Tally.

"So, what do you foresee the future holds for you, Jess?" Matthew asked.

She shrugged her shoulders. "I don't know, I really don't know. I often wish I was a chap so that I could have learned a trade like Ollie and Dad, because I'm not really an academic. It's not fair, things are different for women, aren't they? Because when you boil it all down it seems to be a choice between retail, clerical work, catering or tourism, none of which really appeal, although I do like working in the Pickled Egg, I love baking and like Mum I quite enjoy meeting people."

"You could be a model," suggested Wills, sincerely, "you've a terrific figure."

"Thanks, but I'd be wasting my education if I went in for something as banal as that. Besides, my figure might look alright to you, but I can assure you in reality I'd be regarded as fat in the world of fashion."

"Perhaps some dashingly handsome young millionaire will come to Trengillion and sweep you off your feet," grinned Matthew, "then you won't need to work."

"Ha, ha, not much chance of that, and if such a person were to come here then he'd not give me a second glance. Besides, I wouldn't want to be a kept woman, I think I'd die of boredom if I had everything handed to me on a plate."

Tally gazed thoughtfully at her cousin. "I think you ought to have your own business, Jess. After all you're a Capricorn and they're excellent organisers and good at solving problems too."

Wills looked heavenwards. "Here we go. Tally is about to tell us all what the future holds according to her heroine Taffeta Tealeaves."

Jess giggled.

Wills punched his sister's arm affectionately. "Come on Talls, and tell us what the soppy woman in your airhead magazine predicts will happen today?"

"*Love-in-a-mist* isn't an airhead magazine," said Tally, indignantly. "Many of its articles are very educational and I can assure you that Taffeta is by no means a silly woman."

Wills laughed. "That's as maybe but horoscopes are nonsense and everyone knows they're just made up by people who write the first thing that comes to mind."

Rebecca shook her head. "I can't agree with you there, Wills. I occasionally read my horoscope and sometimes it's spot-on."

"Sometimes, yes, but then you can put that down to the law of averages. If an astrologer really was worth his or her salt they'd get it right every time and everyone knows that wouldn't be possible because a single forecast couldn't be accurate for everyone under the umbrella of any particular birth sign. I mean, there's much more to our makeup than the mere influence of stars, time and the year of our birth: genetics for instance."

Ollie nodded. "I agree, Wills."

"Humph! You're a typical Gemini, Willoughby Edward Castor-Hunt," laughed Tally, "a right clever-clogs and a born intellectual who won't shy away from voicing his opinion, however biased it might be."

Elizabeth left Chy-an-Gwyns with dressmaking scissors, pins, needles and several reels of cotton in various shades of brown in her handbag. After Tally had asked her to take up the hem on Maurice's curtains she had spoken to him on the phone and told him she would be delighted to help out but she had recently cut the index finger on her right hand which made sewing difficult, but not to worry as it would only take a few days to heal. Maurice reiterated that there was absolutely no rush and it was agreed he would leave his house key on the bar with Justin so that she had access to Valley View whenever she was ready.

Elizabeth had never been inside Valley View before even though it was next door to Rose Cottage, the home of her parents, but that was mainly because the occupants were ever-changing tenants and the owner of the house lived somewhere in the Falmouth area. Therefore, as she walked up the garden path she decided to take a quick look around before she started work.

In spite of the warm morning, the house struck cold as Elizabeth stood on the doormat inside the hallway, and a strong musty smell was slightly masked by the pleasant aroma of fried bacon which Maurice must have eaten for breakfast. Elizabeth dropped her bag on the floor and went upstairs.

There were three bedrooms. Originally there would have been four but the smallest had been converted into a bathroom; its chunky white suit was dated and had an electric shower over the stained bathtub, alongside which hung a floral shower curtain, its bottom half blackened with mildew. Elizabeth peeped inside the bedrooms; Maurice obviously used the largest on the back of the house for the other two were devoid of personal belongings.

Back downstairs, Elizabeth glanced into the dining room then the living room where the over-long curtains hung. The more she saw the more saddened she felt. In its hey-day the house would have been grand in a modest way, but now much of the furniture both upstairs and down, was well-worn and drab and the décor was shabby throughout; but she knew Maurice paid a very modest rent due to the house being in need of renovation and were the landlord to try and let it out through an agency, the property would not be up to scratch. All the same, Elizabeth felt sorry for the house. The atmosphere was tinged with sadness; it felt unloved, yet at the same time, creepy, almost sinister. She shuddered at the thought of being there alone after dark and imagined it in years gone by, before electricity when the only light would be from candles eerily flickering in draughts creating ghostly shadows on the dim, dark walls.

In the living room, she was relieved to find the curtains were unlined and so would take up far less time to sew. They were, however, at least two feet too long and so leaving the curtains hanging, Elizabeth carefully measured the required length to be discarded and then carefully trimmed off the excess fabric which she deemed was sufficient to make two matching cushions.

When both curtains were pinned and Elizabeth was happy they were level, she went into the kitchen, as instructed so to do by Maurice, and made a mug of tea which she carried back into the living room where she sat in the fireside chair nearest to the window. She glanced around the room. The furniture was sparse; just the two armchairs, a bookcase, an old television set, a coffee table and a modern desk on which stood Maurice's computer, monitor, mouse and keyboard; the desk, she concluded, no doubt belonged to Maurice. From the coffee table she picked up a glossy magazine and flicked through the pages. The pictures were of computers, printers and other technological gadgets; since they were of no interest she lay the magazine back down and drank her tea.

From her handbag, she heard her mobile phone make a beeping sound. Thinking it indicated a text message, she eagerly pulled the phone from its case but to her disgust the message merely said that her battery was low. With an air of disappointment she stood to return her empty mug to the kitchen, but as she walked towards the door, she thought she heard a deep voice quietly mumbling. She was puzzled; Maurice lived alone hence there should be no-one in the house. What's more, her earlier look around had proved she was quite alone. She left the living room and crossed the hallway. A door at the foot of the stairs was ajar. She peeped inside knowing it was the dining room; no-one was in there. She frowned. Perhaps the voice had come from outside. She opened the front door and stepped out into the garden. All was quiet and no voices emanated from the street. She returned indoors and listened, but the house was silent apart from the ticking of a wall clock in the hallway and the humming of the refrigerator in the kitchen. Thinking she must have imagined the voice, she endeavoured to get back to work, but as she walked into the living room she heard it again; a deep voice, quickly spoken and husky. Elizabeth paused and raised her eyes towards the ceiling. The voice was coming from above.

With heart thumping loudly, she returned to the hallway. At the foot of the stairs she clung on to the newel post and looked up to the landing. The voice was now gaily chattering, although its words were muffled and incoherent. Silently she crept up the stairs. At the top she tiptoed along the landing towards the room from where the voice was coming. Slowly, she pushed open the door. In the corner beside his unmade double bed, red lights flickered up and down on Maurice's clock radio. With relief, Elizabeth laughed and moved forward to switch it off. And as she touched the switch it burst into song.

Chapter Seven

Ned Stanley had retired from his position as headmaster of the village school during the summer of 1992, after thirty nine years of service. To reward and thank him for his many years of dedication, patience and loyalty, a collection was initiated and with the sum raised a camcorder was purchased and presented to him in a tearful ceremony inside the school.

After Ned's retirement, the village waited with bated breath to see who was appointed as the school's new head teacher and to the surprise of many, the successful applicant was a woman. Her name was Alison Turner, Ms Alison Turner to be precise, and very little was known about her other than that she hailed from Paignton in Devon.

Following her engagement she purchased a modest house in Helston. Many villagers thought she ought to have settled in Trengillion; some even felt snubbed, but she told her critics she did not wish to fraternise with the parents of her young pupils as it might influence her impartiality. Trengillion parents did not agree, but by the first Christmas following her September start, most conceded she was doing a good job. The children adored her, admired her and approved of her good looks, but most important of all, they obeyed her and so the criticism stopped.

Since the completion of the Penwynton Housing Estate, pupil numbers at the school had increased twofold, hence a portable classroom was installed in the corner of the playground to accommodate the extra children. It was brought in during the summer holiday in 1987 as a temporary measure and soon became fondly known as the Hut. However, its days were numbered for there were plans afoot to increase the size of the school building with an extension which would provide two more classrooms.

The completion of the Penwynton Housing Estate inevitably doubled the population of Trengillion as well as school pupil numbers. Many people, even those who had lived in the village all their lives, as had their parents before them, frequently encountered unfamiliar faces and knew not whether they were inhabitants of the village or holiday makers.

Nevertheless, in spite of the changes, Trengillion was still a very friendly place to live and all knew their near neighbours even if people further afield were strangers. Furthermore the village had retained the same feeling of camaraderie and community spirit that was prevalent back in the days when it was half the size.

Inside the kitchen of Valley View, Maurice Lamont, the inn's new chef, drummed his fingers on the kitchen table top awaiting the delivery of his new computer. For his old one lacked the capacity he required to store his frequent downloads, and since he was earning well he thought he deserved to be a little lavish with his income.

From the street, Maurice heard the door of a vehicle slam shut. Hoping it was his delivery, he dashed into the living room and looked out of the window but to his disappointment the garden gate was closed; no-one was walking up the path and the only sign of life were the two magpies, Kernow and Kate, strutting across the lawn. With a sigh of disappointment he sat down in one of the fireside chairs and cast his eyes around the room and towards the ceiling. The house seemed eerily quiet, even the ticking of the clock in the hallway seemed to be fainter than usual. Maurice shuddered, and for the first time since he had lived there, wondered if he might be sharing the house with a ghost as suggested to him by Elizabeth.

The carton arrived in due course and Maurice opened it eagerly. When the system was up and running he logged onto his eBay account to browse through the Tobacciana section. For Maurice was a keen collector of Smokeralia, especially old lighters and pipes. After selecting five items, which he put on watch, he checked his emails, mostly from colleagues in the Plymouth area, and then spent an hour responding before he prepared for his evening shift at the inn.

At half past five he left his home, and as he walked past the post office a red Ford Fiesta pulled up. Nessie stepped out looking very happy and smiling from ear to ear. Maurice was rather taken aback. Like everyone else he had heard of her swift departure following, allegedly, an explosive disagreement.

Their eyes met and Maurice grinned nervously.

"Off to work?" she said.

"Hmm, yes, hello, it's um, good to see you back."

Laughing, she opened the boot in which lay two floral suitcases.

"Och, do you mean to say anyone even noticed I'd gone, and after such a wee while too. Wonders will never cease."

"I, umm...sorta heard on the grapevine," said Maurice, clearly embarrassed, "anyway, I must get off, lots of prep work and so forth to do, bye."

Maurice decided not to say anything about Nessie's return when he arrived at the Jolly Sailor for fear of being cast in the same category as the gossips. Therefore, it was a surprise to everyone when Stephen walked in with Nessie on his arm: everyone except for Stephen's brother, David, who came in with his wife, Judith.

"Good to see you back," said David, leaning forward to kiss Nessie's cheek, "you're looking well."

"Thank you. It's nice to be back even though we had a wonderful time." She tightened her grip on Stephen's arm. "And this wonderful man is an absolute treasure for letting me go and leave him to run the place alone."

The bar was almost silent; no locals spoke; all were listening.

Nessie looked askance. "Why is everyone watching us?" she whispered. "Have I grown an extra head or something?"

Stephen grinned as he too lowered his voice. "I forgot to warn you. Everyone assumed you'd left me when you went off on your holiday. It's because you were heard ranting and raving, you see. We'd had a row apparently, at least that's what I've been told."

"A row!" the young Scot, hissed. "When?"

"In the minutes before you left."

"You mean, when I was in a flap because I couldn't find the car keys."

Stephen nodded. "Yep."

"But that's ridiculous. Of course I was in shouting. I was already running late and I had a plane to catch."

"You know that and I know that," whispered Stephen, "but everyone else put two and two together and it seems made five."

"We knew too," giggled Judith, "and it was me who told Stephen what was being said. I heard whispers, you see, when I was doing the egg round, but of course I kept mum."

"Really? So where did I go after this row?" Nessie asked.

"No one knew, but then someone said they'd seen you hugging a man by a gate in Helston," said Stephen, "so it was assumed you had a new bloke."

Nessie put her hand over her mouth to smother a laugh. In reality she had been away because an old school friend in Scotland had phoned and asked if she'd like to take the place of her boyfriend for a holiday. A sudden urgent work load meant that the said boyfriend was unable to go at the last minute and he had begged her to take someone else. On being asked, Nessie had jumped at the chance; the result of which was a prepaid two week holiday in Greece.

Nessie smiled. "Another bloke indeed! Rob will hoot when I tell him. Let's keep quiet about him though and the holiday too. It might even be very good for trade in the post office if the inquisitive make frequent visits to ferret out the truth about him and my unexplained absence."

On Saturday July the seventeenth, the village prepared for its annual summer fayre on the recreation field. As usual it was arranged by the church and school combined and was always a popular event. Because of the eclipse, it had been suggested at a meeting earlier in the year, that the event be put off until August in order to get a larger crowd, but the motion was defeated unanimously as most people would be involved with other activities that week and head teacher, Alison Turner in particular, was not in favour of returning to the village to work during her summer vacation, especially in the mayhem of eclipse week.

Potential poor weather was always a worry for the organisers. Most years they were blessed with a modicum of sunshine and occasionally they enjoyed a heat wave, but there was always the odd year when the weather was miserable or even worse they had to endure torrential rain and hold the event inside the school. In 1999 they were lucky; the day was fairly good and the sun shone from time to time as the stall holders set out their wares during the morning.

At half past two, the Fayre was duly opened by Justin Thornton, for members of both committees thought it would be a friendly gesture to welcome him and endorse their approval of his contribution to the village, especially the wonderful community spirit his Sunflower Competition had evoked.

Gertie, along with Meg Reynolds, both representing the church, had volunteered to run the White Elephant stall. As the afternoon wore on and the crowds dispersed, Gertie chatted about the downside of ornaments being their ability to collect dust to Candy Bingham on the adjacent stall selling plants and garden produce. Candy agreed and then begged Gertie to buy one of the many marrows which weren't selling very well. Gertie turned up her nose, Percy liked stuffed marrow but she thought the dish a little too bland. Nevertheless, she agreed to take a couple off Candy's hands and selected two of the biggest. As she bent down to retrieve her handbag from beneath the stall, she noticed the Moore family slowly amble into the field. It was the first time Gertie had seen her new neighbours all out together and to the best of her knowledge it was the first time they had attended any of the village functions. She handed over fifty pence to Candy and then both watched with curiosity as the family walked around the field viewing the stalls on the opposite side of the field, buying a few bits and pieces but dutifully never letting the children out of their sight.

As they reached the jumble stall, Trevor suddenly leaned backwards, a pained expression on his pale face. Valerie hurriedly took his arm and escorted him to a row of chairs outside the tea tent where he awkwardly took a seat. While he sat in obvious pain and discomfort, Valerie slipped inside the tent and returned shortly after with a cup and saucer along with two beakers of orange squash. From her handbag she then took a bottle of tablets and handed some to her husband who eagerly popped them into his mouth and washed them down with gulps of tea. Valerie then walked rapidly over to the jumble stall from where she returned with two carrier bags bulging with her purchases.

Gertie, out of character, said not a word during the Moores' movements, but nevertheless hoped they would visit her stall so that she might try and wheedle out some personal information. However, to her dismay, they left after the jumble stall visit. Trevor was obviously still in pain, and so Gertie was none the wiser as to their circumstances.

The Summer Fayre did well and to the delight of both school and church committees, took a record amount of money. After everything had been returned to its rightful place and the proceeds counted, Alison Turner thanked everyone for their dedicated, hard work and invited the stall holders and organisers to the inn for a drink at her expense.

"Cor blimey, I wonder what's the reason for this largesse," whispered Gertie to Meg, picking up a carrier bag full of purchases, the marrows and her handbag, "I'd always got her down as a bit of a tight arse because let's face it, she's never done anything like this before and she's been head for seven years now."

"Is it really that long?" queried Meg, picking up beetroot and a marrow she too had bought from her produce stall. "I suppose I should know seeing as I retired just before Ned. It's weird you know, not having much to do with the school now. I was there a long time, practically all my working life, with just a couple of breaks when the children were born."

"I remember your first day," said Gertie, wistfully, "you wore your favourite blue dress because you said it was lucky. Do you remember it? It had a really full skirt and a tight fitting bodice. I used to envy you your figure back then."

Meg laughed. "Not only do I remember it but I still have it. I was wearing it, you see, when Sid proposed to me. We were sitting on Denzil's bench at the time."

"Hmm, happy day, eh, Meg? Shall we pop this stuff home before we go to the inn, it seems daft to lug it down there when we only live up the road."

"Good idea. I can get my warm cardigan then at the same time. I feel quite chilly now the sun's gone round and although this cardigan looks nice, it's rather on the thin side."

Inside the Jolly Sailor, Gertie, sat with her friends near to the fireplace in the snug, where a black cast iron cauldron full of dried blue and white hydrangeas hid the empty grate. From her seat she read a notice taped on the chimney breast.

"I see Justin's looking to recruit more staff," she said, sipping her complimentary rum and diet Coke, "I'm not surprised, he's probably getting a bit nervous about eclipse week. I know I would if I were in his shoes."

"Really, I wonder how many extras he actually wants," said Candy, thoughtfully, "I wouldn't mind having a go."

"Go and ask him," said Meg, glancing through the open snug doors towards the bar, "look, he's not serving anyone at present."

"But don't you think I might be a bit too old?" asked Candy, hesitantly. "I mean to say, most of his staff are youngsters and full of life."

"Our Sue's not much younger than you," said Gertie, "she's in her forties too, in fact she's probably about your age."

Candy wrinkled her nose. "Yes, I suppose so. He might want blokes though, because all his current staff are females, so a chap or two would redress the balance a bit and make a change."

"You're talking yourself out of a job before you've applied for it," laughed Stella, who had been selling raffle tickets at the Fayre, "Faint heart never won fair lady."

"I know, but that's because I lack self-confidence and I'm not very good at being rejected, so I'm exploring obstacles before they arise to soften the blow of an inevitable refusal."

"You timorous twit," said Gertie, rising. "Inevitable refusal indeed! You'd make a brilliant barmaid. Leave it to me."

"No, Gert, please…"

But Gertie, never one to be called bashful, was gone, and within minutes she was standing at the bar chatting to Justin. When she returned to her seat she was holding two packets of crisps and grinning.

"Job's yours if you want it," she said, proudly, pulling open the bags of crisps and indicating to others to help themselves, "Justin agreed you are a bit old, but he said you have a nice personality, good legs and a pretty face, so those assets should compensate."

Candy's cheeks turned crimson. "Oh Gertie, he didn't say that, did he? He must suppose me a right fool. I hope he doesn't think I got you to ask on my behalf because I was too much of a coward."

"Well, yes that's what I told him. And I also said you thought he might want blokes to redress the balance, and he said he's already had Ollie Collins asking for a job so the two of you will be ideal. In fact he said he'll be over in a minute and he asked me to take this notice down."

"Why does young Ollie Collins want to work here?" Meg asked, leaning to one side to enable Gertie to reach the notice. "Isn't there enough work in building?"

"Yes, plenty," said Stella, amused by Candy's anguished expression, "but Anne tells me Ollie's saving for a car and so needs every penny he can get his hands on."

Candy continued to look uncomfortable as she nervously nibbled a crisp. "Justin didn't really say I was a bit old, did he, Gert?"

"Of course not, Candy, he's not that much of a cad. But smile without letting the laughter lines show too much, because your new boss is coming this way."

Chapter Eight

On the last day of the school year, Jane Williams woke in her two bedroomed flat above the Pickled Egg and sighed. The beginning of the school holiday meant the beginning of six or seven hectic weeks, especially so with the eclipse on the horizon.

Smothering a yawn, she stepped from her bed, drew back the curtains and then walked into the bathroom. In the mirror above the wash basin she caught sight of her reflection and groaned. The bright sunlight shining through the frosted glass panes, cast a golden beam on the top of her head, highlighting the grey streaks amidst the light chestnut brown.

Jane looked closer in the mirror and gently brushed a finger across the crow's feet around her eyes. She smiled half-heartedly, her complexion was not bad for a woman of forty four years but the grey hairs were beginning to get a little too many in number.

"Better see if I can get Rebecca to colour it before the madness begins and I don't have the time," she sighed, reaching for her shower cap, "though on reflection, it does seem a little silly when I'll spend much of the summer standing over a smelly deep fat fryer."

After breakfast, Jane walked up the road to Fuchsia Cottage, the home of her parents, Betty and Peter. It was the house where she had grown up along with her brother, Matthew.

At the back of their house, Betty had her own hairdressing business, and as a young girl Jane had helped out on Saturday mornings and earned a bit of pocket money. But since the marriage of Matthew to Rebecca, also a hairdresser, Betty had gradually eased off and let her daughter-in-law take over the business.

Jane made an appointment with Rebecca to have her hair coloured in spite of her inevitable meetings with the fryer, she then went into her parents' living room for a chat with her mother.

"I hope you've plenty of staff lined up this summer," said Betty, spraying window cleaner on the mirror above the fireplace. "From what the media are saying Cornwall could well be swamped with visitors come August. I think it's quite exciting: Cornwall being a good vantage point for seeing the eclipse, that is. Have you got your special 3D viewing specs yet? We have. I got some for me and your dad from the post office yesterday. You must do the same in case they sell out."

Jane smiled as she sat down on the settee. "If the predictions are correct then I'll probably not have time to watch the eclipse anyway with all those extra mouths to feed."

Betty vigorously polished the glass. "Of course you will, nobody will be hungry 'til after it's done and I think it's around eleven in the morning anyway and you don't open 'til twelve."

"Oh, is that right? Anyway, you can be rest assured I've got plenty of staff lined up and a few I can call on if the going gets tough."

"Good, and you know you can always get me in to give a hand too if needs be. I'd be only too glad to make myself useful especially if there's plenty of money to be made by you. As you are well aware, you have to make your money when you can in the holiday trade." She sighed. "That's where I was lucky with hairdressing. Women, and men too, need their hair done all year round."

Betty put the bottle of window cleaner on top of the sideboard alongside a can of furniture polish and sat down in a fireside chair.

"Thank you for volunteering," said Jane, "but I shouldn't think it will be necessary. At present I have Janet's help and also her two daughters, Lucy and Angie. The schools break up today so I shall have them working more or less full time next week. And then of course there's Jess Collins, she was invaluable last summer and I'm sure she'll be just as useful this year."

"Hmm, she's nice is Jess. Has Janet's eldest girl finished school now?"

"Yes, she took her A-levels earlier this year and plans to go to university in the autumn if her grades are good enough."

"Really, and what about the other one?"

"Angie, she'll be starting her A-levels in September and she wants to go into dentistry like her dad, but as a dental nurse not as a dentist."

"She's done her GCSEs then?"

"Yes, and there's no doubt that she'll get good grades because she's really clever, probably even more so than Lucy."

Betty sighed. "Oh dear, it seems like only yesterday the Ainsworths arrived in Trengillion and moved into the Old Police House. Children grow up far too quickly these days. How old are the boys then?"

"Not sure, but I think there's two or three years between the older boy and Angie. Silly, but I can never remember the boys' names but then I don't see them much and probably wouldn't recognise them if I did."

"James and Mick," said Betty, "they're the boys' names. I know that because your dad was telling me only yesterday that the youngest, James, is growing a couple of sunflowers for the competition."

Jane nodded. "Yes, of course. Where is Dad? I've not seen him for a week or two."

"He's in the back garden supposedly cutting the grass, but if I know him he'll be sitting on the bench and probably dozing."

"In that case I'll pop out and see him, but I'll tread carefully in case he's asleep."

"Okay, but if he's awake be sure to comment on his sunflowers, he's really pleased with them and reckons he could be in for the prize."

Jane shook her head. "It's amazing you know, how many people, and men in particular, who at one time wouldn't have known the difference between a daffodil and a dandelion, have suddenly become keen gardeners. Susan tells me the chat in the inn is often dominated by the progress of their sunflowers."

"Don't I know it," laughed Betty, "but I'm pleased, it's the first summer I've ever known your dad talk more about the garden than fishing, but then he and Percy have been retired for three years now."

As Gertie hung out her washing one sunny morning in late July she heard voices emanating from the back garden of Number One. Hoping to hear snippets of the conversation she pricked up her ears, but the sudden rumble of a tractor crossing the field at the back of Coronation Terrace drowned out the voices. Not to be outdone, Gertie put down her washing basket on the back step and moved alongside the tall escallonia hedge which separated the two gardens, looking for a gap through which she might see her neighbours. As she found a convenient spy hole and began to push aside the foliage in order that she might see better, Meg called to her from the back garden of Number Three on the other side.

"Looking for bird's nests, Gert? I think you're a bit late."

Gertie leapt back very red faced, for as Meg had spoken so had the tractor engine stopped; inevitably the Moores would have heard Meg's comment.

"Hmm, no, no, I was um, looking for a peg, yes, a clothes peg, it sprang out of my hand, you see, as I was hanging up this towel and it landed somewhere in the hedge."

Meg suppressed a laugh, realising, when she heard a ball bouncing, that the Moores were in their garden.

"And have you found it?" she asked.

"Yes thank you," said Gertie feebly, holding up the peg she had clenched in her hand all along.

Laughter rang from the back garden of Number One. Gertie's face reddened, convinced the Moores knew the reality behind the situation. She wasn't accustomed to being ridiculed, hence she felt a sudden burst of hostility towards the occupants of Number One.

Sitting at the kitchen table at the Old Vicarage, Jess Collins looked with dismay at her bank statement which had arrived with the morning post. She knew her account must be getting quite bereft of funds but it was far worse than she had anticipated.

"What's up, Sis?" asked Ollie, who had popped home for his mobile phone which he had inadvertently left behind in his haste to be ready for work, "no pennies left to spend in the pub?"

"No pennies left to spend anywhere," she groaned, disdainfully tossing the offensive sheet of paper across the table. "Looks like I'll have to become teetotal until my first full week's pay packet at the Pickled Egg, unless my dear brother wants to give his poor hard done by sister a loan."

"Humph, I'll have to think about it. I'm saving hard at the moment for a new car, and for that reason I'll be doing a few hours at the Jolly Sailor soon. I might be able to spare a few coppers though if you're really skint."

"A new car! It's not fair, I can't even drive yet."

"Well, it was your choice to go to university; you could quite easily have got a job like me and saved all the hardship."

"Oh, come on, that's a bit harsh. You work for Dad and Uncle Steve because they asked you to. Leaving school at sixteen was the obvious thing for you to do. I said all this when we went out in the boat the other day. You've had it easy."

"Just teasing, and you're right of course. There's big money to be made in building and I'm actually getting quite good at many aspects of it, especially carpentry. How much do you want then?"

"Will it be interest free with no set date on which to pay it back?"

"Yeah, alright."

"Then I'll have a tenner, please."

Ollie pulled a ten pound note from his wallet and laid it on the table. "Must go now or Dad will be wondering where I've got to."

Sid Reynolds, sat in the front garden of his home in Coronation Terrace reading the local newspaper on which he had worked many years before. As he was reading about forthcoming events for the area, two little girls skipped by sweetly singing a song which even he in the autumn of his years knew was a recent hit for one of the boy bands.

Sid was enchanted. The girls had tuneful voices and impeccable timing, in fact he decreed they were good enough to perform in front of an audience.

Sid laid the paper down beside his old deckchair and puffed at his pipe. The eclipse was less than three weeks away and it was supposed that it would cause Cornwall to be awash with visitors. In which case, why not hold a talent contest in Trengillion, open to all? The venue would be the village hall, the obvious place, and it would make good use of its little used stage. Sid was delighted with his plan, but he'd need someone to help him organise it. Meg of course would lend a hand, but neither of their children lived in the village now. Diane had moved to Truro two years after her marriage to Mike, and Graham had sold his Penwynton Crescent house in 1997 and moved to Helston to be nearer his job with the estate agents, the office of which he was now the manager.

Sid stood up and called to Meg who was ironing.

"I'm just popping round to see Ned and Stella. I've had an idea regarding a bit of entertainment this summer. Do you fancy coming with me?"

"I can't Sid, I've got a cake in the oven and it won't be ready for another twenty minutes or so. You go and you can tell me all about it when you get back."

"You sure?"

"Yes, of course, love. Give Ned and Stella my regards."

July ended on a warm, dry note and thus began the manic month of August. Across the county eating establishments submitted large orders for food supplies and geared themselves ready for the extra influx of visitors.

Meanwhile, in many Trengillion gardens, bright yellow sunflowers stood tall and proud awaiting judgment day.

On Friday August the sixth, much to the delight of Milly Pascoe, the family who had been staying in Higher Green Farmhouse, left at lunchtime a whole day before the end of their fortnight's stay. They told Milly, when they handed over the keys, they had a long journey home to the Isle of Man and had decided to break up the drive and spend the Friday night in Somerset.

After they had gone, Milly set to stripping the beds and beginning the task of cleaning the house from top to bottom. As she was tackling her least favourite job, the large double oven inside the inglenook fireplace, Johnny, who had found her note about the early departure on his return from visiting his mother-in-law, arrived to give a helping hand.

"Well, that was a bit of luck, them going early, I mean. So who've we got coming in next?" he asked, looking for window cleaner in the cupboard beneath the sink.

Milly closed the oven doors, rose to her feet and peeled off her rubber gloves. "The Americans. Thank goodness that beastly job's done. Their name is Jefferson and I believe there are four of them."

Johnny laughed, as he knelt on the draining board and sprayed the kitchen window, "We've certainly had a good range of nationalities this year, haven't we? The folks from the Isle of Man have just gone, before them were the Germans and after Easter we had the Swedes.

And now we've got Americans coming. Still, they say variety is the spice of life. How long will they here for?"

"Three weeks, until August twenty eighth. But don't forget the Dutch couple who were here around Flora Day."

"Oh yeah, the tulip growers, I'd forgotten them."

Milly washed her hands, took a chocolate bar from her bag and then filled the kettle.

"Do you want a coffee, Johnny? I'm going to have one before I start on the cupboards, I think I've earned it after doing that horrible oven."

"Yes, please. And I think instead of doing any more windows I'll leave you to get on in here and cut the grass instead. I ought to give that hedge a trim too, and by the looks of that sky I reckon we're in for some rain."

On Saturday morning, in the front garden of Rose Cottage, Stella Stanley slowly walked along the path snipping off the faded heads of dahlias in the herbaceous border. As she stood back to double check that none had been missed, the church clock struck eleven, prompting Stella to head indoors and make coffee for herself and Ned. However, before she reached the house she was sidetracked by Kernow and Kate the two magpies flapping around together in the apple tree. Stella folded her arms and watched much amused by their antics. The birds were well known throughout the village for their high jinks and bad behaviour although most of Trengillion's residents were glad they were still around for their entertainment value, even though their young had gained independence.

Stella jumped, startled, as their clumsy movements unexpectedly sent half a dozen small, unripe apples tumbling onto the path below. Tutting, she clapped her hands loudly and shooed them away. Obligingly, they flew off, wings flapping noisily, cawing cheekily in their easily distinguished, mechanical manner.

"Sodding magpies," said Ned, appearing from inside the house. "I was watching them from the kitchen window and that's the second time this week I've seen them knock apples from the tree. At this rate there'll be none left to harvest.

"Well, yes, I agree, but I think it's somewhat charming the way they're always together and you have to admit they are rather funny."

Ned scowled. "Humph, they'll look even funnier when I've taken a pot shot at them and they've lost a few feathers."

Stella looked aghast. "You can't mean it, Ned. You wouldn't shoot at them really, would you?"

"Too right, I would. At least I would if I had a damn gun."

Stella slipped her arm through his. "Come on, coffee time, then I think you ought to take a nap."

"A nap," spluttered Ned, "I've only been up for three hours so why on earth should I want to take a nap?"

Stella grinned, impishly. "I believe it's what grumpy old men do, dear, and you're emitting all the symptoms of rapidly turning into one."

After leaving the locality of Rose Cottage, the two magpies flew over the village and out towards the Penwynton Hotel where they rested on the top step alongside the open door of the main entrance with heads cocked to one side as though listening with interest to the conversation within between a mother and her daughter.

"I must admit I won't be sorry when it's this time next week," said Mary Cottingham, after the first guests for the eclipse had arrived early, left their luggage in the vestibule and then gone off sight-seeing until their room was ready for occupation. "What with all the rooms taken and the dining room booked solid for the week, I think it's going to be like a madhouse here."

"You must learn not to worry, Mum," said Linda, observing a cobweb dangling from the chandelier when she switched on the light to make the vestibule more attractive, "we've lots of staff coming in this week, including my own girls, so I don't see why it shouldn't go as smooth as clockwork. I'm quite looking forward to the challenge and I think Jamie is too."

"I know, love, and you are both doing a magnificent job, but living over the shop, so to speak, I can't help but be aware of the busyness. I wouldn't want it any other way, I suppose. Oh dear, I should be more like your father; he's learned to let go and is enjoying retirement. But I believe half of my problem is I don't like to admit that I'm over seventy now. It sounds so damn old."

"Well, you don't look it if that's any consolation," smiled Linda, taking a feather duster from beneath the reception desk. "You could easily pass for ten years less, but that's still no reason to worry unnecessarily."

After pulling the Regency chair beneath the chandelier, Linda kicked off her shoes, climbed onto the padded seat and knocked away the offending cobweb. She then jumped down. "You, Dad, Auntie Heather and Uncle Bob have done a superb job building this business from scratch to what it is today but it's time you recouped some of its rewards and put your feet up."

Mary smiled and sat down on the chair as Linda returned it to its rightful place. "I suppose that's your way of telling me I fuss too much. Your father says I do and he's quite right of course. He says I don't seem to realise you're a grown-up now, but that really isn't the case, Linda, I'm fully aware that you are grown up and sensible with it. In fact you must be around the same age now as I was when we bought this place."

Linda smiled. "I wish. I think you'll find I'm older, Mum, and by quite a few years too."

As she spoke the last guests due to leave that morning descended the staircase and so Mary left her daughter to finalise their stay.

Inside the Jolly Sailor, Candy Bingham nervously stood in the hallway having reported for her first morning's work. Justin greeted her warmly before putting her in the capable hands of Susan Penhaligon who had emerged from the kitchen on hearing voices.

The letter box clicked and several envelopes fell onto the doormat. "Sorry to have you cleaning on your first day," Justin said, picking up the post with a distinct lack of interest, "but it's all part of the job. I have a separate cleaner for the bar, but I like my bar and kitchen staff to do the guests' rooms on a rota."

"And most of the kitchen staff are the bar staff anyway," added Susan with a grin. "With the exception of Maurice, that is; he never does the bar of course or the guest rooms, which is probably just as well because he's very messy in the kitchen. In fact I don't think he knows what the broom, mop or bucket are for."

"That's because he's a chef not a skivvy," grinned Justin, ducking to miss Susan's blow, "anyway, don't forget Ollie, he's starting this week and being a chap he'll not be doing the rooms either, and quite rightly too. I definitely think it's more of a female thing."

"Humph! The words, male, chauvinist and pig come to mind," teased Susan.

"Please don't apologise," said Candy, surprised by the way Susan spoke to her boss and vice versa, "cleaning's something I'm used to doing because I was once housekeeper up at Higher Green Farm. That was when it was a proper farm of course and not a holiday let like it is now."

"Good," said Justin, gently squeezing her arm, "and I hope you'll enjoy working here. You know us all anyway so it shouldn't be too difficult and please don't hesitate to let me know if there are any problems."

As Justin disappeared into the bar, Susan led Candy along the passageway and showed her the cupboard where the bed linen was kept.

"Only two of the rooms were used last week so that's perfect as we can have one of them each. So I'll do the double on the front and you can do the single on the back. It's all pretty straight forward. Change the bed, dust and so forth and make sure nothing's been left behind."

"That's fine with me," said Candy, taking the single bedding, "as long as you direct me to the right room."

"I'll show you all the rooms while they're empty, they're very basic but quite pleasant, although I'm surprised the inn's full. It's the first time I've known that happen since I've worked here."

"Really?"

"Yes, though I'm glad of course for Justin's sake," said Susan, as they climbed the stairs, "but nowadays, most people want their rooms to be en suite, don't they? I mean, it's considered dead old fashioned to share a loo and bathroom with strangers, isn't it. I don't think it'd suit me."

"Beggars can't be choosers," said Candy, as they reached the upstairs landing. "I think this week most people will be glad of anywhere to stay and I believe Justin's rates are very reasonable." She giggled. "Besides, I think a lot of people, especially blokes, would prefer having a bar downstairs much more than having their own washing facilities. I know Larry would."

Susan nodded. "Hmm, and Steve too. In fact on reflection, I think to lodge in rooms above a pub would be Steve's idea of a dream holiday." She laughed. "You know, if Steve misses coming in for a pint, Justin asks if he's ill."

As promised, Susan showed Candy around upstairs and then they separated to clean their allotted rooms, after agreeing whoever finished first must make a start on the communal bathroom.

Chapter Nine

In the afternoon inside Sea Thrift Cottage as Milly Pascoe was watering the Busy Lizzies on her kitchen window sill, a large black car pulled up alongside the garden gate. Milly promptly put down the small green, plastic can, picked up keys from the hook over the sink and went out to greet the visitors, confident they would be the Americans booked for a three week stay in Higher Green Farmhouse. She was correct in her assumption, for as she approached the open gate, a portly man wearing a white suit, blue shirt and bootlace tie stepped from the driving seat of a luxurious hired car. On his head he wore a white Stetson hat and underneath the brim glinted a pair of gold rimmed spectacles. When he saw Milly, he politely raised his hat revealing beneath a head of thick, white hair.

"Hi, honey, if we've got the right place and this is Sea Thrift Cottage then you must be Mrs Pascoe."

Milly nodded and politely pointed to the house name nailed to the open gate.

"Great! Allow me to introduce myself. I'm Jefferson, Jefferson K. Jefferson. And me and my good family here, have come to stay in the little old farmhouse."

"Good heavens," muttered Milly, dazed by the apparition before her, "I feel as though I've stepped into an episode of Dallas."

"Dallas! No honey, right state, wrong city; me and my family here come from Fort Worth. Gotta nice little ranch there."

"No, I was referring to the TV programme… oh, never mind. Yes, I'm Mrs Pascoe, but please call me Milly."

"Milly! Wow. Lovely name Milly, it was my ma's name and she was a mighty special lady. Come on folks. Where are your manners? Will y'all get out of the car and come and shake hands with Milly here."

Three doors opened and the rest of the family stepped out onto the grass in a line.

"This here is my wife," said Jefferson K. Jefferson, proudly patting the shoulder of a small woman in her early sixties, "and she of course is Mrs Jefferson K. Jefferson."

The wife smiled sweetly and nodded.

"Next here, well you can probably see the likeness, this here is my handsome son, Jefferson K. Jefferson, Jr.."

Junior raised his hat and bowed, "Howdy, ma'am."

Milly smothered the desire to laugh.

"And finally, this here is my daughter in law, Mrs Jefferson K. Jefferson, Jr.."

The daughter-in-law stepped forward and to Milly's horror, curtseyed. "Delighted to meet you, Miss Milly."

"Hmm, pleased to meet you too," said Milly, shaking hands with each in turn, "I hope you'll all enjoy your stay. Cornwall is very beautiful and Trengillion especially so."

"Thanks, lady," said Jefferson K. Jefferson, Jr., "we sure hope so too. You got a mighty fine view up here, a mighty fine view, kinda makes me feel all romantic."

Mrs Jefferson K. Jefferson, Jr. giggled and linked arms with her husband.

"I'm glad you like it," said Milly, overcome by the Jeffersons' impeccable manners, "because the farmhouse has a similar outlook and from the upstairs windows you can see for miles."

"We saw that was the case in the brochure," said Jefferson K. Jefferson, Sr., "in fact it was the views that made us want to come here. Wasn't it folks?"

The family nodded, and at the same time, Jefferson K. Jefferson, Jr. patted the head of his attractive wife.

"I just hope my dear little wife here don't get into one of her sleepwalking phases; it'd be terrible if she went and fell over the side of them cliffs."

Mrs Jefferson K. Jefferson, Sr. shuddered. "Don't say that, son, it's a horrible thought. Better lock the bedroom door at night though and hide the key, just in case. We don't want no accidents while we're here."

"Actually the bedrooms don't have keys," said Milly timorously, "only bolts. So you'll have to hide the house keys instead."

"He was only joking," said Mrs Jefferson K. Jefferson, Jr., "Why, I ain't been a sleepwalking for a long time now, so I reckon I've grown right out of it."

"Yeah you're right there, honey, the last time was way back in 1996 when we went to stay with your old granny before she passed away."

"Well, you would hardly have stayed with the old gel after she'd passed on, son," laughed Jefferson K. Jefferson, Sr., slapping his generously proportioned thigh.

"We sure are looking forward to the eclipse, miss," commented his wife, not wanting Milly to think badly of her husband over his frivolous remark concerning the dead. "It should be quite spectacular."

"Hmm, yes, we're all looking forward to it too," said Milly, attempting to hand over the keys. "Now, would you like me to accompany you to the Farmhouse? It's not far away, you actually passed its driveway on your way up here, but I'd be only too happy to escort you if you'd like me to."

Jefferson K. Jefferson, Sr. shook his head as he took the keys and dropped them in the pocket of his jacket. "No need to do that, miss, we know exactly where to go, and if you don't mind I think we'll be getting along there right now. Got quite a lotta stuff to unpack."

Milly smiled, a little relieved. "Well, it's been nice meeting you and I hope you enjoy your stay."

"Gee thanks, Milly," said Jefferson K. Jefferson, Sr., indicating to the rest of the family it was time to get back into the car, "and thank you for your warm welcome. I hope we see you around sometime during our vacation."

Milly smiled. "You will. I shall be in to change your beds and have a quick whip round with the duster and vacuum cleaner every seven days."

Jefferson K. Jefferson, Sr. put on his hat and patted it firmly into place; he then climbed into the driving seat. "We look forward to seeing you. Bye, young lady."

Late on Saturday afternoon, Anne picked flowers from the Old Vicarage garden, a mixture of asters, white roses and sweet peas, and took them to the churchyard to put on the graves of John's grandparents, Nettie and Cyril Penrose, to honour the sixth anniversary of Nettie's death. She then walked back by way of the recreation field, the bottom of which ran alongside the curtilage of the Old Vicarage.

Several people were erecting large tents as she walked down the field. Anne, shuddered and looked towards the grey clouds looming overhead; the idea of sleeping under canvas had never appealed to her sense of adventure for fear of the weather being wet. But the new arrivals seemed undeterred by the prospect of imminent liquid sunshine and went about enthusiastically constructing their temporary homes with an air of great anticipation.

At the bottom of the field, as Anne neared a gap in the hedge between a rampant buddleia and elderflower entwined with sweetly scented honeysuckle, which led into the Old Vicarage garden, she noticed a bright yellow convertible car, drive onto the field from the adjoining lane. Its doors and bonnet were decorated with large, luminous flowers and colourful cartoon characters.

Anne paused and smiled as the car passed by. Its occupants, four young men all with different coloured heads of hair and none probably more than twenty three or four years of age, sat in the car heartily singing along with a CD playing old sixties tunes. To avoid detection Anne stepped into the gap in the hedge and watched as the car pulled up near to the other campers and whilst exchanging banter and laughing, the four young men jumped from their vehicle and proceeded to unload bags and bundles from the boot.

Anne smiled, it appeared their sense of dress was as bizarre as the car itself, for in spite of the dull weather, all were dressed in garish short sleeved shirts and Bermuda shorts; they wore flip-flops and their eyes were hidden beneath sunglasses made for children in varying brightly coloured plastic frames.

Their antics gave her a warm feeling inside; it was good to see young people having fun and she felt sure their presence would enhance the village for the duration of their stay.

During a shower of rain on Saturday evening as Jess left the Old Vicarage and hurriedly crossed the wet recreational field, a short cut, on her way to meet her friends at the Jolly Sailor, she encountered the new young male campers, peering from the doorway of their very basic, shabby white tent. They appeared to be discussing a venue at which to spend the evening away from the rain.

"Hello darling," said the least bashful, running his fingers through a shock of ginger hair, "can you tell us where the coolest place to hang out around here is?"

Jess abruptly stopped, tilted her umbrella to one side in order to weigh up their potential. "It all depends what your idea of a cool night out is. Personally, I'm quite happy to spend an evening at the pub, the Jolly Sailor, but then of course lots of my friends live here. But if you want a late night with live music, then your best bet would be a trip to Helston or better still Penzance."

"You going to the pub now then, darling?"

"As a matter of fact, yes."

"What, you going to meet your boyfriend?"

Jess winced and her face reddened. She had recently split up with her boyfriend, a fellow student at Swansea University, due to his unfaithfulness, hence the subject was a very sore point which she chose not to discuss with anyone, not even family and close friends. "I am going to meet contemporaries of mine," she retorted, primly, "not that it's any business of yours. Male *and* female friends."

As she flounced off, head held high, she heard peals of laughter from inside the small white tent.

"Silly little boys," she snapped, vociferously, without turning her head.

In the public bar of the Jolly Sailor, Jess waved to her cousin, Wills, her brother Ollie, and her friends, Charlie Bingham and Lucy Ainsworth; she then shook her umbrella and placed it in a stand with numerous others. After getting a drink from the bar she sat down, her face still flushed with anger. To quash suggestions she might be in a bad mood, she told of her meeting with the boys camping on the field.

"Really! Four of them, what are they like?" asked Lucy, eyes shining. "My love life could do with a boost."

"Minging, all of them," snapped Jess, crossly, "minging and uncouth."

"Who's rattled your cage?" teased Ollie, "I saw them when I came over the field and they looked alright to me. And their car's really cool."

"Oh, nothing, they just annoyed me, that's all."

"Poor sods!" persisted Ollie, "You mustn't be too hard on them, Jess. It must be pretty miserable stuck in a tiny tent in a strange place with the rain pouring down."

Jess shrugged her shoulders. "Anyway, I should imagine they'll be in later because if they decide to go to Helston or Penzance, as I'd like them to, then one of them won't be able to have a drink because he'll be driving."

"Sounds good to me," said Lucy, eying the door, "I wonder how long they're here for."

"Well, it's got to be at least Wednesday," said Charlie Bingham, "because I expect they're here for the eclipse. Everyone else is."

Ollie nodded, "Yeah, Mum said the Penwynton's full this week."

"Tally's looking nice tonight," said Lucy, nodding towards the bar behind which Tally was busily working. "Is that top new? The colour really suits her."

Wills screwed up his face. "Don't ask me. I'm not in the least bit familiar with my sister's wardrobe. She could have had it for years for all I know."

"Well, she hasn't and it is new," tutted Jess. "She bought it in Falmouth last week. I was with her when she got it."

"How come Tally can afford a new top and you're always skint?" Ollie asked.

"Because Tally's been working lots of hours ever since we finished university but I didn't start to earn properly 'til the schools broke up, stupid. Anyway, aren't you supposed to be working here now?"

"I'm doing Wednesday and Friday nights this week because of the eclipse, so I reckon I'll be too knackered to do anything by next weekend. Then Justin's going to sort out next week's rota after the madness has died down a bit."

As he spoke the door opened and the four young campers sauntered into the bar. Jess groaned. "That's all I need. That's them," she hissed. "I had an awful niggling feeling they'd be in."

Lucy eagerly turned her head. "Christ, Jess, you need specs. They're not minging they're gorgeous, especially the redhead, bagsy he's mine. I'm fascinated by ginger nuts."

"Weirdo," laughed Charlie Bingham.

"Humph, he's the bugger with whom I had brief words earlier," muttered Jess, casting an evil eye towards the young Titian. "Keep him away from me."

After buying their drinks and attempting to chat up Tally and Demelza behind the bar, the four young men sat at a table within earshot of Jess and her friends, which curtailed all normal conversation as each party was trying to eavesdrop on the other. Lucy, however, decided if their stay might not be for long, then time was of the essence. When she caught the eye of her favoured redhead, she unashamedly, winked. To her delight his reaction was to rise introduce himself as Neil and ask if he and his friends might join the party of young locals. All said yes except Jess, who glowered as they shuffled round the table to make room for the campers.

On Sunday it rained heavily. Around the village all was quiet except for a few holiday makers, each putting on a brave face, and out walking wearing brightly coloured cagoules. Inside the Pickled Egg the place was full with families trying to make the most of the inhospitable conditions.

"I do feel so sorry for holiday makers when the weather's like this," said Janet Ainsworth, moved by the sad face of a little girl with chin resting on her small chubby hand, watching the raindrops streaming down the window, "especially families. It reminds me of when Ian and I went to Scotland with the children before we moved down here. That was a pretty wet week, but of course, the weather was lovely on the day we came home."

The rain stopped briefly at lunchtime but the sky was still overcast. Looming dark clouds threatened a shower of rain as Elizabeth left Chy-an-Gwyns with an umbrella and two carrier bags containing the cushions she had finally got round to making for Maurice using the spare curtain fabric. Once again Maurice had left the key to Valley View at the Jolly Sailor so that she would be able to put them in situ and admire her handiwork. He'd also informed her that because she had refused payment there would be a thank you gift waiting for her collection on the kitchen table.

Elizabeth was looking forward to her second visit to Valley View, for it hadn't occurred to her until after she'd arrived home following her first visit that something must have triggered off the radio on Maurice's alarm clock; without doubt it had not been on when first she had arrived there and taken a quick look around the house. Furthermore, when questioned, Maurice informed her he never used the radio as an alarm for he was always awake long before he needed to arise. This had prompted her to suggest he might have a ghost or a spirit of some kind, a notion which caused him to laugh heartily.

A few drops of rain fell as she approached the house. Eager to get inside before it worsened, she ran up the path and as she closed the door, the heavens opened.

As before, the house struck chilly as she wiped her feet on the mat in the hallway and she shivered as she removed the cushions from the carrier bags and placed them on each of the two fireside chairs in the living room. To her delight, the cushions looked impressive and helped make the room look a little less drab. Pleased with her efforts, she folded the empty carrier bags and stuffed them into her handbag which she dropped onto the swivel chair at Maurice's computer desk; she then returned the hallway, her intention being to listen for any strange noises.

Calculating it to be as near central a position as she could get, she stood at the foot of the stairs. The house again seemed eerie and she found it very easy to imagine that she was not alone. She sat down on the stairs, for if anything unusual were to happen then surely it would again be in Maurice's bedroom. For ten minutes she sat, listening to the clock ticking in the hallway and the gentle pitter-pattering of rain against the dining room window, but there were no other sounds. She then stood up and laughed. She was being silly, her imagination was clearly in hyper-active mode, for common sense advised her she was quite alone and might just as well go home.

As she was about to leave she remembered the thank you present and so went into the kitchen to collect it. On the table stood a beautiful scented orchid. Elizabeth lowered her head to take in the delicate perfume. She sighed with delight; it was exquisite.

With her arm securely wrapped around the plant pot, she left the kitchen and went into the living room to collect her handbag and then returned to the hallway. As she reached out for the Yale latch, a noise from behind caused her to pause. She relaxed her arm and listened. The noise was a cross between a buzz and a hiss and appeared to be coming from the living room.

Quietly, Elizabeth put the plant down on the hall table and peeped around the living room door. The room was just as she had seen it seconds before. Confused she went further inside and looked towards the window where raindrops trickled down the glass panes.

A sudden noise from behind caused her to jump. She turned and to her surprise saw Windows 98 written beside a logo of coloured squares on the screen of Maurice's computer monitor. Elizabeth was intrigued as to why the computer had switched itself on but conceded it had probably been sleeping and she'd disturbed it when fetching her handbag. Assuming she was right she moved towards the desk and sat down on Maurice's swivel chair. Being unfamiliar with computers, she stared, mesmerised, at the moving logo. Suddenly the coloured squares began to fade; they disappeared, the screen went blank and then wavy lines emerged; flickering lines in equidistant rows. Elizabeth leaned back in the chair and watched as the lines slowly began to disperse, revealing behind the mysterious face of an elderly man wearing a dark, flat hat. His skin was grey and transparent; his eyes, dark and sunken and his downturned mouth was framed by a clipped moustache and a pointed, neatly trimmed beard. He stared out from the screen, his piercing gaze fixated on Elizabeth's face, while his head gently rocked from side to side.

With an immense feeling of unease, Elizabeth slowly pushed back the chair; her neck and shoulders felt cold, like ice; her arms tingled beneath the sleeves of her jacket and her mind was confused. Something was wrong. Very wrong. Aware that her breathing was irregular and heavy, she gripped her hands tightly around the arms of the chair. But as she slowly began to rise, she saw to her horror that the socket on the wall, into which monitor and computer were both plugged, was switched off. She gasped; leapt to her feet and fled from the room, hysterical and screaming; leaving behind the mysterious face to stare at the vacated chair as it span round and round and round.

During the afternoon, in spite of the cloud, Ned and Stella, keen to get out of the house for a change of scenery, walked down to the cove to buy locally made ice creams from the Pickled Egg and as they sat on Denzil's bench enjoying their purchases, a couple walked onto the beach and sat on the rocks nearby.

"Who's that chap?" Stella asked, nudging Ned and nodding towards the new arrivals.

"No idea, holiday makers, I expect."

"Well, that's as maybe, but I'm sure I've seen him before, though I can't say the same for his companion."

"Well, that's more than feasible," said Ned, "lots of people come back here year after year."

As he spoke Ned caught the strange man's eye and in both there was an instant glimmer of recognition.

"Of course, you're the headmaster," said the stranger, slapping his thigh and rising, "I knew when we sat down I'd seen you before. What a relief, everyone else is a complete stranger."

"Good God, Freddie Short," laughed Stella, recognising the voice, "the lack of hair, hippy clothes and beads fooled me for a while."

"Severe lack of hair. When I look in the mirror I find it hard to realise I ever had such a mop. It's not much fun going bald."

"Well, I never," laughed Ned, as memories came flooding back, "I'd never have guessed in a million years. So what brings you here after all this time?"

Freddie proffered his right hand; Ned, and then Stella eagerly shook it.

"The eclipse of course. When I heard Cornwall was the place to see it, then I knew there was only one place to come and here we are. By the way, this is my wife, Trish."

Trish came and stood by her husband's side.

"Delighted to meet you," said Ned and in turn Stella, each rising to shake hands, "Where are you staying?"

"The inn of course," said Freddie, "But, oh, the place has changed such a lot. Not so much in layout and décor, but the staff and general way it's run. And the name's changed too, I wouldn't have been able to contact it if it wasn't for the fact I still had the phone number in my address book."

"It's changed several times," said Ned, ruefully, "but by far the best name of all was The Ringing Bells Inn."

Freddie nodded. "I'm sure. And Frank and Dotty have both gone. I guessed they'd have retired of course, but I was very sorry to hear they'd actually both passed away. Such a shame, they were a lovely couple."

"Yes, I'm afraid most of that generation have gone and we're the old timers now."

"Oh, don't say that, I find retirement quite tough, I'm always on the lookout for folks up to no good. Still they say, once a copper always a copper. I suppose you must have retired too, Ned."

"Yes, been retired seven years now but I manage to keep myself occupied and out of Stella's way for much of the time. In fact, sometimes I wonder how I ever found time to work."

Freddie laughed. "I've taken up painting to occupy my time but I'm not much cop, if you'll excuse the pun, but then my eye sight's not what it used to be and I'm determined not to wear specs."

"Stella paints," said Ned, beaming at his wife, "we have a lovely picture of hers over the fireplace. It's a snow scene and she copied it from a photo I took when we had lots of snow back in that bitterly cold spell in January 1987. You must come and see it. I love it and think you'll be impressed."

"We'd like that very much. Are you still living in the Old School House?"

"No, no, we're in Rose Cottage now. It's the house my mother and the major used to live in. Do you remember them?"

"Vaguely, it was a long time ago now."

"Yes, I suppose it must be, but I've no idea of the exact year."

"I know precisely. It was a year never to be forgotten," said Freddie, "1967, the summer of love and flower power. Ah, those were the days!"

Late on Sunday afternoon, as Candy was dropping a letter into the post box a car pulled up outside the post office and from it stepped a dashingly handsome man in his late twenties. Candy felt she had seen him somewhere before and so while she attempted to recall where this might have been, she lingered outside the post office and pretended to read the notices in the shop window. To her surprise he went round the side of the building and knocked on the house door. Nessie answered. "Robbie, darling, you're here already. We didn't expect you for another hour or two yet." She kissed his cheek. "Come in."

"Thank you," said Robbie, a hint of a Scottish accent in his deep voice. "I hope you don't mind me coming over earlier than I said."

"Of course not. In fact since you're here early we can pop down to the pub before dinner and I can introduce you to everyone. I think it's time the locals met my little brother."

Candy felt her cheeks burn as she recalled why his face had seemed familiar. Robbie was the young man with whom she had seen Nessie in an embrace by the gate in Helston.

Amongst the inn's new guests was a young attractive lady, holidaying alone; her name was Doctor Morgana Owen. The doctor, like everyone else, was in Cornwall to witness the forthcoming eclipse. She arrived late on Saturday evening driving an ancient green Morris Traveller, much to the amusement of village youngsters who were unfamiliar with such a vehicle.

On Sunday evening, as the doctor sat in the snug quietly sipping a glass of wine, Gertie and Betty, who had just returned from a short walk, arrived at the inn for a much needed drink and a pizza to share. To their dismay the inn was busy and the only vacant seats were at the table where the doctor sat.

"Is it alright if we sit here?" Gertie asked, pointing to the empty bench.

"Please do," said the doctor with a smile, "I feel like a leper sitting alone. I did intend to read but foolishly left my book in my room."

Gertie and Betty sat down. "Are you staying here at the inn then?" Betty asked.

"Yes, and like everyone else I'm here for the eclipse."

Gertie took a large swig from her pint glass of lager. "Is it true you're a doctor?"

Doctor Owen smiled. "Yes, my colleagues and I have a practice in South Wales."

Betty tilted her head to one side. "Do you get lots of people telling you about their ailments as soon as they know you're a doctor?"

The doctor laughed. "Oh yes, and it can get very tiresome. I'd much rather talk about my hobby, which is astronomy. I find it a fascinating subject."

Gertie wrinkled her nose. "Hmm, I used to be a bit keen on it when I was young but my horoscopes were always rubbish so I stopped reading them in the end. I know it interests some of our grandchildren's generation though, doesn't it, Bet?"

Betty giggled. "Horoscopes and stuff is astrology, Gert. The doctor's interested in astronomy; you know, stars, planets and so forth."

Gertie blushed. "Oh, oh, I see. Silly me I always get the two muddled up."

Doctor Owen smiled kindly. "Don't worry, you're not alone in that respect." She took a sip of her wine. "Are you ladies locals?"

Both nodded and spoke in unison. "Born and bred."

"Ideal, and so you're from Trengillion?"

Gertie and Betty nodded again.

Doctor Owen stood her wine glass on the brass tabletop. "I wonder then, do you have any knowledge of strange happenings in the village following eclipses in days gone by?"

Gertie pulled a face. "What, you mean in Trengillion?"

"Yes, here in Trengillion."

Both ladies looked nonplussed.

"To be honest, right now I can't even remember there being any eclipses, let alone strange happenings. Can you, Bet?"

Betty frowned. "I vaguely remember there being one or two when we were younger but I can't remember any details and I certainly don't recall anything strange happening afterwards."

Doctor Owen laughed. "Actually I wasn't referring to any eclipses that would have taken place in living memory; the ones I'm interested in date back to the eighteenth century. 1715 and 1724 to be precise."

Gertie giggled. "Oh, I see. Yes, that is a year or two before we were born."

Betty frowned. "So what were the strange happenings?"

Before the doctor could answer, Tally arrived with a large plate. "One twelve inch pepperoni pizza," she said, placing the plate in front of the two ladies.

"Wow, thanks, that looks and smells yummy."

"You're welcome," Tally said as she lay down two sets of cutlery and a tray of condiments.

"Sorry about that," said Betty, lifting a slice of pizza from the plate as Tally left. "You don't mind if we eat, do you?"

"Of course not."

"You're welcome to a piece," said Gertie, pushing the plate towards the centre of the table.

"Thank you but I had a very substantial meal a while back."

"So, what were you about to say regarding strange happenings?" Betty asked, eager to hear.

The doctor leaned back, a huge grin across her face. "Actually, you'll probably think me a little unhinged when I tell you." She sighed and then smiled. "You see, because of the forthcoming eclipse I was interested to read all I could about previous ones where Cornwall had been a good vantage point and I came across an article which claimed that following a total solar eclipse in May of 1715 an old house was mysteriously burned to the ground. Now, you will probably think 'so what' and I don't blame you. But then nine years later following another eclipse in May of 1724, for which I must add Cornwall did not have the best vantage point, a similar thing happened again. This time, however, the fire only damaged the upper floor of the house. Needless to say, the locals were very much disturbed by the second incident and for years the second house stood empty. No-one wanted to live in it, you see; people believed it to be cursed, haunted or whatever and so it fell into a bad state of repair and remained empty for a further eighty years."

Gertie was so engrossed in the doctor's information that she stopped eating. "I don't suppose you know where these two houses were that got burned, do you?"

Doctor Owen smiled. "I don't know where the first house was but the second, believe it or not, was your village hall."

Betty frowned. "The village hall! How did that come about?"

"Well, apparently because no-one wanted to live in it, it was eventually decided to turn it into a meeting place where villagers could hold events much as you do today. To do this they removed the damaged remains of the upper storey and capped it with a new roof."

Gertie nodded. "Now you come to mention it, it's always been claimed that the village hall was originally a house. My son, John, is a builder and years ago he told me it was easy to work out how the original layout might have looked."

"That's right," said Betty, "Now you come to mention it, I've heard the same." She turned to the doctor. "So if the fires were both in the eighteenth century, do you know if there were any other such incidents after that?"

Doctor Owen shook her head. "No, there weren't and funnily enough there were no total solar eclipses in the UK between 1724 and 1925 either."

Gertie looked alarmed. "So, do you think something similar might happen after Wednesday's eclipse?"

The doctor shrugged her shoulders. "I really don't know. Common sense tells me it's highly unlikely but I have to admit, curiosity has brought me here."

Gertie shuddered. "Blimey, to be on the safe side I must make sure our house insurance is up to date when I get home."

Chapter Ten

Larry Bingham, who was engaged in a plumbing job for people new to the village, went home for lunch on Monday in order to establish his sunflowers had not suffered any damage since he had last checked them. The competition was due to end the following day and it was essential that no catastrophe should befall his efforts at the eleventh hour. To his delight all was well and so after a bite to eat he left the house to finalise the new bathroom he was installing.

As he opened the front garden gate of his home in Penwynton Crescent and stepped onto the pavement, he observed a silver BMW with tinted glass windows driving into the village. He paused and watched the car pass by. The driver was, without doubt, Iris Delaney the actress. Larry grinned as he closed the gate; the presence of Iris was sure to excite a few of the locals.

The luxurious car also caught the attention of people scattered across the beach as it drove slowly down the steep incline, turned and parked alongside Cove Cottage. Trengillion natives watched, knowing to whom the car belonged, but holiday makers were unaware until Iris stepped from the car wearing dark glasses, jeans and a figure hugging top.

Gertie Collins, sitting on Denzil's bench facing the sea with her friend of many years, Betty Williams, turned her head to see the cause of a spontaneous round of applause. When she saw Iris she nudged Betty sharply in the ribs, for usually Iris visited Cornwall alone, but on this occasion she had with her a male escort and a very attractive male escort to boot. Both ladies sat with mouths gaping.

"Now that young chappie should cause a bit of jealousy amongst Trengillion's hot-blooded males," grinned Betty, noting his head of thick, wavy blond hair.

Gertie blinked to adjust her focus. "And fancy him being here at the same time as Nessie's extremely handsome brother."

Betty looked nonplussed. "I didn't know Nessie had a brother."

"Didn't you, Bet? Sorry, I would have told you had I known." She laughed. "Well, it seems not only does Nessie have a brother but it was him Candy saw hugging Nessie in Helston a while back. You know, when we all thought she had another bloke."

Betty scowled. "So what was he doing in Helston?"

"Well, from what I've heard, he's living there now. Bought a house in Godolphin Road."

"But you just said he was here in Trengillion."

"Yes, he is at present because he's staying with Nessie for a few days. I suppose he's here for the company because I daresay he doesn't know anyone in Helston yet."

"Hmm, interesting. So what does he do? Is he married with a family and so forth?"

Gertie shrugged her shoulders. "I've yet to find out. All I know is that he was in the pub yesterday lunchtime with Nessie and Stephen but he didn't have a wife or girlfriend with him. Our Sue was working, you see, and she said he's absolutely gorgeous. I'll let you know when I've found out more."

Betty sighed. "Two handsome men and both strangers to the village. Oh, to be young again, eh, Gert?"

Gertie nodded, dreamily. "Hmm, we'd certainly have been hot on their tails forty years ago, wouldn't we, Bet?"

By the water's edge, watching Matthew's fishing boat with Wills on board chug towards the shore, stood the four young camping lads. With interest they watched as once ashore the boat was winched up the beach over a path of logs.

"We thought it was you," said Neil, the redhead, to Wills, when the boat was finally at a stand-still. "Where is everyone today?"

"At work, I suppose," said Wills, genuinely pleased to see them. "I know Tally's in the pub this lunchtime but I'm not sure about Demelza, and Jess and Lucy are most likely in the Pickled Egg. Charlie's an electrician so he'll be working too, somewhere or other."

"Oh, what dimwits we are, it never occurred to us that local folks have to work," said Rob. "We've been looking everywhere for you all this morning."

"Who's the bird with the flashy car?" asked Kev, a blond and the most handsome of the four, nodding in the direction of Cove Cottage.

"Must be Iris Delaney," grinned Wills, on seeing the vehicle, "Wow, she usually comes down here while I'm away. Hopefully I'll get to meet her this time."

"Really, you sure about that? I didn't expect to see someone like her in a place like this."

"Well, that's her cottage and there's no doubt about that because we lived there until a year ago and she bought it from us."

"Brill, that'll be something to tell the lads back home," drooled Neil, "I wonder if she'll be wanting a toy-boy while she's here."

"Course not, stupid," chuckled Mac. "She had a bloke with her when she arrived so he must be her boyfriend. Besides why would she want a penniless twit like you who works in a mobile phone shop?"

As they spoke Gertie and Betty rose from the bench, chatting without restraint as they strolled across the beach.

"Hey look, quick, the two old dears are going, so let's go and nobble that bench before someone else does, because I'm tired of standing."

"Old dears!" spluttered Matthew, his shoulders shaking with laughter, "I'll have you know one of them, the slimmer of the two, is my mother."

"Oh no, sorry mate, no offence meant."

"None taken, but don't let them hear you call them old: they'd be mortified."

As the lads took up their seats, Neil read the inscription on the back of the bench. "I wonder who this poor dude Denzil Penhaligon was. It says the poor sod got drowned."

"He was my grandfather," said Demelza, coldly, as she and Tally, having just finished the lunchtime shift at the Jolly Sailor, arrived at the bench.

"Christ, no, I'm so sorry, Demelza. I didn't mean no harm."

Demelza smiled. "No, I'm sure you didn't, but I feel very protective towards his name and this bench, even though I never knew him and my dad doesn't remember him either."

"It looks to me like we're going to have to be really careful what we say around here. I just referred to two biddies who were sitting on this bench as old dears, and it turns out one of them is the mother of the bloke in the boat with your brother Wills."

Demelza giggled. "Hmm, it certainly looks as though you will have to be careful, because the other old biddy was Gertie Collins, my grandmother. It was they who told us you were on the beach when we met them walking past the Jolly Sailor."

After parting with Betty at Fuchsia Cottage, Gertie carried on along the road homeward bound but en route she called in at the post office for a bag of her favourite toffees, hoping she might see or hear something of Nessie's brother.

A family were in the shop buying postcards and stamps. While Stephen served them, Gertie cast her eyes along the jars of sweets on the shelf wondering whether it might be better to have softer toffees than usual as some of her teeth were inclined to wobble. Her decision was still unresolved when she spotted a fairly large parcel on top of a pile of boxes clearly addressed to Nessie at the post office.

Gertie was intrigued, and even though she knew its contents were most likely quite mundane she had to know what lay beyond the brown wrapping paper otherwise she'd not be able to sleep. And so when the family left she stepped up to the counter and innocently nodded in the direction of the package.

"I see Nessie has a parcel. Is it her birthday?"

Stephen laughed. "No, at least I hope not. No, it definitely isn't because I'm sure her birthday is in November or is it December? One or the other anyway. Having said that it might be October. No need to worry though, I'm sure she'll drop plenty of hints when the time comes."

Gertie frowned. Stephen's wordy answer was all very well but it didn't in any way reveal the parcel's contents. Fortunately, Stephen noticed her expression and followed her eyes to the package.

"I assume it's her bagpipes in there," he grinned. "God help us all, eh? Unless of course she's been ordering things from her catalogue again. I keep meaning to take it out the back. Ness hasn't seen it yet, you see, because it arrived just after she'd gone off to the cash n' carry with her brother."

Gertie's face dropped. All desire for information about Robbie vanished. "Bagpipes! You're pulling my leg."

"Wish I was. Her granddad died earlier this year and the old boy left them to her because she always used to be fascinated by them as a kid. He used to play in a pipe band or something like that and apparently they were his pride and joy. I believe there are two of them in there."

Gertie wrinkled her nose. "Two! She'll not be able to play them though, will she?"

"She intends to have a go and she ordered a book last week with instructions for beginners and that arrived on Saturday. Anyway, what can I get you?"

Gertie, excited by the information and eager to pass it on, asked for her usual toffees and then bustled back down the road to Fuchsia Cottage to relay the news to Betty.

In the evening, Iris and her now much talked about fancy-man went to the Jolly Sailor for dinner and ate in the dining room. Tally took their order and waited on them throughout their meal

"Iris's chap asked me convey his compliments to the chef," said Tally to Maurice, as she entered the kitchen with two empty plates. "And Iris asked if you would join them in the bar for a drink after you've finished work."

"Yeah, of course," said Maurice, wiping sweat from his brow, "tell them I'd be delighted. It's a month or two now since I had my ego massaged by the beautiful Iris."

After Maurice had washed his face and combed his hair, he entered the bar to meet Iris and her friend, but as they rose to greet him he stopped dead in his tracks.

"I don't believe it," he laughed, shaking the hand of Iris' escort, "Rusty, Rusty Higgins. Good God man, you've not changed a bit."

"Neither have you, Mo. How long is it now since we last met? Must be fifteen years."

"And the rest. I've been a qualified chef since 1979 and I've not seen you since then."

"Yeah, I suppose you're right. I keep forgetting, accidentally on purpose of course, that I'll be forty next birthday. What will you have to drink, Mo?"

"A pint of Stella, please. Don't worry about being forty, I'm there already and it's no big deal."

Maurice sat on a stool opposite Iris as Rusty went to the bar.

"So, you two already know each other," said Iris, amused, "well that sort of makes sense now."

"How do you mean?"

"I was telling Rusty about this wonderful chef in Trengillion and when I mentioned your name his face lit up but he didn't say why. And then when he heard I was coming down for the eclipse he begged to come with me, even though taking time off work at such short notice didn't go down very well with his boss."

"So, is he still in the antiques business? It was his passion when last I knew him."

"Yes, he works for a large auction house, smoking memorabilia is his speciality."

"Never! That's a stroke of luck, I'll have to get him to have a butchers at my collection of pipes and old lighters then."

"I'm sure he'd love to. So how come you know each other then? It must be going back a bit."

Maurice grinned. "We lived in the same village and we were at school together. We corresponded for a while after we left but then sort of lost touch. I'd moved away you see. I've often wondered what happened to him though."

Rusty returned with the drinks and placed them on the table, "Made any chocolate gateaux lately?" he grinned, taking a seat.

The colour in Maurice's cheeks deepened. "Don't you go reviving that old story, it could well ruin my reputation," he hissed, "I was only a kid then."

"What's all this?" asked Iris, intrigued by the chortles and thigh slapping of Rusty and the obvious embarrassment of Maurice.

"I'll tell her," said Maurice, wagging his finger at his long lost friend, "you'll exaggerate, you bugger."

Rusty grinned. "Go ahead, Mo, but I shall correct you if you leave anything out."

"It was a long time ago, Iris, when we were still at school. And as I've already said back then we lived in the same village." He attempted to smother a smile as the memories flooded back. "Anyway, once a year the village had an Autumn Fayre and in the marquees they had competitions for all sorts of produce including homemade cakes. The Fayre had a good reputation and folks entered their stuff from miles around so the competition was pretty intense." He stopped to sip his lager. "I liked cooking even then and making cakes in particular, though I don't do much of it now, of course, and so I made a Black Forest Gateau using one of Mum's recipes, and my entry, needless to say, went in the gateau category. I thought the result was pretty good and I was confident that I had a good chance of winning a prize."

Rusty smothered a laugh.

"Shut up," said Maurice, before his friend had time to speak. "Anyway, I proudly handed my entry in and went off to look around the other marquees with Rusty while the judging took place. Later we went to see what the results were and to my disgust someone else had also made a Black Forest Gateau and had the cheek to win first prize. What's more, a lemon gateau came second and I was a measly third."

"How old were you?" Iris asked, amused by his refreshed indignity.

"Fourteen," said Maurice, flushed, "so old enough to know better. Anyway, I was rather cross that I'd been beaten and that's putting it mildly. What a brat I was. I can assure you I'm not a bad loser now though. But do you know what I did?"

Iris shook her head.

"I ran round to the village shop and bought six bars of Ex-Lax, you know, the laxative chocolate. I then took them home, grated them, went back to the fayre and while no-one was about, ate most of the real chocolate on the winning cake and then sprinkled my substitute thickly in its place."

Iris gasped. "Oh, Maurice, you didn't, that's dreadfully wicked. So what poor soul ended up eating the cake?"

The colour of Maurice's face went even darker.

"The person who made the cake donated it to the local old folks' home and a few days later I heard they'd closed the place to visitors because they thought they had a sickness bug. I've been riddled with guilt ever since."

"Oh no, it must have been dreadful for those poor carers dealing with the consequences," Iris whispered, biting her lip.

Rusty roared with laughter. "Do you still think he's the best chef in the world, Iris?"

On Tuesday morning, Elizabeth teetered on a wooden step ladder alongside the front periphery of Chy-an-Gwyns, clipping the straggly growth from the top of a tall privet hedge. On the roof top above, Kernow and Kate, the two magpies, sat for their usual rest, unperturbed by the presence of humans below. On the grass twixt the coastal path and the front boundary of Chy-an-Gwyns, sat Susan Penhaligon, merrily chatting to Elizabeth, passing on gossip heard at the Jolly Sailor along with snippets from her mother, Gertie.

"…and," said Susan after telling Elizabeth of Doctor Owen's news regarding fires following eclipses in days-gone-by, "you've no doubt heard about Nessie's brother and how it was him that Candy saw her hugging by his gate a while back. Poor Candy she said she feels such a Muppet. Still, we all make mistakes."

"I had heard," said Elizabeth but I've not seen him yet. Tally tells me he's very handsome."

"Hmm, he is and considering he's a Scotsman he actually talks clear enough for me to understand what he's saying. Some of them I can't understand at all."

Elizabeth laughed. "And I daresay some Scots would struggle to understand the Cornish accent when spoken by some of the old timers."

"True."

"So have you any idea what Robbie does for a living?" Elizabeth asked.

Susan was just about to answer when she saw a party of four approached from the direction of the Witches Broomstick. She promptly sat bolt upright.

"Yikes, they must be the Yanks Mum told me about," said Susan, unsure whether they ought to run inside and hide or greet the foreign visitors.

"Yanks!" Elizabeth repeated, "What Yanks?"

"The ones staying at Higher Green Farmhouse. You must know of them, surely."

"No, I've no idea who's staying there, I never do. But does it matter whether they're American or not? We live in a multi-cultural society now, Sue, so foreign visitors are nothing unusual and I'm a bit miffed by your unsociable attitude; you're usually so out-going."

"Oh, no, I don't give a toss where they come from and I'm not being unfriendly; it's just that this lot are really, really weird. Milly told Mum they all have the same name."

"Well, I expect that's because they all belong to the same family," laughed Elizabeth, wondering if Milly might have spent too long in the sun.

Before Susan had a chance to answer the Americans were in earshot and so she rose to her feet and smiled sweetly in preparation to greet the overseas visitors.

"Hello, you must be the people staying at the farmhouse. I hope the miserable weather at the weekend didn't get you down."

"Gee honey, back in Texas we're always glad to see a bit of rain so it didn't bother us one bit, did it folks?"

The rest of the family nodded obligingly.

"Allow me to introduce myself, if I may, lady" said the Texan, raising his hat. I'm Jefferson K. Jefferson, and this here is my wife, Mrs Jefferson K. Jefferson." Susan shook hands, and Elizabeth, suddenly feeling unsociable, stepped down from the ladder.

"And this fine looking lad here is my son, Jefferson K. Jefferson, Jr., and this pretty little gel is his wife, Mrs Jefferson K. Jefferson, Jr.."

"Oh, and I'm Susan," mumbled Susan, feeling her name was quite inadequate. "Susan Penhaligon, and this is my lifelong friend, Elizabeth Castor-Hunt."

"Pleased to meet you both, ladies. You've a pretty little house here, miss. Nice view, like back at the little old farmhouse. So, do you both live here?"

"Oh, no," said Susan, "I live in the village with my husband at the Old School House. Elizabeth lives here with her husband and two children."

"The Old School House! You're a schoolmarm, then?"

"No, no, I'm a barmaid," giggled Susan, amused that anyone could even think her intelligent enough to teach, "and my husband's a builder."

"That's nice. How about you, Miss Elizabeth, what do you do?"

"Hmm, I...um, well actually...I...um, nothing," Elizabeth mumbled, feeling overwhelmingly lazy, "I've not actually worked since the children were born."

"Well, I expect they keep you occupied. I reckon a mother should stay at home with her kids. So how old are your little ones and how many do you have?"

Elizabeth winced. "I have two ...err...Wills is twenty one and Tally, err, is nineteen and they're both at university. Well, actually they're not at present because it's the summer holiday, so they're both home until late September."

"So you're a little old housewife like the two Mrs Jefferson K. Jeffersons, here. What kind of business is your husband in, may I ask?"

Elizabeth smiled, much relieved that Greg's occupation was at least of some note. "He's a solicitor," she said proudly, "and is in partnership with a colleague in Helston."

Jefferson K. Jefferson, Sr. tutted. "Phew! My Uncle Chuck was a lawyer in Chicago. Ain't now though. A while back he was prosecuting attorney in a case involving gangsters and after he got some guy convicted and sentenced to life, his family had a hit man shoot him down dead. Poor Uncle Chuck! He was putting out the garbage cans at the time, and he didn't stand a chance."

Chapter Eleven

The half a million extra people predicted to invade Cornwall for the eclipse never materialised and many local people blamed the Blair Government for advising people to stay home and watch it on the television instead of overcrowding the county which might not have been able to cope with the influx. Nevertheless, there were still a quarter of a million more people in Cornwall than there would have been for an average August.

The night before the eclipse was extremely busy in every pub, inn, hotel and restaurant across Cornwall, where people gathered together eagerly looking forward to the following day's events optimistically hoping the weather forecast predicting cloud would be wrong.

Inside the Jolly Sailor, Justin, Susan, Candy, Tally and Demelza, worked non-stop serving the thirsty crowds until well after dark.

"Oh, to be young again," sighed Stella, wistfully, as she gently sipped from her glass of sweet white wine, conscious of Jess, Ollie, Charlie and Lucy playing pool with the lads who were camping on the recreation field.

"But we are young, Stell," laughed Rose, optimistically, "at heart anyway and who cares about a few saggy old wrinkles and grey hairs. It's what's inside that matters."

"Hmm, that's as maybe, but on nights such as this it'd be nice to drink too much and let down one's hair without suffering the consequences."

"Wow, so what's stopping you, Stella?" laughed George. "You'll never be as young again as you are today and to see you legless would be a hoot."

"But it wouldn't would it? I'd be labelled a disgraceful old woman who can't take her drink."

"And quite rightly too," said Ned, a little alarmed by Stella's declaration, "a lady of seventy one years should be dignified, like you are and always have been."

"Humph, I know, but it's not fair, is it? The youngsters have all the fun."

"Oh come on, Stella, we had some fun when we were young, didn't we? And you know only too well you don't really want to drink too much because if you did you'd feel like death in the morning."

"I know I would, but that's not the point. It's the fact after two glasses of wine I now start to slur my words so it shortens the length of time I'm able to socialise. I'd like to be able to drink until the early hours instead of succumbing to the need for sleep before the Ten o' clock News has finished."

George gently hummed the tune of a well-known lullaby and Rose prodded him in the ribs. Ned on the other hand thought it best to change the subject.

"Do we know yet who's judging the Sunflower Competition tomorrow?" he asked, "Justin was hoping to rope in one of the guests."

"And he has, it's me," grinned Freddie, standing by the fireplace, "Justin asked me last night, so I may well be quite unpopular by tomorrow evening."

"Surely not," said Ned, "I mean you can't be biased in any way not when the winner will be the person with the tallest flower and I'd say it's pretty certain that all entrants will be keeping a watchful eye on your tape measure to make sure you get it right."

Freddie grinned. "I know, but it's human nature to blame someone else when things don't go to plan, unless of course the fine people of Trengillion are good losers. From what I've been told thirty five people have entered the competition so that means thirty four are going to be very disappointed."

Trish nodded in agreement with her husband. "Does anyone know what the prize is?"

"It's a surprise apparently," said Rose.

"I think you'll find that's another way of saying Justin hasn't decided yet," laughed Ned. "At least that's what Susan told Gertie, but that was several days ago, so I should imagine he has it sorted by now."

Anne and John, also in the Jolly Sailor, were talking with Elizabeth and Greg; something they always said they must do on a more frequent basis but which seldom came to fruition.

"Would you have any objection to these good folk knowing about your recent experience at Valley View?" Greg asked Elizabeth.

Elizabeth scowled. "I thought we agreed it was best not to say anything to anyone."

Greg wrinkled his nose and grinned in a boyish manner. "Yes, but Anne and John aren't just anyone, are they? They're family."

Anne looked at her sister. "You must tell us now, Liz, whatever it is because we're intrigued. Isn't that so, John?"

John nodded. "Absolutely."

Elizabeth took several sips of wine to enable her time to think. "Okay, but I warn you that you might find what I have to say unbelievable, and that's putting it mildly." She then proceeded to tell of her experience regarding the mysterious face on Maurice's computer screen which she had witnessed on Sunday.

John laughed. Anne sat with her hands spread over her cheeks.

Elizabeth, relishing their lack of verbal response, slowly finished off her wine to hide the amused expression on her face. "Now you can see why I was reluctant to say anything."

"Fair enough," said John, a glint in his eye, "but I want you to be utterly truthful, Liz, and tell us just how much are you exaggerating by."

Elizabeth shook her head and put down her glass. "That's just it, John. I'm not exaggerating at all. In a funny sort of way, I wish I were."

"Have you told Maurice?" Anne asked, looking over her shoulder to make sure the chef was not in earshot.

"Good heavens no, nor do I intend to. When I saw him after I'd been round the first time to do the curtains, I told him that the house felt eerie and I suspected he might have a ghost, but to be honest I was part joking and only said it because his radio had played suddenly for no apparent reason and it scared the life out of me. If I told him about the face he'd think I was either crazy or pulling his leg."

"Hmm, and who could blame him?" said Anne.

"So who do you reckon the old bloke was?" John asked.

Elizabeth shrugged her shoulders. "Search me. I've never seen him before in my life, nor anyone like him for that matter."

As they continued to talk, Nessie's brother, Robbie, walked by with a tray of drinks.

"Does anyone know why he's moved down here?" said Greg nodding in the Scotsman's direction. "He must be here to stay if he's bought a house in Helston."

"I hadn't thought of that," said Anne. "For some silly reason I thought he was just visiting Ness for the eclipse. I'd forgotten about his house."

"Perhaps he's in the Navy and has been posted to Culdrose," said Elizabeth. "Although I think that's unlikely as his hair is a bit too long."

John looked towards the table where Robbie was sitting with his sister and her friends. "Oh well, whatever the reason I'm sure we'll find out in due course."

Anne nodded, impishly. "Yes, and I bet it will be your mum who finds out first."

In the very early hours of Wednesday morning, Elizabeth woke abruptly bathed in perspiration and breathing heavily. Shakily she climbed out of bed and crept towards the door hoping not to wake Greg. Once on the landing she went downstairs craving fresh air.

A light south westerly breeze cooled her skin as she walked along the garden path and out onto the cliff top where the tranquillity of the night sky calmed her breathing and relaxed her limbs. Feeling a little unsteady, she sat on the grass and looked towards the deserted beach where the gentle waves of the sea were just visible in the glow from the Pickled Egg's security lights.

Elizabeth sighed; she knew the reason for her unrest was just a bad dream, and its contents, a fire along with the face she had seen on Maurice's computer screen, were no doubt brought about by the doctor's yarn of fires following eclipses in years gone by and her chat with Anne and John the previous evening. But it was not so much the fire itself that had disturbed her sleep, nor was it the face: it was the scream in the fire's mist. Elizabeth shuddered; it was a desperate, piercing scream and she could not banish its clarity of pitch from her mind. Feeling cold, she went back indoors and returned to bed but she did not sleep soundly.

Chapter Twelve

To the dismay of everyone the morning of the eclipse dawned totally dull and overcast. Villagers groaned as they pulled back their bedroom curtains, and on the recreation field, Trengillion's campers woke early due to the hardness of their uncomfortable beds, and fried their eggs and bacon beneath the gloomy sky. Inside the Penwynton Hotel, guests conscious of absent sunlight streaming in through the dining room windows, ate smoked salmon breakfasts, their spirits flat in contrast to the bubbly champagne fizzing in flute glasses.

Inside the Old Vicarage, before breakfast, Jess hurriedly iced a cake she had made the night before to commemorate the eclipse, even though she would be at work for much of the day and unlikely to eat any of it before evening. Anne was impressed by her daughter's efforts; the cake was made with two rounds, one left whole the other cut to a half moon shape and the two were joined together. The whole one Jess iced in black and the half in pale yellow to signify the sun and moon during an eclipse. On the black side she had piped the date in yellow.

"You really are a clever old stick, Jess, I'd never have thought of doing a cake like that. When you said you were going to make one I expected it to be an un-iced fruit cake or a Victoria Sponge."

"Thanks, Mum, I hope it tastes good too."

"I'm sure it will, but it's far too special to be seen just by us, you ought to take it to the Pickled Egg. It doesn't have to be eaten, it can just be on show, like a decoration to enter into the spirit of things."

"Do you think so?"

"Yes, Jane won't mind, in fact I bet she'll be pleased."

By half past ten it was drizzling fine rain and inside the Jolly Sailor, Maurice, Demelza and Tally half-heartedly made preparations in the kitchen for a busy lunchtime, but feared their efforts might all be in vain should the weather deteriorate further. Meanwhile, on the recreation field, the four young male campers donned warm clothing following their hearty breakfast, but still wore their brightly coloured sunglasses and Bermuda shorts.

Inside Chy-an-Gwyns, Elizabeth, Ned, Stella, Rose, George and Anne - who was not due at work until half past one - walked down the hallway to the front door, wearing coats and holding umbrellas should the weather worsen.

"I wonder if it's as miserable as this in Helston," said Elizabeth, locking the door and slipping the key into her pocket, "if not, then Greg might see more than us."

"I doubt it," sighed Rose, "I think this cloud is pretty general but with any luck there will be a break here and there."

Stella laughed. "Not here by the look of things."

"Where are John and the lads working today, Anne?" asked Elizabeth.

"The Lizard, so it's just as likely to be pretty miserable there, I should imagine."

Stella wandered towards the edge of the cliff and looked down into the cove below. "Look, the beach is absolutely deserted. I bet it's a long time since that's happened in August, apart from when the weather's really bad, that is."

"What, like today?" moaned Ned, pushing his hands inside the pockets of his jacket, "we're certainly not going to see the eclipse in its full glory as anticipated. More's the shame."

On the cliff tops on the opposite side of the cove a large number of people had gathered on a large grassy spot where stood two wooden benches, dedicated to the memory of Nettie and Cyril Penrose. The recreation field was also a popular spot, with those who didn't want to clamber up onto the cliffs, and especially with the inn's staff keen to return indoors once the spectacle was over and to get ahead of punters eager to be the first to celebrate with a drink.

Iris and Rusty decided to view the eclipse from the Witches Broomstick and when they arrived there they found that the lads who had their tent pitched on the recreation field had the same idea.

"Do you mind if I take your photo, Iris?" asked Neil, the young ginger head, nervously, "my dad thinks you're drop dead gorgeous and I think you're pretty cool too."

Iris smiled, sweetly. "Then how can I refuse? And if you get it developed before I go home then I'll sign it for you too."

"Wow, thanks."

"But wait 'til after the eclipse," said Rusty, didactically, "the light will be better then."

Away from the Witches Broomstick, the Jeffersons gathered in the one-time farmyard, laden with cameras and camcorders, determined to capture every minute of the eclipse to show to the folks back home.

"Didn't the brochure say something about sunny Cornwall?" wailed Mrs Jefferson K. Jefferson, Sr., looking at the sleeve of her coat where light drizzle rested on the dark fabric resembling cobwebs on a dewy autumn morning.

"Oh, come on Mrs J. K. J, it's only a little drop of water, it won't be doing no harm and yesterday was a mighty fine day. I got me a burnt nose to prove it."

As the long awaited moment approached, locals and visitors, assembled in their chosen places of observation, patiently and quietly waiting to witness the imminent darkening of the skies, when the moon's shadow would sweep above them. And at eleven minutes past eleven, the predicted time, it happened. The sky turned pale, and then steadily darkened like rapidly impending dusk. A ghostly shadow crept over the village. Along the roadside, a dim light from each of Trengillion's streetlamps slowly brightened, and the birds, confused by the abrupt loss of daylight, flew around overhead desperately seeking safe places to roost. The temperature dropped and a sudden eerie breeze whipped around the spectators who stood mesmerised for two minutes beneath the mystical shadow cast by the moon.

"Fast falls the eventide," whispered Stella, linking arms with Ned as a strange silence gripped the village. The road was devoid of traffic. Nothing stirred. No-one spoke. No dogs barked. Only the waves of the sea continued to lap onto the shore, blasé over an occasion witnessed many times before. Then quite suddenly, the sky began to lighten. The birds sang again. The streetlamps went out and the crowds cheered and clapped to show their appreciation.

"That was actually quite spooky," said Rose, rubbing the sleeve of her jacket to dispel hidden goose-pimples, as the small party outside Chy-an-Gwyns turned to go back inside the house to prepare lunch.

Stella agreed. "It was and goodness only knows what they must have thought when such things happened hundreds of years ago. It must have seemed like the end of the world to them."

"They'd have thought the gods were angry," grinned George, "and probably sacrificed a beautiful fair maiden to pacify whom so ever they worshipped."

"Do you think they had beautiful fair maidens back then," laughed Ned, "I always regard our prehistoric ancestors as a pretty ugly bunch."

"So they were," George agreed, "and I should imagine uneducated peasants as recently as just a few hundred years or so ago were no beauties either. Not if the old paintings are anything to go by."

"Ah, but the paintings of yesteryear weren't of hoi polloi, were they? Most were of the rich and prosperous."

"Yeah and great over-fed lumps they were, as well," grinned George.

"What's that blowing around down on the beach?" asked Stella, weary of mundane chat regarding the appearance of womenfolk in days gone by.

Rose crossed to her side. "Looks like ash or dust. I expect some of the holiday makers had a barbecue there last night and the wind had caused it to blow around."

Stella nodded. "Yes, I expect you're right after all the weather was fine last night."

Rose pointed towards the stationary fishing boats. "Look, there's someone on the beach. Can you make out who it is?"

Stella caught a glimpse of the figure as it disappeared behind the winch-house. "So there is, but, no, I can't. It's probably a holiday maker waiting for the Pickled Egg to open up. I suppose astronomy isn't everyone's cup of tea."

"Well, it's not mine either," laughed Rose, "as interesting as the eclipse was, talk of space, stars and suchlike is all gobbledygook to me, and I don't like to be reminded that the earth is a planet floating around in the atmosphere or whatever it does, with its centre on fire. I'd much rather believe we're firmly planted on solid ground."

"Rose still likes to think the earth is flat," roared George. "Don't go out in a boat, sweetheart, or you might fall over the edge."

"I do not," snapped Rose, "I just think space and such like is boring and so are the people who are fascinated by it."

"Don't let our beautiful, sophisticated Doctor Owen hear you say that," smiled George, amused by his wife's lack of interest and understanding, "or she'll be most offended. Anyway, I think it's all very intriguing and I should like to learn more."

"Humph, how come you've taken an interest in astronomy all of a sudden?" grinned Ned, "as if I need ask."

Stella raised her eyebrows. "Let's get the champagne open, Liz, because in spite of the weather, this is a once in a lifetime event which I'm glad to have witnessed, and I think we ought to celebrate, whether we understand the science behind it all or not."

As the party moved towards Chy-an-Gwyns Elizabeth glanced up to the roof and gasped. "Oh no, there's only one magpie here today, there are always two. I do hope the other one isn't hurt."

Rose stopped dead. Her face turned white. "One for sorrow," she muttered, raising her right arm to salute the lone bird, "Hello, Mr Magpie or perhaps it's Mrs Magpie. Oh dear, I don't know which is missing, Kernow or Kate. "

George laughed. "See, my dear wife is more inclined to believe superstition than hard facts. One for sorrow indeed! What a load of tosh."

"It's not tosh," said Rose, feeling hurt, "a lone magpie is a sign of impending doom and gloom, just you wait and see."

"I expect it's Kate that's missing," said Ned, flippantly, "and she's still disorientatated because of the eclipse. Just like a woman, no sense of direction or the wonders of science." He gave Rose a quick hug. "I expect she'll be back tomorrow and then all will be well."

"Leave her alone," snapped Elizabeth, crossly. "You of all people should both know better than to mock folklore and superstition, Dad."

Ned raised his hands in a ghost-like manner, "Ooooo, I do believe my mother has just spoken from the grave in order to castigate me." He then caught Stella's eye and said no more.

At three o'clock that afternoon after the inn closed, Freddie, armed with a tape measure, step ladder and clip board was escorted by his wife, Trish and pub landlord, Justin, around the village in search of the tallest sunflower. As they proceeded from one garden to another so the group increased in numbers, as entrants already judged followed to witness the reading of others. But Freddie refused, under instruction from Justin, to let anyone know the measurements of their rivals, for he planned to have a prize giving ceremony at the inn in the evening, hence the winner must remain unknown until then.

Chapter Thirteen

In the evening, holiday makers and many locals made a bee-line for the Jolly Sailor, for the eclipse, in spite of its visual resplendence having been marred by the disappointing weather, still evoked a feeling of great camaraderie which drew people out to celebrate the infrequent experience with others. The results of the Sunflower Competition were also to be heard later in the evening, an event which raised high expectations in each and every budding garden enthusiast.

Justin was overwhelmed. "Love a duck, how many more are going to cram in through that door? It's not even eight o'clock yet. I expect lots of them will be hungry too; I hope it doesn't send poor old Maurice into a tis-was."

Susan, pulling a pint alongside him, the third in a round of eight, wished she had worn flat shoes instead of high heels. "It's crazy," she whined, "I can't even see the tables because of all the people standing and it's a really hard trying to make out what people are ordering over the racket they're making."

Waving a twenty pound note in her hand, Tally slipped on her way to the till. "Whoa, I'll get a mop if we get a lull," she muttered, slightly shaken, "this floor's getting dangerously slippery, but then I've not helped by spilling that pint of Guinness."

"I don't think there'll be a lull," said Susan, dropping slices of lemon into glasses of gin and tonic, "and I'm dying for a fag. I think it must be the wafts of smoke coming this way from Mr America, Senior's ginormous cigar. It's tantalising aroma is tickling my taste buds."

"Yuck, you've got to be joking," said Tally, pulling three packets of peanuts from a card beside the till. "It smells vile and is stinking the place out."

"Women!" laughed Ollie, enjoying the buzz of his first night behind the bar. "Do they ever stop whinging, Justin?"

"Sadly, no, and fortunately when it's noisy the other side of the bar the punters can't hear the nature of their waffle so we're the only ones that hear it. But don't worry, Ollie, after a while you'll deaden your mind to it and it'll just become a muzzy din in the background."

"Cheeky sod," gasped Susan, subtly elbowing him in the ribs.

"Well, whether it's considered whinging or not, I'm dying for the loo and we're out of pint glasses too," sighed Candy, taking change from the till, "I'll have to go pretty soon because it's affecting the way I walk. I'll collect some glasses at the same time."

"You'll never get out there," said Justin, biting his bottom lip, "we'll have to drag in outside help."

He took the money for the round he was pouring and then to the surprise of everyone, rang the inn's bell.

"Ahoy there shipmates. If there are any empty glasses near you, please try and get them onto the bar otherwise there'll be no more beer."

The loud hubbub of collective voices subsided momentarily and male groans, along with the chinking of glass, filled the air. Within minutes the bar was cluttered with a mixed selection of empty drinking vessels.

"Thought that might work," grinned Justin, pushing some towards the glass washer, "trouble is we don't have time to wash 'em."

Gertie, pinned up tight against the bar where she fanned her flushed face with a beer mat, seized the opportunity to escape. "I'll come round and help, you've got more room that side than this and I could do with a change of scenery."

"Thanks, Gert, you're an angel, and you Candy had better slip upstairs to the bathroom loo before you make the floor even wetter."

Just before nine, holiday makers with children, who had eaten, began to drift away and the bar staff heaved sighs of relief as the pace dropped from manic to busy.

"You can have that fag now, Sue," said Justin, noticing she was very hot and flustered, "and then we'd better announce the winner of the competition. I advertised it as nine o'clock so we mustn't keep folks waiting, because the suspense must be unbearable, ha ha."

"Ta, I'll be no more than five minutes, promise."

Susan took her cigarettes from beside the till and went outside, glad of the opportunity to cool down and breathe fresh air. Outside, she leaned against the nearest window sill, took a deep breath and then pulled a cigarette from its packet. At first she thought she was alone, but then she had a creepy feeling that she was being watched. Glancing towards the direction in which she felt her observer was, she saw the solitary figure of a slim girl strangely dressed in black, sitting on the bench over by the long disused toilet block, watching her she felt, with a scornful air of disapproval.

Susan, oblivious of the stranger's reason for contempt, forced a smile. "You come out for some fresh air too? It is a bit stuffy in there, isn't it?"

The girl smiled with her mouth but her eyes looked tired and Susan thought, tinged with sadness. "Yes," she nodded.

Susan lit her cigarette and conscious she was still being watched, crossed the cobbles and offered one to the stranger.

"No thanks," said the girl, backing away with her hands raised. "I don't like smoke it gets in my eyes and makes me cough."

"Oh, sorry," said Susan, fanning the smoke and retreating towards the door. "I should have realised that's why you were giving me the evil eye."

But when she turned around the girl was gone.

Back inside the inn tension mounted as everyone awaited the results of the Sunflower Competition. Justin, who had joined punters on their side of the bar, stood by the front door on a footstool with Freddie by his side, conscious Ned was standing nearby with the camcorder ready for action.

"Before I announce the winners I'd like to thank everyone for entering the competition. Far more of you took part than I'd ever dreamed would and for that reason there will be three prizes. I must admit I've rather enjoyed listening to the many conversations, boasts and pitfalls regarding the progress of your efforts, though I shall not be repeating any of the expletives I've heard in reference to slugs and snails. I know it's a bit premature, but because of your interest I've already decided that next year we'll see who can grow the biggest marrow. But as we'll not have an eclipse for the dramatic climax we'll probably have the presentation at the Summer Fayre or Harvest Festival instead. Anyway, I'll say no more as I'm sure you're all longing to hear the results which Freddie here will kindly announce. All yours, Freddie."

Justin stepped down from the footstool and Freddie took his place.

"Thanks, Justin. I've been asked to announce the three winners in reverse order to increase the suspense, and so here goes. In third place with a sunflower an impressive eight feet and three inches tall, is our youngest competitor, James Ainsworth. Well done, James."

Everyone clapped, pleased to see a child amongst the winners. From behind the bar, Susan passed Justin an envelope containing a ten pound note which the landlord handed to the young finalist.

"Wow, thanks," he stammered, amazed by his good fortune, "Now I'll be able to buy the PlayStation game my best mate's selling."

Freddie grinned, tickled pink by the delighted expression on the eleven year old's face. As the applause subsided he continued with the announcements.

"In second place, with a massive height of eight feet eleven and a half inches, is your horticultural expert and vegetable grower supreme, Jim Haynes."

"Damn, didn't quite make nine," tut-tutted Jim, as Justin handed him an envelope containing twenty pounds, "Should have put on more manure."

"And now for the moment you've all been waiting for. In first place with a staggering height of nine feet and eight inches is, a garden novice I believe, your local plumber, the one and only Larry Bingham."

"Never," said Larry, genuinely surprised, "I don't believe it. I knew it was big but never dreamt it was that big. Wow, thanks, Freddie you've made my day."

Amidst the laughter and applause were a few good humoured calls from other entrants of 'cheat' and 'fix'. And Jim Haynes cheekily suggested Freddie must have had the tape measure upside-down and the real measurement was eight foot six.

"I'll just go and get your prize," said Justin, amused by the good natured retorts of the losers, "the winner doesn't get money."

Larry laughed. "Well, actually, beating green-fingered Jim is a prize in itself. I can't believe I've done it. Must have been the plant food I used; it said it was good stuff on the label."

Jim smiled. "That, and a huge dose of beginner's luck."

Justin returned in minutes with a brown cardboard box which he placed on a bar stool beside the proud winner. Larry excitedly opened it. When he saw the contents he roared with laughter and lifted out his reward to show the bystanders his prize. The award was a fifteen inch tall garden gnome, crudely painted in gaudy colours, with a cheeky grin on his bright pink face. And in his hands he held a tall, bright yellow sunflower, which looked down at the gnome with an equally impish smile.

"Speech," called someone in the crowd.

Larry gasped. "What! Well, yes, alright. Firstly, thanks to Justin for running the competition and so forth. We've all had a lot of fun growing the sunflowers, but well, some of us were just a lot better than others, ha, ha. Meanwhile, err, what can I say about my prize, I mean, it's actually rather charming. Just what I've always wanted, in fact. Thanks to you too, Freddie, for being such an excellent judge. In fact I shall name this gnome after you in honour of this momentous day."

He raised his glass, "Cheers everyone, and here's to next year and the biggest marrow.

The three prize winners then stood in a row while family members took photographs for the album, and Ned, confident he had recorded the event for posterity, reached for his pint.

By closing time, with aching legs and sore feet, Justin and his staff were ready to sit down and take their ease in spite of the huge amount of clearing up to be done. But their burden was eased by a band of volunteers who helped tidy up on the off chance it might earn them a night cap.

"I don't think we need worry about the Old Bill being around tonight," laughed Percy, helping Gertie wipe down the tables, "I expect there'll be plenty to keep them busy in the towns."

Freddie raised his eyebrows and opened his mouth to speak but a sharp nudge in the ribs from Trish deterred him from making a comment.

"Did any of you see a strange girl in here tonight?" asked Susan, removing her shoes and resting her feet on a stool once the work was finally done.

"Strange," yawned Candy, swirling brandy in her glass, "in what way?"

Susan wrinkled her nose in a puzzled manner. "I don't really know, but I saw her when I went out for a fag. She was on her own and like me had gone out for fresh air. She's a non-smoker, you see, and I reckon the smoke was stinging her eyes. But it was her outfit that was strange, in fact I'd say it was really weird. She was wearing a black calf length dress with a fitted waist, lots of chunky jewellery, her tights were black and she wore great clumpy boots. She had shining jet black hair which was back combed and kind of spiky and around her hair she wore a jewelled headband. Oh, and her nails were painted black too, and her dark eyeliner was really thick and over the top, especially since her face was white. She looked to me like she could do with a spell in the sun. Surely someone other than me saw her."

Everyone nonplussed, shook their heads except Tally. "She'll be a Goth," she grinned, amused by Susan's unworldliness. "It's a trend. Several girls, and boys too, dress that way at university. It's a fad that's been around for a while now, but you don't see much of it down here."

"Well, thank goodness for that, I thought at first I must have imagined it. What a shame though, because she had a really pretty face."

"A pretty face, I can't say that I saw her then," said Ollie. "Next time she's in you must give me a nudge."

Gertie grinned. "If she's that outlandish looking I should think you'll notice her yourself, Ollie."

Tally nodded in agreement. "But surely a Goth would never take your fancy, you're much too down to earth."

"Is that your way of saying, I'm boring?"

"No, not at all, it's just that in all aspects you're very conservative with a small c. I mean the way you dress, your taste in music, your friends and so forth. A Goth girlfriend just wouldn't be you. I think Doctor Owen would be more up your street."

"Oh, come on, Tally, I think that's a bit harsh on poor Ollie," said Candy, "the doctor, as charming as she is, is considerably older than your cousin."

"Well, when I mentioned the doctor I was meaning her as a type of person, not the lady herself, if that makes sense."

"Anyway," said Gertie, "this Goth girl's probably ever so nice under her funny clothes and they might be quite well suited, you just never can tell. Besides, we all wear things when we're young which make us shudder when we get older. Isn't that so, Freddie?"

Freddie laughed, but those who had not known him in the past thought it unlikely he could ever have dressed anyway but conventionally.

"Anyway, said Ollie, rising, "if there's nothing more to do then I'll be off home, if that's alright, Justin. I have to be ready for work at eight tomorrow."

"No, that's fine, off you go. You did a good job, well done."

"Thanks, I enjoyed it and the time went really fast."

"We'd better be off too," said Candy, casting a look of despair at Larry who had overdone his victory celebrations and was trying to get the gnome to eat a cheese and onion crisp.

"And we'll go too," said Gertie, rising, "Come on Percy, we'll escort Candy and Larry home, just in case Larry falls in the hedge or something."

Larry grinned and hiccupped as he unsteadily stood. Candy shook her head. "God only knows how much he's had to drink, but then it's not every day he wins a competition, I suppose. In fact to my knowledge, he's never won one before."

Larry picked up the gnome from the table, "Come on, Freddie Gnome, we're going home. Hey, that rhymes, Cand! Freddie Gnome we're going home."

Chapter Fourteen

Elizabeth woke early the following morning and because she was unable to resume her slumbers, she rose, inspired by the notion of a gentle stroll across the beach. For she liked early mornings, especially if in time to see the sun rise. There was something special and magical about being up when most of the village were still sleeping.

She left Chy-an-Gwyns dressed in jeans and a baggy T shirt, flip-flops on her feet and her hair pulled back in a ponytail, for she assumed, as was usually the case at early dawn, the beach would be deserted unless the fishermen were still on shore. To her delight no-one was about and the tide was low also, exposing a wide expanse of smooth sand and shingle.

Elizabeth slowly strolled towards the sea, across the wet compressed sand, hardened by the ebbing tide, singing quietly to herself, delighting at the defined indentations made by her solitary footprints. Glad to be alive and full of the joys of life, she reached the water's edge and looked to the skies where a solitary seagull swooped overhead.

From the beach she picked up a large egg-shaped pebble and cast it into the surf; she heard it plop and watched as the small ripples vanished beneath an oncoming wave. All was quiet save the murmur of the sea. All was peaceful, tranquil and serene.

She walked along the edge of the crystal clear water, watching as it swirled alongside her feet, magnifying the stones and shingle as it trickled back into the sea.

As she approached the section of beach from where the fishing boats were launched, she paused and picked up another pebble but instantly she dropped it. The pebble was hot and the shingle beneath her feet was gently steaming. Elizabeth stepped back, puzzled. The morning was warm but the rising sun's rays held insufficient heat to warm the shingle to the degree she felt through the soles of her flip-flops. As she stepped into the waves to cool her feet, a small posy of wild, red and white clover, brought in by the rising tide, brushed against her ankles. Forgetting the unexplained heat, she picked up the bedraggled flowers from the salty water and feeling sorry for them, took them home where she placed them in a small vase of water to help them revive after their ordeal.

Because of the fine, warm weather, Trengillion was, by mid-morning, awash with people milling around, thrilled by the cloudless blue skies and the warm sunshine. On the beach, bathers bronzed beneath the sun's rays, built castles in the sand, paddled and swam in the cool waters of a calm sea and idly chatted over matters of little importance with newly-made friends. And one comment which cropped up time and time again, was an expression of sorrow, saying, it was a shame the previous day's weather had not enjoyed the same degree of sunshine and clear vision as the present.

Inside the Pickled Egg, Jane and Janet cooked and produced hot meals, snacks and cream teas for holiday makers, and Janet's two daughters, Lucy and Angie, waited on the clientèle along with other girls from the village. Jess was not due in until evening as she had the lunchtime off.

By mid-afternoon demand for food lessened and Jane made tea for herself and Janet and poured Coke for the girls which they took outside to drink in the shade of the colourful umbrellas. As they sat, glad of a break, Janet subtly pointed across the beach to the lonely figure of a slim girl with long black hair. "Look, she's still there, and in the very same spot as she was sitting when we got here this morning, how odd."

"What's odd about that?" scowled Lucy, blowing bubbles into her Coke through the straw, "lots of people stay put for the day once they get on the beach."

"I know, but I just think it's odd that she hasn't moved and she looks kind of lonely. I mean to say, if she's on holiday then she ought to be laughing and having fun with friends, like those crazy lads camping in the Rec."

Lucy raised her eyebrows and smirked on hearing reference to the crazy lads.

"Perhaps she's shy," suggested Angie.

"Or she's foreign and doesn't speak English," said Jane, "But then if that's the case I suppose she'd have to have come over here with someone. People seldom go abroad on their own, do they?"

Lucy glanced over towards the lone figure. "Shall I go and interrogate her and ask why she's a Billy-no-mates?"

"That's a good idea, Lucy," said Janet, "find out who she is and if she is on her own, then perhaps you could be friends with her."

Lucy scowled, put down her glass on the table, stood and casually walked across the beach. Near to the strange girl she stopped, sat down and it seemed to onlookers, struck up an amicable conversation.

"I'd never be able to do that at her age," gasped Jane, admiringly, "I'd have been far too shy and I'm not much better now."

"Oh, Lucy will talk to anyone, I've never known her to be lost for words. Angie's not much different either, are you, Ange? But the boys are both quite shy, so I was delighted when James came third in the Sunflower Competition, the compliments brought him out of his shell a bit."

Lucy returned shortly after and sat back at the table. "She's not an alien, a foreigner or anything like that. She's a Goth, her name is Morwenna and she's here because of the eclipse."

"Morwenna, isn't that a Cornish name?" said Jane, "there used to be a Morwenna in our class when I was at school and she always claimed it was."

"Cornish or Welsh," said Janet, confidently, "and it means maiden or white sea, something like that. In fact it's very similar to Doctor Owen's Christian name. Ian tells me she's Morgana."

Angie scowled. "How do you know where the name comes from? You're not Cornish or Welsh."

"Because it was in the book of Cornish girls names I had from the library when I was looking for a name for Miriam. And I had it on my short list for a while, Morwenna that is, not Morgana."

Lucy groaned. "Well, thank goodness you didn't choose it. Morwenna is alright for a girl but it'd sound stupid for a dog, having said that Miriam's a pretty stupid dog name too. God only knows what made you choose it."

"What's she like?" Jane asked, "Girl I mean, not dog."

"She seemed quite nice," said Lucy, "friendly and all that, but her clothes look a bit weird on a summer's day."

"Goths are real freaky," said Angie, "that's probably why no-one's chatting to her."

Janet cast a sympathetic look across the beach. "Poor kid!"

Angie scowled. "Why do you say, poor kid? Being a Goth is her own choice, there's nothing stopping her being normal like everybody else."

"Goth?" Jane looked puzzled.

"It's a fashion," said Janet, "You must have noticed a few girls wearing a lot of black, often having hair part-dyed in un-natural colours, wearing dark satanic lipstick, lots of thick eye make-up, black nail varnish, undignified clumpy boots and so forth."

"Well, yes, but I didn't realise it was a fashion, I just assumed they had no dress sense. Oh dear, I must be getting old."

Angie giggled. "But they don't have any dress sense."

Janet nodded to endorse her daughter's comment. "It's not a very flattering fashion and there seems to be something sinister about it to me. I'm glad neither of my girls dress like it."

Lucy shook her head. "I think you're being a bit unfair, Mum. From what I know of Goths, they find beauty in things that others might consider to be dark. You know, things that are mysterious but by no means evil. In fact they're usually gentle and kind by nature and abhor cruelty and violence, although from what I know their sense of humour does lean towards black comedy."

"Humph, they sound like morons, if you ask me," said Angie.

"Oh, but they're not morons; in fact quite the opposite. They're usually intelligent and are often romantics. Some people reckon they're just remnants of the Punk era but that just isn't so."

"How come you're so knowledgeable about Goths?" Janet asked, surprised by her daughter's empathetic comments.

"There's a boy at school who's a Goth. He's ever so nice, even the teachers think so."

"But surely he doesn't dress Gothish at school?" said Jane.

Lucy shook her head. "No, he doesn't. He toes the line and wears school uniform like the rest of us, but he's a Goth at heart and I've seen pictures of him taken out of school hours."

As her words faded a family approached the Pickled Egg and looked at the menu on a table and so the gathering ceased talking and returned indoors.

Seeing the weather was fine and sunny, Robbie Macdonald left the post office where his sister, Nessie and her boyfriend, Stephen were hard at work and headed to the cliff tops for a walk to the Witches Broomstick. Nessie had recommended he take that route because she found the spot intriguing and thought its name very appropriate. For the Witches Broomstick was a stretch of sand surrounded by a formation of rocks which caused the shape of the sand to resemble that of a broomstick.

Robbie left the village behind and climbed the steep cliff path. At the top he paused to regain his breath and sat down on the grass to relish the spectacular views. The turquoise sea was crystal clear, visibility was perfect and he was able to see for miles along the rugged coastline in both directions. He felt tired and so he lay back on the grass and closed his eyes. The sun was warm and the sound of the sea lapping against the cliffs below was very soothing. He smiled to himself, confident that he had made the right decision. For Robbie was a successful writer whose acclaimed books were popular on both sides of the Atlantic. The first two series he had written were detective crime novels, gritty and harsh, his protagonist, headstrong and determined and both were set in his native Scotland. But he felt it was time to do something a little different, hence a change of location seemed a good proposition and as his only sister was already living in Cornwall, Cornwall seemed the obvious place to come.

Once he had resolved to make the move, Robbie, after much consideration, decided not to sell his house in Scotland so that he would always have somewhere to stay when he wanted to go home for a visit. He chose to buy a house in Helston because of its close proximity to Nessie; it was also quite central to reach other destinations.

The sound of a helicopter in the distance gradually grew louder. When it was very near, Robbie sat up and watched as it flew overhead. There was a time when he'd rather liked the idea of being a pilot but as he'd grown older, the idea had appealed less as he'd realised that all he really wanted to do was to write. Hence, when he left school he took a job with a local newspaper and worked by day and wrote his first story by night.

Because the helicopter had disrupted his train of thought, Robbie rose to continue his walk. He met several people as he followed the winding coastal path and greeted them each with a nod and a cheery 'good morning' as he continued on his way.

As he approached the area where the footpath left the edge of the cliffs and ran towards the stile leading into the dandelion field, he paused. Had he heard the cry of someone in distress or was it a trick of the wind? Attentively, he stood very still and listened but no further call met his ears and the southerly wind was little more than a breeze. He walked on but as he reached the stile he heard a call again. Confused, he looked all around but he was quite alone. Nevertheless, in case someone was in trouble, he thought he had better investigate if for no other reason than to clear his conscience. Hastily, he retraced his steps and then walked towards the cliff edge. He knelt and looked down onto the rocks below; as he expected there was no sign of life and all was quiet save the whooshing of waves gently lapping against the cliff base.

Satisfied that it must have been the wind he'd heard, Robbie attempted to stand but before he was fully vertical, a sudden sharp pain, like a knife, shot through his left shoulder blade. He shrieked in agony and fighting to catch his breath, gripped his shoulder to ease the pain. Simultaneously, his ears began to buzz, he felt dizzy, and as he tried to stand up straight, he stumbled, lost his footing on the damp grass and slid feet first over the side of the cliff.

Ten feet below the cliff's edge, several rocks formed a substantial, flat ledge and fortunately for Robbie, he landed on his backside right in its middle. Badly shaken, he laid back his head and thanked God that he was not lying a crumpled heap at the foot of the cliff. He sat for a while to compose himself and moved his limbs to make sure not one was broken. Once confident that his arms had regained sufficient strength to aid his climb, he rose and clambered back to the top of the cliff where he sat down on the grass, and as he rested, he watched a lone magpie pecking at the undergrowth beneath a spread of wild gorse.

A fairly large crowd gathered at the Jolly Sailor in the evening and amongst them, to the delight of many, were Iris Delaney and Rusty Higgins. Iris, dressed in a flattering white, backless sun dress, mingled with the locals and holiday makers alike, signing autographs for those visiting the area and skirting quickly over any questions asked regarding her career. Her private life, however, including her relationship with Rusty, was a no-no subject.

When the attention ceased, Iris gracefully sat on a stool at the bar vacated for her by an ardent fan and crossed her long, bronzed, bare legs. Rusty stood close behind, taking on the guise of a devoted bodyguard. Iris then ordered drinks which Jefferson K. Jefferson, Jr., overwhelmed by her presence, insisted on paying for.

"Iris had some jewellery stolen yesterday." said Rusty, casually stroking the back of her head, waiting for Susan to pour his pint. "A bracelet. The thief must have broken into the house while we were watching the eclipse. Not a very nice feeling knowing someone's been poking through our belongings."

Freddie, overhearing the comment, stepped forward and looked Iris in the face. "I hope you've reported it to the police."

"No," said Iris, emphatically, casting a frown in the direction of Rusty, "I haven't, nor shall I. The bracelet wasn't worth anything so I'm not in the least concerned."

She leaned forward and took a cigarette from her handbag which hung on a brass hook attached to the bar, and to the surprise of all but Rusty, placed it in an old-fashioned cigarette holder. On seeing this, Jefferson K. Jefferson, Jr., dashed forward and lit the cigarette with an ostentatious silver lighter. Iris drew smoke and then released it above her head as though to emphasise her obstinacy.

"It's unlikely the thief would ever be caught even if you did," agreed Doctor Owen. "We had a spate of burglaries at home a while back but no-one was ever brought to justice."

"But you should still report it," persisted Freddie, wagging his finger, annoyed by her unreasonable behaviour. "If there's a thief around the police should be made aware so they can keep their ears to the ground."

"If there were other break-ins at the same time then I'm sure others will have reported them," said Iris, loftily, "but it's more likely I was the only target. I frequently have items of jewellery stolen, you see, and often when I'm wearing it too. Fans are always after mementoes and for that reason the jewellery I wear is always paste, unless it's a very special occasion of course, such as the BAFTAs or a film premiere."

"Humph, alright, but have you any idea how the thief got in?" continued Freddie. "Any signs of a break in?"

"None," said Rusty, sympathising with the ex-policeman's concerns, "but foolishly we left the kitchen window open, so anyone slight of build could have got in without disturbing anything. And as the bracelet they took was lying on the dressing table in Iris' room, they didn't even have to look far."

"Not much to go on then," said Freddie, "but I still think it should be reported whether it was a fan or not. Theft is theft whatever the motive."

"We saw someone on the beach just after the eclipse," said Ned, recalling the lone figure from the previous day spotted by Rose and Stella.

"Really, were they anywhere near our cottage?" Rusty asked.

"Well, yes, I suppose they were. Rose pointed the figure out because it seemed the beach wasn't a good place to view the eclipse, it being down in a dip. Having said that I've no idea who it was or what they looked like because we were too far away. I didn't take too much notice and so couldn't even say whether it was a male or a female. Could you, Stell?"

Stella shook her head.

"Humph, not much help then," sighed Freddie, "perhaps more news will come to light in due course. Meanwhile, I suggest everyone be a bit more security conscious than usual."

Chapter Fifteen

After Maurice finished work on Thursday evening, he went home for a shower and a change of clothes. He was feeling tired and his muscles ached; the evening had been really busy, the dining room full and it felt as though he had fed just about everyone in Cornwall. Once clean and refreshed, he finished off the remains of a bass he had baked earlier in the day and then sat at the kitchen table and wrote a birthday card for his mother in Plymouth. He thought about spending a while on the computer or watching the television, but his eyes were tired so he decided since he had to post his mother's card anyway, that he'd do it en route to the inn where he'd enjoy a nice cold pint of lager instead.

Maurice always enjoyed the brief walk to the inn; he appreciated the fresh air and the opportunity to stretch his legs, especially after dark when there was no-one around. On this occasion the night sky was clear and a gentle breeze was blowing from the south west; to savour the tranquility he sat down on a wall outside the village hall and lit a cigarette.

Inside the curtilage of the village hall, stood the old sycamore tree, its roots hidden beneath the uneven, cracked concrete through which it grew. It had been there for many years, and no-one could remember when it had first emerged as a self-set seedling. However, in spite of the lack of sustenance during its former years, it had survived against all odds and was now a substantial tree, much loved by many villagers, especially the children who regarded it as the home of Kernow and Kate.

As Maurice sat enjoying the peace, the leaves on the sycamore rustled overhead in the gentle breeze, creating dappled shadows in the light of a streetlamp beyond. Above the tree, a new moon glowed in the night sky amidst an array of twinkling bright stars.

Maurice sighed, a contented man. He liked Trengillion, even though he had known the village for only seven months. The inhabitants were friendly, he liked the people he worked with and he enjoyed the quietness of village life, especially at night when he had the opportunity to be alone and enjoy the peace following a hard day's work.

When the cigarette was finished, Maurice stubbed it out and flicked the butt into a rubbish bin on the other side of the wall. He then stood, stretched his arms and turned in preparation to walk down the road to the inn. But before he had completed two steps, he heard a startling whoosh from behind; he turned quickly and saw flames five feet in height leaping from the rubbish bin. Swearing profusely, Maurice leaped across the wall, kicked over the bin and turned it upside down to rob the flames of oxygen. When he was convinced the fire was extinguished, he turned the bin upright and returned it to its usual place.

"What on earth happened there?" asked a female voice from the shadows.

Maurice turned as Doctor Owen walked into a pool of light from the nearby lamp post.

"God only knows," he growled, hoping she had not heard his ungentlemanly expletives, "I couldn't have put the damn fag out properly, I suppose."

The doctor smiled. "You should give up, it's a disgusting habit and you'll never grow into a big strong lad."

"You sound like my mother."

"Yes, I suppose I do, and no doubt it's a prophecy used by most parents. Are you going back to the inn? You look as though you could do with a drink after your ordeal."

Maurice stepped back over the wall. "Yes, that was my plan. How about you?"

"Same here. I came out after my dinner for a walk and some fresh air. My steak was cooked to perfection by the way, as always."

"Thank you. Do you like walking in the dark then?"

The doctor laughed. "I never really feel it's dark, not with the stars to guide me. I never tire of seeing the night sky."

"Hmm, it's looking good tonight I must admit, but I'm afraid one sky looks pretty much the same as any other to me. I mean, there's either stars or no stars, but then it wouldn't do for us all to have the same interests, would it?"

"Absolutely not."

"Sorry about my language back then."

"Apology accepted."

"Do you mind if I walk with you back to the inn?"

"No, I should enjoy your company."

"Thank you."

As they began to walk, the doctor glanced around. "Do you live near here?"

Maurice nodded. "Yes, back there in Valley View." He pointed to the house.

"Very nice. There must be money to be made in culinary art."

Maurice sighed. "Sadly I don't own it; it's rented, more's the shame. Still, who knows, if the owner ever decides to sell I might give it a go." He laughed. "I've been told by a fairly reliable source that it might even have a ghost."

"Really, how interesting. Is it very old, do you know?"

"The ghost or the house?"

"The house."

"Apparently yes. It, and the village hall, are two of the oldest buildings in the village. I'm told both date back to the early sixteen hundreds."

"I knew the village hall was that old and I daresay both are listed buildings then."

"Yes, both Grade Two."

"Interesting. So, tell me Maurice, what do you enjoy doing when you're not cooking?"

"I spend a lot of time on my computer, especially eBay. I collect Smokeralia, you see, and I already have quite a collection."

"How fascinating. I keep meaning to register but as yet I haven't got round to it. I believe there are bargains galore to be had."

Maurice laughed. "Yes, as long as you're careful. As with any auction it's easy to get carried away when bidding."

"Oh yes, that's something I understand only too well. My father is a great fan of auctions and attends them whenever he's able, but sadly not all of his purchases are welcomed by my mother."

On reaching the inn they went their separate ways. Maurice joined Iris, Rusty and the small gathering drawn around them, and the doctor, after exchanging pleasantries with Justin, bought a glass of wine which she took outside to drink while she studied the night sky further.

"I think I'm probably going mad," said Stella, as she entered the living room of Rose Cottage. "I just went into our bedroom to put the washing away and saw flames leaping upwards in front of the village hall and then suddenly they went out. Weird don't you think?"

Ned raised his eyebrows. "Probably a reflection of the light bulb in the window and it just looked like flames."

"I didn't put the light on," said Stella, annoyed by her husband's flippant response. "I left the washing on the bed, that's how I could see. It was quite unnerving because at first I had a horrible feeling the hall was on fire."

Ned tut-tutted. "Surely you're not anticipating a fire based on the cock-and-bull story Doctor Owen has been spouting. Come on, Stell, be realistic."

Stella sat down on the settee. "Anyway if it was anything earth shattering I expect we'll hear about it."

"Hmm, we shall if it reaches Gertie's ears," said Ned.

Inside the second largest bedroom at Higher Green Farmhouse, Jefferson K. Jefferson, Jr. was woken by a sudden loud crash. At first, unsure where he was, he lay awake staring at the ceiling where a thin strip of dim light peeped through a chink in the curtains.

"Hey, did you hear that noise, Julie May?" he whispered, reaching out gently to prod his wife. But to his dismay she did not answer for she was not there.

Hoping she was in the en suite bathroom he sat up in bed, but no light shone from beneath the bathroom door. Alarmed he sprang out of bed, reached for his dressing gown and peeped out onto the landing. The house was in darkness. Not wishing to disturb his parents he crept down the stairs and went into the kitchen. As he had feared the backdoor leading outside was wide open and the key lay on the floor.

From beneath the dresser, Jefferson K. Jefferson, Jr. pulled out his sneakers. No socks were present and so he slipped the shoes onto his bare feet, hastily tied the laces, reached for the torch hanging on the back of the door and stepped outside.

There was no sign of Julie May in the farmyard and so he ran out into the lane flashing the torch in both directions; to his relief he could see her in the distance walking down the hill towards the village wearing only her flimsy nightdress and with slippers on her feet.

Making as little noise as possible he ran to catch up with her, hoping he might take her hand and lead her safely back to the farmhouse. But Julie May seemed determined, even in her sleep to continue with her nocturnal adventure and so Jefferson K. Jefferson, Jr. had no choice but to escort her wherever she chose to go, for he was only too well aware that a sleepwalker must never be forcibly woken from their sleep. He was also curious as to where she might be going.

At the foot of the hill Julie May turned up into the village, past the inn, past houses, past the post office and the village hall. By a turning which led to the Old Vicarage she turned and walked down the narrow lane. Jefferson K. Jefferson, Jr. was alarmed and prayed in desperation that his wife did not intend to make an unannounced visit to the good folk who lived in the Old Vicarage. He heaved a sigh of relief when she suddenly left the lane and walked through an open five bar gate and onto a track in a field.

At the end of the track they reached a stile beside a closed gate. Julie May clambered over the stile with ease, Jefferson K Jefferson, Jr. followed and to his surprise saw they were at the village allotments.

Julie May continued along a strip of grass lying between rows of vegetable plots and on towards the edge of the field. Beside an old well she abruptly stopped.

In the east, daylight was beginning to peep through the night sky casting a golden beam of light across distant fields. Jefferson K. Jefferson, Jr. switched off the torch and looked at the face of his wife. To his surprise she was staring at the sunrise and tears were trickling down her cheeks.

"You okay, Julie May?" he asked, grabbing her arm without thinking.

She jumped and woke with a start. Her moist eyes flashing as she tried to make sense of the location.

"Julie May, I'm sorry, honey, I shouldn't have shouted like that. I woke you and that was a mighty stupid thing to do. Are you alright?"

Julie May began to shiver. Her teeth chattered as she attempted to speak, "Where are we, Jeff? I'm so cold. Why are we here?"

Jefferson K. Jefferson, Jr. quickly took off his dressing gown, wrapped it around the shoulders of his shivering wife and hugged her tightly. "You were sleep walking, honey. I followed you here. The sunrise made you cry."

Julie May looked towards the sunrise. "Well, it is mighty pretty, I must admit, but I can't think why it should have made me cry. Where are we? I don't recognise this place."

"We're where the local folks grow their vegetables, honey. You'll see them in a minute when we go back across the field."

She stepped forward, touched the side of an old well and glanced around at their surroundings, "Why is there an old well here, Jeff? There are no houses round about."

"I don't know, honey. I guess they had it built to water their gardens with. You know how fanatical the English are when it comes to gardening."

Julie May tried to smile. "Yeah, you're probably right."

Jefferson K. Jefferson, Jr. took her hand, "Come on, honey, let's get back to the farmhouse before Ma and Pa are up and local folks are about too. Because if anyone were to see us, they'll think us mighty peculiar walking about in our nightwear."

Julie May giggled. Her husband was much relieved. It seemed her brisk awakening had done no harm.

Chapter Sixteen

Friday dawned another fine day, but as Jim climbed onto his bicycle after a morning's work at the Penwynton Hotel where he had replaced the glass pane in a window accidentally broken by a high-spirited guest, the sun disappeared behind a mass of grey cloud. Nevertheless, Jim was not downhearted. He didn't like handling glass and so was far too relieved that the job was over and done with to be bothered by a grey cloud or two. In a good frame of mind he happily peddled down the winding driveway of the Hotel, tossing over in his mind the vegetables he needed to get from his allotment for the Jolly Sailor.

At the end of the drive, a solitary magpie sat perched on the open gate, cawing. When Jim came into view, whistling, 'Livin' la vida loca', it flew off noisily into the shrubbery, startling Jim and causing him to lose his balance.

"Whoops, better be careful," he laughed, quickly taking his right foot off the peddle and resting it on the gravel, "after all it is Friday the thirteenth."

Once calmed he resumed his journey home and as he approached Ebenezer House he was surprised to see much of the produce he had left out for sale on his barrow that morning had gone. Jim's spirits rose even higher, but then his heart sank. Had the fruits of his hard labour actually been sold or had they been taken by thieves, or even worse, tossed into a hedge by meddlesome children?

His heart began to pound as he recalled talk at the Hotel of jewellery belonging to Iris Delaney being stolen from Cove Cottage. Anxiously he rested his bicycle against the wall and shook the cash box he kept padlocked through its handle to the gate. He swore beneath his breath, it did not sound promising, only a few coins appeared to rattle inside.

Jim fumbled in the pocket of his jeans for the key and unlocked the lid. Two fifty pence pieces and a five pence coin lay on the bottom of the tin. Jim swore, over six pounds worth of vegetables were missing, spring onions, peppers, tomatoes, courgettes and aubergines. He put the coins in his pocket, slapped shut the lid, locked it, and wheeled his bicycle up his path a very unhappy man. He had never had any of his vegetables stolen before and it left an unpleasant taste in his mouth. However, after short consideration he decided against reporting it to the police for he thought the likelihood of anyone ever being caught was nil.

"I hear that Iris' hunk and Maurice are old friends," said Gertie, taking a seat at the kitchen table inside Rose Cottage later that same morning, "and Maurice was dead chuffed to see him again."

"Really, who told you that?" said Stella.

"Our Susan," said Gertie, "It's brilliant having a daughter working at the inn, it reminds me of when I was there. God, those were the days, eh Ned?"

Ned smiled. "And now it's our grandchildren who are the young set and there seems to be quite a lot of them going around together from what I've seen."

"Yes, Sue tells me they've all become really good friends with the cheeky lads camping on the field and that Goth girl too, I think she's having quite an influence on them. Demelza tells me she's a student of alternative medicine or something freaky like that and she rinses her hair in rosemary. God only knows how she does that."

"I suppose she boils the rosemary or just steeps it in water for a while and then uses the liquid," said Stella, "must be something like that anyway."

"That would have impressed my dear old mum," Ned sighed, "she was very interested in herbal remedies, beauty treatments and that sort of thing."

"Hmm, well I suppose some of them work, Morwenna's certainly got pretty hair. It shines like satin."

"Coffee, Gert?" Stella asked, reaching for the kettle.

"Yes, please, then I must go home and sort out some stuff for tomorrow's jumble sale. I've been meaning to do it all week but what with the eclipse and so forth I've never quite got round to it. Not that the eclipse affected me at all; I mean, I didn't have to do anything because of it, but Sue said the inn's been crazy every day this week and it certainly was on eclipse night, wasn't it? I think I'd have died of fatigue if I'd not volunteered to wash glasses and get myself some more space."

"Yes, we've been in once or twice and found it very busy," said Stella, "Justin must be pleased."

"Yes, he is and he was thrilled to bits with the interest in the Sunflower Competition, but he's tired now, poor chap."

"Yes, I expect he is. Liz said Tally has been finding it hard to get out of bed this week."

Gertie nodded as she glanced out of the window at the grey clouds. "I hope the weather will be nice for the outing next Tuesday. I shouldn't think there'll be much to do in Mevagissey if it's wet."

Ned laughed. "I'm sure we'll find something even if it's just sitting in a pub all day."

"Hmm, that'd suit Percy, but I expect he'll be talking to the fishermen and looking at the boats if it's fine, so I'm not sure that I wouldn't prefer it to be wet."

Following her visit, Gertie left Rose Cottage and walked up the road towards her home in Coronation Terrace. Outside the village hall she stopped to see if there were any new notices pinned on the board. But there were no forthcoming events with which she was not already acquainted and the next happening was the aforementioned jumble sale in aid of the Christmas Lights due to take place the following morning.

As she turned to resume her walk, a pleasant smell wafted by on a sudden gust. Gertie wrinkled her nose and sniffed the air. The scent reminded her of an expensive aftershave. As she glanced around to see if there were any dashing young men nearby she saw Nessie's brother, Robbie Macdonald taking something from the back seat of his car parked alongside the road.

From above, Gertie heard a piercing squawk. She glanced up; on the ridge tiles of the village hall roof sat a solitary magpie.

"Oh dear, still on your own, I see. Poor you, I hope your mate hasn't gone missing permanently."

From nowhere, a sudden strange whooshing noise echoed along the street. It made Gertie jump and she stumbled forwards. After regaining her balance, she looked over her shoulder to see the source of the noise and to her surprise she saw Robbie lying face down on the pavement.

A car, a silver BMW with tinted windows, pulled up on the opposite side of the road. Rusty Higgins jumped out and sprang to Robbie's aid. "I say, are you alright?" He knelt by his side and touched a gash on his forehead. Gertie, having composed herself, went to see if she could help too.

"Just winded," Robbie gasped, blinking as though dazed. "It's daft, but something appeared from nowhere and hit me in the back but I didn't see what it was."

Rusty glanced around the pavement. "Perhaps something fell on you from somewhere."

Robbie shook his head. "I don't think so because if it had then surely it would have hit my head and not my back."

"Hmm, so what exactly happened?"

Robbie's voice was a little shaky. "I heard a funny whooshing noise behind. Then I was hit, but when I looked up there was nothing or no-one there."

Rusty turned to Gertie. "Did you see anything or hear the noise?"

She nodded. "I heard the noise: it was all very sudden and caused me to stumble but it didn't hit me and I didn't see anything either."

Rusty shook his head. "I'm at a loss as to what it might have been then, unless it was a bicycle or a kid on a skateboard and they fled indoors quickly to avoid confrontation."

Robbie laughed as he sat up. "Feasible I suppose, but I'm sure we'd have seen a bike and the same goes for a skateboard."

Gertie nodded. "And we'd have heard a skateboard too because they're bloomin' noisy when they're rattling along."

Rusty helped Robbie to his feet. "Do you think we ought to inform the police?"

"No, no, definitely not," said Robbie, brushing the knees of his trousers. "I'm alright, just shaken and it'd be no use wasting police time if I'd be unable to give them any useful information."

Gertie nodded her head. "I agree. I was a witness but likewise wouldn't be able to say anything useful."

"I daresay Freddie would disagree," said Rusty, grinning.

Gertie raised her eyes heavenwards. "Then we'll have to make sure he never finds out, won't we? Or we'll all get a lecture."

When Percy returned home after chatting with fishermen on the beach, Gertie told him of Robbie's ordeal. He was intrigued.

"How about popping down the pub for lunch. You never know, someone else might have seen what happened."

"I doubt it, because only Rusty and me went to help Robbie. Having said that I'm starving and so lunch is an excellent idea."

Freddie and Trish were in the bar eating ham and tomato baguettes when Gertie and Percy arrived, and much to Gertie's annoyance, Freddie overheard Percy excitedly telling Justin about Robbie's misfortune when he went to the bar to order scampi and chips. When Freddie caught Gertie's eye he promptly beckoned her to his side and asked what had happened. Gertie grudgingly reiterated Robbie's ordeal but deliberately played it down hoping to avoid castigation from the retired police officer.

"He must notify the police," Freddie promptly replied, "Something of this nature should not go unreported, and he might have been seriously injured."

Just at that moment Robbie, feeling in need of a pint, walked in. Freddie wasted no time in remonstrating with the young Scot.

Robbie sighed deeply. "No, I really can't be doing with all the hassle. I'd not be able to say what it was anyway because I didn't see anything. They'd think me a little foolish if I'm unable to provide any kind of information at all." He touched his forehead. "And the wound I received was nothing more than a graze anyway."

"But this is ridiculous. What is the matter with everyone here? Iris Delaney won't report her stolen jewellery and now you won't report a possible assault. Both are serious offences, and I consider the two of you are being bloody-minded, if you don't mind me saying so."

Robbie smiled. "I suppose we just want a quiet life, that's all. Anyway, I'm alright and that's the main thing." A puzzled expression crossed Robbie's face. "The funny thing is, a similar thing happened the other day. I was out walking the cliff path and thought I heard a voice. I looked all around and no-one was there so I went near to the cliff's edge in case someone was in trouble down below. No-one was there either but a sudden stabbing pain in my back caused me to fall over the side. I'd be dead were it not for a ledge several feel below as I fell onto it."

Freddie scowled. "Are you sure there was no-one around?"

"Absolutely. I mean the cliff paths are pretty open so there's nowhere that anyone could have disappeared to in just a few seconds."

Freddie shook his head. "How strange. There's definitely something odd going on here."

Jim, who had just made his usual delivery of produce to the kitchen overheard the conversation between Gertie, Robbie and Freddie which prompted him to tell of his stolen vegetables, but like Robbie he also refused to report the incident. Freddie groaned and then laughed. "You know, I was a copper for thirty five years, but I've come across more obstinate people in this last week than I did in the whole of my career. It's just incredible, absolutely incredible."

"I reckon in both your cases it was just a stroke of bad luck," said Gertie, cheerfully. "After all it is Friday the thirteenth so odd things are bound to happen. What's more, I saw one of our magpies on his own again this morning just seconds before Robbie's err...mishap, so that had to be a bad sign."

"Did you?" said Jim, surprised, "so did I, and I wouldn't be surprised if I saw him at the very time my veg was being nicked. A magpie on his tod is definitely a bad omen."

Gertie scowled. "On his tod?"

"Todd Sloan," laughed Jim, "Todd Sloan, own, cockney rhyming slang."

Gertie giggled. "Oh, I see, well then, there you are, Freddie, the date and the magpie on his tod are to blame."

Freddie shook his head in utter disbelief. "I've heard everything now, you lot really are as mad as hatters. Ill omens and bad luck indeed, what utter nonsense."

On Friday afternoon, and feeling sleepy after a couple of pints at the Jolly Sailor, Jim Haynes was relaxing outside on a bench beside the arched door to Ebenezer House, when he saw Morwenna approaching the chapel gates from the direction of the crossroads, wearing a daisy chain crown on her jet black hair and softly singing to herself.

Jim watched. He had heard much of the Goth girl down for the eclipse who had befriended the village youngsters and he was intrigued by her interest in alternative medicine. When she reached the open gate and saw him sitting on the bench she stopped and gave him a quizzical look.

"Do you live here?" she called, bluntly, "I see there are curtains at the window and the vibes I pick up are of friendship and not religion."

Jim sat up straight. "Yes, I bought the place several years back when it was unloved and derelict."

Without being invited Morwenna walked between the gate posts and up the path to the bench where she sat beside Jim. "How absolutely fascinating. To live here amongst the dead, I mean. Oh, what tales they could tell."

Jim laughed. "Well, fortunately for me they've never uttered a word since I've been here, but it's nice to hear the views of someone who doesn't think I'm a crackpot. Most people do, you know, though the locals have got used to me being here now and think little of it."

"Well, I think it's fantastic, the place must be steeped in history. May I take a peep inside, please?"

"Of course."

"My name's Morwenna, by the way."

"I know. I've seen you around. I'm Jim."

"Delighted to meet you, Jim."

They shook hands and laughed.

"Likewise," he grinned.

Jim escorted his impromptu guest inside. She was overwhelmed. "It's fascinating, and I like the way you have restored the arches and oh, the memorial plaques on the walls are so much more interesting than commercially bought, run-of-the-mill pictures."

Jim smiled. "Well, I do have a few run-of-the-mill pictures on the stud walls that make my kitchen, bathroom and bedroom, but I think they should meet with your approval since most of them are herbs and wild flowers."

"You know of my interest in such matters then."

"Yes, you have become quite a talking point in the village, though I might add I've heard no-one say a bad word against you, but your sense of dress has raised a few eyebrows."

"Good," laughed Morwenna, "how dull it would be if we all dressed in the same conventional way."

"Hear, hear."

"Shall we go back outside? It's too nice to be indoors."

Jim nodded.

"I take it you came here for the eclipse," said Jim as they sat back down on the bench."

"Yes, and so it seems did the world and his wife."

Jim laughed. "I watched it from the clifftops. I had intended to go as far as the Witches Broomstick but left it a bit late so didn't quite make it."

Morwenna frowned. "What do you mean by the Witches Broomstick?"

"It's the name given to rocks at the bottom of the cliffs that form the shape of a broomstick around sand. You'd really have to see it to understand what I mean."

Morwenna tossed her hair. "Humph, sounds silly to me. Witches and broomsticks, that is. Whoever gave it such a daft name?"

Jim shrugged his shoulders. "No idea, but I'm told that once upon a time the locals believed it was the home of evil spirits."

Morwenna cast her eyes over gravestones. "Really...so, where do you grow the vegetables for your stall? It can't be here unless you've up-rooted a few old bones in a quiet corner somewhere."

Jim laughed. "Christ, I wouldn't dare do that, the owners of the bones might come back and haunt me. Anyway, I don't own the graveyard but I have use of it as long as I treat the graves with reverence and keep it in a reasonably good state, which I do. The veg are grown at an allotment I have in the village."

"Really, I should like to see it sometime, I'm fascinated by herbs and vegetable gardens and so many people are ignorant of the goodness they provide."

"We can go up there now, if you like. I've been up there once today to get stuff for the inn, but I'm quite happy to go again, because I've nothing else planned until I pop back to the inn for a pint tonight."

Morwenna nodded. "Snap, that just about sums up the conclusion of my day too."

They walked together back into the village, turned down the lane towards the Old Vicarage, and then half way down, left the road and followed a bridle path. After climbing the stile, they were in the field where much of the land was taken with allotments.

"How come you're not out with your friends today?" Jim asked, as they crossed the field. "I got the impression you were quite inseparable."

"Usually, but the locals are all working today and the chaps camping have gone to Penzance because they fancied a trip over to the Scillies. They did ask me if I'd like to join them but I prefer to stay ashore."

"Me too," said Jim, "I went fishing for a spell a few years back but it didn't suit me at all because I'm prone to sea sickness."

They reached the garden plots and Jim proudly pointed out his neat rows of flourishing crops.

"Very impressive, you've a very comprehensive selection. And they look in exceedingly good health."

"Thanks for the compliment. I must admit, I am very proud of my efforts."

Morwenna cast her eyes over the neighbouring plots. "I see your garden is much bigger than the others."

Jim nodded. "Yes, it is, and that's because I actually have three plots combined but you wouldn't know because I've taken down the fences that were the boundaries. I found that one just wasn't big enough for the amount I need to grow."

Morwenna nodded. "I see." She then pointed to the corner of the garden where multi coloured, sweetly scented blooms covered a construction made with long, leafless branches. "What are those flowers?"

"Sweet peas," said Jim, "I grow them there to hide the compost heap. I occasionally take a bunch home as well because their scent is wonderful."

Morwenna moved towards the flowers and took in a breath of their strong perfume. She closed her eyes. "They really are beautiful. Do you know the meaning of their name?"

Jim nodded. "I do actually. Their name means blissful pleasure, good-bye and thank you for the lovely time we've had."

"Goodbye and thank you for the lovely time we've had," repeated Morwenna, "that's really nice. I like the sentiments of your sweet peas, Jim, and their name."

Jim laughed. "Their correct botanic name is Lathyrus Odoratus; it derives from the Greek word lathyrus meaning pea or pulse and the Latin word odoratus meaning fragrant. At least, that's what Elizabeth told me."

"I'm impressed, and who is Elizabeth? I don't think I've come across anyone with that name yet."

"Elizabeth Castor-Hunt. She's the mother of your friends, Tally and Wills."

"Oh, I see." Morwenna glanced around the field, a bewildered expression on her face, "What do you do for water?" She asked. "Surely you don't put your faith entirely in the Almighty to provide rain."

Jim pointed to the corner of the field where a blackthorn hedge dripped with unripe sloes. "There used to be a few old cottages here many moons ago, built in the early fifteen hundreds so I'm told and just over there, beyond the blackthorn, is an old well, which amazingly enough still contains water, so we use that. Though it has to be said, with the climate in Cornwall it isn't very often needed, only really when the plants are very small. Come and see."

Through long grass peppered with golden buttercups, they followed a path worn down by present day gardeners.

"Well, I never," muttered Morwenna, as they reached the far side of the blackthorn hedge, "fancy the old well still being in use."

Jim followed and together they looked at the old well. "We thought it was fantastic too when we discovered it. Of course the walls around the side had collapsed and the hole was covered with several huge sheets of rusting metal, but it didn't take long for us to re-build the sides once we'd established there was water down there."

Morwenna smiled. "You speak with great enthusiasm. I'm impressed."

"I love this spot, it almost feels magical. Often I'm the only one up here, especially on weekdays when the others are at work. And then I'm happy just to sit, watch the birds and listen to the wind whistling through the long grass. I suppose that sounds a bit sad."

Morwenna shook her head. "No, it wouldn't do at all if no-one appreciated what Mother Nature has given us."

Jim grinned, pleased to have her approval. "You know, I'd love to go back a few hundred years and see the folks that lived up here and watch them going about their daily chores and using the well. In comparison with then, things today are so mundane."

Morwenna threw back her head and laughed.

"Oh, come on, Jim. I don't think you'd find life was a bed of roses back in the sixteenth century. In fact for the poor it was quite the opposite. All cottages wouldn't have been like those depicted on chocolate boxes, they would have been little more than huts and many with no glass in the windows to keep in the warmth of log fires because glass was expensive. The floors would have been compressed earth; the furniture very basic, just benches, stools, tables and wooden chests. And as for the mattresses in which the poor slept, they would have been stuffed with straw and thistledown."

Jim gazed warmly at Morwenna. "Wow that was some history lesson! I wish you lived here, Morwenna. You're so in touch with Mother Earth and I feel I should like to know you better. We seem to be on the same wave length, you and I. And that's a very precious gift indeed."

Gently she patted the back of his hand. "It's best not to know me too well," she smiled. "I wouldn't want to see you hurt. I can see that you're a thoughtful man, Jim, kind and sensitive. But please believe me, I would not be good for you. Besides I shall be gone soon."

Jim decided it might be best to change the subject and instead focused on his herbs and vegetables, determined to enjoy her presence while she was in his company.

The inn was busy again on Friday night, for a good many people were due to leave the following morning and return home.

"I can't say that I'll be sorry to see some of them go," yawned Justin, his eyes tired through lack of sleep and working very long days, as he unlocked the door at opening time, "though of course, I shall miss the money. I believe it's going to be pretty quiet everywhere next week."

Demelza smiled, as she straightened the beer mats on the bar, "But I understand Doctor Owen has decided to stay another week since her room isn't needed for anyone else. I wonder why that is."

"Has she? I didn't know that," said Tally. "She's alright anyway, if you can steer her away from astronomy."

"That's as maybe, but does she have any other interests?" asked Demelza.

Justin laughed. "As a matter of fact she does, apparently she likes to study and press wild flowers."

"Really," laughed Demelza, "we used to do that at primary school so I think I could just about keep up with her on that subject."

"I wouldn't be so sure," said Justin, "I got a lecture on the decline of the lesser Butterfly Orchid the other day. They used to be quite common in the British Isles apparently, but not anymore."

"A lecture on an orchid, eh?" grinned Demelza, "so that's what the tête-à-tête I saw you both engrossed in was about."

Justin's response was a cross between a smile and a smirk and there was without doubt a twinkle in both eyes.

The credits were rolling on a late night film Elizabeth had been watching when Tally and a slightly intoxicated Wills returned from the Jolly Sailor.

"Gosh, you still up Mum," Tally yawned, "it's nearly half past one."

"I know, but I saw this old film years ago and so I wanted to see it again. I know I could have recorded it on video but I'd never get round to watching it if I did."

"Is Dad still up?"

"No, he turned in hours ago."

"And I'm doing likewise," slurred Wills, "Goodnight."

"Goodnight, love and don't wake your father."

"I'm having a coffee," said Tally, "would you like one?"

Elizabeth switched off the television with the remote control and followed her daughter into the kitchen. "Yes please. Was the inn busy tonight?"

"Yes, but lots are going home tomorrow so it should be much quieter next week. At least I hope so, I could do with some time off. I've hardly seen my friends this week, except from the other side of the bar."

"I know, poor you. Are the lads camping on the field going home tomorrow?

"No, they're here for another week, in spite of the weather, thank goodness."

"Thank goodness," repeated Elizabeth, her eyebrows raised.

Tally laughed. "They're very funny, Mum. At least that's what I'm constantly being told, so I'd like to see a bit more of them before they go."

"Where are they from?"

"Essex."

"Oh, and do you have any idea what they do?"

"Mum, there's not a prospective son-in-law amongst them if that's what you're thinking."

Elizabeth smiled. "I was only asking."

"But if you really want to know, Mac works for the Inland Revenue, Neil's in a mobile phone shop, Kev works in a supermarket stacking shelves and Rob's a trainee undertaker."

"A trainee undertaker," repeated Elizabeth, surprised.

"Well, someone has to do it," said Tally, practically, handing her mother a mug of coffee, "and Morwenna thinks it's really cool."

Chapter Seventeen

Saturday began dull and light drizzle fell throughout much of the morning. Inside Rose Cottage Ned looked from the living room window cursing the lack of sunshine and the rapidity with which the years went round. It was his seventy third birthday.

"Trengillion should be a lot quieter after today," said Stella, plumping up the cushions on the settee. "Anne says at least half of the Hotel's guests leave today and there are vacancies then right through the rest of the summer."

Ned turned away from the window and sat on the arm of a chair. "Hmm, but the summer's as good as gone anyway once we're half way through August and reach my damn birthday, and the nights are drawing in rapidly now."

"Well, I'm not sorry about that," smiled Stella, "I usually find by this time of the year I'm beginning to tire of the garden, weeding, dead-heading and so forth and I look forward to long winter nights when we can put the central heating on, light the fire, shut out the weather and be cosy. In fact we ought to order some coal before long."

Ned tutted. "What is it with women and being cosy? Mum was just the same and so is our Liz."

Stella smiled. "And so is Doctor Owen; she was really enthusiastic when I told her how cosy the Jolly Sailor was on a winter's night with the fire blazing in the hearth and the wind howling outside and down the chimney. She said it sounded wonderful and if nothing else crops up she might come down for Christmas or New Year's Eve."

"Well, Doctor Owen is here for another week yet anyway, so if this weather continues she might well witness howling gales before she goes home. The Shorts are here for another week too, so they tell me, and I believe so are the crazy lads camping on the field."

"That should keep the grandchildren amused. And what about Iris, is she off today?"

"No, no, she isn't, so I discovered to my surprise. She and Rusty reckon they'll be here for another day or two yet."

"Really, Iris doesn't usually stay for long, does she? And she's already been here since Tuesday. Are you sure you've got your facts right?"

"Absolutely, I was talking to her only yesterday outside the village hall. She wants to stay as long as possible and hopefully until next weekend. She's off to the States in September, you see, filming some epic or other, so she'll not be able to visit Trengillion again 'til well into the New Year."

Stella sighed. "So we won't see her not only 'til next year and the next decade but the next century and the new millennium also. I can't believe we're going into the year 2000 in a few months' time. It sounds so weird and well, you know, futuristic."

"Hmm, it does, I'll never get used to saying two thousand and so forth. It's such a mouthful, whereas nineteen something or other just trips off the tongue."

"Yes, but I'm sure it'll come naturally eventually, if we live that long."

Ned cast a glance out of the window and then stood and looked again to make sure his eyes were not deceiving him. "Good heavens! What on earth's happened to the rowan tree? It looks as sick as a parrot, Stella. Its leaves are all brown and so are the berries. It must have heard you saying you usually get tired of the garden by August so it's gone into winter mode early."

Stella walked to Ned's side and looked from the window. She frowned. "Oh no, I thought you were joking! It looks really dreadful. Whatever can be wrong?"

"Probably some obnoxious bug sucking the life and colour from the leaves and berries," said Ned, lazily, watching a snail chomp its way through a leaf on the asters beneath the window. "The veg get all sorts of pests and diseases so it stands to reason trees must too."

"Yes, I know, but it's a bit sudden. I'm sure it was fine yesterday, in fact it was alright when I looked out of the bedroom window this morning. Your mum would not be impressed, would she? Everything flourished under her watch, I shall have to consult my gardening book."

"Yes, or it might even be the weather," said Ned, walking away from the window, sitting down heavily on the settee and picking up the daily newspaper, "I don't think any living creatures like this much wet, not even ducks."

Inside the village hall, members of the Christmas Lights' Committee sorted through bags of jumble donated by well-wishers and laid out the contents on relevant stalls. Then at ten o' clock, when the work was done they opened the door of the hall to the waiting crowd. To their delight the attendance was good and the great heaps of clothes, toys and household goods decreased rapidly.

Lucy Ainsworth, on her way to the post office with a letter her father had asked her to post, walked past the village hall and glanced at the open door with curious interest. She had not been to a jumble sale since her primary school days when they had been an annual fund raising event, but for some reason she felt compelled to go inside and have a quick look through the items for sale. With a subtle glance over her shoulders to make sure none of her contemporaries was around, Lucy, telling herself she was just supporting a worthy cause, put down her umbrella and slipped inside the hall. After quickly casting her eyes around the room, she headed for a pile of ladies' clothes thinking they would be the most interesting.

After tossing aside items she wouldn't be seen dead in, Lucy found a long black crumpled dress not dissimilar to the one worn by Morwenna. She stepped back from the table, looked at the size label and held the dress against her slim body. She grinned, overwhelmed by a sudden desire to be outlandish, crazy and mischievous. "Damn it," she tittered, "I'm going Goth." For on reflection she realised a lot of Morwenna's appeal was the fact she dressed differently and that was possibly the very reason she was admired by her friends, herself, and especially the boys. For not only was she popular with Mac, Neil, Kev and Rob but she had some of the local lads drooling too.

A self-satisfied smirk crossed Lucy's face as she paid twenty pence for the dress, her imagination dominated by the look of admiration on Neil's face when he was confronted by her drastic change of appearance. For Neil was great fun to be with: she enjoyed his company immensely and it was just such a shame that he and his friends had only a week of their holiday left.

However, as Lucy stuffed the dress into a Gateway carrier bag, given to her by Candy Bingham, manning the stall, her thoughts were suddenly tinged with apprehension regarding her parents' inevitable reaction to her new look. Momentarily she paused in the hall doorway, her face flustered at the prospect of an ugly confrontation. There were only another five days to go until the A-level results came out and she wasn't one hundred per cent sure her grades would be good enough to get her into her favoured university. If she failed, they might well say her failure was due to frivolous behaviour and lack of dedication, their supposed qualms confirmed by her reckless attitude to fashion, and she did not want to encounter their wrath and forgo any financial rewards that might be forthcoming.

Lucy sighed as she slipped the carrier bag on her arm and put up the umbrella. Well, it was a risk worth taking. Besides, she had no intention of staying a Goth forever, it would only be until the end of the summer holiday and she was sure, if needs be, she could get round her father. Furthermore, Morwenna was a student and no-one could say she wasn't dedicated to her studies, for she talked frequently with great authority of alternative medicines, herbs and their uses by monks back in the distant past and most people were impressed.

Jim Haynes, wearing his waterproofs, spent a couple of hours working in the walled vegetable garden at the Penwynton Hotel on Saturday morning. After he'd had lunch back home at the former chapel, he observed the weather had brightened up, so cycled to the allotments to tend his own garden and pick vegetables to put on his stall the following day.

Inspired by the growth of his prize winning sunflower, Larry Bingham was chopping down weeds with a scythe on his newly acquired allotment in order to dig it over and cultivate the ground. Jim nodded to Larry and then after leaning his bicycle against his shed went to speak to the newcomer.

"I think you'll need a rotavator to tackle that," Jim grinned, appreciatively looking heavenwards as the sun finally broke through the clouds, "I did when I started up here and it saved a lot of time and effort."

"I think you're probably right," Larry sighed, standing to ease his back, "the ground's rock hard. I think I'd better take your advice and go into Helston to hire one."

"No need," said Jim, kicking aside a ball of couch grass, "they've got one at the Hotel and I know there'd be no objection to you borrowing it. I'll ask Jamie if you like, I'm going up there again in the morning so I can bring it back with me in the trailer at lunch time."

"Really, that'd be great, because I reckon by the time I've cut down the weeds I'll have had enough today anyway, which means I can go home and watch *Grandstand*."

"So what are you planning to grow? I assume it won't be prize winning sunflowers."

Larry laughed. "No, though I might grow some in the garden at home again next year to see if I can get them bigger than I did this. They were a huge success as you're only too well aware, although I can't say the same for our young rowan tree. Candy planted it in our front garden a couple of years ago and I don't know what she's done to it but it looks proper miserable. In fact I wouldn't be surprised if it's dead."

"She probably doesn't have the Midas touch," grinned Jim, impishly, "but seriously, that's a shame, rowans are usually at their best in August and September and the birds love the berries."

"I see you've a lovely display of sweet peas, but why do you bother growing then up here where no-one sees them?"

"I see them," grinned Jim, "but seriously, I grow them to hide the compost heap and also because I love the smell."

Larry nodded. "Makes sense. So who do you get your horticultural talents from? Your mum or your dad."

"Dad, without question. He was a brilliant gardener but sadly he died when I was eighteen. That's part of the reason why I moved to Cornwall. Mum met another bloke, you see, after which she left the village we lived in. After she'd gone I didn't see any point in staying there even though I'd taken the Council house over from Mum."

"So you wanted to make a fresh start?"

"Yes, and I'm pretty happy with my lot in life, in fact I couldn't be happier."

"Good for you, there's a lot to be said for contentment."

Jim nodded. "So, putting my doings aside, may I ask what you intend to grow up here?"

"Ah, simple: my plan here is to grow vegetables, lots of them, like you. It's daft really, and you may well snigger, but the competition has convinced me I have green fingers. Whether I have or not we'll have to wait and see. I'm looking forward to the challenge though and Candy is looking forward to lots of fresh veg."

"Well, if I can be of any help you only have to ask, I've been growing veg for years and I find it very rewarding."

"Thanks, Jim, you've certainly got a good crop this year and you can give me some advice next year on how to grow the biggest marrow."

Jim laughed. "I'll do that but we'll be in competition with each other there, because I have every intention of entering that too and I don't intend to come second next year either."

Inside Trengillion's hairdressing salon, Rebecca was drying Janet Ainsworth's hair which she had just coloured, while Anne sat awaiting her turn for a trim.

"It's good to see that horrid bit of grey gone." said Janet, admiring her reflection in the mirror, "I just wish hair didn't grow as quickly as it does then the ghastly white stripe would be kept at bay for longer."

Anne laughed. "I bet Rebecca doesn't agree with you there, she'd be out of business if hair grew too slowly."

"I certainly would, in fact I sometimes wish it grew quicker."

"You won't wish that once the grey starts to take over," said Janet, wagging her finger, "that's one of the downfalls of having dark hair, the grey shows up more than it does on a blonde."

"That strange girl Morwenna has beautiful hair, doesn't she?" said Anne, "I wish my hair was that dark and in that condition too. It's quite superb the way it catches the light."

"I reckon it's dyed," nodded Janet, "it looks too shiny to be natural, either that or it's a wig. You can get very good wigs these days."

Rebecca smiled. "No, I'm sure it's not a wig, I think it's natural enough, she has very dark eyebrows and thick dark lashes to back up that theory. In fact all in all she's a real beauty: it's no wonder the lads are all besotted with her."

Anne nodded to endorse Rebecca's sentiments. "Jess tells me she rinses her hair with rosemary water. I've never heard of anyone doing that before. Is it a good idea, Rebecca?"

"I don't really know, I must admit. But some herbs can definitely enhance hair, so if Morwenna uses rosemary, then it must be effective. The proof's in the pudding and all that. I might even give it a try when I have a quiet day because we have rosemary growing in the garden at home, but we seldom use it."

Anne stood and removed her jacket as Janet rose from the chair, "Changing the subject," she said, "Has anyone heard any more about Nessie's brother's accident?"

Janet frowned as she picked up her handbag. "I didn't know he'd had one."

"Really, well it happened yesterday. He was knocked over and quite badly shaken but nobody saw what knocked him over so it's a bit of a mystery."

"Poor old thing."

"He didn't need medical treatment though, did he?" said Rebecca, as she took money from Janet, "but the poor bloke was pretty shaken by it and he's not going back to his own house for a day or two because Nessie wants to keep an eye on him. "

"That's good to hear," said Anne, "although he seems to spend quite a lot of time at the post office already."

"Well, I don't suppose he's got to know many people yet," said Rebecca, "He's not been down here long."

"I wonder if he's learning the bagpipes too," said Anne.

Janet laughed. "Don't tell Ian if he is. He hates them but I must admit I think they're rather charming."

"Hmm, no comment," smiled Rebecca, as Anne took her place in the chair, "but while you're both here, can either of you tell me if Madge is David's gran? I know I ought to know by now but I always get a bit muddled with that family for some reason."

"Yes she is," said Anne, who had been in the village all her life. "Madge is Milly's mother and David and Stephen's grandmother. And as you know, Stephen runs the post office and David and his wife Judith, run Home Farm where Madge has her bungalow. You're probably confused because Albert, who used to run the farm, wasn't Milly's real father, Madge had her you see before she met Albert, though he always treated Milly's boys as though they were his own grandchildren."

Janet laughed as she slipped on her jacket. "Now I know why I've also never been able to get my head round the relationship of that family. Bye girls."

As Janet left the salon Rebecca clasped a cape around Anne's shoulders. "I think she's amazing," said Anne, "Madge that is, she must be nearly ninety yet you say she still comes in for a perm."

Rebecca nodded. "Yes, she told me she wants to look nice for the outing on Tuesday, bless her. I think the old folks really look forward to the little trips out, don't they? I do hope the weather's better for them though than it was for the eclipse."

Jefferson K. Jefferson, Jr. and his wife, seeing the weather was improving, told the senior Jeffersons, after consulting a map they had found in a drawer at Higher Green Farmhouse, they had decided to take a walk across the cliff tops to a little fishing village called Polquillick, after which they intended to walk back to Trengillion by way of country lanes. Jefferson K. Jefferson, Sr. deemed the walk too far for himself and his wife and wished the younger family members a safe and enjoyable trip.

The young Jeffersons left the farmhouse and walked hand in hand across the cliff tops determined to take as long as possible and enjoy their time alone. For Jefferson K. Jefferson, Sr. could be a bit over powering and though the son loved his parents dearly, he loved his wife more.

The sun was shining brightly by the time they reached Polquillick, and so they wandered down to the beach, walked amongst the fishing boats and bought cornets of Cornish ice cream to pass away the time. When they tired of watching the boats, they walked through the village along the main street, calling in the numerous gift shops and enjoying the quaintness of the thatched houses.

The lane which left Polquillick and led back to Trengillion thrilled them even more. They were enthralled by its narrowness, its tight bends and walls so high in places it was impossible to see what lay on the other side of cascading red and purple fuchsias, scented woodbine and brambles dripping with blackberries ripening in the August sun.

When they reached the crossroads at the top of the hill, they stopped to rest on the grass verge. And whilst they relaxed, both simultaneously observed an old chapel peeping through the canopy of trees. Surprised it was in an area around which no houses stood, they went to take a closer look.

"Gee, it looks as though someone lives here in this old chapel, Julie May," said Jefferson K. Jefferson, Jr., pointing to the name on the gate, "Ebenezer House it says, so I guess the guy's name must be Ebenezer."

"Not necessarily, Jeff," said Julie May, "Ebenezer is a type of chapel over here. Their non-conformist chapels have all sorts of different names but share similar religious beliefs. I was reading about them in the Old Farmhouse just last night while you and your ma and pa were watching that quaint little old programme Gardeners' World."

"Wow, I'm some glad I chose me a smart wife," laughed Jefferson K. Jefferson, Jr., "I'd have looked a right ass if I'd spotted some guy in the yard here and said 'howdy there, Ebenezer'."

Julie May laughed. "Well, you never know, he might be called Ebenezer, but I think it unlikely."

Jefferson K. Jefferson, Jr. picked up two aubergines. "These are mighty fine looking eggplants, Julie May, I'm gonna buy them for Mom and then she can make a moussaka tomorrow."

"But your ma should be taking her ease more, honey, and not cooking for us every day."

"But she loves cooking, Julie May, and she don't get much chance to do it back home since Pa employed that cook lady. And I know too that moussaka is one of her favourite dishes, and has been since they took that vacation in Greece many years ago."

He pulled out a handful of change from his pocket and dropped the correct amount into Jim's cashbox, and then turned to his wife, "So how come you was reading a book about old chapels, Julie May? I didn't think you was that religious."

"I just happened to see it on the shelf in the bedroom we're not using and thought it might be interesting. My family emigrated from this country you know, many years ago and I thought I might learn something."

Jefferson K. Jefferson, Jr. stopped dead in his tracks. "You don't say, Julie May. I never knowed that. How come you never told me before?"

"Well, I never really thought about it 'til I saw the book. My granny used to tell me her great, great granny's folks emigrated from England to the States when she was a babe in arms, but that's about all I can remember just now and of course poor old Granny's gone now, so I can't ask her for any details, not that I think she knew a great deal anyway."

"So, I not only got me a smart wife, I gone and got me an English wife too. Well, I'll be dammed! Your ancestors probably sang in this little old chapel, Julie May."

"Gee, Jeff, I don't think I can claim to be English: it were a mighty long time ago. In fact I daresay it were long before this here chapel was even built. Besides, I said my ancestors came from England, I didn't say whereabouts. England's a big place, honey, and it could've been just about anywhere."

Jefferson K. Jefferson, Jr. threw back his head and laughed. "You sure got a sense o' humour, Julie May. England, big! Why, it's tiny, honey, tiny compared with the good old U. S of A."

Julie May smiled. "Come on, it's getting chilly standing about."

They left the chapel each carrying an aubergine.

"Shall we pop into the Jolly Sailor on the way back?" said Jefferson K. Jefferson, Jr., licking his lips, "because if my memory serves me right then this road should take us past it, and all this walking has made me mighty thirsty."

"Yes, if you want, but we mustn't be long because your mom's making a fish pie tonight."

"We'll just pop in for a couple of drinks then, because I must admit I rather like that Doom Bar beer, I reckon if we had that back home I might become addicted to the stuff."

Chapter Eighteen

On Saturday afternoon, as she finished off her housework, Betty, seeing the weather had brightened up, decided to go out for a breath of fresh air. After returning the vacuum cleaner to the cupboard beneath the stairs, she combed her hair, put on her lightweight jacket and left the house for a stroll down to the beach. She planned to visit her daughter Jane, whom she had not seen since before the eclipse due to hurting her back whilst washing the bathroom ceiling.

On nearing the church she realised she had forgotten to put on her watch and so glanced towards the church tower to check the time; to her surprise, she noticed the leaves of two rowan trees visible from the road were no longer green, but lustreless rusty brown, as were the usually bright orange berries.

Betty stopped in her tracks to question whether the month was really August or if it might be November, for the trees in the churchyard looked much as they always did in the autumn. Seeing a couple of women walk by wearing shorts, she was reassured and continued on her way muttering to herself.

"Must be the peculiar weather we've been having; warm and sunny one day and wet the next." Though on reflection she conceded unsettled was frequently the weather pattern for a British summer.

Inside the Pickled Egg, Betty found Jane spreading thick layers of strawberry jam and clotted cream on freshly made scones for Freddie and Trish Short who were sitting outside in the sunshine awaiting their cream teas. Jane looked up as her mother closed the door.

"Hello, Mum. How's the back?"

"A lot better now, thanks. What a week to get laid up! I've felt so guilty because I'm sure with all the eclipse people about you could have done with an extra pair of hands."

Jane smiled. "Don't worry, we coped, although it was pretty manic at times. I must admit I've felt equally guilty not having had the time to get up to see you." She laughed. "Most of the time I was even too tired to go to the inn when I'd finished here in the evenings."

"Oh no, you poor thing, but at least it seems a bit quieter today, although having said that I've seen several familiar faces, the Shorts included, so I guess some folks are down for the fortnight."

Jane finished off the scones and laid them neatly on a tray alongside a pot of tea, milk jug and sugar lumps. She then called Jess, busily folding paper serviettes, who took the tray outside to Freddie and Trish.

"You look tired, Jane," said Betty. "You ought to take a break. Is it just you and Jess here today?"

"Yes, Janet came in and covered lunch time with me but I insisted she went home at two because she looked shattered; after all she does have her own business to run, not to mention a family. I'll be alright now, anyway. I don't think we'll be too busy this afternoon or this evening either for that matter."

"Then take a break now and I'll look after things for a while. It'll do you good."

"But, Mum…"

"No buts, I've helped you out before so I know what's what and you'll not be far away if I get overwhelmed. Besides, Jess is here so she can put me right. Go on, Jane. Take a couple of hours off and lay on the beach in the sun while it's fine. It'll do you good."

"Are you sure? I mean it really would be very nice, I must admit."

"Then go and I'll stay put 'til you get back, but don't rush."

Jane ran upstairs for a blanket, sunglasses, book and sun cream. She then kissed her mother, left the café and strolled across the beach to find an appealing vacant spot. The tide was out and she found the ideal place near to the island. With blanket spread out, she applied a generous layer of sun cream to her face, arms and legs to protect her fair skin, then lay on her front and opened up her book on the pages separated by a bookmark. But before she had read one page her eyes felt heavy and tired, the warmth of the sun relaxed her body and within minutes she was sound asleep.

She slept for forty five minutes until she was woken abruptly by someone gently shaking her arm. She jumped, startled and confused. Kneeling beside her was a man with whom she was not acquainted. He was laughing, and suggested she move, for the tide was coming in and her feet and the bottom edge of the blanket were damp with splashes from the quickening waves.

Jane scrambled to her feet, picked up her book and the man picked up the blanket. Both then walked further up the beach where Jane's Good Samaritan laid the blanket on dry sand and shingle.

"Thank you," Jane muttered, rubbing her eyes in an attempt to wake properly. "I didn't even realise I'd gone to sleep. It was very silly of me. I should have known the tide would soon be on the turn."

"Are you a naïve holiday maker then, like me?"

Jane laughed. "No, I've lived here all my life and I ought to be familiar with the sea's habits seeing that my brother is a fisherman, as was my father until he retired a few years back."

The stranger laughed. "Lucky you. To live here, I mean."

"Yes, I think so too. Currently I run the little beach café over there."

The stranger watched the direction of her pointing fingers. "The Pickled Egg," he grinned, "well I never! I'm surprised I've not seen you before then. We're near neighbours, you see. My name is Rusty, Rusty Higgins and I'm staying at Cove Cottage with dear Iris."

He held out his hand.

"Oh, oh yes, I see," muttered Jane, surprised to realise she was disappointed to discover he was spoken for. "I heard on the grapevine that Iris was not alone this visit."

They shook hands and then Jane sat down. "Sorry," she stammered, "I feel a bit light headed. I don't think I'm properly awake yet. My name's Jane, by the way, Jane Williams."

To her surprise, Rusty sat down on the blanket beside her. "Have you finished work for the day now?"

Jane shuddered as his bare arm brushed against hers.

"No," she mumbled, "Mum's looking after the place for a while to give me a break, but I shall have to return for the early evening trade."

"So what time will you be finishing then?"

"What? Oh, we close at eight," said Jane, puzzled.

"In that case, Jane, I'd be really thrilled if you'd join us at the pub for a drink tonight. You must have worked pretty hard this week. The place has been packed every time I've walked by. You need to let your hair down."

Jane looked up, convinced the gaze of his blue eyes reflected hints of amusement.

"But, but won't Iris mind?" she asked, feeling flustered. "I mean, I'd love to, but I don't want to get in the way."

"You'd not be in the way, I can assure you. Iris would be delighted to think I'd even asked you."

Jane arched her eyebrows. "In that case I'll join you, but it'll be about nine by the time I've closed up and changed."

"Whenever you're ready, no rush." Rusty rose from the blanket and patted her shoulder affectionately. "See you later, Jane."

Jane nodded and watched as he ran up the beach towards Cove Cottage, her thoughts much confused by his strange invitation.

Inside the Old Police House, Janet Ainsworth, who had fallen asleep on the sofa following her lunchtime session at the Pickled Egg, was woken suddenly by the banging of the front door. Still half asleep she slid off the sofa and stumbled into the hall to see who it was. Lucy stood on the doormat wiping her feet.

"You alright, Mum? You look really weird and your hair's standing on end."

"What! Is it?" Janet looked in the hall mirror and flattened the offending strand of hair. "I can't believe you're back already, it seems like only a few minutes ago I got back from work and found your note."

"We've been gone for ages, we went at half past one and it's gone five now. Is tea ready yet?"

"Tea! No, no, I was going to do a salad so I've not even started it yet since it doesn't take long. Are you hungry then?"

Lucy wrinkled her nose. "Not really; I had a huge slice of chocolate cake and a cup of coffee in town. Is Angie here?"

"No, not unless she came in while I was asleep, but I doubt it, she and Sam have gone for a walk. They popped into the café to tell me that about half two, so she should be back soon."

"Damn, never mind."

"Did you buy anything nice?" Janet asked, eying a Boots carrier bag which Lucy had dropped at the foot of the stairs.

"Only make-up and stuff, and Demelza bought a pair of jeans."

"Oh, that's nice, I didn't realise you'd gone with Demelza though. Did you go on the bus?"

"No, her mum and dad gave us a lift, they were going into town anyway to get some stuff. Well, if tea's not ready I might as well go and have a shower."

"Alright, I'll get a salad together then and you can have it when you want it. Would you like cheese or tuna mayonnaise?"

"Tuna please, but don't mix any onion with it."

"But you like onion, Lucy."

"Mum, I'm going out later and I don't want smelly oniony breath, do I? That'd be a right turn off."

Thirty minutes later, Lucy entered the kitchen wearing her dressing gown and with a towel wrapped firmly around her head. Angie was home and already at the table eating her salad. Beside her sat Ian, their father.

"Why've you got that silly towel on your head?" Angie asked, her forehead wrinkled, as Lucy took her seat opposite. "I thought you were going out tonight. Your hair will never dry like that."

Lucy scowled and kicked her sister on the shins beneath the table. "I know that, don't I, stupid? Anyway I can always use the hair dryer if it's still wet."

"But that's daft and a waste of electricity, isn't it, Mum?"

Janet nodded.

"See! Take the towel off and don't be so obstinate."

"Shut up and leave me alone. How I dry my hair is no concern of yours?"

Janet placed Lucy's plate of salad before her and then she too sat at the table. "You alright, dear? You seem a little edgy this evening."

"Yes, of course I'm alright," she snapped, pulling forward the towel to make sure no strands of hair were showing, "Why shouldn't I be?"

Janet shrugged her shoulders. "I don't know, but you just seem to have a very short fuse."

"Well, that's because everyone's nagging."

"We're not nagging," snapped Angie, "we're just making sensible observations."

"No you're not, you're nagging and it's irritating, so why don't you all just shut up and leave me…" She caught sight of a look of disapproval on her father's face. "Sorry," she mumbled, hanging her head, "sorry."

"And so you should be," said Ian, solemnly.

"That's alright, love," said Janet, patting her daughter's hand. "I know it's not easy growing up and I expect you're a little on edge knowing you're A-level results will be out next Thursday. So, are you going anywhere nice tonight?"

Lucy pulled away her hand and scowled.

"Sorry, sorry," said Janet, "no more questions."

Later that same evening, Rose and George joined Ned and Stella at Rose Cottage for a meal to celebrate Ned's birthday. They had thought about going to the inn but changed their minds when their grandson, Wills, brought them a fresh crab, hence they decided to stay in and have, melon for starters, crab salad for the main course and rhubarb pie and ice cream for pudding.

They ate in the kitchen in order to save moving around the furniture in the study, a necessity to accommodate the increased volume of the drop-leaf dining table should they have chosen to dine there.

After discussing the week gone by with its eclipse, the extra influx of holiday makers and the Sunflower Competition, George mentioned he had heard the long range weather forecast and it was not looking good for the Over Sixties' Club outing the following Tuesday. In response Stella cast a pitiful glance in his direction, "Please don't let's discuss the weather," she begged, "it's been Ned's favourite subject for much of this month and it's becoming a little tiresome."

"So is the weather," replied Ned, promptly, "so is the weather."

George roared with laughter, but Rose heeded Stella's cry and steered the subject towards the construction of the Millennium Wheel in London, knowing it was something about which George had much to say. Although it had to be said his thoughts on the Wheel were of little consequence compared with those he held on the Millennium Dome.

After the main course was finished, Rose and Stella cleared the table and as Stella put the dirty plates on the draining board they heard a sharp crack.

"What on earth was that?" Rose asked.

"Sounded like thunder," said Stella.

Ned shook his head. "No, the sky is clear tonight, for a change. Must have been a car back firing."

While Rose served up the rhubarb pie, Stella went outside to the shed which housed their small chest freezer to fetch ice cream and as she walked along the path with the cold tub in her hands, she thought she could smell burning; not the pleasant smell of an autumn bonfire, it was more toxic and decidedly disagreeable. Stella paused and shrugged her shoulders, someone was probably burning rubbish amongst which were plastics. The ice cream tub began to deaden her fingers and so she returned quickly indoors.

As they finished off their puddings they heard the blare of an emergency vehicle siren. Intrigued, they all sat in silence to listen and were surprised when the vehicle appeared to stop nearby. Ned hastily pushed back his chair and went into the living room, but he was unable to see the vehicle accountable for the siren from the window because of the shrubbery. Eagerly, he stood on a chair and opened the window. "Good grief, something's wrong," he said, alarmed, "I can smell smoke."

He closed the window abruptly and headed for the front door in the hall closely followed by Stella, Rose and George. Once outside they were able to see thick, black smoke pothering into the darkening night sky, high above the shrubbery.

"Christ, where's that coming from?" shouted George, as all four scurried down the garden path. His question was answered as a second fire engine pulled up alongside the first. The village hall was on fire.

Chapter Nineteen

The second fire engine was closely followed by two police cars and officers who abruptly proceeded to push back the rapidly gathering crowds pouring into the road and footpath from all directions. The area was then cordoned off.

The horrified spectators watched, stunned, their chatter fast and furious, asking questions and expressing dismay as the leaping flames and thick, black smoke briskly engulfed the building amidst a sea of flashing blue lights and powerful jets of water.

Throughout the village news of the fire spread as fast as the fire itself, bringing further spectators to witness the blaze from the inn and houses on the Penwynton Estate. All stood, shocked, bewildered and stunned in disbelief as the inferno grew in power, strength and intensity, but no one noticed a solitary magpie standing on a nearby telegraph pole.

"Well, I'm pleased to see that someone in the village has the nous to call out the emergency services when needed," muttered Freddie, as he and Trish arrived on the scene.

Gertie raised her eyebrows. "Oh, come on, I don't think you can compare this horror with Robbie's silly little tumble?"

"It wasn't just a tumble and Ms Delaney's jewellery wasn't taken by a fan either and neither, of course, were young Jim's vegetables. My instincts tell me there's something fishy going on here and these incidents are probably all linked. Someone's up to no good, mark my words, but you're quite right of course, none of those incidents do in any way compare with a fire on this scale."

As he spoke there was a mighty crash and the crowd gasped and stepped further back as the village hall roof collapsed and fell into the ferocious flames.

Stephen Pascoe arrived with Nessie and Robbie; with them was a fireman who had gone to the post office to establish whether or not there was likely to have been anyone inside the hall. Once the fireman was able to report the building was empty and no lives were at risk, the expression on the chief officer's face was clearly one of relief. The fight, however, to extinguish the fire did not ease up and water continued to pour down on the fierce, crackling flames with relentless force.

"My face is hot and feels burned by the heat," said Stella sadly, wiping tears from her eyes, "but at the same time I'm shivering with cold."

"It's shock, love," said Ned, putting his arm around his wife and pulling him towards her. "Shock and disbelief. What a dreadful waste!"

Close to the gate of Valley View, stood Doctor Owen. Her face looked pale and her eyes were moist with tears. George went to make sure she was alright. She assured him she was fine but just shocked and deeply saddened that fire had followed an eclipse as in days gone by: something she never really expected to happen and especially to the same building.

"They say lightning never strikes twice," she whispered, "but in this case it has. It's so disconcerting. I feel I must be dreaming."

Also amongst the spectators were Ian and Janet Ainsworth, who had heard about the fire from Angie who had rushed in with boyfriend, Sam to pass on the news.

"It's just as well there's quite a gap between the hall and Coronation Terrace," said Ian, observing the distance, "otherwise the houses would have to be evacuated."

"God forbid," agreed Ned, "that wouldn't go down very well with Gertie."

"Did someone say my name?" Gertie called, from amongst the crowd."

"Only in a nice way," said Ned.

Gertie moved closer and when Ned repeated Ian's comment her face dropped. "Oh, God, don't. The thought of losing everything I've collected together over the years, diaries, photo albums and so forth is just too terrible to even think about."

"Ah, but at least your house is owned by the local authorities so you wouldn't have to worry about the loss of the building," said Janet.

"Actually, we own it," snapped Gertie, indignantly. "We bought ours in the early 1980s, when Maggie Thatcher gave us the option, and so did Meg and Sid. The other two are still owned by the local authorities though."

"Oh, I see, sorry, I didn't realise that."

Gertie grinned smugly, and nodded towards the bystanders watching the fire at the end of the row. "I see your daughter's gone all freaky. I didn't recognise her at first. I don't know, the youngsters of today, eh, Janet, they're nearly as outrageous as the kids were in the late sixties early seventies."

It was Janet's turn for indignation. "Freaky!" she repeated, "Whatever do you mean? I can assure you that neither of our daughters are in the least bit freaky."

As she spoke she caught sight of Lucy hanging on the arm of one of the camping lads, her hair as black as coal and backcombed into spikes. Her eye make-up was thick and dark. Her painted false nails were long and black; around her neck she wore a studded leather choker and the tight waisted dress she wore, hung unevenly below her knees, its colour every bit as black as her hair.

"Oh, my God," gasped Janet, feeling the colour drain from her face. "No wonder she wouldn't take the towel off her head earlier and rushed off out shouting goodbye without coming in the sitting room to see us. Just you wait 'til she gets home. You'll have to have words with her, Ian, she'll listen to you."

But when she looked at her husband she saw he was smiling. "It's not funny," she said, irritated by the smug look on Gertie's face, "it's humiliating. People will think we've allowed her to dress like that and it just isn't so."

"Janet, she's eighteen; she's past the age of consent and in the eyes of the law is a grown up. It's just a fad, she won't stay like it forever. One day we'll look back at this and laugh, meanwhile, make sure you admire her new look with exuberance, that way she'll probably discard it sooner rather than later."

"Good philosophy there, Ian," agreed Ned, "it's the sort of thing Stella would say. Isn't it, old girl?"

Stella raised her eyebrows and opened her mouth to object to his comment but quickly decided the compliment far outweighed the insulting reference to her age.

On Sunday morning, Trengillion's inhabitants woke to the bitter memory that their village hall was no more, and many, keen to witness the extent of the damage in daylight, ventured to the spot where they could view the smouldering remains from behind a police cordon.

Smoke still rose from the burnt out shell, the smell was foul and all that was left were the blackened outside granite walls. Nothing else had survived the intensity of the harsh flames.

"Thank God we had insurance," said Susan, close to tears, "otherwise we'd never be able to raise enough money to rebuild it. I just hope it wasn't arson. It'd be dreadful to think someone from here could be spiteful enough to cause such damage."

"Well, if it wasn't arson I can't see what else might have caused it," said Meg, practically. "I don't think there's been anything on in there since Keep Fit on Wednesday. So it couldn't have been a cigarette butt or anything like that."

"Keep Fit was cancelled this week because of the eclipse," said Candy Bingham, "but we used it yesterday morning for the Christmas Lights jumble sale."

"Oh, yes of course, I'd forgotten that. I intended to go but completely forgot. That's old age for you. Did you do alright?"

"Absolutely, we made one hundred and fifteen pounds and five pence, so we're really pleased with that. And before you ask, no-one was smoking. Ironically enough, no smoking was a new policy dreamed up by the Village Hall Committee at their last meeting and to make sure everyone knew they've put up notices everywhere inside the hall saying so. At least they did, they're not there now of course."

Gertie scowled. "That's a bit freaky. The Committee being afraid of fire, I mean, and then it burns down. I wonder if someone had a premonition."

"Or maybe they were influenced by Doctor Owen's story," said Candy.

Meg smiled. "I think the decision's more likely to have been influenced by the cost of insurance, not to mention the horrible smell left behind when lots of people have been smoking."

"The poor old sycamore looks a bit sick," said Candy, surveying the blackened withered leaves and branches, "but I'm sure it'll pull through alright unlike the hall, because surely its roots must go down for miles."

"Actually they don't go down very far at all," said Jim, who had arrived on his bicycle just in time to hear Candy's comment. "Most of their roots only go down a few feet, but there are lots of them. I shouldn't worry about it though, because even if it was felled new growth would spring from the stump; sycamores are as tough as old boots."

"That's nice to hear," said Meg, "because that tree's been here for as long as I can remember, and that's a very long time."

"At least the young magpies have flown," sighed Susan, "it would have been awful if the poor things had perished in the flames and smoke."

Jim scowled. "Magpies are horrible things. They kill little birds, damage crops and are real pests."

"And they bring bad luck," added Gertie, "don't they, Jim?"

Candy's face dropped. "But they're such fun to watch and they look so cheeky. I love the fact they're renowned for collecting shiny things too. In fact I wouldn't be surprised if it wasn't a magpie that took Iris's jewellery."

Susan laughed. "And it probably nicked your veg, Jim."

"Ha ha. But seriously, look at the poor hall. I thought the chapel was in a sorry state when I bought it but it was rudely healthy compared with this wreck. It's a dreadful shame."

"Well, at least the fire brigade have ways of finding out the causes of fire," said Susan. "God only knows how though, I wouldn't know where to start looking."

"Me neither," agreed Jim. "Anyway, I must be on my way, ladies. See you around."

"Bye, Jim," the ladies chorused.

"He's such a nice lad," sighed Candy, "and we still haven't found him a wife."

Gertie wasn't listening. "I wouldn't be surprised if that Trevor Moore bloke wasn't involved somehow," she said, in a lowered voice, glancing towards Coronation Terrace where Trevor stood on the front doorstep of his house gazing at the remains of the village hall.

A puzzled look crossed Meg's face. "What on earth are you talking about, Gert?"

"The fire of course. I mean he could easily have had something to do with it, living so close."

"Don't be ridiculous," snapped Meg, "that's a preposterous thing to say. Poor bloke."

"But he was here last night, didn't you see him? Watching the hall burn down. Which I thought was a bit odd seeing as how he's never taken the slightest bit of interest in the village or its people."

"Oh, come on, Mum, that's a bit harsh," said Susan, "whatever motive could he possibly have for burning down our hall?"

"I don't know, but I'm sure he's a fraud. I mean to say, why doesn't he work? He seems more than able to me except for a bit of a hobble. I reckon he's conned the benefits people and is work shy. And have you noticed the curtains in the front room and dining room are always drawn so no-one can see in? That's pretty suspicious, you have to admit. I wouldn't even be surprised if it turns out he's growing cannabis plants in there, because I read about someone doing that up-country recently and they kept the curtains closed too."

Susan and Meg laughed but Candy nodded. "I have noticed the curtains and I agree, it does seem a bit odd. But even if he was growing cannabis, which I'm sure he isn't, it wouldn't make him an arsonist."

"And the family have attended one village event," said Susan, in their defence, "they were at the Summer Fayre, all four of them."

Before going downstairs to begin preparations for the Sunday lunchtime trade, Jane looked from her sitting room window towards Cove Cottage, wondering if Rusty were there or whether he had gone out, for the car was missing. She sat down, still in somewhat of a daze. For the previous evening, before the drama of the village hall fire had erupted, she had timorously gone to the inn thinking, as did everyone else, that Rusty and Iris were romantically attached. It came as a surprise, therefore, to hear they were half brother and sister. They shared a mother but had different fathers, and had been brought up in different households; they kept these facts quiet as it helped deter unsolicited attention towards Iris from amorous males.

Jane looked dreamily out to sea. Rusty was only thirty nine and so several years younger than herself, but deep down she had a strong feeling that he would play a large part in her future; or was it just wishful thinking? Jane was unsure. She was also afraid. For the bitter manner in which her last romantic encounter had ended twelve years earlier had left her reluctant ever to let herself fall in love again. The pain of losing her last love had been so intense, so bitter, that during the first difficult twelve months she thought the scars would never heal. But at the same time she conceded life without a partner was very lonely and she envied her friends their happy relationships and marriages.

A rap on the door below brought Jane back to reality. Assuming it was Jim with supplies, she put down her empty coffee mug and walked down the stairs. When she opened the door her heart skipped a beat. Rusty stood on the doorstep clutching a huge bunch of deep red roses and a massive box of chocolates.

Chapter Twenty

On Sunday afternoon, after finishing work at the Jolly Sailor, Tally and Demelza walked down to the beach in search of their friends, old and new. As anticipated they found them stretched out on the sand dozing in the hazy sunshine.

"It's alright for some," grinned Demelza, sitting down beside Kev who was snoring gently. "Wake up, you lazy sod."

"What, oh, yes, good heavens, Demelza, hello, what time is it?"

"Half past three. I thought you weren't drinking this lunchtime."

"Well, we didn't intend to, but it didn't seem right to go into a pub and not drink beer. Dinner was smashing anyway. I'm still full."

"So, what have you been doing with yourselves while we've been slaving away in a hot kitchen? Tally asked, "apart from boozing and having a roast, that is."

"Actually, we've been quite busy," said Neil, turning onto his side and resting his chin in the palm of his hand, "before lunch we walked up to see what's left of your village hall and you'd never believe the heat still coming from the pile of rubble."

Tally groaned. "Goodness knows where we'll hold events 'til it's rebuilt. I feel really cheated, I was enjoying learning Cornish."

"Cornish!" laughed Neil, "what's that about? Do they teach you to grunt and growl?"

"Don't be cheeky," Tally replied, ruffling his hair with a mock slap, "Cornish is a language in its own right, though sadly it's no longer used. It's quite fascinating when you get into it."

"But it must have been dead for yonks," yawned Lucy, turning over to tan the backs of her legs having removed her black Goth tights, "I've never heard anyone speak it and we've lived here for twelve years now."

"Well, admittedly it has been dead for a while because it was superseded by English way back in the sixteenth century. A few people carried it on though and allegedly it was last spoken by Dolly Pentreath who lived in Mousehole and she died back in 1777. Though it's claimed a few other folks still spoke it after her demise."

"How can you be studying Cornish here when you're away at university for most of the year?" Mac asked.

"It's only a short course for beginners which started in June just after I got home and it finishes at the end of September."

"I see; so what's the Cornish for beer?" grinned Mac, with a challenging smirk.

"Korev," Tally replied, triumphantly.

"Hmm, I'm impressed," he laughed, and laid down with his arms behind his head.

"I've never been able to get on with learning languages," said Demelza, "I'm a dunce when it comes to pronunciation, you see, because I make all languages sound the same."

"What, you pronounce foreign words the same as you would do English?" laughed Neil. "Same here."

Demelza nodded.

"I find Cornish interesting because it teaches a bit of history," continued Tally, "for instance, it's believed Trengillion was at one time called Tremellyonenn or something similar and the name changed over the years, as most names do."

"Blimey, no wonder they changed it, what a mouthful."

"Well, I've heard a lot worse," said Kev, "some of the places in Wales have ridiculously long names."

"Llanfairpwllgwyngyllgogerychwyrndrobwllllantysiliogogogoch," laughed Tally, "is that what you're referring to."

"Big head."

Rob grinned. "Which means, the Church of St Mary in the hollow of white hazel near the rapid whirlpool and the church of St Tysili's by the red cave, or something like that."

"Now I know why I stock shelves in a supermarket and you lot don't," said Kev, with an air of self-pity, "I couldn't remember that if my life depended on it."

"It's not really being clever," said Tally, generously, "it's just having the sort of brain that retains facts. Whether or not that's a good thing is debatable."

Lucy addressed Morwenna. "Your name's Cornish, Morwenna, isn't it? At least my mum said it is. Cornish or Welsh, anyway."

Morwenna nodded.

"Mor is Cornish for sea," said Tally, "so Morwenna means sea waves or sea maiden, something like that."

"So how about Morgana, what does that mean?" asked Demelza.

"More or less the same; edge of the sea or sea shore," Tally answered,"

Ollie looked puzzled. "Who is Morgana?"

"Don't you know? It's Doctor Owen," said Demelza.

"Oh, is it? I wasn't aware of that."

"I only know because I heard her and Justin talking the other night in the dining room and he called her Morgana," giggled Demelza. "I reckon he's nuts about her."

"Oh, dear, don't tell Jess, she thinks Justin's the Bee's Knees," sighed Tally, "but then Charlie Bingham is on her hot list too and she quite likes the temporary postman currently doing the round. It's a shame she split up with her boyfriend in Swansea: she's been a bit lost this summer."

"And don't forget Robbie the Scot," said Lucy, "she goes all googly-eyed whenever she sees him."

Morwenna scowled. "Humph!"

Mac tilted his head to one side. "What's the matter, Morwenna? Don't you like Robbie?"

Morwenna continued to scowl.

Tally attempted to smother a smile. "Robbie and Morwenna aren't what you might call kindred spirits, Mac. He mocked her clothing, you see, which wasn't very nice, I must admit. And when Morwenna retaliated with a verbal attack he asked her where she'd parked her broomstick."

Mac laughed. "Take no notice of him, sweetheart, I expect he was only joking."

Ollie nodded. "Yeah, Robbie's a bit of a clown. I often have a game of pool with him. He's a great laugh and Dad tells me his books are brilliant. Apparently he's read them all."

"He seems to be accident prone too," said Lucy. "Robbie, that is, not your dad, Ollie. I mean, not many people get knocked over twice in one week and for no apparent reason."

Morwenna smirked. "That'll teach him not to mock others."

"Are we going to the Talent Contest later?" Neil asked, feeling it might be wise to change the subject. "I think we should, it could be a laugh."

Tally nodded. "I agree, it's only right we show our support, after all Mr Reynolds has put a lot of time into organising it."

Lucy groaned. "Must we? My horrible little brother's proposing to do some magic. It'll be really embarrassing."

"Blimey, so your brother not only grows big sunflowers but he's a magician too," Neil laughed, "rather puts you in the shade, doesn't it Luce?"

"Actually, it's not the same brother. James grew the sunflower but it's Mick who likes to think he's a magician. Silly arse."

"That's a bit harsh, Lucy," commented Demelza, "after all he is a member of the Magic Circle so he must have some skills at his fingertips."

Mac scowled. "But surely the contest's been cancelled. I mean to say, how can it go ahead without the village hall?"

"It's going to be in the school instead," said Tally, "there was a notice in the inn saying so. Everyone was talking about it this lunchtime and I must admit it might be fun seeing how many plates Jim smashes."

"Plate smashing! What sort of act is that? No, don't tell me, it's an ancient Cornish tradition started by your Dolly Pentreath."

"Ha ha," mocked Tally, "Jim's act will be spinning plates, so my reference to breakages obviously referred to his accidents."

Morwenna suddenly shuddered.

"Hey, you alright, Wen?" Rob asked.

Morwenna nodded. "Yes, I just felt all cold and shivery. Ugh, weird."

"That means someone just walked over your grave," laughed Neil, "that's what my gran would say anyway. Isn't that right, Rob?"

"Leave him alone," said Tally, defensively, "you mustn't keep teasing him just because he has a slightly unusual occupation."

"Hear, hear," said Demelza, "instead can we rewind a bit and return to the Cornish language, because I'd like to know what, whatever Trengillion used to be called, means."

"Tremellyonenn," smiled Tally, "roughly it means a settlement in clover and I think that's quite feasible because there's clover in every field, even today."

"Clover," scoffed, Kev, "why name a place after a weed?"

"A weed," squealed Demelza, "Clover isn't a weed, you moron, it's a wild flower and a very pretty one at that."

"Weed, wild flower, same thing, surely."

"Actually, red clover has many uses in herbal medicine, doesn't it, Morwenna?"

"Hmm, that's right, the flowers when dried make excellent tea which sooths a cough and settles upset stomachs. The rest of the plant is used too and can be a healthy addition to salads, even the seeds once they've begun to sprout are edible."

"Ugh, salad."

"So what else does it cure apart from coughs and dicky tums?" asked Mac, always eager to learn facts.

"Just about everything," said Morwenna, adjusting her headband which had slipped onto her forehead, "eczema, psoriasis, gout, whooping cough, some cancers. All sorts of things."

Tally laughed. "And according to my mum, who's quite knowledgeable when it comes to folklore, different numbers of clover leaves are significant too. For instance, in medieval times clover was used to ward off evil spirits and witches, and today, everyone knows a four leaf clover is meant to be lucky, but few know that a five leaf clover is thought to have been worn by witches to enhance their evil powers."

"I didn't even know there was such a thing as a five leaf clover," said Demelza.

"Yes, there is apparently, although I've never seen one, but then I've never seen a four leaf either, not that I've ever looked. And apparently there are two leaf clover too, but that has a more innocent meaning as it's supposed to lend foresight to a maiden to see her future lover."

Neil groaned and sprang to his feet. "Right, that's enough about flowers and maidens. Everyone huddle together for a group photo."

Lucy looked heavenwards. "For heaven's sake, Neil, haven't you finished off that film yet? You said it was nearly full the day before yesterday."

Neil grinned. "Oh yeah, that film's done but I've put another one in now. Can't have too many holiday snaps."

The change of venue for the Talent Contest had been a hasty decision made in the early hours of Sunday morning, when Sid, unable to sleep, conscious cancellation would disappoint a large number of children, decided to ring Alison Turner and ask if it would be possible to use the school. To his delight she agreed providing the school governors raised no objections, and after several phone calls to those concerned, permission was unanimously granted.

The Contest was scheduled to begin at six o' clock and so throughout the day, Sid and a band of volunteers dutifully erected a portable temporary stage borrowed from Polquillick village hall. The Contest, however, would have to go ahead without curtains, for even if there had been a track on which to hang them, no-one had drapes large enough to fill the great void and the lush velvet curtains custom made for the village hall, lay in ashes on the hall's smouldering floor.

By six o'clock the school was packed to full capacity. Alison was a little alarmed that the over-crowding would seriously contravene Fire Regulations, but they were reluctant to turn anyone away and so the show went ahead with fingers on the hands of all organisers firmly crossed.

In the infants' classroom the performers patiently awaited their turns, some seemingly nervous, others full of confidence. First to set foot on the temporary stage was eight-year-old Loretta Young, a girl whose family had been in the area for just over a year. Loretta graced the stage and showed off her newly acquired ballet skills, accompanied by music from a compact disc player. Her efforts left the audience quite enchanted by her energy, elegance and flexibility.

Second on stage were the two little girls whose singing had prompted Sid to organise the talent contest in the first place. To his delight they sang the same song he had heard whilst in his front garden.

Much to the embarrassment of Lucy, the third act was her brother Mick Ainsworth. She watched his tricks through the fingers on her hand stretched across her face, praying he would not embarrass her in front of her friends and especially Neil. But to her amazement, his tricks were impressive, his timing impeccable and the audience were enchanted. And after his final trick a loud rapturous round of applause filled the room.

Mick's performance was followed by a couple of holiday makers who attempted to sing in harmony, but whose nerves produced a few bum notes which triggered off an infectious bout of giggles.

Next was Jim and his spinning plates.

Morwenna sat up straight when Jim took to the stage and to her surprise she found herself nervous on his behalf. But his performance was perfect, not one plate misbehaved and his talents earned him a standing ovation.

"Where did he get all those plates from?" Demelza asked, as Jim lifted the stack of plates from the table prior to making his exit.

"Car boot sales," said Ollie, still clapping, "he and Mum are good friends and to help him she always looks out for old cheap plates when she goes to a car boot, because needless to say, a few get broken when he's practising. He was pretty impressive, wasn't he?"

Jim's act was followed by a pianist who expertly played 'Greensleeves' on the old school piano. And a female guest staying at the Penwynton Hotel followed the pianist with a monologue and a few jokes. She was funny both in the contents of her act and her appearance and she too earned a richly deserved round of applause.

A break followed the comedienne and raffle tickets were sold, the proceeds of which were to go to the Christmas Lights' funds. When the tickets were drawn Morwenna was surprised to find she had won a box of chocolates but as she did not eat sweets she passed them onto her friends.

Trish Short started off the second part of the show with a beautiful rendition of 'Ave Maria'. Her performance was followed by a less skilful interpretation of 'Climb Every Mountain' by another holiday maker.

A juggling friend of Alison Turner followed the two singers. His act was frivolous as the items he chose to juggle were Cornish pasties.

After the stage had been swept to remove broken pasties, four young children nervously sang a lullaby. The performance would have been perfect had not the freckled faced girl with the loudest voice forgotten the words and ad-libbed for two out of the three verses.

The final act was Nessie and her brother, Robbie; both walked onto the stage carrying bagpipes.

Morwenna raised her hands in horror as the siblings nodded to each other and raised the blowsticks to their mouths. "I hate bagpipes," she muttered, "they drone and set my nerves on edge."

Rob laughed. "You'll not be getting up for a jig, then."

Nessie looked down at the audience with an amused smile on her face, fully aware that many in the village were not enthralled with the bagpipes, hence she and Robbie had impishly chosen to play a complex piece of music knowing full well many notes were beyond their capabilities and so would jar on the nerves of their adversaries.

They began their performance with confidence and skill, but towards the end many hands were held over ears. Some, however, were in fits of laughter and compared the siblings' performance with the late Les Dawson, who with a deadpan face, had expertly played the piano but with the inclusion of several incorrect notes.

"Oh, God, this is painful," whinged Morwenna.

Suddenly there were two loud bangs and the air quickly escaped from the bags of Nessie and Robbie's bagpipes. Somewhat surprised they held up their instruments. The audience gasped. The sheepskin pipe bags in both cases, were torn from top to bottom, leaving gaping holes.

Morwenna giggled. "Who says there isn't a God?"

As the laughter and loud applause subsided all the performers collected together on the small stage and the panel of judges announced the winners in reverse order. Third was Loretta, the eight year old ballet dancer, second was Jim and in first place was Mick for his conjuring. And when Mick was awarded a cheque for twenty five pounds, Lucy beamed with pride.

Chapter Twenty One

On Sunday night as Trengillion slept beneath a starless, moonless sky, an unpredicted, brisk, south westerly wind, swept in from the sea, swirled across the cliff tops and down into the valley. Gathering speed, it whipped around the village, roaring and screaming, rattling windows, bending trees and tossing lightweight garden furniture across lawns and terraces into untidy heaps beneath fences, hedges and walls.

From the charred remains of the village hall, ash and debris danced along the deserted road, partnered by withered, blackened leaves from the stricken sycamore tree.

Out in the fields, corn and wheat crops swayed and bowed as the strong gusts reached gale force. And in the Bingham's back garden, the huge head of Larry's prize sunflower, snapped from its thick stem and plunged with a thud onto the damp earth below.

On the beach, huge waves energised by the ferocious wind crashed onto the shore, rearranging vast areas of shingle and cobbles as they merged with the sodden sand.

Up on the cliff tops beyond the Witches Broomstick, the Jeffersons leapt from their beds in Higher Green Farmhouse and switched on the lights, convinced Cornwall was besieged by a tornado twisting its way around the old house. Julie May, however, showed no signs of fear. Mesmerised by the call of the wind, she ran down to the kitchen unlocked the door and stepped out into the old farmyard. With the wind tearing at her long dark curls, she ran onto a lawned area, laughing and dancing, twisting and twirling, her bare feet skimming over the surface of the coarse grass; her short satin nightdress flapping hard against her slim legs.

"Julie May, you get back here now," shouted Jefferson K. Jefferson, Jr., "you'll catch your death of cold."

"You should have stopped her drinking all that there Baileys stuff," said Mrs Jefferson K. Jefferson, Sr. wagging her finger, "the poor lamb's gone daft."

Jefferson K. Jefferson, Sr., however, slapped his thigh, leaving an imprint on his thick, brown dressing gown and laughed. "Dag nab it, if I were twenty years younger I'd go out there and join the gel. The wind's kind of exhilarating, ain't it? Y'all leave her alone."

In the recreation field the young occupants in the only remaining tent were abruptly woken by the canvas flapping like masts on a storm ridden sailing ship. The boys, alarmed by the noise, sat up in their sleeping bags, switched on Mac's powerful torch and prayed the pegs would hold. Alas, their prayers were not answered. A sudden gust took away their temporary home and blew it across the field, gliding in the wind like an enormous white kite down into the valley below, its eerie image caught in a beam of Mac's torchlight.

Shocked, and with the wind tearing at their hair, the boys, still tucked snugly inside their sleeping bags, huddled together on the crumpled groundsheet, locked in a state of disbelief, unsure whether to laugh or cry. When the tent finally came to rest, its bulk caught in the branches of a tree, they heaved a sigh of relief with the knowledge they would at least be able to retrieve it after daybreak.

Suddenly, a flash of lighting streaked across the dark sky, lighting up the field and the surrounding buildings. It was instantly followed by the booming crash of thunder. The boys looked heavenwards and instinctively held out their hands as the first ice cold raindrops fell from the heavens.

"Quick, the car," yelled Mac, shivering, as he clambered out of his sleeping bag, "let's get in the car."

With sleeping bags clutched in hands, they grabbed as many items of clothing and possessions as possible from the flapping groundsheet and dashed to the car before the rain, mingled with large hailstones, fell heavily. Thankful the car roof was already up, they threw their possessions into the boot and then clambered into the seats. For the rest of the night they sat watching and listening, until finally the storm abated, the rain and hail stopped and daylight emerged with the rising of the sun.

When Trengillion's inhabitants arose, the only subject on anyone's lips was the storm, and inside most homes, people switched on Radio Cornwall eager to hear what damage the storm had caused throughout the county. But to their amazement no mention of it was made at all, and it was only after phone calls to friends and relations in neighbouring towns and villages that it became apparent the storm had occurred in Trengillion only and nowhere else.

On the front lawn of Rose Cottage Ned and Stella looked around for signs of damage but the only casualty appeared to be a section of the wooden fence between their house and the garden of Valley View, which was lying on the grass smashed into small pieces.

"Sodding wind," cursed Ned, "why did it have to blow our fence down?"

"But it's only one section," said Stella, bending to gather together a few of the smaller pieces of wood. "It could so easily have been the whole fence and at least it didn't flatten the sweet peas."

"Humph, I suppose so."

"Anyway, at least it means we won't need any kindling wood for a while next winter."

Ned frowned and then laughed. "I've never known anyone to be as optimistic as you. The old adage, every cloud has a silver lining should be your catchphrase."

Stella smiled. "It's just a bit of fence, Ned. John will have it repaired in a flash, you see."

On rising inside the inn, Justin noticed the boy's tent was no longer in its usual place. Concerned for their welfare he wandered onto the field to see if they were in need of help. He found them in the valley; Mac and Kev up a tree, swearing and cursing as they attempted to free the tent from its jagged branches, while down below, Neil and Rob looked on amused by the desperate efforts of their friends.

When finally the tent succumbed to their hard labour, the boys triumphantly laid it out on the grass, but their euphoria was short lived; the tent was in tatters and a gaping hole stretched the entire length of the top ridge.

"Looks like it's time to pack up and go home," said Kev, sadly, kicking the canvas, "what miserable, rotten luck."

"Oh no," said Justin, "you're not going home yet. Come on, gather your things together and come with me. You can stay at the inn for the rest of the week, the family room's free now."

"That's ever so good of you, Justin, but we really can't afford it," said Kev, "our finances are getting quite low now."

Justin smiled. "I'm not going to charge you; it's an act of friendship. Besides you've spent enough at the inn to have paid for a room anyway and I'd hate to see you go in these unfortunate circumstances and so would your many new friends."

After a morning's work at the Penwynton Hotel helping the head gardener replace panes of greenhouse glass broken during the storm, Jim Haynes went up to his allotment prepared for the worst, but to his delight his greenhouse and small polytunnel were still intact and none of his vegetables seemed to have suffered any long term damage. Delighted by his find he then gathered tomatoes, cucumbers, peppers and chillies, put them in the basket on the front of his bicycle and rode into the village to the Jolly Sailor to deliver them before the inn closed following lunchtime opening.

On arriving at the inn he dropped the produce in the kitchen where Tally took charge of them, he then went into the bar to collect his money from Justin.

Percy Collins and Peter Williams were in the bar telling Freddie, Trish, and Doctor Owen, all in for lunch, of storms gone by and the damage done thereof.

"Well, last night's storm was a weird one," mused Trish, pushing aside her empty plate, "I used to work for the Met Office, and believe you me, that one appeared from nowhere and the fact it was so localised is very odd. I reckon this village is definitely jinxed."

"Jinxed," Percy laughed, "but surely Trengillion can't be the first place ever to have had a localised storm."

"Well, no, but I'm not basing my theory on just that, I'm taking into consideration all the other odd incidents that have happened too. The jewellery stolen from Iris for instance, the village hall fire, young Robbie being knocked down by nothing apparent, not once, but twice, the withering of the rowan trees in the churchyard and elsewhere in the village, Robbie and his sister's bagpipes bursting at the talent contest and now this localised storm. It's all very strange, very strange indeed."

"And some of my veg was nicked too," added Jim.

Freddie smiled, and patted his wife's shoulder in a condescending manner. "Trish reads lots of murder mystery books, and so I'd take everything she says with a pinch of salt. Having said that, it's more than possible there is a link between the acts of criminality, by that I mean the thefts and Robbie's assaults, but to suggest those crimes might also encompass the weather, plants dying and so forth, well that's just ridiculous, and as for the place being jinxed, I'll not even comment."

"Yes, I expect we'll find there's a perfectly good scientific reason behind each incident," smiled the doctor, "I mean, take the trees for instance, there's nothing unusual about them withering up and dying, it happens all the time. They are after all very susceptible to the weather, pests, diseases and so forth. That's why some wild species are becoming extinct."

"That's as maybe," said Trish, "but it seems odd to me that all rowan trees in the village have suffered, and the weather's not been that unusual except for last night's storm, that is."

"Perhaps someone's been spraying weed killer on the trees because they don't like them," suggested Percy, frivolously, "I mean, I daresay they're not everyone's cup of tea; just as dahlias aren't mine. I think they're too gaudy and garish."

"Well, as regards dahlias I fall into that category too," said the doctor, "but I wouldn't dream of harming someone else's pride and joy and the same goes for the rowans. Although I really can't see why anyone would dislike them because the berries are very attractive and a good source of food for birds."

"Maybe someone doesn't like birds and so vandalised the trees with weed killer," said Peter.

Jim grinned. "You might have a point there, Pete. Magpies aren't too popular with everyone and there only seems to be one of the sycamore pair left now."

Percy shook his head. "No, according to the dotty women, the missing magpie has been gone since the day of the eclipse so that would have been before the trees got sick."

"I still think this village is jinxed," said Trish, "and nothing any of you say will convince me otherwise."

In the afternoon, Candy Bingham left her home in Penwynton Crescent for a stroll down to the beach. Outside the village hall she stopped like many before her to survey the fire damage. Gentle puffs of smoke still escaped from the smouldering, blackened rubble, but the atmosphere seemed one of peace in spite of the destruction. With a sigh, Candy continued along the road, past Coronation Terrace where Gertie chatted to Meg over the front garden hedge about the storm, and on towards the cove.

Several people were sitting outside the Pickled Egg eating fish and chips. The smell made Candy feel hungry even though she had only just eaten her lunch.

The beach was quiet in comparison with the chaos of the previous week; a few people were sitting on the sand and shingle wearing jackets and cardigans, but no-one was in the sea, for it was still very rough and looked most uninviting with limp seaweed and debris swirling around in the dirty, frothy, tumbling waves.

Candy looked across the shore towards Denzil's bench. To her dismay someone was already seated there and the island was out of the question because the tide was coming in. She decided, however, since the bench seated four, it would not be untoward to sit alongside the present occupant, even if he might well be a stranger.

Candy crossed the beach avoiding wet strands of seaweed, and debris washed up by the storm. As she sat, she was relieved to see the man was not at all a stranger, but Rusty Higgins.

"Phew, I'm glad it's you sitting here, but I never dreamt it might be; for some reason I thought you and Iris had gone home. But then of course, you haven't because you were in the pub on Saturday night, weren't you? I remember seeing you when we all dashed up to see the fire."

Rusty nodded. "You'll not be rid of us yet, we've decided to stay until the weekend."

"That's good. How did you fair in the storm? It must have been a bit rough this close to the sea."

"Alright, but neither of us slept much. I daresay that can be said for most people in the village though. Did you suffer any damage?"

Candy giggled. "Only to Larry's prize sunflower. Its head got snapped off. I must admit I found it hard to keep a straight face when he told me. When it was growing it was often all he could talk about, you see, and then when he won first prize, well, I longed for it to go over so that I could watch the birds eat its beastly seeds."

"And now you feel guilty," smiled Rusty.

"Well, yes, in a way I do. After all it really was very breathtaking and he deserved to win. It was a good few inches taller than the runner up, you know, but I think a lot of his success was brought about by the lashings of rotted chicken manure he'd scrounged from David Pascoe when he was up at Home Farm putting in a new bathroom suite. That and the plant food he fed it with every other day."

Rusty smiled, but his blue eyes lacked lustre.

Candy tilted her head to one side. "You look pale. Is that lack of sleep or is something worrying you?"

Rusty raised his eyebrows.

"Sorry," said Candy, shaking her head, "it's none of my business. I had no right even to ask, I don't know what came over me."

"Well, actually, you're very perspicacious. There is something bothering me. At least there's something puzzling me."

It was Candy's turn to raise her eyebrows.

"It's Jane," sighed Rusty, attempting to force a smile. "One minute I think she really likes me and then the next she's as cold as a fish. I know we've only known each other for a couple of days, but it's driving me mad because I really, really like her, the chemistry's right and we could have a future together. Oh, I don't know, perhaps it's my imagination."

Candy felt saddened. "If I tell you why, or at least why I think she's like she is, do you promise you'll never let on I told you?"

Curiosity raised, Rusty nodded his head. "I promise."

Candy bit her lip, "Has Jane ever mentioned a previous boyfriend to you?"

Rusty shook his head. "No, so who was he?"

"I don't want to mention any names as it might seem disloyal to Jane and really it must be her decision to disclose personal details. She met him back in the 1980s; he lived around here and everyone liked him and assumed one day they'd get married, Jane thought so too, but he never popped the question."

"Why ever not?"

Candy shuddered. "Let's just say he had to go away, never to return, and leave it at that. After all, it's not really for me to spread gossip even if it's true. The person in question really did love her though, but because of a guilty secret he could never ask her to marry him; he told me so himself and so I know it's true. Poor Jane. After he had gone she never saw him again. He did write to her though; just the once; she showed me his letter. He begged her to find someone worthy of her love, but she told me she couldn't. Her faith had been destroyed, you see, and she vowed she would die an old maid."

Chapter Twenty Two

Much to the dismay of Over Sixties' Club members, Tuesday dawned cool, damp and dull.

"Typical," said Ned, as he slid out of bed and drew back the curtains, "trust the forecast to be right on the one day I hoped it wouldn't. God only knows what we'll find to do in Mevagissey all day."

Stella yawned. "Well, I guess we'll have to do what we said the other day and spend it in a pub; they've quite a few to choose from."

Ned laughed. "Don't you think we're all a bit too old for a pub crawl?"

"Not really, I quite like the idea."

"Well, I suppose if the weather doesn't improve we could leave Mevagissey early and ask Bert, if he's driving the mini bus, to pop over to St Austell so we can take a peep at the Eden Project's construction. I'm sure most of us would like to see that."

"Can you see anything from the road though? I mean from what I've seen of it on the telly it seems quite tucked away and access might not be permitted if it's off the beaten track."

"I don't actually know, but it's food for thought if we all get bored."

Stella nodded. "I agree. Now, is your mobile phone fully charged?"

Ned shrugged his shoulders. "I suppose so, considering I never use the damn thing."

"Well go and check and make sure you remember to take it with you."

Meanwhile, at the post office, Stephen and Nessie were in a bit of a dilemma because Bert, who usually drove the mini bus for Trengillion's excursions, had phoned up early that morning to say he wasn't at all well and had been up half the night coughing.

"I'll take the old folks out," said Robbie, on hearing the news, "it'll make a nice change and I've nothing else to do today."

Nessie frowned. "But are you feeling well enough?"

Robbie sighed. "I'm fine, Ness. Absolutely fine."

Nessie looked at Stephen. "What do you think?"

"If you're up for it, Rob, then I think it's an excellent idea. We can't let the old timers down, that's for sure."

Before lunch Elizabeth gathered together the ingredients to make a cherry cake, Greg's favourite, but when she went to the fridge for butter she found there wasn't enough, and so she put on her jacket with the intent of going into the village to get some from the post office. There was a break in the cloud as she stepped outside and so she opted to walk rather than take the car.

On her way home, with butter in hand, a few spots of rain began to fall and by the time she had reached the inn it was raining steadily. Elizabeth quickly considered her options. She could either make a dash for it or pop down to the Pickled Egg and seek refuge there. As the raindrops increased she opted for the latter and stumbled inside the café door just as the heavens opened.

Jane laughed when she saw the look of disgust on Elizabeth's face. "I bet you're not as fed up as the outing lot."

"Ugh, no, poor things. I shall have to keep out of Dad's way for a while after this, because Mum says he's constantly moaning about the weather these days. Not that I can blame him; I hate getting wet too."

"Hmm, likewise: having said that, trade's still quite busy here when the weather's grim, but not as busy as it is when folks can sit outside."

Elizabeth smiled. "Well, seeing as I'm here, I'd better boost trade a bit and have a coffee."

Jane nodded, poured a coffee and handed it to Elizabeth. Elizabeth fumbled in her purse for change"

"Don't be silly, Liz. It's on me, I don't see you often enough."

"Thanks, Jane."

As Elizabeth lifted her coffee, a bedraggled family came in also to shelter from the rain, and so Elizabeth left the counter to make room for the new arrivals.

"Hello Mum," called a voice from the corner. Elizabeth turned and saw Tally sitting with Demelza, Morwenna and the four lads whom she recognised as the campers. With coffee in hand she crossed to acknowledge her daughter's greeting.

"Well, I never, I didn't know this was your mum," said Morwenna, with a look of approval. "Please, come and sit with us. I've seen you around quite a bit and always admired you." She shuffled along the bench to leave a substantial gap. "Jim mentioned you to me regarding the meaning of sweet peas but I didn't realise you were one and the same person."

"You admire me! Good heavens! That's flattery indeed," said Elizabeth taking the seat offered.

"Why do you admire my mum?" Tally asked, puzzled. "I mean, I admire her of course, but then that's because she's my mother."

Morwenna laughed. "I feel we're on the same wavelength when it comes to folklore and so forth and I simply adore the outfits she wears. The colours are so vibrant and the styles, well, so sort of..."

"Old fashioned," finished Tally, "Mum's dress sense is very old fashioned."

"There's nothing wrong with that. We should all dress as we please and be individual."

"Absolutely," said Rob, "Morwenna's quite right."

"Thank you, turtle."

Rob's face dropped. "Are you implying I'm slow?"

Clearly confused, Morwenna shook her head.

"You called me turtle and they are slow."

Morwenna blushed. "Sorry, I didn't realise I had, it must have just slipped out. But please don't be offended, it's a term of endearment, you see, and frequently used by my parents when addressing each other. And it doesn't mean turtle as in a tortoise, it means turtle as in turtle dove."

"Really, that's beautiful," said Elizabeth.

Morwenna smiled. "I think so too."

"Anyway, please let me introduce myself properly. My name is Elizabeth and it's really nice to meet you all because I've heard so much about you."

"Mum! That makes me sound like a gossip and I'm just not," Tally spluttered.

"There are others apart from you in the village, Tally, who have made observations regarding your new friends." She turned to the boys. "Right, so which of you lads is which, and who does what?"

"I'm Kev, the thicko, and I stock supermarket shelves."

"I'm Neil and I work in a mobile phone shop."

"I'm Rob, and I'm a trainee funeral director."

"Undertaker," roared Kev.

"I'm Mac, and I work for the Inland Revenue."

Elizabeth nodded. "I see, so what is Mac short for?"

Mac squirmed. "It's short for Mackenzie."

"Ah, so is that your Christian name?" persisted Elizabeth.

"Mum, don't ask so many questions," hissed Tally, annoyed.

"No, his Christian name is Wilfred, Wilfred Mackenzie," laughed Neil, slapping the table.

Tally's face dropped. "What! It's not, is it?"

Mac blushed. "Afraid so. Unfortunately I was named after my granddad. Don't get me wrong, he was a smashing bloke, but I just wish he'd had a cooler name, Wilfred's just so dead old fashioned and even if you shorten it you're left with Wilf or Fred, and they're both just as bad."

"That's the trouble with names, we seldom like our own," said Elizabeth, "although to be perfectly honest, I've never had a problem with mine."

"What's Tally short for?" asked Mac, concerned by the frown on her brow and the fact she had released his arm from her grip on hearing her name. "I've been meaning to ask for ages."

"Nothing," said Tally, gloomily.

"It's short for Talwyn," said Elizabeth, ignoring her daughter's pleading look. "It's an old Cornish name and we named Tally after one of the Penwyntons of long ago."

"Winnie," snorted Neil. "Like it! Wilf and Winnie."

"It's a pretty name," said Mac, scowling at Neil, "Talwyn and William, both nice names for your offspring, Mrs, C-H. Well done!"

"Actually, Wills isn't William," said Elizabeth, "he was named after his grandfather, Willoughby, and so his full name is Willoughby Edward Castor-Hunt."

Kev groaned. "And I'm just plain old Kevin Thomas, the supermarket shelf stocker."

Neil punched his arm. "Don't worry, turtle, we'll always love you whatever your name is."

Elizabeth turned to Morwenna who was listening to the banter, a look of amusement on her pretty face. "I do wish my grandmother was still around, Morwenna: from what I hear you and she would have had a lot in common. I refer to your studies of herbal medicines and suchlike."

"I should like to have met her," said Morwenna, "Tally's told me a little of her. Was she born in Trengillion?"

"Oh no, there was nothing Cornish about Grandma. I'm not quite sure where she actually grew up but she'd been here since before I was born. I think it was about 1952. Dad was teaching at a school in London back then and he came down here to convalesce after he'd been ill with something or other. Grandma joined him and while she was here she met Major Smith and they got married."

"She wasn't married before that then?"

"Well, yes, she was married to Dad's dad, but they got divorced because he ran off with his secretary. All a bit racy for back then."

The Over Sixties' Club members, who had gathered ready for their departure outside the remains of the village hall at ten o'clock, were, in spite of the weather, in high spirits. For the weather could not suppress the pleasure they took from meeting up. The outing gave them a chance to dress up, catch up with local gossip of which there was no shortage, and at the end of the day they knew they had a sing-song on the journey home to look forward to.

It was still raining when they had arrived in Mevagissey but this did not deter them from making the most of a different environment. So that no-one was left out or dragged off to do something they did not enjoy, they split up into three groups. One group went shopping, another went to look at the boats and chat to the fishermen, and the third went straight to the pubs.

Ned and Stella were in a group with Rose, George, Gertie and Betty; their choice of activity was for a brief browse round the shops and then go to a pub for lunch; seeing he looked a bit lost, George asked Robbie to join them. Robbie accepted with gratitude, much to the delight of Gertie and Betty; for since the ladies had discovered that he was not only dashingly handsome but also a successful writer, he had become quite a celebrity in the village.

Because the weather failed to improve they were all back on the mini bus before the allotted time and so at Ned's request, they left early and went on a detour to view the early stages of the Eden Project's construction. All were overwhelmed by the enormity of the project and agreed that when it was finished it would certainly be the destination for a future summer outing.

At the request of Madge, who because of her age, was very much aware that any outing might be her last, they called at another pub en route home, for it was custom to arrive back in Trengillion around nine o' clock, and they would have felt cheated had they returned home earlier.

At half past eight, with arms linked, each full of the joys of life, they returned to the mini bus huddled beneath umbrellas, laughing, joking and ready for the last part of the journey home. And even before the bus had left the car park, Sid Reynolds was leading the singing with his fine tenor voice.

It was ten minutes to nine when the mini bus turned off the main road and headed for Trengillion; the rain was lashing hard against the windows, but no-one noticed nor cared, everyone was heartily singing 'Trelawney', including Robbie, the driver, who had been a member of a male voice choir in Scotland and so had a passion for singing.

They passed Ebenezer House, where Jim was inside watching the television; they passed the cross roads and the main gates of the Penwynton Hotel, and just as they were approaching the village, from nowhere, a wet, tattered carrier bag blew up from the middle of the road. Robbie swore as it hit the windscreen and attached itself to the wipers. The wipers stopped, jammed in a vertical position and Robbie, unable to see, lost control. The bus swerved, left the road and toppled towards a ditch beneath an elm tree on which sat a solitary magpie.

Chapter Twenty Three

Robbie was unconscious by the time the mini bus came to a standstill, for although the seat belt he was wearing saved him from colliding with the windscreen, he still suffered a nasty blow when his head hit the driver's side window.

The passengers, however, with seat belts to restrain them, were not too badly thrown around, hence, as the bus finished up leaning on its side against the elm tree, everyone was still seated.

Fortunately the interior lights remained on throughout, and this enabled Ned, who deemed himself uninjured, to scramble to his feet and stumble outside by means of the emergency exit. Beside the back wheels of the mini bus, still spinning, and in a state of shock, he managed to press the nine digit three times on his mobile phone and call for much needed help.

In all, eight of the Club members were taken to hospital, and the others, mostly the younger ones, were allowed to go home after a quick check up. Thankfully, no-one suffered any life threatening injuries; bruising was the main damage, although one or two, including Madge, had broken limbs. Only Robbie, the driver, was severely concussed.

The following morning, Wednesday, Gertie was sitting by her living room window, resting her bruised ankle and wondering how the Club members who had been taken to hospital were faring. As she sighed, a Royal Mail van pulled up alongside the path. Hoping he might have something of interest for herself or Percy, she watched as the postman lifted out a parcel and carried it up the path of Number One, home of the Moores. Two minutes later he walked back down the path, parcel still in his hands. As he reached the van he saw Gertie in the window, he waved and opened the gate of Number Two. Gertie met him on the doorstep.

"This is for the folks next door but there's no-one in. Could I leave it with you?"

Certainly," said Gertie, eagerly, "they must be out because their car's not there. I'll pop it round as soon as I see them come back."

The postman thanked her, returned to his van and drove off.

After shaking, prodding and sniffing the brown paper all over, Gertie, unable to verify the contents, placed the parcel on her hall table. She felt rather excited as she returned to her chair, for at last she would have the chance to peep inside the Moores' house, a house she had known well many years ago when her daughter, Susan and son-in-law, Steve had lived there.

Two hours later, as Gertie was finishing off her lunch, she heard a car pull up in front of the houses. Without hesitation, she pushed her empty soup bowl to one side, rose from the kitchen table and hobbled into the living room. With a quick peep around the curtains she was just in time to see the Moores and their children walking up their garden path.

"I'll leave it for ten minutes," Gertie thought, gleefully clenching her fists, "after all, it's only fair to let them get settled before I call. Besides, I don't want them to think I've been spying on them."

Exactly ten minutes later, with parcel beneath her arm, Gertie hobbled up the path of Number One and rapped the brass knocker, firmly. From inside, she heard children's voices, but no-one answered the door. She rapped again, but still no-one replied. Knowing they were in, Gertie walked to the living room window hoping to get a glimpse inside through a chink in the curtains, but they were pulled tightly together. She tried the dining room window, but that was just the same. Frustrated, Gertie returned to the door, lay down the parcel on the path and peeped through the letterbox. To her surprise she saw the hallway was completely empty. No furniture, no shoes, just the carpet laid by the people who had moved in when Susan and Steve had gone to the Old School House many years before. Gertie was cross, and puzzled. She didn't like to be ignored, and so she hammered with renewed vigour and crashed the letterbox flap at the same time.

Presently, she heard the sound of someone opening the door. Quickly she composed herself and picked up the parcel. It was Trevor Moore who answered.

"Sorry to bother you," she said, in an un-Gertie-like sweet voice, "but the postman tried to deliver this earlier and you were out so he asked me to see that you got it."

"Oh, I see, thank you. Is it heavy?"

"Well, yes, fairly. Why?"

"Because I can't lift heavy things and Val's in the loo, but if…"

"That's no problem," said Gertie, ignoring his looks of discomfort, "I'll carry it in for you."

Without giving him a chance to respond, she crossed the threshold and marched down the hallway into the kitchen. In the kitchen doorway she stopped dead. The room was so bare. No pictures hung on the walls, the work surfaces were devoid of utensils, save a kettle. And in the corner, an old Formica top table and four utility chairs were the only pieces of furniture.

Gertie laid the parcel on the table and without seeking permission walked back into the hall and opened the dining room door. The room was absolutely empty and echoed as she closed the door. She then looked in the living room. A few toys lay on the carpet and cushions were scattered over the floor, but again the room was devoid of furniture.

"What on earth's going on?" asked Gertie, bluntly, her normal voice resumed. "Where's your furniture?"

She turned to see Valerie Moore standing at the top of the stairs, the two children by her side clutching her legs. Her face was pale and her bottom lip quivered.

"I'm sorry," said Gertie, suddenly ashamed of her discourteous behaviour, "I'm so sorry, I really don't know what came over me. Please ask me to leave and mind my own business."

As Gertie moved towards the front door, Valerie ran down the stairs and grabbed her arm. "No, please, please stay. Would you like a cup of tea?"

Trevor raised his eyebrows. Valerie read his thoughts.

"She's seen how we live now, so there's no longer any need to be so unsociable."

"Yes, please," said Gertie, feeling very uncomfortable, "but only if you're having one."

Valerie didn't answer. All returned to the kitchen. Valerie filled the kettle and took a box of cheap teabags from the cupboard, which Gertie was pleased to see did at least contain some food.

"Better sit down then," said Trevor, unsteadily sitting himself, as Valerie took mugs from another cupboard.

When the tea was made, Valerie also sat at the table and the children went to play in the living room.

"They gave us beds, she whispered, lowering her head, "so we do have something to sleep on."

"Who are they?" Gertie asked.

"The authorities or a charity, I'm not sure. It's all a bit of a blur," said Valerie, tears beginning to trickle down her cheeks. Trevor reached across the table and patted her shuddering hand. "I'll tell her," he said.

"My name's Gertie, by the way. Gertie Collins."

"And I'm Trevor, Trevor Moore and this is my wife, Valerie."

All nodded in acknowledgement.

"We used to live in Truro," said Trevor, leaning back in the chair, "and when we were first married we rented a tiny flat. But then we struck lucky and won enough money on the Lottery to buy a three bedroomed house with the aid of a loan from an aunt of mine. We spent everything on that house, new furnishings, electrical goods and gadgets. You name it, we had it all. I was a self-employed painter and decorator at the time, so even though we saved a few bob with the decorating, we still managed to blow the lot. Every damn sodding penny."

Gertie attempted to smile, puzzled, as she was unsure where the story might lead. "And?" she asked.

"One night I went down the pub with a mate and when I got in I opened a can of lager, put the telly on and lit a fag. Val was in bed and I should have joined her straight away because I was really tired. I'd been up early that morning, you see, to finish off a job in St Mawes. Anyway, I dozed off in the chair and then woke suddenly, switched off the telly and dashed to bed while I was still sleepy."

Tears welled in his dark eyes. Gertie was shocked, she hated to see a man cry.

"Don't blame yourself," said Valerie.

"I must, it was my fault, my own stupid fault." He lowered his head to hide his tears. "The cigarette I'd lit, but didn't finish, must have fallen down the side of the chair. I didn't see it, nor did I think of it. I left the room quickly and was asleep again as soon as my head hit the pillow. The fire…" His voice trailed away.

"It was our dog who raised the alarm," said Valerie, continuing for her husband. "He started to bark and it woke me up. When I opened the bedroom door I could smell smoke and ran downstairs to investigate. Foolishly, I opened the living room door and a ball of flames lashed out. I ran into the kitchen and dialled 999. When I went back into the hallway the stairs were on fire. I ran outside and woke the neighbours."

She looked at Trevor who had partly composed himself.

"Val's screams woke me," he said, "I grabbed the children from their beds, took them both into our room, closed the door and opened the window. Val was down below on the lawn with the neighbours, bless them, who were dragging mattresses from their own beds for us to jump onto."

"Everyone was so good," whispered Valerie, "they all tried so hard to help, but there wasn't time to think. The glass cracked and then shattered in the downstairs windows, and the heat of the flames which leaped from the burning frames forced us back. It was horrible. I could see Trevor with the children at the bedroom window, but there was nothing I could do."

"I could hear the flames on the landing outside the bedroom door," continued Trevor, "I knew time was running out. The children were both screaming. Everyone was screaming. In turn I threw the children down onto the mattresses and then I climbed onto the window sill ready to jump myself. I remember hearing a great whoosh. I looked behind, the flames had forced open the door. Then I lost my balance and toppled forward. As I fell my sleeve caught on the window latch and it threw me off course. I missed the mattress by inches and smashed my back against a stone urn. I don't remember anything after that."

"He was so brave," sobbed Valerie, "and the fire brigade arrived along with an ambulance, as he hit the ground. The girls were unscathed, but Trevor was unconscious. He was rushed off to hospital where tests showed he had broken his back in several places."

Gertie opened her mouth to speak but was unable to think of appropriate words.

"We all survived," said Trevor, "but at the same time we lost everything."

"Everything," repeated Valerie.

Gertie looked around the kitchen for a basket or old blanket but neither lay on the floor. "Does everything include your dog?" she asked, finding her voice.

Valerie nodded. "She was a beautiful black Labrador and her name was Esmeralda, we called her Esme for short. The children adored her."

Gertie looked puzzled. "I know it wouldn't have brought back your dear dog, but surely your house insurance covered you for the loss of the building, its contents and so forth."

Trevor laughed, sardonically. "We had no insurance. We spent all our money, a lot of which went on unnecessary things, but didn't have the nous to buy the most important thing of all, house and contents insurance. It was such a stupid thing to have done, but I suppose like so many others, we thought, fire and so forth would never happen to us. Anyway, knowing we'd never be able to afford a rebuild, we had no choice but sell off the burned out plot in order to repay my aunt, who, I might add was absolutely disgusted by my incompetence, and quite rightly too."

"The Council were ever so good," said Valerie, "they put me and the girls in Bed and Breakfast while Trevor was in hospital, but by the time he came out we knew he'd never be able to work again."

"It was a bitter pill to swallow," said Trevor, "knowing I'd never work again. And that on top of losing the house and everything, was a living nightmare. I wouldn't wish what we went through on my worst enemy."

"When they offered this house in Trengillion we took it," said Valerie, "because with Trev unable to work it didn't really matter where we were living."

"But, why didn't you tell anyone?" asked Gertie. "We'd all have rallied round to help."

"I was too ashamed," said Trevor, "too proud. And after all it wasn't an accident, was it? It was all caused by my own stupidity."

"We haven't even told our old neighbours where we are now," added Valerie, "we didn't want them to know we had no insurance. And so we deliberately lost touch to cover the embarrassment."

"Still, one good thing came out of it," said Trevor, attempting to put on a brave face, "It forced me to give up smoking, something I'd been trying to do for years."

"No! Two good things came out of it," smiled Gertie, standing to hug them each in turn, "You've been blessed with a new life here in Trengillion, and believe you me, it's all going to be uphill from now on."

When Gertie left the Moores' house she did not go home but walked determinedly down the road, caring not a jot about resting her bruised ankle. Her destination: Rose Cottage, where she hoped to find Ned and Stella. To her delight, both were in and sitting out on their front lawn, reading. On hearing the garden gate latch click, Ned and Stella simultaneously looked up. After giving a little wave, Gertie pottered along the path and sat down unceremoniously on the front door step. "I'm here for two reasons," she said, before either Ned or Stella had a chance to speak. "The first is, of course, to see how you both are and the other to ask a favour of you. You look awfully pale, Stella. Ought you not to go and see the doctor? We were told we must if we had any sort of relapse."

Stella smiled. "I'm fine, thanks, Gertie, still a bit shaken and my shoulder aches, but it could all have been so much worse. How are you?"

"I'm okay, got a few bruises and my damn ankle's showing off, but apart from that I've nothing to moan about."

"I popped in the post office this morning to ask if there was any news about Robbie and Madge," said Ned. "Nessie told me Madge is making very good progress and Robbie's on the mend too. Apparently it helped them getting prompt medical attention."

"Well, that's because of your mobile phone, Ned," said Gertie. "Percy and me were talking about it this morning and saying what a good thing you had it on you, otherwise we could all have been stuck there a lot longer."

"You're quite right," Ned conceded. "Even I have to admit that. Liz always said it'd come in useful one day."

"Absolutely: that's why Percy and me are going to get one each next time we're in Helston. Anyway, pushing mobile phones and the accident aside for a mo, as I said earlier, I've come to ask a favour, but it's not for me, it's for my new friends."

"Really," said Ned, smiling, as he lay his book on the grass amused by the fact Gertie had obviously been longing to tell the real reason for her visit whilst commenting on the accident. "So who might these new friends be?"

"My neighbours, you know, Trevor and Valerie Moore."

Stella gasped and leaned forward in her chair. "What! Since when have they been your friends? I'm told that only the other day you implied poor Trevor might have started the fire in the village hall and is likely to be growing cannabis."

Gertie squirmed. "I know, that was a real bitchy thing to say, but it's taught me to reserve judgment on people until I've learned the true facts. I was very harsh and I take back every cruel word I've ever uttered about the Moores. In fact, I take back every horrible thing I've ever said about anybody, and there have been plenty, I have to admit. You see, I know their story now, the Moores, that is, and believe me, Trevor Moore is the last person in Trengillion that would ever start a fire deliberately. The poor, poor man!"

"Well, now you've managed to have us both desperately intrigued perhaps you'll tell us what you've found out," said Stella, watching Gertie's head shake back and forth, "and then I'll put the kettle on."

"Certainly." Gertie then proceeded to relay the story she had learned from the new residents at Number One, Coronation Terrace. When she concluded her piece of news, it was Stella's turn to sit with head shaking back and forth.

"Oh, the poor, poor things. I can think of nothing worse than losing everything, especially through fire. And the poor little dog! How terribly sad. The fire in the village hall must have brought back some horrendous memories, Gert."

"Hmm, and I assume the favour you wish to ask has something to do with our surplus furniture," said Ned, thoughtfully.

"Well, yes, it just seems to me..."

"Say no more, Gert. As far as I'm concerned they're welcome to as much of it as they want, all of it even. What say you, Stella?"

"Absolutely, I agree, of course. My sister said some time back there's nothing else of Mum and Dad's that she wants, and Liz and Greg don't want any of their old stuff either, so it's all in need of a good home as far as I'm concerned."

Ned nodded. "And I'm sure Anne and John will be relieved too, because it means they'll be able to find another use for their garage."

Gertie clapped her hands gleefully. "I knew you'd help. So is it alright with you if I nip back now and tell them? They don't know anything about your furniture yet, because I thought I better ask before I said anything."

Stella rose. "Have a cup of tea first and then I'll go back with you. Once done, I'll ring Anne and then we'll take the Moores to the Old Vicarage to see what they'd like. And if he's willing, your John can then drop whatever they want round to them in the truck this evening."

"I think," said Iris, sitting on a sun-lounger in the front garden of Cove Cottage on Wednesday afternoon, "that since the weather looks to be fairly settled for the next few days, it might be nice to have a barbecue on the beach this Friday for the locals and the holiday makers who came down for the eclipse. It's been such a nice break and I've no idea how long it'll be before I can get down again. What do you think, Rusty?"

"Whatever you like. It's a nice gesture and I must admit I do feel sorry for the locals. They've had a rough time lately, what with the loss of their village hall, all the mishaps and the dreadful accident on the way back from the outing last night."

"Yes, I know, poor lambs, but at the same time I think it's drawn some folks closer together. You know, a bit like during the War, not that either of us were around then of course."

"We'll need to get a barbecue," said Rusty, lazily, "unless you've got one tucked away somewhere unbeknown to me."

"No, I haven't and I suppose for things to run smoothly we'll need more than one. You'll also need someone to get help with the cooking. I don't want to stink of smoke and I shall be looking after the drinks anyway, that's more my line."

"I'll ask Greg. I like him and we had a smashing chat in the pub on eclipse night. I think we ought to start the barbecue quite early, too, because it would be nice to go to the pub later, seeing as it'll be our last night here."

"Good idea, and we don't want to take trade away from Justin anyway. He's such a nice bloke, in fact we'll ask him if he can get away for a while to join us."

In due course Rusty went shopping and bought two large barbecues and Iris put up notices around the beach, in the post office window and with Justin's permission, inside the Jolly Sailor. And finally she called at the Pickled Egg with one for Jane.

That same afternoon, youngsters from the village gathered with their new friends in the recreation groud and amongst other things, discussed the accident involving Trengillion's elderly residents.

"I hope poor Robbie gets better soon," said Jess, "and that his lovely face wasn't injured."

"Serve him right if it was for inflicting those horrid bagpipes on us at the talent contest," said Morwenna, unsympathetically.

"I can't agree with you there," chortled Neil, "I thought he was a good sport doing that. Nessie too. It certainly made me laugh."

"My horoscope predicted bad news yesterday," said Tally, leaning her head on the iron chain supporting the motionless swing on which she sat. "I'm so glad no-one was seriously hurt."

Demelza was clearly impressed. "Did it really?"

"Yes, poor old things."

Rob frowned. "Humph, that's probably the first time a horoscope has ever been accurate. They're usually a complete waste of space."

Demelza ignored Neil's remark. "What's your birth sign, Morwenna?"

Morwenna shook her head. "I don't know."

"Really? When is your birthday?"

"August the eleventh."

"Wow, eclipse day," said Demelza, surprised.

"That makes you Leo, Morwenna," said Tally. "Leo is a fire sign ruled by the sun."

"I like it," laughed Neil, "fancy having a birthday on the day of the eclipse when you're ruled by the sun. It's kind of weird and freaky."

"I'm Taurus the Bull," said Mac, "I know that because my sister told me. What sign are you, Tally? Not that I have any interest in such things."

"I'm Aries, the Ram and a fire sign. How about you, Demelza?"

"I'm Pisces, the Fish and a water sign."

"I think I might be that too," said Kev.

Tally smiled. "You think, don't you know for sure?"

"Well, it sounds sort of familiar."

"When's your birthday?" Tally asked.

Kev wrinkled his nose. "It's a bit of a tricky one really. I was born on February the twenty ninth, you see."

"Wow, so you were a leap-year baby," said Demelza, "how fascinating. So when do you celebrate your birthday?"

"On the twenty eighth because I was born shortly after midnight which makes it the nearest to the twenty ninth."

"In 1980, I assume."

"That's right."

Rob did a quick calculation using his fingers. "So, if you only have a real birthday every four years then on your next birthday you'll only be five." He gave Kev a friendly slap. "Be time for you to start school then."

Kev ignored Rob and turned to Demelza. "So does that make me a Pisces like you?"

She nodded. "Yes, it does."

"Cool."

Tally smiled. "That doesn't mean you're compatible, Kev,"

His face dropped. "Doesn't it?"

Tally shook her head. "Having said that two people of the same sign may well get along fine." She sighed. "It's all rather complicated and there are many conflicting views anyway."

"I don't seem to be any good when it comes to girls, love and all that stuff," said Kev, "so I don't expect I'll ever get married and settle down."

Lucy tilted her head sympathetically. "Don't be silly, Kev. You're still very young, as are all of us, and everything comes to he who waits."

Morwenna nodded. "Quite right, and of course, the course of true love never did run smooth."

"Shakespeare," said Tally.

"Spot on," said Morwenna, "*A Midsummer Night's Dream*, written in 1598, and never were truer words spoken."

Rob nudged Kev's arm. "There you are, Kev, a quote from the Bard himself…the course of true love never did run smooth. I like it."

Kev, nonplussed, quickly changed the subject. "So who writes the horoscopes you read, Tally?"

Tally giggled. "Taffeta Tealeaves and she writes in the magazine *Love-in-a-Mist*, but I daresay it's not her real name."

"*Love-in-a-Mist*," said Morwenna with a frown, "what a strange name."

"Oh, do you think so? I've always considered it to be rather charming," said Tally, "it takes its name from the flower, of course."

Tally saw that Morwenna looked puzzled. "Oh come on, Wen, you must have heard of love-in-a-mist. The flowers are blue or white and are really pretty, as are the delicate feathery leaves."

Morwenna shrugged her shoulders. "Doesn't sound familiar but then I'd probably recognise it if I saw one." She suddenly laughed. "I do know what a sweet pea looks like though because Jim has them growing at his allotment. They smell absolutely gorgeous too and their name means blissful pleasure, goodbye and thank you for the lovely time we had. Isn't that wonderful?"

Tally smiled. "Yes it is, and they are very pretty too. My grandparents have them growing in their front garden at Rose Cottage but I didn't know what their name meant. I must admit it's very romantic."

Neil nodded. "Hmm, if these sweet pea things mean goodbye and so forth, we might have to give bunches of them to you girls when we go home on Saturday."

Chapter Twenty Four

The village hall had finally stopped smouldering and on Thursday morning fire officers were able to access the remains in order to try and establish the cause of the fire. Several hours later, grapevine news indicated that there seemed to be no evidence of arson and the most likely reason was an electrical fault. However, the investigation was ongoing and would continue until officers were completely satisfied that no criminal activity had taken place.

Most of Trengillion's inhabitants were slightly relieved to hear this news, even though there was still a modicum of uncertainty and the disclosure was not official. But for some the source of the fire was of little interest, for establishing it would not bring back their hall.

In the afternoon, Gertie called round to see Trevor and Valerie Moore. As she walked up their path she saw the curtains were pulled back in both front room windows and her knock was answered instantly.

"I was just thinking," said Gertie, as Valerie beckoned her inside, "there's Karaoke on at the Jolly Sailor tonight and I think you ought to go, that's if you you'd like to."

Trevor, sitting at the kitchen table doing a crossword, sighed. "Lovely idea. From a musical point of view I'm tone deaf, but Val has a nice voice and likes singing, but we won't be able to go because of the children."

"But, that's why I'm here," said Gertie, proudly, "I'm volunteering to baby-sit. I'm well qualified being the mother of three and grandmother of four, even if they are all grown up now."

"Are you sure?" Valerie asked, her face flushed with excitement. "I mean, won't you be wanting to go yourself?"

"I'm getting a bit long in the tooth for making a fool of myself and so I'd much rather you went."

"Then we'd love to go," said Valerie, her eyes shining, "we've not been out for ages and it'd do Trev good to get out and socialise. It's no life for him stuck at home all day with me and the kids."

"Good, well Karaoke starts at half past eight, so if it's alright with you I'll come round just after eight. Now, will you be alright to walk down, Trevor, or would you like Percy to give you a lift. I wouldn't advise you to take your car because there's not a great deal of room for parking, especially this time of the year."

"I can walk a short distance like that, so I'll be alright as long as I can sit down when I get there."

"That won't be a problem because some of my friends are going and so I'll ask them to save you both a seat. They always go early when it's likely to be busy so that they don't have to stand."

"Brilliant, thanks, Gertie. I can't believe I ever thought you were a misery."

"Did you indeed," laughed Gertie, bustling towards the door. "I must go now because I left a cake in the oven. See you later."

Jim Haynes spent Thursday working up at Long Acre Farm harvesting along with Tony Collins. When he finished at seven o'clock, he decided to walk home by way of the coastal path thinking the fairly long stretch might help ease his aching back. As he passed the row of Coastguard Cottages he caught sight of Matthew and Rebecca Williams seated in the front garden of their house, eating their dinner.

"Something smells good," he commented, leisurely passing their gate.

Rebecca smiled. "Chicken and bacon lasagne. We're eating early tonight because we thought we'd give the Karaoke a go. We've missed the last two."

Jim slapped his forehead. "Damn, I'd forgotten about that. Had I remembered I'd have taken the quicker route home. Now I shall be hard pushed to get there for when it starts."

"Well, I don't think much happens 'til the drink flows a bit," said Matthew. "Most people are too self-conscious and I for one don't usually join in 'til the end. In fact old Sid Reynolds seems to be the only one who has the guts to sing whilst sober."

Jim nodded. "Yes, dear old Sid. I don't know whether or not he'll make it tonight though, I've heard he's still a bit shaken because of the old folks' accident. I hope he does though, because I think it's nice to see all the generations having a laugh together and so many things today are age divisive. Anyway, must go or I won't even get there for the grand finale."

Jim walked quickly for the rest of his journey home, eager to get to the Karaoke in good time to see Morwenna. For even if he had no reason to speak to her, there was nothing to stop him admiring her from afar.

When Ebenezer House finally came into view he heaved a sigh of relief. But before he went indoors he checked his produce stall and emptied money from the cashbox. To his delight he had done well; all money seemed present and correct and only a few carrots and runner beans were left unsold. Jim picked up the unsold goods, placed them in one of the boxes he kept beneath the stall, carried them up to his front door and rested them on the step.

Before he went inside, he walked back down the path to see if he had any mail in his post box, and to his surprise he found a white envelope addressed to The Gardener. Puzzled Jim opened the envelope and inside found a ten pound note along with a brief letter.

Dear Gardener,

Please find enclosed £10 for produce recently taken from your stall. My wife and I are on holiday and staying over at Polquillick and we came across your excellent stall whilst out walking the other day. But as neither of us had any money on us we took the produce with every intention of returning with the money later in the evening. Regrettably though the head gasket went on our car that night - Friday the 13th if you remember - and so we've been somewhat prepossessed getting that sorted. Anyway, here is the money now with a little added interest.

Sorry for any inconvenience caused,
With regards,
Bill Grayling.

The smile on Jim's face stretched from ear to ear, "It's just so good," he said, "to know there are still a lot of decent, honest folk out there."

Once inside the chapel he took a pizza from his freezer, popped it in the oven and while it was cooking took a quick shower in order to get to the Jolly Sailor as quickly as possible.

Karaoke had become a popular and regular event at the inn since Justin had first introduced it in early February. And though it usually started off with only competent singers with pleasant voices taking to the floor, it could be guaranteed that by closing time even the bashful had been lured by the microphone and the evening usually ended with a chorus of the inebriated along with the untalented.

Ned, Stella, Rose and George were already at the inn when the Moores arrived, whereupon Ned and George, having received a phone call from Gertie, beckoned them over to their reserved seats in the snug.

Morwenna arrived just in time to greet Lucy as she emerged from the dining room with her parents, two brothers, and sister, Angie. All were in high spirits due to Lucy's excellent A-Level results which she had received that morning.

Lucy took Morwenna's arm and the two girls went to watch the karaoke. Angie meanwhile met up with boyfriend, Sam Bingham, who was chatting to his brother, Charlie.

"Your mum and dad are obviously pleased with your results," said Morwenna, picking up a list of Karaoke songs. "Your mum's positively beaming."

Lucy giggled. "I should be able to get away with murder for a day or two now; they're as pleased as punch. I did better than I ever dared hope."

During the course of the evening Morwenna learned of the Moores' misfortune; after which she seemed subdued and for a while even lost her usual sparkle. In particular she seemed saddened by Trevor's back injury which had made it impossible for him to work.

A little later, while Lucy was being questioned about her A-Level results by Jess Collins, Valerie left her seat and went to sing. Morwenna seeing her leave, quickly took her place beside Trevor.

"Where does your back hurt?" she asked.

Trevor, enjoying a pint of real ale was surprised by her question. "Everywhere," he said, "here, there and everywhere, depending on the time of day and what I've been doing."

Morwenna frowned. "Yes, but which part does the pain appear to stem from?"

Trevor, realising she was serious, pointed to the most troublesome parts of his back.

She lifted his T shirt. "I will cure you."

"Really?"

She nodded. "Yes."

Trevor took a sharp intake of breath as she touched his back. "Yikes! Your hands are freezing."

"Sorry, but you must keep still."

Trevor's expression was a cross between embarrassment and ecstasy. He hoped Valerie would understand if she noticed this weird but very attractive young woman caressing his back. But Valerie was oblivious of his therapy and sang, 'I will always love you', the song she and Trevor regarded as their song, for it was in the charts when they had first met in November 1992.

Skillfully, Morwenna continued to knead, rub and massage parts of Trevor's back with her slim hands. He felt his temperature rise and so put down his pint glass. He felt strangely on edge, and at one point he thought he was going to faint.

"Done," said Morwenna, abruptly, dropping his shirt. "Your back will never trouble you again."

"Thanks," said Trevor, dubious and amused by her conviction, for all types of physiotherapy, acupuncture and remedies had been tried but nothing had had a lasting effect.

"You don't believe me?"

"I'd like to, but I have to admit I'm very, very sceptical about jiggery-pokery."

Morwenna laughed as she stood. "Jiggery-pokery indeed, you'll see."

"When Valerie's song finished, Morwenna promptly left and joined Mac, Kev, Neil and Rob who had just arrived and were chatting to Lucy, Jess, Wills and Charlie Bingham.

"You alright?" Valerie asked, taking a seat, her faced flushed by the sound of spontaneous applause. "You look rather smug."

"Do I? You did well: that's not an easy song to sing."

"Hmm, but that's no reason for your seeming smug."

Trevor laughed. "You always were very astute, Val. My smugness is because she reckons she cured my back. Morwenna, that is. You know, the girl over there with the long black hair. What do you think? It'd be brilliant if she had."

Val looked puzzled. "Hmm, and how, may I ask, has she cured it?"

Trevor shrugged his shoulders. "To be honest I haven't the foggiest idea. For some reason I didn't like to ask in case she scolded me, because well, she looks that sort. But it was probably Reiki, something like that anyway. But whatever, it was the most enjoyable treatment I've ever had, in spite of her cold hands. So I won't be too upset if it fails and I need a second dose."

From his seat on a stool by the bar, Jim Haynes, whilst chatting to John and Anne Collins caught Morwenna's eye. She promptly waved and beckoned him towards her. Jim excused himself from John and Anne and eagerly went to her side.

"You must join me for a song," she smiled, handing him a laminated list. "You choose."

"What! But I can't sing, not very well anyway."

"Neither can most other people here. Come on, it'll be fun and something to remember me by. After all I shall be gone soon."

The thought of her gone brought a lump to Jim's throat. "Okay, but you choose something and I'll tell you whether or not I know it."

Morwenna nodded but after looking through the list, she sighed. "Oh dear. Nothing seems to jump out at me."

Jim looked relieved. "How about you sing something and I just listen."

Morwenna laughed. "Coward." She turned to Lucy. "I heard a song the other day playing on someone's radio. It was really pretty but I don't know what it was. Can you help me?"

Lucy shrugged her shoulders. "I'll give it a go, if you can sing or hum a bit of it."

Morwenna hummed a few notes.

"That's 'Unchained Melody'," said Lucy. "It was a big hit donkey's years ago when my parents were kids but it became popular again because of *Ghost*."

"*Ghost!*" Morwenna repeated. "What do you mean?"

Lucy looked taken aback. "I mean the film with Patrick Swazi and Demi Moore. You must have seen it."

Morwenna shook her head. "Anyway, whatever it is or wherever it's from doesn't matter, but that's what I'd like to sing for Jim."

"But it's a love song," said Jim, feeling himself blush.

"Most are, turtle," she said, turning to put in her request.

Chapter Twenty Five

Elizabeth woke early on Friday morning and knowing she wouldn't be able to get back to sleep she got up, made a mug of tea and went outside where she sat on a grassy patch outside the garden gate of Chy-an-Gwyns, watching the sun rise over the old mine on the cliffs across the bay.

The morning was cool in spite of the first rays of sun glinting through the thin cloud, lighting up the spot where she sat. The air smelled clean and fresh, like newly laundered washing, its fragrance enriched by the sweet scent of honeysuckle creeping across the privet hedge, its curved stems firmly grasped by the leaves of a deep ruby red clematis.

When she finished her tea, she lay down her empty mug on the grass and leaned back her head on the granite gatepost. The morning was beautiful. The sun was fully out. The sea stretched as far as the eye could see, its surface sparkling as though sprinkled with dazzling crystals; while above, a brilliant azure sky hinted the probability of a warm sunny day.

Absently, Elizabeth watched a fluffy white cloud as it drifted in slowly from the distant horizon; as it reached the shore it temporarily blocked out the sun and then floated away over the village and inland.

A gentle breeze ruffled Elizabeth's hair. 'A good day for drying washing,' she thought, optimistically. She then remembered she had promised throughout the summer to wash the drawing room curtains. She returned her mug to the kitchen and walked to the drawing room where she proceeded to remove the curtains from the curved brass track.

"Is there anything you'd like us to do for you?" Rob asked Justin, as he and his friends descended the stairs on Friday morning, heading for the dining room and breakfast. "I feel we ought to do something to help earn our keep and we'll be gone tomorrow, so it'll be too late then."

"Well, actually you could do the bottling up for me. I've a dental appointment at ten o'clock, so it'd save me some time as I'm running late. I was going to leave the cleaner a note asking her to do it when she'd finished the bar, but if you'd do it it'd save her the bother."

"Brilliant, of course we will. Shall we do it now?"

"No, have your breakfast first and then come into the bar when you've finished. I'll still be there and I'll show you what's what."

Accordingly after breakfast the boys met with Justin in the bar and he took them through the trap door to the beer cellar where bottles and barrels were stored.

"Blimey, look at all the pipes," said Kev. "So that's how the beer gets to the pumps. Silly, but I'd never thought about how it got up there before."

Justin grinned. "Please don't disturb any of the barrels, especially the real ales. The bottles are all over there."

He pointed to crates stacked down the side of one wall. "I won't insult you by telling you how to bottle up as it's pretty elementary, but you'll find a note pad beside the till to write a list on, unless of course you have infallible memories. I must go now, thanks for your help and I'll see you later."

When he was gone the boys looked around the cellar. "I wouldn't want to be down here for too long," grumbled Rob, rubbing his arms to dispel goose pimples, "it's flipping freezing."

"Bit like the mortuary, eh Rob, I'd have thought it'd make you feel at home."

"Ha ha, come on let's go upstairs and see what's needed."

When they had crates full of the necessary bottles to fill the numerous gaps, they quickly topped up the shelves.

"Do it neater than that," commanded Kev, scowling with disapproval, "the labels need to face outwards."

"Yeah, but this isn't your poxy supermarket, is it?" laughed Neil, "I'm sure the punters won't give a toss whether the labels are straight or not."

"No, but Justin will, I've noticed before how neat and precise everything is here and I don't want him to think we can't even do a simple job like bottling up."

"Kev's right," said Mac, "put 'em straight, Neil."

"I'm gonna miss this place," said Rob, watching the cleaning lady walk through the bar towards the toilets with a mop, and bucket full of steaming hot water, delicately scented with pine disinfectant, "I've really enjoyed this holiday and I don't want to go home one jot."

Mac nodded. "Same here. In fact I shall definitely come back again another year, maybe even next, and meantime I hope to keep in touch with Tally. She's already given me her address for when she's back at university."

"Hmm, and I might even send Demelza a Christmas card," grinned Kev. "Our last night should be good anyway. Demelza tells me the local band Iris has got is really brilliant. And I agree with you about coming back again, because it'd be great to see everyone again. How about you two?"

Neil nodded, as he straightened the last of the bottles. "I'll keep in touch with Lucy because she's a great laugh, but they'd never be anything serious between us because I don't think we're that compatible. Having said that, I'd like to see her again and she'll be off to university too in the autumn. But students get damn long holidays, don't they? So that's no problem."

"Before we come back again, I think we ought to try and save up some money," said Mac, "that way we'll be able to stay in here all the time. Being indoors is so much better than sleeping in a miserable tent, unless of course the weather's brilliant, but you can never be sure of that in this country, can you?"

"You've got a good point there," said Neil, "because if we did stay here we wouldn't have to wait 'til summer, we could come back in the winter when the sea's crazy and the fire will be lit. In fact if we came down at Christmas, the girls would be back then too."

Rob looked dejected. "Yeah, it's alright for you lot, you're lucky. But Morwenna's on holiday, isn't she? So whenever we come back she won't be here." He sighed. "I'd say the chances of me ever seeing her here again are zilch."

Kev pulled a mock sympathetic face. "Poor you, turtle, but if you remember the lady in question said the path of love wasn't smooth or something like that, so you might see her again."

Rob scowled. "Actually to be precise, it's the course of true love never did run smooth."

"There you are then," said Neil, "you just gotta be patient."

Rob shook his head. "No, I'll never see her again and to be honest I think she's more interested in Ebenezer Jim than me anyway. I mean, it's obvious he likes her because he went all gooey when she sang that soppy song to him last night."

"Yeah, but she doesn't go gooey over him like he does her. I think she only likes him because she thinks living amongst the spooks is gothish."

"I dunno, I get the impression she's quite smitten with him."

"Smitten, eh," laughed Neil, "that's the sort of word my granny uses. Look the sun's shining, let's go for a quick dip and then we can play football for an hour until lunch."

"How can you think of lunch already, we've only just had breakfast."

"No, that was well over an hour ago, it's coming up for eleven now and I'm already feeling peckish. Anyway, we'll need to eat early today so we've lots of room left for all the lovely grub Iris will be showering us with later."

"Cool! And I think for today's lunch we must go the Pickled Egg, because I rather fancy one of their pasties and today will be our last chance."

As Justin drove into Trengillion on his return from Helston, he passed Doctor Owen emerging from the post office. Minutes later, as he was taking shopping from the boot of his car outside the inn, she turned the corner, crossed the cobbles and kissed him on the cheek.

"I nearly stopped to offer you a lift, Morgana," he grinned, lowering three carrier bags to the ground, "but it seemed a bit pointless when you were nearly here."

"And I'm not staying anyway," she said, gaily, skipping from foot to foot, "I'm on my way down to the beach for a large ice cream, but thought I'd just stop to say hello en route. How was the dentist?"

"Fine, it was only a checkup and no treatment is needed, thank goodness. You've bought a book I see. Surely you didn't find one on wild flowers or astronomy in our humble post office."

"I did not, nor did I want to either. I sought and found something a little more light hearted, you see, and I'm happy with my purchase."

She held up the book so that he might see the cover. To his surprise it was a frivolous romance, the type where the heroine always gets her man or vice versa. He laughed, life just wasn't like that!

"I must go," she said, leaning forward to kiss his cheek again, "or it will be time to return and change for the barbecue before I've even got my teeth into the book. I hope you're still going to that, the barbecue that is."

"Of course, Morgana, I wouldn't miss it or your wonderful company for anything."

She smiled coyly and with a pronounced wiggle, walked away without glancing back. Justin watched until she was out of sight.

"Roll on this evening," he grinned, lecherously rubbing his hands.

Chapter Twenty Six

In the hallway of the Jolly Sailor, Justin, laden with shopping, was greeted by Demelza hanging up her fleece having just arrived for the lunchtime shift. Inside the kitchen he found Maurice frantically drinking from a pint glass containing cold water and ice cubes which rattled with every soothing guzzle.

"Christ, Mo, looks like you might have overdone it last night," sighed Justin, "I thought you and Ian looked a bit sloshed and when you both sang I knew you were."

"Oh for Pete's sake, did we sing? I can't remember much after I'd finished cooking and the end of the night is a complete blur. God only knows how I ever got home or how I'll get through the rest of today. I shall have to lie down after lunch and I've only just got up."

"Well, thank goodness you don't have to cook breakfast these days," Justin tutted, "otherwise the guests might have had a long wait this morning."

"Ugh, I couldn't have done it. The sight of fried eggs would have made me sick."

"Dad took you home," said Demelza, filling the condiment sets as she listened to the chat, "and Mum told me he put you to bed too."

Maurice groaned. "That's all I need, the whole village will know by now."

Demelza tried to look offended. "Are you saying my mum's a gossip?"

"Well, Sue certainly does…um…um, you know, like her mother, Gertie, she um…"

Justin came to his chef's rescue. "Well, I hope Ian feels a lot better than you, gazing into people's mouths must be nauseating when you're hung-over. I'm glad he wasn't my dentist this morning."

"He should be alright, I do remember he stuck to beer, but being a silly sod I went onto whisky."

Demelza giggled. "And then liquors, you tried several. In fact you emptied the Drambuie bottle."

"That's enough about drink," said Maurice, feeling his innards churning, "and instead let's go back to the karaoke. Break it to me gently. What did Ian and me sing?"

Unable to control the giggles, Demelza spilt salt over the floor.

Justin chuckled. "You sang, 'You're the one that I want' from *Grease*, and you took the part of Sandy. It was a hoot!"

Inside the Old Vicarage, Jess quickly drank a mug of coffee and took a handful of custard creams from the biscuit tin. Her mother, who was putting away shopping following a trip into town, tutted.

"You really should get up earlier, Jess, it's not fair to Jane to be late and the same goes for any job. Punctuality is a virtue."

"Yes, yes, I know, Mum, you tell me every day, but getting up sucks and I am supposed to be on holiday."

"Are you ever punctual for your lectures?" Anne asked.

Jess turned away to hide the guilty look she knew betrayed her. "Um, I do my best," she answered, feebly.

Anne shook her head as Jess dashed for the door to avoid further questions.

"See you later, Mum. Enjoy your day off. Love you."

Outside, as the fresh air cooled her burning face, Jess rapidly ate the biscuits as she hurried down the driveway. Her mother was right of course, Jess was only too aware of that, but she didn't need to be reminded every day. If the truth be known Jess severely lacked motivation and she felt her life was going in the wrong direction. To be fair she had not been pushed into a university education, she had gone through choice, but at times she doubted it would ever serve any purpose other than to boost her ego should she achieve a degree of any note.

As she passed the post office Mary Cottingham emerged looking as sprightly as ever, having delivered a poster for display in the post office window advertising a Murder Mystery weekend scheduled to take place at the Hotel in the autumn. They briefly exchanged pleasantries.

Jess hurriedly continued on her way. It was all very well for her mother to remonstrate, she thought, for she had known from a very early age what she wanted to do on leaving school, that being to work at the Penwynton Hotel. Hence she'd left school at sixteen with just her O-Levels, knowing that was more than sufficient to achieve her objective. She sighed, her mother had obviously made the right choice for she had returned to the Hotel years later in spite of the fact that there was no financial need and was still there.

Jess arrived at the Pickled Egg, flustered and breathless, just as Jane was opening up.

"I'm so sorry," she panted, "really I am. I bet you'll be glad to see the back of me in September."

Jane smiled. "No, no, not at all: in a funny sort of way you remind me of myself when I was your age. Come on in."

"But surely you were never a scatterbrain like me," said Jess, somewhat surprised. "I mean this place is a success and Mum and Dad tell me it's all your own doing. You could never have been as disorganised as me."

"Yes, you're right, this is all my own doing, but there was a time when I felt I was in a rut. I worked in a shoe shop after I left school, you see, and hated the fact my friends had Saturdays off when I had to work. It made me very discontented and I must admit, I felt dreadfully hard done by."

"Really! So what happened? How did you get this place started?"

Jane tipped the contents of several money bags into the open till. "I had a boyfriend who was a chef at the Penwynton Hotel and he got me interested in catering. At the time Dad and your Granddad Percy owned these premises, well actually they still do and I pay them a modest rent. I saw the need for a café here, something like the beach café in Polquillick, and so I took a gamble and went for it. I must admit it's been more successful than I ever dreamt it could be, and Ben was right, he said it'd be a goldmine."

Jess nodded. "I should do something like you because I'm not really an academic. I like doing things and being creative like Mum and Dad. Mum's brill when it comes to gardening and decorating and Dad's a top notch builder, everyone says so."

"Does Ollie enjoy building?"

"Oh, yeah, and Dad says he's getting really good, so one day he and Denzil should be able to take over when Dad and Uncle Steve want to retire."

"Good idea, keep it in the family. I sometimes wish I had someone to take over from me, but I'll never have children now: it's much too late."

"How about Matthew and Rebecca, do they want children?"

"I don't know but I hope so. Mum's longing to be a granny although she never complains, but it must be frustrating to see that her lifelong friend, Gertie, has four grandchildren."

"One of which is me," giggled Jess.

"Yes, one of which is you. Will you and Ollie be twenty one next birthday?"

"Yes, and on New Year's Eve too, so what with that and the Millennium it'll be a big night of celebrations."

"Good heavens, yes, won't it?"

"I'm glad you see yourself in me," mused Jess, thoughtfully, as she took a lettuce from the vegetable rack and plunged it into cold water. "It's a wonderful compliment and has given me hope. Because now I believe there probably is something out there waiting for me, I just need to find it."

Jane patted her arm. "Yes, I'm sure there is. You have personality, Jess, oodles of it and with the dedication you must have inherited from both your parents, I don't see how you can fail. Just be patient and keep an open mind, and then one day, hopefully, the opportunity you've been waiting for will show itself."

Jess nodded. "I will."

"Good girl."

"And have you got everything you've ever wanted from life?"

Jane laughed. "Not quite. When I was a girl I always rather fancied playing the piano. Mum had lessons when she was young but said she wasn't musical enough to enjoy it and Dad was much the same so the opportunity never arose for me. Silly really, but it's still something I wish I'd done, but I never will now and I couldn't fit one in here anyway."

"You could get a keyboard," Jess suggested.

"I know, I tinkled around a bit on one they had for sale at the Christmas bazaar last year, but I knew then I'd never get on with it. I mean it's just not the same, is it?"

Jess nodded in agreement. "A bit like riding a moped when you long to drive a car. I mean, they'd both get you from A to B, but one would seriously lack style, elegance and poise."

Jane laughed. "I couldn't have put it better myself."

Inside Rose Cottage, Stella entered the living room with a bunch of brightly coloured dahlias which she had gathered from the garden. She handed them to Elizabeth who had called to visit her parents for a chat.

"Before you go down to the churchyard would you be a dear and post a letter for me, please? It will save me going out."

Elizabeth rose with the flowers. "Of course."

Stella took the letter from the sideboard and handed it to Elizabeth who dropped it into her pocket. "I think I'll get off now before these flowers start to droop."

Inside the churchyard, Elizabeth replaced the wilting sweet peas on her grandmother's grave with the fresh dahlias, she then discarded the dying flowers onto the compost heap and returned to the gravel path which ran all around the church.

As she walked towards the lichgate she could see in the far corner a young woman sitting amongst the oldest graves. Elizabeth shaded her eyes from the sun; the woman was dressed in black and was chattering freely, yet she appeared to be alone. For some reason Elizabeth was curious, especially so when she realised the person was Morwenna.

Leaving the path she walked amongst the graves towards the area where Morwenna sat, but when she got there Morwenna had gone. Elizabeth cast her eyes around the graveyard. Morwenna was nowhere to be seen but on the spot where she'd sat, lay a tiny posy of red and white clover. Elizabeth knelt and picked up the posy. Above it towered a crooked gravestone, cracked down one side and part covered with green and yellow lichen. Elizabeth ran her hand across the stone's surface; the inscription was illegible but she was just able to make out one word, the name Cardew.

Chapter Twenty Seven

Iris Delaney, very much aware that she would have to return to the hustle and bustle of her career and life in the media spotlight the following day, pulled on a lightweight jacket having decided to take a walk. Rusty had gone into Helston to collect burgers, sausages and sesame seed buns from the butchers and bakers, hence she knew she would not be missed and there was not much she could do until his return anyway.

Given the choice, Iris would have preferred to walk along the coastal path, but to do so would inevitably mean she would encounter holiday makers who would want to chat and ask for autographs, and because it was her last day, she wanted to walk alone with her thoughts unhindered by small talk, as so often was the case when listening to unbridled flattery and sweet compliments from the general public.

Iris left Cove Cottage and walked through the village wearing a multi-coloured headscarf and dark glasses until she reached the top of the lane between the school and the School House. There, hoping no-one would be around, she removed the scarf, draped it around her neck, and pushed the glasses onto the top of her head amongst her blonde curls.

The morning sun was shining brightly as she sauntered down the hill, glad to be alive and thankful that her lifestyle permitted her the opportunity to savour precious moments such as those spent in Trengillion. For prior to the purchase of Cove Cottage, her only refuge had been a visit to her parents' home in Sussex, where she could be sure her mother would not let the media or the general public within a hundred yards of her.

At the bottom of the hill, Iris sat on the granite wall of the bridge overlooking the stream and thought of Rusty. Poor Rusty! He really had had a rough time. Well, perhaps not rough, but he certainly hadn't enjoyed a lifestyle such as she, neither before nor after she had become famous. This meant there were times when she felt a little bitter towards her mother for having abandoned him so.

Iris picked up a twig, threw it into the stream and then crossed the road to watch it emerge from beneath the bridge on the other side.

If her mother had not put Rusty up for adoption then she would always have had a big brother to look up to and play with, especially during the long winter days when the weather was too inclement to play outdoors with her friends. As it was she had spent her formative years believing she was an only child, unaware she had a sibling until he had stepped into her life just two years back.

On the other hand she could see her mother's point of view. She had a career on the stage, albeit modest, and she could not afford the time or the expense of bringing up an illegitimate child. And so Rusty had been adopted, never to be told by his new parents this was the case. It was not until after their death following a car accident, that he found the adoption papers, learned the truth and set out to find his birth mother.

Still, at least their mother had done the honourable thing when he turned up on her doorstep. She had welcomed him with open arms; cried on his shoulder and begged his forgiveness. Rusty of course forgave her, but then he would, because well, Rusty was just like that. And so she, Iris, finally got what she'd always wanted, a big brother.

Iris left the bridge and walked slowly up the hill towards Long Acre Farm. In the front garden of a house in a row of recently refurbished cottages, a teenage girl was pushing a mower, filling the air with the sweet scent of freshly mown grass. Iris loved the sound of an old fashioned mower, it reminded her of the hot sunny days in her childhood when she had helped her father rake up the freshly mown grass and put it onto the compost heap.

On the side of the road opposite the cottages, montbretia grew in a huge clump, its long spear-like leaves gently quivering in the light breeze. Iris picked a flower and held it up to the light. It was very pretty, such a vibrant shade of orange, and the red markings were exquisite. What a shame, because its growth was so rampant and intrusive in Cornwall, clumps were often discarded and dumped in hedgerows and on grass verges.

Iris tucked the flower in the lapel of her jacket and continued up the hill. At the signpost indicating a bridle path towards the cliffs she paused and decided to follow the path.

As she walked she thought of her career. Back in the days when she had followed in her mother's footsteps and opted for a life in show business, it had been because she was insecure, not able to pinpoint her own identity and therefore she enjoyed playing the parts of people she was not. But over the years things had changed. She had become a famous face and frequent good reviews from both sides of the Atlantic had boosted her confidence. Iris sighed. She was always a little apprehensive about going to the States but on each occasion she'd had an enjoyable time whilst there. But there was no place like England and she was always glad when she stepped from the plane and set foot back on English soil.

As she neared the coastal path she contemplated whether to go on or retrace her steps and go back the way she had come. By a five bar gate she stopped. In front of her lay the sea, sparkling in the dazzling sunlight, and without hesitation she climbed over the gate and walked to the edge of the cliff path to drink in the view.

From behind the walls of the old Penwynton mine, a family appeared. One of the party recognised her and rushed forward, fumbling in her bag, searching for pen and paper, and at the same time asking for an autograph. Iris smiled sweetly. It was such a small gift to give; she was a very lucky lady and when all was said and done, it was the fans who had elevated her to the status she held.

Iris signed the paper and wished her admirers a good day. She then turned and walked back to Trengillion looking forward to meeting everyone at the barbecue in the evening.

"What time are we going to the barbecue?" asked Jefferson K. Jefferson, Jr., as he and his wife loaded up the dish washer with crockery used for lunch.

"Well, your mom and me will want a nap later this afternoon before we go, so I reckon about six o'clock. But you and your good lady wife can go down earlier if you like because I believe it starts around five."

"Yeah, well if that's alright with you that's what we'll do, eh, Julie May? We'd like to walk you see, seeing as the weather's good and it's a fair way down from here, especially if we dawdle, which I expect we will."

That's fine with me, son. We'll take the car of course so you can have a ride home with us. Your mom will drive back so I can have a whisky or two at the Jolly Sailor. Won't you, Mrs J. K. J?"

"Sure, honey," said Mrs Jefferson K. Jefferson, Sr., sitting by the window where the sun shone through the spotless glass panes, "as long as you remember to buy me that pretty little necklace we saw in town the other day."

"Dag nab it, I don't reckon there's much fear of my forgetting that, Mrs J. K. J, you remind me just about every day."

When Matthew and Wills returned from hauling the crab pots on Friday afternoon they found the cove much transformed. On a ladder propped against the wall of the winch-house, Rusty was hanging a lantern to light the area below where he and Greg would be barbecuing burgers, sausages, chicken and mackerel for the carnivores and vegetable kebabs for the vegetarians. From the mizzen masts of boats already ashore, bunting borrowed from the committees who ran the summer fayre, fluttered in the light sea breeze.

"Need a hand with anything?" Matthew asked, once his boat was alongside the others. "You're doing a grand job."

Rusty acknowledged the compliment with a coy grin, "You could decorate your boat, that's if you don't mind. Iris has the bundle of bunting and she's hanging it up the incline somewhere. You can't miss her because she's being helped by a gaggle of admirers."

"No problem," said Matthew, "we'll do that, we don't want to look like party poopers and be the odd boat out."

Rusty descended the ladder and then put it back inside the winch-house where it belonged. "I reckon there could be quite a good crowd tonight if the weather holds. I hope you and your wife will be coming."

"Of course, I've had my instructions from big sister, but we were going to come anyway. No need to worry about the weather, it'll stay fine tonight and tomorrow as well, so you'll be able to leave most of the clearing up 'til morning."

"Good thinking. I know Iris is keen to get to the pub later since it's our last night and I can't say that I want to be left here on my own clearing up."

"You'll be alright as long as you move everything up above the high water mark, otherwise you might find a few things have gone for a swim in the morning."

"Point taken: that's what nearly happened to your sister. That's how we met."

Matthew grinned. "So I've heard, but Jane never was one to fully understand tides."

After Wills returned with the bunting he had fetched from Iris, he and Matthew draped it around the mizzen mast to match the other boats.

"Is Tally working at the pub tonight?" Matthew asked.

"No, Justin has given all the youngsters the night off. Tally would have been gutted if she'd missed out. I reckon she's quite taken with Mac and he goes home tomorrow."

"So I've heard. It's going to be damn quiet here next week without the lads, and Morwenna too, of course."

"Yeah, and from what's being said, I reckon Justin's going to miss the doctor too."

Meg, like Gertie, was a close neighbour of the Moores, and as she was still suffering the after effects of the coach accident on Tuesday night, she offered to baby sit for Trevor and Valerie on Friday evening in order that they could attend the jollifications on the beach. Valerie was delighted, although at first she expressed reluctance thinking it unfair to deny Meg the pleasure of enjoying the festivities the barbecue would bring. Meg, however, insisted they go, and told Valerie if the truth be known she was not over fond of barbecued food and even less of being out on a chilly night with nothing comfortable to sit on.

Valerie was overjoyed, for since they had confided in Gertie, just two days earlier, about their misfortune life had improved one hundred per cent. The house was nicely furnished and comfortable and the two living rooms had all been decorated by a whole band of well-wishers. But most of all she was thrilled with the transformation in Trevor. Gone were the days of relentless, self-inflicted retribution. Laughter had returned to their lives: laughter and a large, wonderful dose of optimism. But the icing on the cake had to be Morwenna's manipulation the previous evening to his back, for since said treatment, his back had been absolutely pain-free, and he was even beginning to think, maybe, one day, he might be able to return to work. Nevertheless, he did not want to tempt fate by telling the world. It was early days yet and there was always the chance that one morning he might wake and find the agony had returned. But deep down, he had faith that that would never be the case, and for that reason, on Friday, his face seemed set in a permanent grin.

Jim Haynes was down on the duty rota to do a shift in the lounge bar at the Penwynton Hotel on Friday night, but when Linda heard of the barbecue she insisted he go there instead. For Jim had worked hard during the summer months and had often dropped everything at the last minute to come to the aid of the Hotel when he was needed.

"Jamie shall work in your place," Linda told him, categorically. "He quite likes working on the bar as long as it's not too busy, so he should be alright as it's much quieter now and I think a few of our residents will be going to the barbecue anyway."

Those words had been music to Jim's ears because he had feared Morwenna would be leaving Trengillion on Saturday morning and after that the chances were they would never meet again. Not that Jim foresaw any future with Morwenna; she had more or less told him so and deep down he was convinced she preferred Rob to him. After all, Rob was much younger and his job prospects much higher, for when all was said and done there would always be a need for undertakers. Jim laughed, his place of residence and young Rob's occupation were not dissimilar. Morwenna was obviously bent towards the dearly departed.

As Jim showered he weighed up the likelihood of ever finding a wife or whether he even wanted to marry. He had always considered being a bachelor was a great way of life, and in the summer he still believed it was, for there was always plenty of work to be done and what better ending to a summer's day than a walk into the village for a pint at the inn. But in the winter it was different; the weather was often wet and the nights long. Jim sighed as he dried his hair on the towel. Perhaps Susan Penhaligon was right when she had said life as a bachelor in old age would be lonely. Oh, well, he would have to leave his future in the lap of the gods.

While the senior Jefferson K. Jeffersons were taking a nap, the junior Jeffersons, as pre-arranged, left the Higher Green Farmhouse for a gentle stroll over the cliff tops and into the village where they planned to sit on the beach for a while to await the beginning of the barbecue. They walked holding hands across the grassy track until they reached a stretch where the path narrowed to single file as it twisted and turned through bracken and gorse. When the path reached the Witches Broomstick they stopped to view the small beach below, the only access to which was via the sea.

"You seem pretty quiet today, Julie May, is something wrong? You've hardly said a word since we left the farmhouse."

"Yeah, I'm fine, honey, but at times such as this it's just nice to admire the flowers, listen to the rhythmic song of the sea and the cry of the gulls."

"Why, Julie May, that's some poetic. I think it must be your little bit of English coming out. Why, I wouldn't be surprised if you weren't a descendent of Mr William Shakespeare himself."

Julie May laughed. "I know that's not possible, honey. Mr Shakespeare's only son died aged eleven and although both his daughters had four children between them, one died in infancy and the other three never produced any offspring, and so there the lineage ended."

Jefferson K. Jefferson, Jr. took a deep breath. "Julie May, you're talents are wasted just being a little old housewife. You should be a school ma'am or something clever like that."

Julie May yawned. "But I wouldn't want to be a school ma'am, Jeff. I'm more than happy just being a housewife and staying home, waiting for you to return when you finish work."

"Gee, that's an awful nice thing to say, Julie May. Sometimes I think I don't deserve you: you never put yourself first."

"That's the way I was brought up. My granny always said I was to think of others and their needs before my own."

Jefferson K, Jefferson, Jr. frowned as his wife yawned again.

"You look awful tired, honey, let's sit down and rest a while."

"I am a little tired, I must admit. I didn't sleep too well last night."

"I know, I was conscious of the fact you were a tossing and a turning. Perhaps you ate something that disagreed with you. Maybe it was the lobster Pa bought from that old dude in Saint Ives."

Julie May laughed. "No, it wasn't the lobster, Jeff. It were, well, I don't know, but I sorta had a funny dream last night. It disturbed me and I couldn't get back to sleep."

Jefferson K. Jefferson, Jr. leaned back and looked his wife in the face. "What sorta dream, Julie May?"

"It's difficult to say because dreams never make sense, do they? But there was a fire. I could feel the heat. Someone was crying and I was sobbing bitterly. It was horrible, Jeff. I woke up feeling ever so low and I've felt the same on and off all day. You know, sorta weird like I'm not here."

"Well, that's easily explained. The dream was obviously occasioned by the fire in the little old village hall and I expect your sorrow was just empathy with all the poor folks here who loved that little old building."

Julie May smiled, lovingly took her husband's hand and kissed it. "I expect you're right."

Chapter Twenty Eight

As the afternoon slipped into early evening, Greg, wearing shorts and a T shirt, left Chy-an-Gwyns and walked down the rugged path to the cove with a large bowl of onions which he had dutifully peeled and sliced since returning home from work in order to lighten the load when making preparations for the barbecue. Meanwhile back home, with several chores she wanted to do before dusk, Elizabeth said she would join him later.

When Greg arrived on the beach he found band members busy setting up their equipment and plugging vast quantities of wire and cables into extension leads trailing from inside Cove Cottage. And on a patch of sand beside the winch-house, Rusty already had the barbecues alight and glowing. Besides the Jr. Jeffersons, a few other people had gathered early, each offering their services in turn should the part-time chefs need an extra pair of hands to assist with the cooking.

Jane closed the Pickled Egg early. She knew it was safe so to do, for it was very unlikely anyone would want to eat in her café when there was barbecue food going free on the beach. So, once showered and changed, she walked onto the beach carrying two large iceboxes, to give a helping hand to the two novice chefs.

"Bit of a busman's holiday for you, eh, Jane?" Greg laughed, as she laid out bowls of pasta salad, three quiches, a green salad and homemade cheese straws, along with mustard pots, salt and pepper, bottles of brown sauce and tomato ketchup from the café.

"Sort of, but at least I'm in the fresh air out here and not being driven mad by the constant whirring of a noisy fan."

"And you're in the company of two dashingly handsome males," grinned Rusty.

Jane laughed. "I like the way you've decorated the boats; it's good to see the fishermen have joined in with the spirit of things."

"Yeah, they were brilliant and told us to do as we liked, but your brother did his boat himself."

"What! Didn't he trust you then?"

"No, no, it wasn't that, he got in later than the rest and seeing us hard at work volunteered to help."

Jane nodded. "I see. Do you think there will be enough food?"

Rusty grinned. "More than enough. We've got loads of stuff to cook and several people have made sandwiches which Iris has put in the cottage until they're needed."

"That's good. Where is Iris, by the way?"

"Making herself beautiful. You know, her last night and all that, she wants to make a good impression. Mind you, she worked damn hard this afternoon getting everything ready, so I don't grudge her a chance to relax."

"Oh, well she won't find it difficult to make herself beautiful, I'd give my eye teeth to have her looks."

"Don't be daft, I think you're lovely as you are," said Rusty, kissing her cheek as he separated a string of sausages. "In my opinion there's no room for improvement."

"Ha ha, not much! Iris has such a dazzling personality, she lights up a room when she walks in, whereas I'm just plain Jane."

"Why are women never satisfied with their looks?" Greg asked, placing a pan of onions on a camping stove. "Liz is the same, she goes on a diet at least six times a year. God only knows why. I wouldn't swap her for anyone, not even the beautiful Iris."

"I should hope not," laughed Iris, looking immaculate as she approached from Cove Cottage. "I'd hate to cause the breakup of a perfect marriage, but thank you for the compliment, even if I wasn't meant to hear it."

Greg grinned. "My pleasure."

"And now," said Iris, glancing over her shoulder, "I have a confession to make, which when it meets the ears of dear Freddie Short will make him tut very loudly regarding my stupidity, and I shall not blame him."

She held up her arm. From her slim wrist dangled a bracelet of blue and white stones.

"Good God, your stolen bracelet," gasped Rusty. "Wherever did you find it?"

"Behind the chest of drawers. My lipstick rolled down the back just now, so I pulled it out and lo and behold the bracelet was there along with my favourite comb which I thought I'd left in London."

"You nincompoop," laughed Rusty.

Greg pointed towards the incline. "And here comes Freddie. You'd better explain your find to him Iris, because at present he eyes all of us here with suspicion. Having said that, surely the bracelet's reappearance will back up your reluctance to get the police involved."

Iris pulled a bottle of white wine from a half barrel filled with ice and proceeded to remove the cork. "Good point, and it turns out Jim's vegetables weren't stolen either. He was telling me so when he popped in with mint and cucumber for the Pimms. So all in all it looks as though folks around here are much more honest than Freddie originally thought."

"Pimms," Jane smiled, eyes sparkling, "did you say Pimms?"

Iris laughed. "Yes I did, I have gallons of it made up in the house for later. Is it a favourite of yours?"

"Oh, yes, I adore it and I think this is going to be a perfect evening. What time will you be bringing it out?"

"I was thinking around sevenish, but if you're that fond of it I'll get you a bumper glass of it right now."

Rob, Kev, Neil and Mac each managed to find enough items of clothing still clean enough to wear for their last evening, but they all agreed that since the night air was likely to be chilly, it might be better to wear jeans rather than their usual Bermuda shorts. Nevertheless, the sunglasses remained part of their outfits. When they were all ready they left the inn by the side door and swaggered down to the beach to meet the girls as prearranged.

"Who's working on the bar tonight if you've both got the night off?" Mac asked Tally and Demelza, who, with Lucy were waiting on Denzil's bench.

"Mum's opening up on her own," said Demelza, rising to link arms with Kev, "but Justin will have his mobile on him if it gets busy. We don't expect it will though, because absolutely everyone's coming to the barbecue."

"Then later on, after the barbecue, Candy's going to work and Auntie Anne and Uncle John have volunteered to help out too," said Tally, "even though neither of them have done any bar work before."

"Well, if Demelza can do it I should think anyone can," laughed Kev, ducking to avoid her flying shoulder bag.

"Dad even said he'd give a hand too," giggled Lucy, with an amused scowl. "Imagine that! Although he often says if he wasn't a dentist he'd liked to have had a pub."

"I think I'd like my own pub one day," said Tally, dreamily, "when I'm older, that is. I wouldn't like the commitment needed for it yet awhile. But when I'm in my thirties I think it'd be really nice."

"Anyone seen Morwenna?" Rob asked, casting his eyes across the beach. "She said she'd be here, but I can't see her."

"I saw her earlier this afternoon when I was on my way home to change," said Tally. "We had a quick chat and I thought she looked a bit glum, but that's probably because she's going home tomorrow."

"Yuck, we know the feeling," said Neil, "come on girls, let's party and make this a night to remember. Morwenna will find us when she gets here."

Elizabeth stood outside Chy-an-Gwyns and looked down from the clifftops onto the activity below. Sheltered beneath the canvas of a large, green gazebo, a popular local band was playing contemporary music. Several people were dancing on the shingle, loud voices and laughter echoed between the cliff walls and from the barbecues, the strong smell of smoke wafted up into the night air.

Elizabeth sighed, she had a throbbing headache and so regarded the barbecue with a severe lack of enthusiasm. She knew she must go down at some time, but feeling unable to indulge in lively chat and boisterous merry making, she thought it best to stay at home a while longer.

Elizabeth looked to the sky; it was twilight, which along with dawn, was her favourite time of day. The sun had disappeared beneath the roof tops of Higher Green Farmhouse and the night air felt chilly in the gentle breeze blowing up from the sea. Rubbing her bare arms to dispel the goose pimples, she absent-mindedly returned to the house and from the bedroom fetched her thickest cardigan. She then made a mug of coffee and took a couple of aspirin to relieve her headache. As she finished her drink, the clock in the hall struck half past eight. Elizabeth sighed, conscious that Greg would be wondering where she was. Reluctantly she placed her empty mug on the draining board, locked up the house and walked down the cliff path into the village.

From his place of work by the winch-house, Greg waved a pair of tongues as she walked onto the beach, she raised her arm and smiled to return his welcome. She was relieved when he resumed turning burgers and sausages alongside Rusty, for she was in no frame of mind to have to converse by shouting above the noise of the band.

Iris appeared from nowhere, thanked Elizabeth for the loan of her husband and pushed a brimful glass of red wine into her hands. Elizabeth smiled feebly, thanked Iris for the drink, and congratulated her on the excellent efforts she had made to ensure the evening was a success. Iris smiled with pride and then bustled away back to her guests.

No expense had been spared by the party's hostess; large flame torches illuminated the beach casting flickering shadows beneath the silver light of a waxing moon. Around the barbecue area, tables groaned with food and drink and further down the beach, a brazier provided heat for those wishing to warm their hands.

Elizabeth sipped her wine, avoiding eye contact with her friends as she tried to relax. She felt the need to be alone: an onlooker rather than a participant. She wandered to the far side of the beach away from the crowd and the noise and sat on a rock in the dark, illuminated by neither flame torches nor moonlight.

Music drifted across the beach, Elizabeth absently swayed to the rhythm as the band played her favourite tune. The joyful ambiance boasted the ingredients for a perfect evening, but Elizabeth wished she were tucked up in bed. She yawned as her eyes darted over the movements of her friends and neighbours; holiday makers too were enjoying their last evening.

Dancing near to the gazebo, Doctor Owen swayed her curved hips, her arms draped lovingly around Justin's neck, her head resting on his shoulder. Beside the brazier, stood Robbie Macdonald chatting to Stephen's brother, David. Elizabeth was pleased to see that he had recovered from the accident and was looking well.

The camping lads were energetically dancing with girls from the village, but not Morwenna; she stood nearby watching, a blank expression on her pale face. Elizabeth was surprised, according to Tally, Morwenna had been the life and soul of the party since her arrival and was much admired by all the youngsters for her unconventional thinking and impish sense of fun.

Near to the winch house, Anne was talking to Jim. Elizabeth smiled: no doubt they were talking gardens, a hobby they both shared passionately. However, Jim looked a little downcast, probably because Morwenna was due to leave in the morning and it was unlikely he would ever see her again. Poor Jim. She had heard of his infatuation with the young Goth and it seemed such a shame that his fancy was taken with someone not of the area. Although Elizabeth had to admit she didn't actually know from where Morwenna hailed, but on reflection that could be said for most of Trengillion's visitors.

Elizabeth jumped when Morwenna suddenly stepped from the shadows, grabbed a flame torch from the end of the row and began to walk slowly backwards up the incline, furtively watching the boisterous crowds as though to make sure her movements were unobserved.

Elizabeth frowned, her curiosity rose and instinctively she knew she must follow. With careless haste she stood her wine glass on a rock where she sat; it toppled from the uneven surface and smashed down on the shingle below. Elizabeth cursed. No-one appeared to have heard or witnessed her clumsiness and as there was no time to pick up the pieces she told herself she must do it later.

Leaving behind her hiding place, she dashed across the beach in order to pursue the young Goth, praying with each step that her sudden uneasiness was unfounded and that Morwenna was just going to the inn or for a guiltless stroll.

At the top of the incline Morwenna's slight figure passed alongside the Jolly Sailor; her black hair shining in the light of a streetlamp and swaying with each step she took. Elizabeth crept forward, her footsteps light, her body bent as she hid in the shadows of parked cars to avoid detection.

Morwenna continued walking, her pace brisk and she did not slow down until she reached the gate of Valley View, home of Maurice the Chef, where she turned and walked along the garden path. Elizabeth was confused; Maurice was at work so why had Morwenna gone to his house? Unable to answer her own question, she quickly followed but decided to go no further than the path by the gate and instead to hide in the dense shrubbery.

Once concealed beneath a buddleia, she nervously peered through the leaves of fuchsia bush causing small pink flowers to drop onto the earth. To her surprise Morwenna was standing on the lawn facing the house, quietly muttering.

Elizabeth's ankles began to ache; cursing middle-age she carefully adjusted her position and knelt. When she resumed her surveillance, she saw that Morwenna was striding towards the house. On the edge of the grass she stopped and looked up towards the landing window where a dim light flickered casting shadows across the glass panes. Slowly, the light intensified and above it appeared the face of an elderly man holding a candle. Elizabeth smothered a scream; the face was that of the old man she had seen on Maurice's computer, but now his gaze was transfixed on Morwenna, who, with a toss of her head, pointed the flame torch towards the house and shook it in a defiant manner.

The flickering light and the face of the old man vanished. Morwenna stepped forwards but then again stopped abruptly, for the elderly man had re-appeared, minus the candle, and was now hovering above the garden path by the front door; his hands clasped together in a pleading manner.

A sudden breeze blew the skirt of Morwenna's dress and tousled her long black hair. She turned her head towards the garden next door and sniffed at the air. She then bent down and pushed the unlit end of the flame torch into the earth and crossed to the boundary where sweet peas were growing in the garden of Rose Cottage. Casually brushing aside montbretia leaves, Morwenna walked through the gap left by the fallen fence and, standing in the herbaceous border, she rubbed the palms of her hands across the petals of the sweet smelling flowers.

Kneeling amongst the shrubs, Elizabeth watched in disbelief. The figure of the old man was still hovering outside the house. Meanwhile, Morwenna was picking sweet peas from her parents' garden and tucking them one by one into the band she wore around her hair. Elizabeth pinched herself. Was she dreaming?

The haunting sound of an owl hooting echoed through the night sky from deep in the valley, as Morwenna, her headband decked with sweet peas, returned to the garden of Valley View. In front of the old man she stopped and together they conversed, quietly, in words Elizabeth could not understand.

Suddenly the old man fell onto his knees but with his legs still hovering above the ground. He reached out to Morwenna with both hands, his eyes dull with sadness. Momentarily, Morwenna hesitated. When she took his hands, a smile crossed his grey, transparent face and a ghostly silence fell over the garden. When their hands parted, the old man looked to the skies and clasped his hands together in prayer. He then raised his hat, bowed to Morwenna and vanished.

Morwenna remained still for a while and then pulled the flame torch from the earth. When she turned, Elizabeth saw that her face was lit by a huge, happy smile. With a laugh, she fled down the path and out into the street, singing at the top of her voice.

Dumbfounded and in a daze, Elizabeth scrambled to her feet, stumbled towards the gate and ran out onto the pavement where Morwenna was just visible in the lamplight ahead. Hastily, Elizabeth followed but as they reached the inn, Morwenna stopped abruptly and quickly turned. With a smile, she waited for Elizabeth to catch up. When both were side by side, Morwenna reached to her headband and pulled out a stem of sweet pea and pushed it through a buttonhole on Elizabeth's cardigan and whispered, "I'm grateful for the kindness everyone here has shown me. Thank you, but I must go now." She smiled sweetly. "It is good to have learned how to forgive and I'm truly sorry for the disquiet I have caused." She then turned and continued to walk towards the beach. Elizabeth followed very slowly. At the bottom of the incline she stopped. Morwenna's words didn't make sense. Nothing made sense.

In front of her, Morwenna ran onto the beach, waving the torch as she span around, laughing and dancing to the music. Her friends, delighted to see she had returned with regained party spirit, waved and beckoned her to join them. She waved back and as she danced past Jim she pulled a sweet pea from her hair and thrust it into his hands; with a smile she blew him a kiss and then turned towards her friends and gave each a flower. To everyone's surprise, she gave the last one to Robbie. She then turned on her heels: laughing, singing, dancing, lost, it seemed to all, in a world of her own.

At the water's edge she ceased dancing and watched as the foam of a gentle wave trickled over her feet. She stood perfectly still on the compact, wet sand and then slowly, softly humming along with the tune the band were playing, she waded into the tumbling waves beyond. At first everyone laughed. They thought it was a prank. Morwenna was going for a swim, fully clothed. Just the sort of thing she'd do on her last night. Rob called her name, but she kept on going. When the water was waist deep, the laughter ceased.

Rob and Mac, assuming she must be drunk, frantically tried to go in after her, but their efforts were thwarted by a sudden strong, off shore wind which took away their breath and forced them to retreat. The band stopped playing. The baggy sleeves on Morwenna's dress flapped and snapped in the crushing breeze. Using both hands, she raised the flame torch above her head and the sleeves of her dress slipped to reveal her long slender arms. She turned to face the crowd and as the swirling water reached her shoulders, her long black hair floated on the bobbing waves. She caught Elizabeth's eye and smiled as though she thought she might understand. And then, with a final step backwards, her voice sang out incomprehensible words, her image faded, the torch slipped from her hand and she vanished.

Above the rippling waves, a ghostly mist, like smoke, swirled in the strong breeze, and for a brief moment the torch's flame cast a bright shimmering light over the water's surface; it then fizzled and went out. And as the wind dropped, darkness descended.

With the wind gone, Mac, Rob, Kev and Neil waded into the sea closely followed by Jim, all anxiously calling Morwenna's name. But she was gone. Lost without trace, except for the blackened torch which floated on the waves until it reached the shore.

The crowd, dumbfounded and baffled, fell silent, stunned by the incident they had all witnessed, and Elizabeth, feeling faint, leaned on the wall of Cove Cottage, white faced, shocked and confused.

The barbecue ended abruptly when the reality of Morwenna's demise sank in. Some became hysterical and all were mystified not only by her apparent, unprovoked suicide, but by the eerie manner in which she had gone. Heads were bowed to hide tears and the night air which had, such a short time before rung with optimism and love, was now heavy with sorrow.

Freddie took charge of the situation and rang for the police and ambulance on his mobile phone, though he knew from experience the latter would be too late even if Morwenna were found. Gradually people drifted off to the inn to discuss the evening's events, for the night air had turned chilly and they were cold with shock.

Freddie, Greg and Rusty remained to await the arrival of the police, and Elizabeth, mentally exhausted, excused herself and wandered home to Chy-an-Gwyns alone to seek solitude.

Elizabeth was still up when Greg, Wills and Tally returned home. They found her sitting on the settee, a blanket around her shoulders and a hot water bottle in her arms.

"You alright, Liz? You're awfully pale," Greg asked.

She attempted to smile. "Just shocked and saddened like everyone else."

Greg patted her shoulder. "Yes, events don't come much more horrific than that. You don't mind if I go to bed, do you? I'm shattered and I've agreed to help Rusty and Iris clear up in the morning and we want to try and get it done before the police divers return."

"Of course not, you go. I shall be alright, but I'd like to sit for a while longer yet because I'm not tired."

"Poor old Iris, she must be devastated that something so awful should happen at an event she's organised," yawned Wills. "I saw her crying, but then nearly everyone was."

As Greg and Wills left the room to retire to bed Elizabeth grasped Tally's wrist. "Stay a minute longer, there's something I want to ask you," she whispered.

"Okay, but can I make a cup of tea first? All the crying has made my throat sore."

"Of course, and make me one too, please."

Tally returned in due course with two mugs of steaming tea and sat down on the sofa beside her mother. "So what is it you want to ask me?"

Elizabeth took the proffered mug. "If it's not too painful for you, I'm curious to know what Morwenna's last words were. It wasn't English so I wondered if it might have been Cornish."

Tally nodded. "Yes, you're right, it was. And I must admit that's been puzzling me, because the other day when I mentioned I was learning the language she didn't comment on it, which seems most peculiar because she must have been familiar with it too, to have said what she did."

"And what was it she said?"

"Well, I'm not too sure because it didn't make much sense, but it sounded like, 'Peace be with you all. Revenge is not sweet and I am sorry. I have learned to forgive and shall not return again."

Elizabeth frowned. "But that doesn't make sense...unless."

"Unless what?"

"Unless she started the fire in the village hall and caused all the recent mishaps."

"What! But that's absurd, Mum. Whatever reason could she have had for being so wicked?"

"I don't know but she said she was sorry so must have done something she regretted."

Elizabeth glanced at the sweet pea tucked through her cardigan. "I do understand why she handed out the sweet peas though."

Tally smiled. "Yes, she told us of their meaning the other day. I wonder where she got them from."

"Umm...probably someone's garden." Elizabeth was reluctant to tell of her experience earlier in the evening.

"Yes, I suppose so. Poor Morwenna. She always seemed so happy, in fact I don't ever recall seeing her miserable," Tally smiled, "not even when it rained."

Elizabeth hugged her daughter. "I wish Grandma Molly was here. I'm sure she'd have much to say about all this. There are so many unexplained things in life, Tally, but Morwenna must have had her reasons for doing what she did, and now she is at rest."

Chapter Twenty Nine

At first light the following morning, police divers arrived in the village to resume the search they had abandoned the previous night. They found nothing. Other police officers made house to house enquiries in order to try and establish Morwenna's identity to enable them to notify her next of kin, but they were unable even to establish where she had been staying whilst on holiday, let alone find someone who knew her home address. In fact, the only piece of information anyone seemed to know for sure, was she called herself Morwenna and claimed she was a student of alternative medicine. Even Rob, who got to know her better than most, confessed he knew nothing to assist with her identity for she had always brushed his questions aside when he had asked of her family and friends. For a short time, Neil thought he might be able to help, as two days before he had taken three films to the post office to be developed. But when he collected them with a police escort, Morwenna was not to be seen on any of the photographs; in every one, the space she had occupied was blank, even the one where she had been sitting on Rob's lap. Everyone was mystified.

The police eventually gave up their investigation and a report was written up regarding the death of a female, possibly in her late teens of whom nothing was known save her Christian name.

Later in the morning, inside Chy-an-Gwyns, eager to keep busy and stop her mind from wandering, Elizabeth pulled the ironing board from the cupboard beneath the stairs and ironed two of Greg's shirts along with the curtains she had washed the previous morning. Once the task was completed she took the curtains into the drawing room, and whilst standing on the ottoman in the large bay window, rehung the curtains on the brass curtain track. When finished, thankful they had not shrunk, she stood back to admire her handiwork, swearing the curtains looked several shades lighter. At the same time, she noticed one of the castors on the bottom of the ottoman looked slightly askew and it was off balance. Keen to remedy the lopsidedness, she knelt in front of the ottoman and ran her hand underneath. One of the screws was loose, and so she went to the shed and brought in a selection of screw drivers to tighten it. To make the job easier she lay the ottoman on its back with its lid tight against the wall to prevent the contents spilling out.

To her delight, the first screw driver she tried was the right size. She tightened the screw and took the tools back to the shed.

On her return, she pulled the ottoman forward to stand it upright, but to her annoyance it slipped backwards on the parquet floor, the lid flew open and the contents tumbled out into a heap. Elizabeth groaned. The ottoman had once belonged to her late grandmother and it contained treasured possessions in the order she had always kept them, plus a few things Elizabeth too had added as keepsakes, such as items of jewellery, a brush and comb, knitting needles and old photographs.

Elizabeth knelt on the floor. The treasured possessions were mostly items of clothing, including a shawl wrapped around Molly's controversial crystal ball, a relic from the days before she met the major, when she had lived in Clacton and tried her hand at fortune telling.

Elizabeth smiled wistfully: apparently for these sessions her grandmother had also worn a long flowing gown. But that gown was gone now forever, for Molly had let it be known she desired it be her burial shroud and the family had dutifully honoured her wish.

Other items which the ottoman held were books: a few novels, a bible and two cookery books, but mostly reference books about the occult, folklore, myths and spiritualism. Ned had wanted to throw them away, "burn them on a bonfire," he'd said, dispassionately. But Elizabeth insisted they must be kept and said she would keep them in her possession.

She picked up the books one by one and neatly placed them back in the bottom of the now upright ottoman. She then laid the clothes on top and last of all, the shawl wrapped around the cherished crystal ball. But as she stretched up to close the lid she saw one book had escaped her notice and lay partly hidden beneath the hem of the curtains.

Elizabeth bent forward and picked up the book; to her surprise it was entitled *Sixteenth Century Witchcraft*. She laughed, dropped it in the ottoman and then noticed a bookmark peeping from the bottom pages. Instinctively she lifted the book and opened it on the page where the bookmark lay. It was at the beginning of a chapter titled, Cornish Witches.

Realistic thinking told Elizabeth to push the book in the ottoman out of sight. Forget it and hastily withdraw from the room. But intrigue enticed her to find out more. With book in hand she scrambled to her feet, closed the ottoman lid and sat down.

Scanning the pages, she half hoped the passage would contain nothing of relevance and focus on Cornwall far away from the Lizard peninsula. It seemed likely, for many names in East Cornwall dominated the pages, and then she saw the name Tremellyonenn. She shuddered. Her hands began to tremble as she recalled Tally, after her first Cornish class, saying Tremellyonenn was the ancient name of Trengillion.

Elizabeth leaned against the curtains. She glanced out of the window and then back at the page. When she felt composed she began to read, very slowly at first, so as to digest every word thoroughly.

The brief account entitled 'The Tremellyonenn Witch,' was an extract, the prologue claimed, from the diary of Elowen Cardew of Tremellyonenn. The excerpt was an English translation from the Cornish diary, loaned to the publishers by a local historian to whom it had been donated in 1827 by the Cardew family, who were unable to read the contents.

The excerpt was dated 1598. It began:

Today my beloved sister died. Put to death for no just reason. Hitherto I shall never be able to forgive those who condemned her, especially Rabbie, the Scot.

She was a young woman in her prime, born of this village with a wonderful gift. A gift which first materialised at the age of eight, when it was acknowledged she exhibited the art of brewing herbs and making potions capable of curing all ills. Many villagers were in awe of her talents, for her medicinal skills surpassed those of all other womenfolk in our midst. Some quipped they believed she was capable of raising the dead, but alas, her talents were not enough to save her from an untimely death, nor will her foolish claim of life everlasting materialise with her passing.

In our village there lives a Catholic philosopher of Scottish descent called Rabbie, who left Edinburgh in 1587 following the execution of Mary Queen of Scots; his intent was to seek revenge against us wicked English who supported our sovereign Queen Elizabeth when she placed the death sentence upon his beloved martyr. After travelling far and wide, however, he found his hate of the English lessened and eventually he arrived here to Cornwall where he settled in our village, Tremellyonenn, and married a local girl, Rozen, whose family he found was sympathetic to the late Scottish queen's religious beliefs.

As the years unfolded, we village folk did come to like, trust and respect Rabbie for without doubt he was a wise and clever man. He played the Scottish bagpipes, one of few items he had carried wrapped in a blanket when first he did arrive in our village. And on many a summer's evening we did listen to him play the pipes for he played with great skill and expertise putting to shame our Cornish bagpipe player, Gurci, who was but a novice. However, Rabbie did not mock Gurci, but did instruct and improve his skills and soon Scottish and Cornish bagpipes played together side by side. But the good times did not last. Misfortune struck with devastating results.

It was in December of last year that first we saw the beginnings of change. It began with a harsh and bitter winter which brought hardship and continued its soul destroying ways past Christmas and through into the beginning of this year. Animals died for no apparent reason. Stored foods rotted in the barns and famine eventually swept through the village.

At the homestead of the Scottish philosopher, fever spread amongst his family. Most survived but his young wife, Rozen, died an agonising death; neither my sister nor any other womenfolk were able to save her. But the following day a lad of little intelligence was cured, even though his elderly parents believed his life was beyond redemption. And it was my sister to whom this miracle was attributed.

Rabbie the Scot was distraught after the death of Rozen and called the people to a meeting to discuss the reason for our bout of bad luck, for neighbouring villages, he declared, were not affected by misfortune, hence the cause, he believed, had to be amongst us.

At the meeting, attended by all, the philosopher, angered by the inability of my sister to save his wife and desperate that someone take the blame, declared she was a devil woman, who brought about the wrath of Holy God with her claims of eternal life. 'She saved not the life of a good woman,' he shouted, 'but that of the worthless imbecile'. With finger wagging and his face puce with rage he accused her of practising the abominable art of witchcraft. Her response was to laugh in his face, and many of us, I do confess, thinking he did jest, did likewise.

Up until the beginning of this century witchcraft was not a punishable offence in this country. It was a part of everyday life, welcomed by those whose crops flourished at a witch's behest and praised by the sick who were cured with the aid of magic. However, when things went wrong then a witch was often blamed and today the offence, if proven, is punishable by the most cruel penalty of all - death.

We village folk were aghast when we did realise that Rabbie the Scot was earnest in his accusation, but all were too afraid to disagree. For had we not all witnessed with our own eyes, following a dispute between my sister and a young man whose attention she forcefully rejected, that he fell the next day from his horse and was instantly killed.

Yesterday she was tried. Rabbie elected himself as judge and chose two men, Conneck the Clerk and Pethick the Priest, both entranced by his intelligence, to act as jury. With her hands tied behind her back she was then walked over many, many fields to a spot where a dam in a fast flowing brook did make a deep pool. We all followed and watched as by the pool her right thumb was tied to her left toe to prevent her escaping or resisting her ordeal. She was then thrown into the water with a rope around her tiny waist. If she drowned, he deemed, she be innocent, but if she floated then, she be guilty. My sister did not drown, hence the Scot declared it proved her guilt and condemned her to death. His sentence was endorsed by the mindless group of sycophants, our village priest and clerk included, who dared call themselves jurors, but who in reality were spineless cowards, afraid to speak the truth.

As Rabbie spoke cruel and untrue words of my weeping sister, I did watch his flashing eyes, convinced he believed her passing might at least part avenge the wrong done to his wife and his beloved Queen, for the look on his pitiless face was one of sweet retribution.

It is normal practice in England today to hang a convicted witch should he or she be guilty of evil. But the barbaric philosopher declared hanging too good for the wickedness brought about by the 'devil witch' and he insisted they did as in Scotland and she be burned at the stake. We said 'This should not be so. Cornwall is in England and we live by English law'. But he declared were she and her sins not burned then the bitter suffering would long continue. In desperation we begged our priest to plead on her behalf, but he said 'Nay, he would not, for she had sinned in the eyes of Almighty God'.

Today, in the presence of the whole village, my dear, kind hearted sister was taken to the beach and tied to a wooden stake pressed deep into the sand. Her beautiful hands, which had healed so many, were tied behind her back with coarse rope and her bare feet were rested on faggots piled high. She spoke not a word as the philosopher read out a list of her crimes and no-one, not even our family, dared speak in her defence. But the sadness in the eyes of my mother will haunt me the rest of my days, and even my father, a learned man, who skillfully taught our family to read and write, felt himself no match for hard-hearted Rabbie the Scot.

Once the faggots were ignited and the flames began to engulf her frail body she shrieked in a terrifying manner. She screamed, cursing all who had sided with the evil Scot, vowing she would return again to seek her revenge. And as she cried her last words, 'Rejoice not for I shall return and avenge this unjust and brutal deed.' so the daylight vanished. A sudden strong breeze blew in from the sea and the temperature dropped. The sky blackened like night, and the birds, disorientated, flew aimlessly in circles seeking safe places to roost. Darkness fell over the village like an evil black cloak and the sun in confusion, collided with the moon and we all fell to our knees quaking with fear, begging Almighty God for forgiveness of our sins.

When lightness returned my sister was dead and free from pain. Her remains were left to burn on the sand until eventually her ashes, all that was left, were washed away by the incoming tide. And when she was gone I did lay on the spot where her precious life ended, a posy of sweet clovers, red and white, to remember her by.

A footnote dated June 1827 added, that on the third day of May in the year 1715, following a total eclipse prominent in the South West of England, the house in which Rabbie the Scottish Philosopher had once lived, was burned to the ground. Reputedly, the fire was started by the spirit of the Tremellyonenn witch, Morwyn Cardew, thus causing inhabitants of the village to believe she had, as she claimed, the gift of eternal life. Nine years later in 1724 shortly after another eclipse the dwelling in which Pethick the Priest had once lived was part-destroyed by fire. The house stood abandoned and empty for many decades and eventually fell into a state of disrepair. It remained uninhabited until 1817 when it was converted into a village hall. Gwel-an-Nans, the former home of Conneck the Clerk was abandoned for fear it should suffer the same fate as the two other houses and it too fell into a poor state of repair. However, it suffered not and was eventually restored to its former glory.

Elizabeth sat with the book on her lap in a state of shock and disbelief, for its contents she realised gave her every reason to suppose that Morwenna was none other than Morwyn Cardew and she had returned to seek further revenge. The footnote claiming she had returned in 1715 and again in 1724 backed up that supposition. The first house she had issue with was long gone and now the village hall also. But what of the third, Gwel-an-Nans the former home of Conneck the Clerk? Elizabeth could not recall seeing or hearing a house of that name in Trengillion or anywhere else.

"Morning, Mum."

Elizabeth jumped. "Tally, you startled me."

"Sorry." Tally kissed her mother's cheek and sat down beside her on the ottoman. "What's that you're reading?"

"Oh…umm…it's one of your great grandmother's old books. I just found it in the ottoman."

Tally sighed. "Oh."

Elizabeth glanced down at the closed book. "Tally, I know this might seem a rather odd question, but how do you say Valley View in Cornish?"

Tally frowned. "Eh…umm, I think it would be Gwel-an-Nans."

Elizabeth shuddered. "I was half hoping that wouldn't be the answer."

"Mum, are you alright? You're as white as a sheet and you're acting really weird this morning. It's freaking me out."

Elizabeth opened the book on the page where the bookmark lay and handed it to Tally. "I think you had better read this and then you'll understand why."

Chapter Thirty

Just before lunch, the Jefferson family went to the Jolly Sailor, where they sat, still baffled as to why the pretty young lady the previous night had taken her own life.

"Are you alright, Julie May?" asked Jefferson K. Jefferson, Jr., "you've not said a word since we came in here, you've not touched your drink neither and you look mighty pale."

Julie May nodded. "Yes, I'm alright, honey; that is to say I'm not unwell or anything like that. It's just that I didn't sleep too well again last night because I kept seeing the face of that poor girl, you know, the one who drowned. It's crazy but for some reason she reminds me of someone back along and I can't remember who it was."

"Probably someone you've seen on TV," said Mrs Jefferson K. Jefferson, Sr., "she was a right beauty anyway, whoever she was. God rest her soul."

They continued to chat quietly, stopping whenever they heard someone nearby making a comment which they thought might clarify the situation. And then suddenly, Julie May sat bolt upright.

"Cardew," she said, slapping the table. "Granny had a picture on her dresser of her mother when she was a girl and she was called Mary Cardew, and it was the Cardews who left England and emigrated to America. Back in 1827 it was. It's all coming back now. Granny used to tell me about the Cardews when I was a kid, though I must admit I don't recall a great deal of what she said."

"Wow, Julie May, that's real cool. Perhaps we might be able to find out something of your ancestors while we're here, now you've remembered the name, that is."

Julie May smiled. "Not unless I can remember where the family hailed from, and I can't; right now I haven't a clue."

"Can you remember why the family emigrated to the States?" asked Jefferson K Jefferson, Sr.. "If it were because of the potato famine then they'd have come from Ireland."

"No, it was definitely England. But then in England they speak English, don't they."

Jefferson K Jefferson, Jr., laughed. "I sure hope so, honey or we'd not be able to understand a darn word the folks here say."

Julie May frowned. "Exactly, but I remember Granny saying something about a diary. It'd been written in the sixteenth century but her ancestors didn't take it to America with them because they couldn't read it. It wasn't written in English, you see, and so they gave it to a historian or something like that. I wish I'd been more attentive now."

"Wow, that's weird, Julie May," laughed her husband, "but I think you've got your facts all muddled up somewhere. Anyway, who'd like another drink before we order our food? I for one just gotta have another pint of that Doom Bar."

Just before lunch, Elizabeth left Chy-an-Gwyns to call on her parents at Rose Cottage, but before that she was keen to visit the scene where the previous evening's drama had taken place.

As she walked towards the cliff path she stopped to admire the mesembryanthemums which grew in profusion on the surface of rocks in many parts of Cornwall. They seemed such happy little flowers and had been part of the Cornish landscape for many, many years. What a coincident, thought Elizabeth, that they should choose to look so impressive on such an extraordinary day.

At the foot of the cliff path she stepped onto the beach; a few police officers were present but all traces of the barbecue had disappeared: the gazebo, the bunting, the barbecues, the brazier, the torches and the litter, all gone. In fact, were it not for the police officers and their vehicles, the scene would look as on any other day.

Elizabeth wandered down to the water's edge near to the spot where Morwenna had entered the sea, and as picked up a pebble to throw into the waves, she heard voices from behind and a car door slam. Outside Cove Cottage, Jane was saying farewell to Rusty as he loaded up the car. Elizabeth kept her distance, but when the car's engine started and drove away she crossed the beach to speak to Jane, who she was saddened to see, was crying.

"Oh, Jane, I didn't realise you and Rusty were that serious."

Jane laughed as she dried her eyes. "Nor did I. In fact I'm not even sure that we are, but whatever the case, I'm very sorry to see him go. And it's such a shame last night turned out to be so horrid. Poor Iris. Poor everyone."

Elizabeth put her arm round Jane's shoulder. "But you'll no doubt keep in touch and I expect before you know it he'll be back down here for another break."

"Maybe," said Jane, "but I'm not sure he'll bother once Iris has gone to America. I know his job is pretty stressful and this holiday was frowned upon by his boss."

From the doorway of the Pickled Egg, Janet stood on the step waving a twenty pound note. "Can I have the safe key please, Jane, I need some change."

"Better go," said Jane, pulling the key from the pocket of her apron, "bye, Liz."

Elizabeth watched Jane return to the Pickled Egg and then left the beach bound for Rose Cottage. Outside the Jolly Sailor, more people were saying their farewells. Kev, Mac, Rob and Neil, having loaded their boot with bags of dirty washing and memorabilia were exchanging phone numbers and addresses with Lucy, Tally, Demelza, Ollie, Sam and Charlie. Elizabeth walked quietly by not wishing to draw attention to herself and spoil the goodbyes, but she could not help but notice the lack of laughter which everyone in Trengillion had come to associate with the lads and their outlandish convertible.

Elizabeth walked on. As she passed the church she noticed the rowan trees were flourishing once more. She thought it seemed incongruous that they could ever have looked so sick and no doubt all but she would be astounded by their miraculous recovery.

Elizabeth continued up the road to Valley View where she paused tentatively by the gate. The scent of the buddleia brought back memories of the previous evening, but everything looked and felt so different now it was daylight.

Elizabeth walked back to next door and the gate of Rose Cottage. As she walked up the path she observed the rowan tree there was also looking fit and healthy again.

Inside the cottage, Stella was preparing a salad for lunch.

"I see your rowan tree has recovered," said Elizabeth, her eyes twinkling.

"Yes, amazing isn't it? You know, I really thought it'd had it, but I bought some plant food in Helston yesterday and I reckon it must have worked wonders." She gave a girlish laugh. "Of course, your dad insists its recovery is purely because he threatened to chop it down and use it for firewood if it didn't buck up its ideas."

Elizabeth smiled. "I don't think plant food would be much use to a tree whose roots no doubt go down a very long way."

"Hmm, that's what your dad said."

Elizabeth glanced into the living room. "Where is Dad?"

"Oh, he's gone round next door to see George and Rose, no doubt to discuss last night's drama."

Elizabeth nodded. "Oh, I see."

As she spoke they heard a truck pull up on the road.

"Ah, that'll be John come to drop off the new section of fence," said Stella, "and your dad's not here to help him carry it up the path."

"Not to worry," said Elizabeth, jumping up. "I'll give him a hand."

As John and Elizabeth lifted the section of fence from the truck Ned returned from Ivy Cottage. He shook John's hand and kissed Elizabeth on the cheek. "I thought you'd be round today, Liz."

Elizabeth's eyebrows rose. "You did?"

"Oh yes. Now you run along back in the house and I'll help John carry the fence into the garden."

Once the section of fence was leaning on the side of the house John left vowing he'd return in the morning to put it into place. Ned thanked him and went indoors. He met Stella in the back porch.

"Just popping to the greenhouse for some tomatoes," she said, "I'll be back in a jiffy."

Ned nodded. "Okay."

Inside the sitting room he sat down on the settee. "So, Liz, what do you think last night's little drama was all about?"

Elizabeth tried to act casually. "Umm...I don't really know."

"Don't know or won't say?"

"A bit of both, I suppose."

Ned laughed. "Well there's definitely been something odd going on and what's more that rowan tree was beyond help. The leaves had all withered up and the branches were as black as coal. Whatever she says it wasn't your mother's plant food or my threats that brought it back to life. It must have been something much more powerful."

Elizabeth raised her eyebrows. "And what do think that something might have been then?"

Ned tilted his head to one side. "Well, if I remember correctly according to folklore the rowan was used as protection against fire and against witches. It was also thought to prevent the dead from rising again which is why it is often found in graveyards, sometimes even on graves."

Elizabeth's jaw dropped. "Oh...but..."

"You're not the only one, Liz, who had to listen to your grandmother's tales. So, are you able to shed any light on last night's drama?"

Elizabeth bit her bottom lip. "Dad, I don't really think you'd believe me if I told you what I witnessed last night."

Ned grinned. "Try me, sweetheart."

With reluctance Elizabeth told Ned about the time when she had seen the face of an old man on the screen of Maurice's computer and then, how the previous evening, she had followed Morwenna to Valley View where the apparition of the old man had appeared again and of the events which followed. She finished by telling of the chapter she'd read in her grandmother's book.

A strange look crept across Ned's face. "So, there really was a grain of truth in all that old nonsense about Morwyn Cardew the witch. How very extraordinary."

Elizabeth was surprised. "So you already knew about her."

Ned threw back his head and laughed. "Of course. Mum bought that book and several others at a jumble sale years and years ago. She was really excited when she came across the name Trengillion or whatever it was called back then, but of course she never mentioned it to the major and I forbade her ever to mention it to you, your mother or Anne. But if you're right, as daft as it sounds, it certainly would explain why nothing appears to be known about the twentieth century Morwyn or Morwenna as she called herself. Nothing other than her name."

"Are you talking about that poor girl?" Stella asked, placing a handful of tomatoes in the colander, "Such a tragedy. I can't get the image of her wading into the sea out of my mind. Her parents will be devastated when they find out. I do hope she'd not been taking drugs, but with no body and no post mortem, I suppose we'll never know the truth." She sighed. "Although of course her body may well be washed up in a day or two, but if it is I hope none of the youngsters are around to witness it. Poor lambs, what a terrible tragedy and they'd all had such a lovely time together too."

Ned glanced at Elizabeth who said nothing.

"Stay for lunch, Liz, and then you can keep me company this afternoon while your mother pops into Helston with Meg."

Elizabeth nodded. "Okay, Greg's out this afternoon anyway so I'll not be missed."

During lunch Stella attempted to talk again of the tragic death of Morwenna, but neither Ned nor Elizabeth felt able to contribute much and so Ned turned the conversation around to Madge Treloar who he had heard was out of hospital. This prompted the discussion to return to memories of the Over Sixties' Club outing.

After Stella had been picked up by Meg, Elizabeth and Ned went into the garden to sit on the front lawn, but before they sat, Elizabeth pointed to two magpies in the apple tree, chatting and squawking amongst the fruit laden branches.

"Shoo, clear off," shouted Ned.

"No, no," said Elizabeth, "please don't scare them away, Dad. If you remember, it was after either Kernow or Kate went missing that everything started to go wrong."

Ned laughed. "Well, yes, but I think the blame for all of Trengillion's mishaps must surely be attributed to Morwenna and not the disappearance of a silly bird, don't you?"

Elizabeth wrinkled her nose as she sat down. "I'd like to think it was a bit of both."

"You know, Morwenna was the first...um...I don't really know what to call her... apparition, I suppose, that I've actually seen," said Ned, thoughtfully, as he too sat. "Weird when you think of it."

Elizabeth cast her eyes towards the missing section of fence and the garden of Valley View. "Yes, it is, and even though we know a small something of Morwenna's past, the fact that she was able to return will always be a mystery to me and I find it a little unnerving."

Ned sighed. "Yes, I have to agree with you there. In fact the whole episode has been a funny old do, but then who knows what mysteries and powers lie beyond the grave."

Elizabeth gently bit her bottom lip. "Dad, do you think we ought to tell the police what we know about Morwenna?"

"Not unless we want to be a laughing stock."

"But...yes, I suppose you're right and it would probably do more harm than good. After all there are no living relatives to inform anyway."

"Precisely."

"Poor Morwenna or should I say Morwyn. Fancy being labelled a witch! How daft is that? I think she was just as she claimed in her present day form, a student of herbal and alternative medicines and Trevor Moore would be the first to testify to that."

"I agree." Ned leaned back his head and looked up towards the sky. "I wonder where she lived all those years ago. Wherever it was has obviously long gone because there are very few houses in Trengillion more than two hundred years old now."

"Hmm, I can only think of the church, the village hall, and of course Valley View, next door, one time home of Conneck the Clerk," said Elizabeth. "It's a shame we don't know where the long gone home of Rabbie the Scot stood either."

Ned grinned. "Ah, yes, Rabbie the Scot, I'd forgotten all about him. People had some strange ideas and beliefs back then, didn't they?"

"They certainly did." Elizabeth smiled. "And how unfortunate that Nessie's brother, Robbie, should appear on the scene during Morwenna's brief stay. Unfortunate for him, I mean. To her his name must have been like red rag to a bull. No wonder she didn't like him or the bagpipes and no doubt she was responsible for his accidents too."

"But back then bagpipes weren't thought of as a Scottish instrument, they were played pretty much all over the country, all over the world in fact."

"Yes, of course. Oh, how I wish it were possible to go back in time to see just how things were."

"I've been saying that for years, Liz."

Elizabeth looked towards the now flourishing rowan tree. "It's been a funny old summer but I think what I shall remember most was what Morwenna said before she slipped beneath the waves."

"Ah, so were you able to make sense of that?"

Elizabeth nodded. "Yes; because I suspected it might have been Cornish, I asked Tally if she knew what it meant. Would you like to know what she said?"

"Of course."

"Peace be with you all. Revenge is not sweet and I am sorry. I have learned to forgive and shall not return again."

Chapter Thirty One

By Christmas, the year, the decade, the century and the millennium, were rapidly coming to an end, and Trengillion, like everywhere else, was ready to celebrate and welcome in the year two thousand. For the first time in its history Trengillion was decked with Christmas lights stretching from one end of the village to the other, and high on the church tower, a string of bright, white stars hung from the turrets. The money had been raised throughout the year by a dedicated group of enthusiasts and the full amount needed was finally reached after a generous donation, sent by cheque, was received from Iris Delaney.

On the plot where the village hall had once stood the area had been cleared of debris ready for the re-build project to begin in January. And on the charred branches of the sycamore tree, small buds awaited Mother Nature to summon their opening with the coming of warm spring sunshine.

At Chy-an-Gwyns, Elizabeth having finished hanging the Christmas decorations, left the house to walk down to the Old Vicarage for some holly, in spite of the fact Anne told her the tree bore no berries. En route she met Jim Haynes and stopped for a chat, during which she mentioned the lack of berries on the Old Vicarage holly tree.

"Then get some from the allotments," said Jim, with enthusiasm, "there are loads of berries on the trees up there."

"Really, I'll do that then, as long as I won't be trespassing."

"No, you won't be. Lots of people have had holly from up there already and most don't have allotments, so don't worry, no-one will say anything. In fact, if you want to go up there now I'll go with you because I wouldn't mind a few sprigs to put in my place to make it look a bit festive."

"Well, that would be nice, and Anne's not expecting me anyway. It only occurred to me that I ought to do the decorations this morning when I realised Tally and Wills will be home tomorrow."

They walked briskly up to the allotments for the day was chilly in spite of the faint sunshine; once they were amongst the vegetable gardens, Elizabeth looked around with approval.

"You know, I've never been up here before and it's really rather interesting. I can understand why people get so attached to their allotments."

"It's even nicer in the summer," said Jim, with enthusiasm, "the plots look a bit sad now with just a few brassicas amongst an abundance of weeds."

Elizabeth laughed. "There are weeds in our garden too, I see them every time I look out of the window, but at least when they're up here you can pretend they're not, if that makes sense."

Jim smiled. "Yes, it does, but I don't mind them, it's a sign of fertile ground, better weeds than a barren earth."

"So, which is your plot?"

"Over there," said Jim, pointing, "I'll show you."

They walked along a grass path which ran between numerous plots and stopped by one housing a shed, greenhouse and small polytunnel.

"This is it, this is my pride and joy, though it doesn't look much now. And over there are the holly trees. See, the berries are even visible from here. I'll get a piece of twine and my secateurs from my shed and then we'll cut some."

As Jim cut the festive holly, Elizabeth cast her eyes along the hedgerows and through a gap between blackthorn bushes, the top of the old well caught her eye.

"Am I seeing things or is that a well on the other side of the hedge?"

"Yes, it is, come and see." He laid down the holly in the long grass.

The old well lay nestled in a corner of waste ground; Elizabeth looked all around, puzzled as to its purpose in such an isolated spot.

"There was nothing much here when this field was first opened up as allotments," said Jim, "and we discovered the well quite by chance. It was just a hole covered over with sheets of metal, you see, and much of it was overgrown by grass."

"So you rebuilt it."

"In a nutshell, yes. When we discovered there was water down there we realised it could be very useful and so several of us got together and built up the sides, put on a roof, inserted a spindle, rope and bucket. I think we did a pretty good job considering we had no idea what it originally looked like. It's reckoned to be pretty old apparently, possibly even dating back to the sixteenth century."

"The sixteenth century," repeated Elizabeth, conscious of the colour draining from her face.

"Yes, there used to be a few old cottages up here, but I won't make the mistake of saying what idyllic times they must have been to live in, not with you being a school teacher. That's what I said to poor Morwenna, you see, and she went nuts and gave me a lecture on the conditions people would have lived in back then. I must admit it spooked me out a bit. Poor kid, I can't believe she took her own life like that, having said that, I know it sounds daft but in a way I'm pleased because I feel like part of her is still around, especially up here." He sighed deeply. "I really liked her."

Elizabeth sat down on the side of the well; her legs felt weak. "I'm glad that you feel she's still here and I'm sure in spirit she really is." She looked around. "Whereabouts were the cottages you speak of?"

"Over there," said Jim, pointing, "come and see, there are several huge lumps of granite still around which were probably used in the fireplace or as lintels."

Elizabeth followed Jim to the large pieces of stone. "So what were the cottages built of, if stone was only used in the fireplace or as lintels?"

"Cob," said Jim, with confidence, "most old places were built of cob back then, modest cottages anyway. Grander houses of course were built entirely with granite."

"Of course, such as the house which later became the village hall."

"Absolutely, and the house that became the village hall at one time housed the village priest. An early vicarage, so to speak. I found that out after I'd bought the chapel, I've always been interested in old religious buildings, you see."

When Jane went to draw the curtains in the living room of her flat above the Pickled Egg as darkness fell on Christmas Eve, she saw a silver Mercedes drive down the incline and park beside Cove Cottage. She was intrigued. It was not Iris' car, and she was away in the States anyway. When a man stepped out, her heart skipped a beat. Surely it was Rusty.

Jane watched as the figure lifted luggage and boxes from the boot of the car and took everything inside the cottage. Once the front door had closed, she drew the curtains, made a mug of tea and sat back down. It couldn't be Rusty. He would never visit Cornwall and spend Christmas alone.

It was her intention to go to the inn in the evening and to meet up with family and friends. But if it was Rusty staying at Cove Cottage, then he too might be go the inn and that could be awkward.

As she finished her tea there was a knock on the door below. Jane's heart skipped a beat and with haste she ran down the stairs. When she opened the door her face dropped with disappointment. It was Janet Ainsworth with a Christmas present in her hand.

"Expecting someone else?" Janet asked, a hint of amusement in her expression.

"Jane sighed. "Yes and no. Come in; it looks chilly out there."

"I see there's a car outside Cove Cottage," persisted Janet, as she stepped inside, "and of course it can't be Iris. I wonder who it is."

Jane closed the door. "It could be anyone, I suppose. I'm sure Iris must have loads of friends and acquaintances. Would you like a cup of tea?"

"No thanks, I can't stop long, we're going to the inn later and I've just popped a casserole in the oven."

"Oh."

"I brought this down for you tonight because no doubt I'll not see you tomorrow. Open it. I want to see what you think."

Jane obediently opened the parcel. Inside was a quality handbag very similar to one owned by Janet which she had admired.

"It's beautiful," said Jane, "and I love the colour. Thank you, Janet. I have your present here and one each for the girls too."

From beneath her Christmas tree Jane pulled three small parcels and handed them to Janet, "I hope you like them."

After Janet had gone home, Jane transferred the contents of her old handbag into her new, she then showered, put on her favourite outfit and did her hair and make-up with care just on the off chance that the occupant of Cove Cottage was Rusty. But at the same time she was very apprehensive; she had not answered his last letter. She had meant to but somehow time had passed by and then it seemed too late to respond. Jane sighed, she half hoped the visitor was Rusty and she half hoped it wasn't.

Inside Number One, Coronation Terrace, after the children had excitedly gone to bed, Trevor Moore, who was thriving once more in his own business as a painter and decorator, raised his glass to the people of Trengillion who had given him and his family back the will to live. Valerie sitting on the floor happily wrapping presents paused to take a sip of wine. As she put down the glass there was a knock on the front door.

"I'll go," said Trevor, putting his glass on a coffee table which at one time had stood in the Old School House, "mustn't delay Father Christmas' good work.

On the door step he found Gertie, cheeks glowing and with hands hidden behind her back. "I've...um...a little present for you all. It's to share. I hope you'll like it, and...well...happy Christmas."

From behind her back she carefully produced a shopping basket and in the bottom, lying on a small folded blanket, slept a black Labrador puppy.

Chapter Thirty Two

The Jolly Sailor was hectic on Christmas Eve: cheerful festive music rang out from small speakers, mulled wine flowed and silver dishes of nibbles and canapés, made by Maurice, stood on all tables and corners of the bar.

On the ceiling, every other beam was decorated with holly and fir, and on the wide sills, dried flowers sprayed silver and red, lay around ceramic pots containing poinsettias.

"Someone has a tasteful touch," said Meg, who had not been to the inn recently to witness the festive décor, "I can't believe it was done by Justin."

"It wasn't," said Gertie, proudly, "our Sue did it, but she asked Janet for ideas first and she didn't get charged for her suggestions either."

Stella grinned. "You're still not too keen on Janet, are you, Gert?"

"She's alright, and I know Bet thinks a lot of her because of the way she helps out Jane, but I don't think we could ever be friends, we're just not on the same wave-length."

A fresh southerly wind was blowing when Jane left the Pickled Egg and made her way to the Jolly Sailor. Outside, on the cobbled area, stood a twelve foot tall Christmas tree, swaying in the strong gusts of wind, causing its multi-coloured lights to flicker and cast eerie shadows across the front wall of the old building. Jane pulled up her collar to protect her hair as she crossed the cobbles and opened the door of the inn.

The warmth in the bar was greatly welcomed by Jane as she lowered her collar, straightened her hair and cast her eyes around to see who was present. When she spotted Rusty, sitting at the bar, talking to Greg and Elizabeth, she gasped. Unsure whether to move in his direction or seek out her family and friends, she remained perfectly still. As luck would have it the decision was made for her when Rebecca, walking through the bar on her way back from the Ladies, insisted Jane join them.

For ten minutes, Rusty was unaware of Jane's presence. Then he caught sight of her reflection in a mirror behind the bar, helping Matthew carry the family's drinks towards their table in the corner. When he saw her sat bolt upright.

"Excuse me," he muttered to Elizabeth and Greg, "I must go and have a word with Jane."

Jane felt her face redden as he neared their table; he looked slightly irritated but greeted her family with sincerity and warmth.

"Jane, may I have a quick word, please?"

Jane's heart skipped a beat as she rose and followed him to the door where he led her outside.

"Jane, what goes on?" he asked, before the door had even closed properly. "You didn't reply to my last letter. Was that your way of saying I was no longer of any interest to you?"

"I...I don't know," she whispered, wishing she had not removed her coat. "I did intend to write back, really, I did, but time went by and then suddenly it seemed discourteous to reply and at the back of my mind I even thought maybe, perhaps it was for the best."

Rusty walked away a few feet and then turned to face her. "So in other words, it's all over, just like that. I can't believe it, Jane. You and I are so good together. What have I done wrong?"

Jane shivered with cold and discomfort. "Nothing! Oh, it's not you, Rusty, it's me. That is to say, I'm afraid, afraid of getting hurt again. Oh dear, you can't possibly understand."

She dropped her head to hide her tears. He promptly stepped closer and lifted her chin.

"If it's because you think I'll leave you in the lurch like the other bloke did, then you're wrong. I won't, my love, I can assure you of that. Please believe me, Jane."

Jane bit her bottom lip. "How come you know of my past?"

"Because someone told me about you and him back in the summer. But don't fret, it wasn't in a gossipy way, it was done to try and help me understand your mood swings."

Jane attempted to laugh. "I suppose I was a bit unpredictable in the summer. I'm sorry."

"You had every right to be, after all you had been tearing around like a headless chicken the previous week. But seriously, well...Oh, this is ridiculous, Jane. I can think of little else but you. I love you, I know I do and I need you by my side."

Jane felt her heart flutter. "But we've known each other for only a short while."

"I know but I can think of nothing I'd like more than spending the rest of my life getting to know you better."

"But what will Iris say?"

Rusty took her cold hands in his. "We have the blessing of Iris. I had a long chat with her over the phone last night and told her you'd not replied to my last letter and how I didn't think I could live without you. It was she who insisted I come down and sort things out." Rusty fell onto one knee. "Please say you'll marry me, Jane and then I'll be the happiest person in the world."

"Marry you! Good grief, I..."

"You won't have to leave Cornwall if you don't want to. I could quite happily find another job and live down here. Having said that I'm sure you'd like my house in Buckinghamshire. Oh, please say yes."

A sudden glow swept through Jane's body and her face broke out into a huge grin, "Yes," she cried, "yes, yes, yes. And right this minute I don't care where we live, as long as we're together."

On Boxing Day, Rusty drove Jane to see his house in a picturesque Buckinghamshire village. He told her nothing about it beforehand, but instead talked of his friends, neighbours and his work colleagues. Jane therefore had no idea what to expect.

They arrived just after dark hence she was unable to see the gardens, but the house overwhelmed her. Formerly a farmhouse it had a fireplace so huge there was room to stand inside it. The stairs with oak balusters, were wide, curved and bordering on grand. The rooms were large, the kitchen was bigger than the whole ground floor of the Pickled Egg, and in the corner of the biggest reception room, stood a baby grand piano. Jane was awestruck.

"Do you play?" she asked.

"Yes, but I'm not as good as I should like to be. How about you?"

"I don't play and never have, but oh, I've always wanted to learn. Will you teach me?"

Rusty laughed and took her in his arms, "Does that mean you would like to live here then?"

"Yes, please."

"Good, and in the morning you shall see the garden. It doesn't look much this time of the year but then gardens seldom do, but in the spring and the summer it's beautiful. I love to sit out there and listen to the birds singing and the gentle babbling of the stream."

"You have a stream nearby?"

"Very nearby. It runs across the corner of the orchard and then down to the woods."

"Stream, orchard, woods, tell me I'm not dreaming."

"You're not dreaming. I'm so glad you like my home, Jane. I love it here and hoped you would too." He kissed her. "So do you think you'd be happy here?"

"I know shall be very happy here. We'll both be very happy here and we can still visit Cornwall often."

Rusty leaned back his head. "Phew! It's such a relief to hear you say that and I agree about visiting Cornwall as it only takes a few hours to drive down there." He bit his bottom lip. "But what I wonder will become of your Pickled Egg."

Jane smiled as she brushed her hand against his cheek. "Don't worry about that. I have a plan, which I think might be the perfect solution."

Jess, home for the Christmas holiday, was sampling a mince pie from a batch she had just made. When her mother came into the kitchen with a visitor, Jess looked up. "Oh, hello, Jane. So how was Buckinghamshire?"

"Wonderful, I loved the house, the village and everything about it so I've decided to settle there."

Jess looked surprised. "Good heavens, I really didn't think you would."

"Well it's a case of practising what you preach," said Jane. "Do you remember what I said to you in the summer about seizing the opportunity?" Jess nodded. "Well that's exactly what I'm doing."

"Good for you," said Jess, sincerely. "And I hope you'll be very happy. Do have a mince pie, Jane, they're wicked, even if do say myself." She passed Jane a plate. "But what about the Pickled Egg? You've worked so hard building it up."

Jane took a mince pie. "It's because of the Pickled Egg I'm here. I've come to see if you'd like to take it over."

"Me!" Jess gasped, amazed. "I'd love to, but…well, I don't have any money and I don't finish university until June. Oh, dear, I really don't know what to say."

"I've thought of that," Jane said, "and I've had a word with Janet and she says she'll open it up at Easter and run it until you're ready."

Jess looked at her mother. "And your father and I will buy the business for you as a twenty first birthday present. Jane's letting it go for a very good price. It's really an opportunity not to be missed."

"And would my running it be alright with Granddad and your father?" Jess asked. "Because you told me they own the premises and you pay them rent."

"No problem there and the rent stays the same."

Jess crossed the kitchen and gave Jane a big hug. "Thank you so much. I shall be delighted to take over from you and I promise I'll not let you down."

"I knew you would and if these mince pies are anything to go by, then you can't go wrong. Meanwhile, do you fancy going round to the inn for a drink to celebrate? Rusty's already there."

"Oh, yes, please, and you and Dad must come too, Mum. Just give me two minutes to change and then I'll be ready."

In the years since the children had grown up, Anne and John had ceased to hold their New Year's Eve parties at the Old Vicarage and instead had gone to the inn along with everyone else. 1999 however was special, for it was the 21st birthday of twins, Ollie and Jess, hence they had a party in the early evening with drinks and nibbles after which they changed into fancy dress costumes with a nautical theme, and moved round to the Jolly Sailor where Justin had arranged Karaoke.

Inside the inn, pirates in abundance mingled with mermaids and sailors, and one or two scantily clad WRENs. Behind the bar, Justin, inevitably dressed as a sailor, had beside him Doctor Morgana

Owen, wearing a long white dress with silver wings attached to her back; when asked what she was meant to be, her prompt reply was 'an angel fish'. However, the costumes which caused the greatest amusement were two floppy crabs, a baggy seagull and a lobster whose claws refused to stay in an upright position. Beneath the feathers, claws and numerous legs were the four camping lads, Rob, Kev, Mac and Neil, down for the twins' birthday and to see in the New Millennium.

Very few chose not to dress up, even the older generation joined in with the spirit of things, although it was questionable whether the fishermen who arrived in their normal attire were in fancy dress or not.

Karaoke was set up at the far end of the public bar, where the youngsters sang, danced and laughed the night away. While in the snug, the older residents of Trengillion sat and nostalgically reminisced of days gone by and those they had lost along the way, sentiments which prompted Rose to put in a request for herself and her contemporaries to sing Mary Hopkins' 'Those Were the Days'.

When they sat back down after their song, Ned noticed Stella was very quiet. "What's the matter, Stell? I can see tears in your eyes."

She attempted to smile. "Just me being silly. I always feel a bit sentimental in the dying minutes of any year, but this year, well it's different. Not only are we going into a new year and a new decade but a new century and millennium too. This last century has been good to us, it's been ours, Ned. But it struck me that at the end of the next century no-one who currently lives in the village will still be here then. Others will come along and life will go on, but everyone here will be gone. We'll just be names on gravestones in the churchyard." She laughed. "I think maybe I've had a little too much wine."

Ned reached out and put his arm tightly around her shoulder. "I think you have but I can see where you're coming from, Stell, and I agree. But don't get maudlin, not tonight. Tomorrow will be just like any other day. Admittedly it'll have a new date and the year will seem strange, but everything else will be the same." He laughed. "And you can bet your bottom dollar that we won't get through the day without seeing rain."

Just before midnight young and old linked arms and as Big Ben struck twelve on Justin's radio they heartily sang 'Auld Lang Syne' and wished each other a happy New Year with kisses and handshakes. They then went outside to watch a fireworks display to welcome in the new millennium.

As the noise brought about by the fireworks subsided everyone returned indoors to continue the jollifications, everyone except Elizabeth. Feeling in need of a little peace and quiet, Elizabeth sat outside the inn and looked up to the stars. She had not thought about Morwyn Cardew since she and Jim had collected holly from the allotments, but earlier in the evening she overheard Rusty ask Jane if Morwenna's body had ever been washed ashore, and this innocent question consequently raised Morwyn's plight to the uppermost region of her thoughts.

Inside the celebrations continued with hearty handshakes, hugs and affectionate kisses as everyone wished all and sundry a happy new year.

"I wonder what the new millennium holds for us all," said Tally, as she and her friends huddled together in a corner.

Lucy reached for a local newspaper lying on top of a cigarette vending machine and handed it to Tally. "One way to find out," she said, "I know a local astrologer can't possibly be up to your Taffeta Tealeaf's standard but it might be a bit meaningful."

Tally laughed. "I'll read them out in no particular order and you must guess which one you think might apply to you."

However, after Tally had shuffled through the newspaper and found the horoscope page, she frowned. "But this is bonkers there's just the one horoscope and it's for all twelve signs. Look."

She held up the paper for all to see.

"That's odd," said Demelza, snuggling closer to Kev to let someone pass by, "but at least it means you won't have so much to read."

Rob laughed. "I like it, one horoscope fits all, now that's what I call hedging one's bets."

"Read it out loud, Tally," said Jess.

"Okay." Tally folded the paper into four so that only the horoscope was visible on the top and then scanned the first sentence.

"It looks a bit weird and appears to be written in a very old fashioned manner," she said, "still, here goes." She cleared her throat.

"It says: *The new millennium shall bring forth in its wake numerous challenges, fostering much hope, causing much pain, raising much laughter and inducing many tears. There shall be good times for which ye shall be thankful, bad times and heartache when tis best to forget. If ye are wronged then learn to forgive for revenge is never sweet. Seek and ye shall find. Your fate is governed by the moon and the sun. Your destiny is written in yonder stars. Be patient, my dear, dear turtles, and remember always, that the course of true love never did run smooth.*"

THE END

Printed in Great Britain
by Amazon